THE STONEHENGE LEGACY

THE STONEHENGE LEGACY

SAM CHRISTER

THE OVERLOOK PRESS
NEW YORK, NY

This edition first published in the United States in 2011 by
The Overlook Press, Peter Mayer Publishers, Inc.

141 Wooster Street
New York, NY 10012
www.overlookpress.com

For bulk and special sales, please contact sales@overlookny.com

First published in Great Britain in 2011 by Sphere, an imprint of
Little, Brown Book Group, an Hachette UK Company

Cataloging-in-Publication Data is available from the Library of Congress

Reformatting by Bernard Schleifer Company
Manufactured in the United States of America
ISBN 978-1-59020-676-8

To my son Elliott in his last year of sixth form – I couldn't be prouder of everything you've done or how you've done it.

PART ONE

The stones are great
And magic power they have
Men that are sick
Fare to that stone
And they wash that stone
And with that water bathe away their sickness

Laghamon

1

NEW MOON, SUNDAY 13 JUNE
STONEHENGE

Mist rolls like vaporous tumbleweed in the dead of the Wiltshire night. Out in the flat, sprawling fields hooded Lookers tilt their heads skyward to witness the first sliver of silver. The moon is new, showing only a faint flash of virginal white beneath a voluminous wrap of black-velvet haute couture.

On the horizon, a pale face turns in its cowl. A fiery torch is raised in an old hand. Hushed but urgent words pass from Looker to Looker. The sacrifice is ready. He has been brought from his fast. Seven days without food. No light, nor sound, nor touch, nor smell. His body has been cleansed of the impurities he has ingested. His senses sharpened. His mind focused on his fate.

The Lookers are robed in handwoven sackcloth, belted with string plaited from plants, their feet shod in rough animal skins. It is the way of the ancients, the creators of the Craft.

The Cleansers remove the man's grimy clothes. He will leave this world with no more than he entered it. They pull a ring from his finger. A watch from his wrist. And from around his neck, a crude gold chain dangling a symbol of some false god.

They carry him, fighting, to the river and immerse him. Cold water fills his mouth and gurgles and froths in his corrupted lungs. He struggles like a startled fish, seeking a safe current to escape the hands of his captors.

It is not to be.

Once purified, he is dragged spluttering to the shore. The Bearers fall upon him and bind him with strips of bark to a litter made from pine, the noble tree that stepped with them from the age of ice. They hoist him high on to their shoulders. Carry him like proud and loving men bearing the coffin of a beloved brother. He is precious to them.

Their walk is long – more than two miles. South from the ancient encampment of Durrington. On to the great avenue, down to where the bluestones and the forty-ton sarsens are sited.

The Bearers make no complaints. They know the pain their forefathers suffered moving the mighty stones hundreds of miles. The astroarchitects trekked through hills and valleys, crossed stormy seas. With antlers of red deer and shoulder blades of cattle, they dug the pits where the circle now stands. Behind the Bearers come the Followers. All male. All dressed identically in hooded, coarse brown robes. They have come from across Britain, Europe and all corners of the globe. For tonight is the new Henge Master's first sacrifice. An overdue offering to the gods. One that will rejuvenate the spiritual strength of the stones.

The Bearers pause at the Heel Stone, the massive chunk of leaning sandstone that is home to the Sky God. It dwarfs all around it, except the gigantic sarsens standing eighty yards away.

In the center of the megalithic portal a bonfire flickers in the darkness, its smoking fingers grasping at the moon, illuminating the Henge Master as he raises his hands. He pauses then sweeps them in a slow arc, pressing back the wall of energy surging between him and the horseshoe of towering trilithons.

'Great gods, I feel your eternal presence. Earth Mother most eternal, Sky Father most supreme, we gather in your adoration and dutifully kneel in your presence.'

The secret congregation of hooded figures sinks silently to the soil. 'We, your obedient children, the Followers of the Sacreds, are gathered here on the bones of our ancestors to honor you and to show you our devotion and loyalty.'

The Master claps his hands and leaves them joined above his head, fingers pointing in prayer to the heavens. The Bearers rise from their knees. Once more they lift upon their shoulders the naked young man tethered to the rough litter.

'We thank you, all you great gods who look over us and who bless us. In respect to you and the ways of the ancients, we dedicate this sacrifice.'

The Bearers begin their final journey, out through the giant stone archways toward the sacrificial point that lies on the line of the solstice.

The Slaughter Stone.

They lay the young man upon the long gray slab. The Henge Master looks down and lowers his joined hands to touch the forehead of the sacrifice. He is not afraid to look into the terrorized blue eyes beneath him. He has prepared himself to banish all feelings of compassion. Just as a king would exile a traitor.

He slowly circles his joined hands around the man's face as he continues the words of the ritual. 'In the names of our fathers, our mothers, our protectors and our mentors, we absolve you from your earthly sins and through your mortal sacrifice we purify your spirit and speed you on your journey to eternal life in paradise.'

Only now does the Henge Master separate his palms. He spreads them wide. His body is in balance with the lunar phase. His silhouette against the great stones is that of a cruciform.

Into each outstretched hand the Bearers place the sacred tools. The Henge Master grips them, his fingers folding around smooth, wooden shafts carved centuries ago.

The first flint axe strikes the head of the sacrifice.

Then the second.

Now the first again.

Blows rain down until bone and skin collapse like an eggshell. With the death of the sacrifice comes a roar from the crowd. A triumphant cheer as the Master moves back, his arms spread wide for them to see the sacrificial blood spattered on his robes and flesh.

'Just as you shed blood and broke bones to assemble this godly portal to protect us, so too do we shed our blood and break our bones for you.'

One by one the Followers come forward. They dip their fingers in the blood of the sacrifice, mark their foreheads. Then they walk back into the main circle and kiss the trilithons.

Blessed and blooded, they bow before silently disappearing into the dark Wiltshire fields.

2

LATER THAT MORNING

TOLLARD ROYAL, CRANBORNE CHASE, SALISBURY

Professor Nathaniel Chase sits at a desk in the oak-walled study of his seventeenth-century country mansion and through the leaded windows watches morning twilight yield to a summer sunrise. It's a daily battle that he never misses.

A colorful male pheasant struts the lawn, cued by the first light on the dew-soaked grass. Dull females follow in the bird's wake, then feign disinterest and peck at fat-filled coconut shells strung out by Chase's gardener.

The male proudly spreads his wings to form a cape of iridescent copper. His head, ears and neck are tropical green and his throat and cheeks an exotic glossed purple. A distinctive white band around his neck gives him a priestly stature while his face and wattle are a deep red. The bird is melanistic – some kind of mutation of the common pheasant. As the professor looks closer, he suspects that a few generations back there must also have been some crossing with a rare green pheasant or two.

Chase is a successful man. More than most ever dream of being. Academically brilliant, he has been hailed as one of Cambridge's finest brains. His books on art and archaeology have sold globally and built a following beyond those bound to buy them for study. But his vast fortune and luxuriously refined lifestyle don't come from his learned ways. He left Cambridge many years back and turned his talents to sourcing, identifying, buying and selling some of the rarest artifacts in the world. It was a practice that earned him a regular place in the rich list and a whispered reputation as something of a grave-robber.

The sixty-year-old takes off his brown-framed reading glasses and places them on the antique desk. The matter in hand is pressing but it can wait until the floor show outside is done.

The pheasant's humble harem break from their feeding to pay the cock the attention he craves. He stomps out a short, jerky dance and leads the buff-brown females toward a stretch of manicured privets. Chase picks up a pair of small binoculars that he keeps by the window. At first he sees nothing except gray-blue sky. He tilts the glasses down and the blurred birds fill the frame. He fiddles with the focus wheel until everything becomes as sharp and crisp as this chilly summer morning. The male is surrounded now and warbling short bursts of song to mark his pleasure. Off to the right lies a shallow nest at the foot of the hedge.

Chase is feeling sensitive, emotional. The display outside his window touches him almost to the point of tears. The male with its many admirers, at the peak of life, vibrant in color and potency preparing to raise a family. He remembers those days. That feeling. That warmness.

All gone.

Inside the grand house there are no pictures of his dead wife, Marie. Nor any of his estranged son, Gideon. The place is empty. The professor's days of plumage-spreading are done.

He puts the binoculars down beside the fine casement window and returns to the important paperwork. He picks up a vintage fountain pen, a limited-edition Pelikan Caelum, and savors its weight and balance. One of only five hundred and eighty ever made, a homage to Mercury's fifty-eight-million-kilometer orbit of the sun. Astronomy has played a vital role in the life of Nathaniel Chase. Too vital, he reflects.

He dips the nib into a solid brass antique inkwell, lets the Pelikan drink its fill and resumes his chore.

It takes Nathaniel an hour to finish writing on the fine cotton-blend paper that bears his own personalized watermark. He meticulously reviews every finished line and contemplates the impact the letter will have on its reader. He blots it, folds it precisely into three, places it into an envelope and seals it with old-fashioned wax and a personalized stamp. Ceremony is important. Especially today.

He places the letter in the middle of the grand desk and sits back, both saddened and relieved to have completed the text.

The sun is now rising above the orchard at the far side of the garden. On another day, he'd walk the grounds, perhaps take lunch in the summerhouse, watch the wildlife in the garden, and then enjoy a midafternoon snooze. Another day.

He opens the bottom drawer of the desk and pauses as his gaze falls on what lies in there. In one determined move, he takes out the First World War revolver, puts it to his temple and pulls the trigger.

Outside the blood-spattered window, pheasants squawk and scatter into the gray sky.

3

THE FOLLOWING DAY
CAMBRIDGE UNIVERSITY

Gideon Chase quietly puts the phone down and stares blankly at the walls of his office where he's been reviewing the findings of a dig at a Megalithic temple in Malta.

The policewoman had been clear enough. 'Your father is dead. He shot himself.' Looking back, it's hard to see how she could have been any clearer. No wasted words. No hyperbole. Just a verbal slap to the guts that sucked his breath away. Sure, she'd thrown in a 'sorry' somewhere, murmured her condolences, but by then the twenty-eight-year-old's brilliant professor-in-waiting brain had shut down.

Father. Dead. Shot.

Three small words that painted the biggest imaginable picture. But all he could manage in reply was 'Oh.' He asked her to repeat what she'd said to make sure he'd understood. Not that he hadn't. It was just that he was so embarrassed that he couldn't say anything other than 'Oh.'

It has been years since father and son last spoke. One of their bitterest rows. Gideon had stormed out and vowed never to talk to the old goat again and it hadn't been difficult to keep to his word.

Suicide.

What a shock. The great man had wittered on all his life about being bold, daring and positive. What could be more cowardly than blowing your brains out? Gideon flinches. God, it must have been ugly.

He moves around his small office in a daze. The police want him to travel over to Wiltshire to answer a few questions. Help fill in some blanks. But he's not sure he can find his way out of the door, let alone to Devizes.

Childhood memories tumble on him like a row of falling dominoes. A big Christmas tree. A melting snowman on the front patch of lawn. A preschool Gideon coming downstairs in pajamas to open presents. His father playing with him while his mother cooked enough food to feed a village. He remembers them kissing under the mistletoe while he hugged their legs until they had to pick him up and include him. Then comes the thump. As a six-year-old, enduring the pain of his mother's death. The silence of the graveyard. The emptiness of their home. The change in his father. The loneliness of boarding school.

He has much to think about on the journey south to Wiltshire, the county where his mother had been born, the place she'd always lovingly called 'Thomas Hardy Land'.

4

WILTSHIRE

Few know of its existence. A secret vault of cold stone, scaled to epic proportions by prehistoric architects. A place unvisited by the uninitiated.

The Sanctuary of the Followers is an unseen wonder. It is the size of a cathedral and yet a mere bump in the turf on the fields above, almost invisible to the human eye. Belowground, it's the jewel of an ancient civilization, the product of a people whose brilliance still baffles the greatest brains of modern times.

Fashioned three thousand years before Christ, the place is an anachronism, a vast temple as out-of-time, breathtaking and impossible as the Great Pyramid of Giza.

Buried in its subterranean tombs are the architects of both Stonehenge and the Sanctuary. Their bones rest in the midst of more than two million blocks of stone, quarried from the same sources. Just as the Giza monument was a near-perfect pyramid, the Sanctuary is a near-perfect semi-sphere, a dome arcing over a circular floor, a cold moon sliced in half.

Now footsteps resound through the Descending Passage as though rain is falling into the cavernous chambers. In the candlelight of the Lesser Hall, the Inner Circle gathers. There are five of them, representatives of the giant trilithons sited inside the circle of Stonehenge. All are cloaked and hooded: a sign of respect for generations past, those who gave their lives to create this sacred place.

Upon initiation, Followers become known by the name of a constellation that shares the initial letter of their own first name. This shroud of secrecy is another age-old tradition, an echo of an epoch when the whole world was guided by stars.

Draco is tall and broad and exudes power. He is the most senior, the Keeper of the Inner Circle. His name comes from the Latin for 'dragon' and the constellation that almost three thousand years ago cradled the northern world's all-important pole star.

'What is being said?' He gives a flash of perfect teeth beneath his hood. 'What are they doing?'

The '*they*' in question are the police, the Wiltshire constabulary, the oldest county police force in the country.

Grus, a thickset man in his early fifties, pounces. 'He shot himself.'

Musca paces thoughtfully, candles casting spectral shadows on the stone walls behind. Although the youngest of them all, his large physical presence dominates the chamber. 'I never expected him to do this. He was as devoted as any of us.'

'He was a coward,' snaps Draco. 'He knew what we expected of him.'

Grus ignores the outburst. 'It presents us with *certain* problems.'

Draco steps closer to him. 'I read the signs as well as you. We have time enough to ride this storm before the holy nexus.'

'There was a letter,' adds Grus. 'Aquila knows someone working on the investigation and a suicide note was left for his son.'

'Son?' Draco casts his mind back and a vague memory surfaces. Nathaniel with a child, a skinny youth with a mop of black hair. 'I forgot he had a son. Became a teacher at Oxford?'

'Cambridge. Now he'll be coming home.' Grus lays out the implication. 'Back to his *father's* home. And who knows what he might find in there.'

Draco creases his brow and looks fixedly to Musca. 'Do what must be done. We all thought well of our brother. In life he was our greatest of allies. We must ensure that in death he does not turn out to be our worst of enemies.'

5

STONEHENGE

An evening mist swirls around the base of the stones, a meteorological sleight of hand creating an archipelago in a sea of clouds. To motorists zipping past on the nearby trunk roads it's a scenic bonus but to the Followers it is much more.

This is twilight. *L'heure bleue.* A precious, twice-a-day time between dawn and sunrise, sunset and dusk. When light and dark are in balance and the spirits of the hidden worlds find a fragile harmony.

The Henge Master understands. He knows that nautical twilight comes first, as the sun sinks between six and twelve degrees below the horizon and gives sailors the first reliable readings of the stars. Astronomical twilight follows, as the sun slides from twelve to eigh teen degrees below the horizon.

Degrees. Geometry. The position of the sun. A sacred triangle mastered by men like him from century to century. Stonehenge wouldn't be here without them. Its location is not accidental. Divined by the greatest of ancient augers and archaeoastronomers, its siting was planned by the most advanced of minds. Such was the precision of its build, the circle took more than half a millennium to complete.

And now, more than four millennia later, the Followers lavish upon the stones a similar rapt attention to detail.

The Henge Master assumes his position at exactly the moment that nautical twilight enters astronomical twilight. He stands as still as the bluestone soldiers circled around him, guarding, protecting.

He is alone.

Like an ancient haruspex, he waits patiently for the gods.

And soon, in a soft rustle of voices, they speak. He absorbs their wisdom and knows now what to do. He will worry less about the professor's suicide and more about the son. He will check that the sacrifice was given a proper burial – it would be disastrous if the remains were to be unearthed. Above all, he will ensure that the second stage of the renewal is completed.

The ceremony must be finished.

The milky vapor rises around his legs. In the wondrous half-light the sarsens come alive. A trick of the eye? A *trompe l'œil*? He doesn't think so. The new moon is barely visible to the uneducated but to an archaeoastronomer like him it is a beacon in the cosmos. Across the vaults of heaven, orbital maps arrange themselves, celestial cycles spring into being and with every atom of his body he senses completion of the sun's shift from Beltane to the solstice.

Seven days to *solstitium* – the moment the sun stands still. And all attention will be on the dawn. When it really should be on the dusk that will follow.

Five full days will pass after midnight on the solstice, then in the fertile evening twilight of that mystical evening will come the first full moon following *solstitium*. The time of renewal. When he must return to the Sacreds and complete what he has begun.

The sky has darkened now. The Master looks for Polaris, the North Star, the Lodestar, the brightest light of *Ursae Minoris*. The closest blink of godliness to the celestial pole. His eyes fall down the black curtain of the sky to the prehistoric earth, to the Slaughter Stone, and he shudders as he hears the command of the Sacreds.

The gods will not tolerate failure.

6

WILTSHIRE POLICE HQ, DEVIZES

DI Megan Baker wants to forget this particular day. And it's still a long way from over. The stick-thin thirty-one-year-old has a sick child at home, no husband to help since she kicked him out, and an arsy DCI who has landed her with a messy suicide. Now she must stay late to see the grieving son, face to face. That, and the combination of unpaid bills cluttering her handbag, is enough to start her smoking again. But she doesn't.

Her parents have said they'll have Sammy again, they always do – and it's 'never a problem', unless you count the patronizing lecture and the scalding looks when she collects her poor four-year-old daughter several hours later than promised.

But she won't give up. Being police is what she always wanted. What – despite a failed marriage – she still wants.

A shot of coffee and several sticks of gum take away the craving for nicotine. Her mobile rings and she looks at the caller display. CB – short for *Cheating Bastard*. She couldn't bring herself to enter her ex-husband's real name. *Cheating Bastard* seemed more appropriate. He is a uniformed inspector in another local division but their paths still cross. Too often. At work and during painful access visits.

CB doesn't want agreed visits. Oh no. That would cramp his shag-everything-with-a-pulse lifestyle. He expects to turn up whenever he wants to see Sammy. And that's just not fair. To her daughter or to her.

The urge to throw the ringing mobile at the wall is almost irresistible. She snatches it off her desk a beat before it trips to voicemail. 'Yes?' she snaps.

CB also has no time for pleasantries. 'Why didn't you tell me Sammy is sick?'

'She's got a fever, that's all. She'll be fine.'

'You a doctor now?'

'You a parent now?'

He emits a labored sigh. 'Meg, I'm concerned about my daughter. You'd shout at me if I didn't ring, now you're shouting because I have.'

She counts to ten and spits out his name, 'Adam, Sammy's fine. Kids pick up bugs at playschool all the time. Her temperature's high, she was a little sick last night, that's all.'

'It's not measles or one of those things?'

'No.' Megan suddenly doubts herself. 'I don't think so. Mum's with her, there is nothing to worry about.'

'*You* should be with her. When she's sick a little girl wants her mum not her grandma.'

'Go to hell, Adam.' She hangs up and feels her heart pounding. He always does that to her. Winds her up. Brings her to snapping point.

The desk phone jangles and she nearly jumps out of her skin. It's reception. Gideon Chase is downstairs. She tells them she is on her way and takes a final slug of the now-cold coffee. Talking to the family of the deceased is never easy.

Reception is empty except for a tall, dark-haired man with shock etched on his pale face. She takes a long breath as she approaches. 'I'm Detective Inspector Baker. Megan Baker.' She offers a hand and instantly notices the well-worn blue plaster on her index finger is in danger of coming off.

'Gideon Chase,' he murmurs, careful not to dislodge the dubious Band-Aid. 'Sorry I'm late. The traffic.'

She smiles sympathetically. 'It's always bad. Thanks for coming so quickly. I know this must be difficult.' She opens a door with her swipe card. 'Let's go through to the back. We can find somewhere quiet to talk.'

7

DEVIZES

To an archaeologist like Gideon Chase, locations and first impressions are of particular importance. A stretch of scorched red Egyptian sand or a dark-green field of English countryside say much about the possible discoveries that lie ahead. The cheap, windowless, wooden door that DI Baker opens and ushers him through does the same.

It's a dull box, floored in black carpet tiles and walled in shades of scuffed gray. Decor as welcoming as a grave. The only bright thing in the room is the woman DI. Reddish-brown hair, sharply dressed in a russet jersey top and flared black trousers. Gideon perches on an uncomfortable molded chair and out of curiosity nudges the edge of the table in front of him. It's bolted to the floor.

Megan Baker is big on first appearances too. With a background in psychology and criminal profiling, she is already appraising the man with dark, Hugh Grant-style hair. He has brown eyes, a full mouth and good cheekbones. His fingernails show no trace of nicotine and have been cut not chewed short. No wedding ring. Many married men don't wear them but those with strong values do, and he radiates traditionalism. They are epitomized in his blue wool blazer with its leather-patched elbows, an item of dress cultivated in college cloisters rather than council estates. And it doesn't go with the black cashmere pullover or floppy green shirt. Any woman in his life could have told him that.

She slides an opened envelope over the table. 'This is the note your father left.'

Gideon looks at it but doesn't move. It's spattered with dark marks.

She realizes what has caught his attention. 'I'm sorry. Putting it in a different envelope didn't seem the right thing to do.'

The right thing to do.

So much of his upbringing has been about the right thing to do. All of it inadequate preparation for the moment you get handed an envelope spattered with the blood of your dead father.

'Are you all right?'

He fingers a flop of hair from his face and looks up at her. 'I'm fine.'

They both know he isn't.

He glances down at the envelope and his own name staring up at him in his father's copperplate capitals.

GIDEON

For the first time in his life, he is pleased that his father preserved his own eccentric style and used a fountain pen instead of a Biro or felt tip, like the rest of the world seems to do.

Gideon catches himself thinking fondly of the old man and wonders if it's just a passing moment, if one effect of death is that you suddenly find respect for the things you used to despise. Does it somehow wipe the slate clean and compel you to think only good of those you thought badly of?

He touches the corners of the envelope. Lifts it a little but doesn't turn it over.

Not yet.

His heart is thumping, like it used to when he and his father argued. He can feel the old man in the letter. He can feel the presence through the parchment. He flips the envelope and pulls it open. As he unfolds the letter, he feels annoyed that the police have read it before him. He understands why: they needed to read it. But they shouldn't have. It was addressed to him. It was private.

Dearest Gideon,

I hope in death the distance between us is less than in life.

You will find out many things about me now that I am gone. Not all are good and not all are bad. One thing you may not discover is how much I loved you. Every moment of my life I loved you and I was proud of you.

My dearest son, forgive me for how I pushed you away. Looking at you every day was like looking at your mother. You have her eyes. Her smile. Her gentleness and her sweetness. My darling, it was too painful for me to see her in your every breath. I know that is selfish. I know I was wrong to banish you to that school and ignore your pleas to come back home, but please believe me, I feared I would have fallen apart if I had acted otherwise.

My sweet, wonderful child, I am so proud of what you have become and what you have achieved.

Do not compare us. You are a far better man than I ever managed to be and I hope one day you'll make a far better father too.

You may wonder why I have taken my life. The answer is not a simple one. In life you make choices. In death you are eternally judged on them. Not all judges are good ones. I hope you judge me well and judge me kindly.

Believe me, my death was a noble one and not as pointless and cowardly as it may seem. You have a right to understand of what I speak and a right not to care a jot and to live your life without giving me a second thought.

I hope you choose the latter.

My solicitor will be in touch and you will find that all I have amassed is now yours. Do with it as you will, but I beseech you not to be *too* charitable.

Gideon, as a child we played games – do you remember? I would devise treasure hunts and you would follow clues I left. In death I leave you clues as well and the answer to a mystery. The greatest treasure of all is to love and be loved – I hope beyond hope that you find it.

It is best that you don't search for the answers to other mysteries, but I understand you may wish to, and if you do, then you do so with my blessing and my warning to be careful. Trust no one but yourself.

Dearest son, you are a child of the equinox. See beyond the sun of the solstice and focus on the rise of the new moon.

Things that you first think are bad will prove good. Things you think good will be bad. Life is about balance and judgment.

Forgive me for not being there for you, for not telling you and showing you that I loved you and your mother more than anything in my life.

Your humble, penitent and loving father,
Nathaniel

It's too much to take in. Too much to understand all at once.

He runs his fingertips gently over the letter. Feels the words 'Dearest

Gideon'. Lets the fingers of both hands rest on the line 'My sweet, wonderful child, I am so proud of what you have become . . .' Finally, almost as though he's reading Braille, his fingers find the words that moved him the most: 'Forgive me for not being there for you, for not telling you and showing you that I loved you and your mother more than anything in my life.'

Tears well in his eyes. He feels, impossibly, like his father is reaching out to him. The sensation is that of a prisoner and visitor divided by glass, putting their hands together to say goodbye, touching each other emotionally but not physically. Invisibly divided by life and death. The letter has become a wall of glass, the way his father has chosen to say goodbye.

Megan watches without interrupting and with only occasional glances at her wristwatch to quell the rising guilt about keeping her sickly four-year-old waiting at Grandma's. She can see the suicide letter is tearing Gideon apart.

'Would you like some time alone?'

He doesn't react. Grief is packing his head like cotton wool.

She clears her throat. 'Mr. Chase, it's getting very late now. Would it be possible to make an appointment to see you tomorrow?'

He climbs out of the numbness. 'What?'

She smiles understandingly. 'Tomorrow.' She nods to the letter. 'There are some things we would like to ask you about. And I suspect you'll have questions of your own.'

He has a lot of questions and now they start to spill out. 'How did my father die?' He looks pained. 'I know you said he'd shot himself, but what happened exactly? Where was he? What time . . .' His voice breaks with emotion. 'When did he do it?'

Megan doesn't flinch. 'He shot himself with a small handgun.' She can't help but add the details: 'A Webley Mark IV, a First World War pistol.'

'I didn't know he even owned a gun.'

'No one did. We found no records of its purchase. Probably picked up man years ago before the law tightened up on gun ownership.'

His shock deepens.

She moves on to the more difficult bit. 'You can see him, if you like. We've had official identification from his cleaner, the lady who discovered him, so there's no need, but if you want to, I can fix it.'

He's not sure what to say. He certainly does not want to see what remains of his father after he put a bullet through his head. But he feels obliged to. Wouldn't it be wrong not to? Isn't it *expected*?

The DI pushes her chair back and stands. If she doesn't take the initiative, the dead guy's son will still have her sitting here at midnight. 'I'm sorry, we really have to wind this up now.'

'Forgive me. I know it's late.' He picks up the letter, folds it and slides it back into the spattered envelope. 'Is it all right to take this?'

'Yes. Yes, of course.'

He places it gently inside his jacket. 'Thank you. And thank you for staying so late.'

'No problem.' Megan produces a card with her details on it. 'Call me in the morning. We can fix a time then.'

He takes it and follows her out of the room. She guides him through the security-locked doors and out into the dark cold of the night and now-empty streets.

As the door clacks shut behind them, Gideon feels numb.

He unlocks the old Audi and sits frozen in the driver's seat, keys shaking in his hand.

8

TOLLARD ROYAL, CRANBORNE CHASE,
SALISBURY

The estate is set in a singularly beautiful, historic chalk plateau straddling Dorset, Hampshire and Wiltshire – not far from the palatial retreat that Guy Ritchie and Madonna once shared.

Gideon has never been here before and trying to find it in the dark has taken more than an hour and proved exhaustingly difficult. He wishes he'd thought things through a little more – booked into a hotel or asked the police to find him somewhere. Now he's faced with nowhere to sleep unless he breaks into the house.

The fruits of his dead parent's dubious labor are impressive. The mansion must be worth ten million pounds, maybe more. Perhaps his father's 'trade' – grave-robbing, as Gideon had often called it – was one of the reasons why he had taken his life.

Gideon drives through tall metal gates into a darkened garden as foreboding as a cemetery. The driveway winds on for nearly half a mile before it sweeps around a marble centerpiece with an elaborate fountain that's lit but not working. Soft, yellow garden lights cast a jaundiced glow through the leaves of ancient trees. He kills the engine and sits for a minute looking at the old house. It's a shell – empty of life.

He gets out and walks a flagged path around the east wing. While he has no keys, he reasons that he's unlikely to get into trouble for breaking into a property that's just been left to him.

He trips another set of security lights and the intense burst of white forces him to blink. There's a scurry of activity in hedges and undergrowth not far from the house – foxes or rabbits, he guesses.

A security box on a far off wall catches his eye. It probably isn't primed. If you commit suicide, you don't set the alarm. And given that the police were sloppy enough not to padlock the front gates, it's unlikely that they've already phoned the company for the key code and appointed someone custodian.

He peers through the panes of a quaint orangery attached to the side of the building and can't quite bring himself to break in. A little further down he looks inside a laundry-cum-storage room. The door is modern. Less expensive to replace than anything else he's seen so far.

A good whack with the heel of his boot should do it. A solid boot somewhere around the lock. He takes a closer look. Best to get things right before you go hoofing away.

The door jamb around the handle looks already splintered.

He gives it a push and it opens.

'Damn.' Gideon curses the police. Unlocked gates and now a damaged door that should have been secured.

The air inside the house is stale and dry. Was this how the police entered? A crazy kick and rush by local plods after a call from a hysterical housekeeper?

He switches the light on and realizes his last thought didn't make sense. The cleaner who found his father most probably had a key. There would have been no reason for them to break in.

The place must have been burgled.

Or worse still – is in the process of being burgled.

9

Musca has found nothing.

He has ransacked the lounge, searched all eight bedrooms, several bathrooms and two reception rooms and so far he's found nothing of any value to him. Sure, the old guy's house is stacked full of fabulously expensive stuff. No doubt a regular burglar would be swinging a full swag bag over his shoulder and whistling a merry little tune as he strolled down the plush halls, but luxury goods are not what Musca came for.

Books, diaries, documentation, photographs, computer files and any form of tape recordings are what he's hunting in the treasure hunter's lair.

He's already wrecked the library. Yanked down, opened up and shaken loose hundreds upon hundreds of old books. Now he's heading into the study – the place he's told the professor killed himself.

He walks over to the casement window and closes the thick red curtain. He shines his torch on to the desk, finds an antique brass lamp and flicks it on. In the mellow light, his eyes fall first on the revolving walnut chair, then the Victorian desk and the large dark-red map of blood spread across the cream blotter.

He shivers. The darkness of the house seems to close in on him. Tower above him.

Click.

Musca whirls toward the door. *Just natural noises of an old building?*

Crack.

He lunges for the lamp switch. Eases away from the desk and slides back toward the door. Leaning against the wall, he wills his heart to slow down.

All is silent.

Then again the soft creak of wood.

He knows now exactly where the sound is coming from. The rear of the house is full of old wooden floorboards, many warped and loose. As he discovered when he came in. He slips his kit bag off his shoulder and dips a hand inside. His fingers close around a small iron crowbar. Perfect for busting open a flimsy back door or a skull.

A moment passes.

Then another.

And another.

He starts to wonder if he's alone or not. Whether someone's come in and spotted him. Maybe even called the cops. Musca can't stand the waiting any longer. He rummages in his trouser pockets and finds his cigarette lighter. If he can't find anything incriminating, then the least he can do is ensure no one else does.

He pads back to the desk, gingerly slides open a drawer and finds a pack of A4 printer paper. Perfect. He tears open the cover wrapping and holds the flame to a wad of paper until it starts to smoke and catches ablaze. He carries the burning bundle to the curtains, flames flailing into the darkness, and holds the blaze beside the long cloths until they ignite.

The curtains create a roaring column of fire, a furious wash of orange and black. Musca retreats two steps. A tide of smoke rises around him.

As he turns, he sees a tall figure in the doorway.

There's a small burst of light, like a switch being turned quickly on and off, and then the ghostly silhouette suddenly pulls the door shut. Musca drops the flaming paper and rushes to the thick mahogany door. A key in the lock clicks twice.

He's trapped.

10

Gideon is no hero.

The first and last time he had a fight was at school – and even then it wasn't much of a brawl. He took several punches in the face from the year bully and was left with a bloody nose and no money for tuck shop.

He's filled out a lot since then. Grown bigger and broader. The former is down to genes and the latter to years of rowing at Cambridge. But ever since that harrowing moment he's developed an acute instinct for danger and an understanding that a quick brain is almost always better than a bully's quick hands.

Gideon's already called 999. Now he's picking his way as silently as possible through the place just to make sure he hasn't made a silly mistake.

The door to the study yawns open and the light from the hall shows the big, chunky key in the lock. When he sees the figure torching the curtains he makes up his mind to lock the door and keep him there until the cops come.

But now he's thinking it over.

He's trapped someone in a burning room and if he doesn't let them out, they're going to die. So what? A bit of him really asks that. *So what* if he dies? Will the world actually miss the kind of lowlife that breaks into a dead man's house and steals from him before he is even laid to rest?

Gideon opens the door.

There's a roar of flames as the draught blows in. He steps back, arms up to his scorched face. Through a molten wall of orange, a black shape hurtles at him. He is slammed against the wall. His body shudders with the impact. A fist smashes into his left cheekbone. A knee thuds into his crotch. He doubles over in pain. Takes a boot full in the face.

Flat out on the floor, his breath shallow and his lips leaking blood, the last thing Gideon sees before dizziness swallows him is the giant wave of flames and smoke rolling his way.

11

Musca charges across the sprawling lawns behind the manor house, his heart flinging itself against his chest. Above the fizz of the flames he hears the siren – just one car by the sound of it. It's way past midnight and he knows the police won't be coming mob-handed. At best, they'll have dispatched that single squad car, with probably a couple of PCs in it.

Still, it was wise to have parked in a lane far behind the estate. The lawns are clear and open and he's soon able to escape the glare of the lights. Problem is, the darkness is virtually total and he can't find the exact place in the wall he climbed over – the point that will guide him back to the car.

He stumbles through a clump of thick rose branches and is almost sent sprawling by a molehill so large its owner could probably run for the governorship of California. Finally, he finds the landmark he'd made a mental note of: a greenhouse, the lower half built out of brick and the top of hard wood and double-glazed glass. He counts thirteen paces along the wall and finds the spot he has to climb.

There's a snag.

When he'd entered the grounds, he'd climbed a small tree on the other side. Dropping ten feet hadn't been difficult. He's just over six foot tall, so he'd been able to sling his bag over, dangle from his fingertips and then drop the rest of the way.

Now he can't get back.

No matter how high he jumps, or even *runs* and jumps, he can't get close to the top of the wall. Musca puts the kit bag down and frantically searches for something to stand on. An old compost bin, maybe a spade or garden fork to lean against, or if he's really lucky a ladder.

There's nothing.

He glances across the dark lawns. Flames spilling out of the side of the house. The cops have their hands full. He calms down. There's time enough to do this without making mistakes.

The greenhouse.

He rattles the door. Locked. Through the window he sees wooden racks full of plants. One of those would do just fine. He rushes back to his bag and realizes he's left the crowbar in the old man's study. Never mind. Brute force will do.

Musca steps back and hammers a heel through the glass and hardwood frame. He jerks the doors open and slips inside.

He's right, the wooden tables are perfect. He pulls one free from the soil that it's sunk in, sending dozens of tomato plants spilling as he pulls it outside. He looks again toward the house.

Suspended in the blackness is what appears to be a bouncing ball of light. Torchlight. A cop with a flashlight is checking the grounds – moving quickly towards him.

Musca has killed and is ready to kill again if necessary. He peels away to the left of the light and heaves a heavy stone into the side of the greenhouse.

'Stop, police!'

He smiles as the torchlight rushes toward the noise. A second later he's behind the beam and the policeman is slumping unconscious to the ground.

Musca returns to the planting table and jams it against the garden wall.

Twenty seconds later, he's gone.

12

Megan is listening to her four-year-old's snuffling and labored breathing. Every half-hour she wakes and passes a hand over the child's head. Sammy's on fire. For the eighth time that night she wets a washcloth and gently lays it on her daughter's forehead.

Her mobile rings. It jerks her out of a tense state of half-sleep and she grabs it before it wakes Sammy.

'DI Baker.'

'Inspector, it's Jack Bentley from the control room.'

'Hang on,' she whispers as she climbs out of bed. 'Give me a second.' She works her way on to the landing. 'Okay, go ahead.'

'We just had an incident in Tollard Royal, the beat officer asked me to call.'

'Bit off my patch, Jack.' She glances down the corridor. Her mother is standing at her bedroom door, scowling.

'I know that, ma'am. There's been a fire in one of the big houses out there. A burglary too, according to the report. A police officer was assaulted by the offender as he fled the scene.'

'You need to call me about this?'

'They've taken a civilian to the hospital. They found your business card on him.'

Megan turns away from her mother's accusatory gaze. 'Do you have a name? What did he look like?'

'I don't have a physical, but we ran a trace on a car parked there, an old Audi A4. It's registered to a Gideon Chase from Cambridge.'

She thinks she knows the answer but still asks the question, 'Who's the house owned by?'

Bentley taps up the info on his computer. 'Property is in the name of a Nathaniel Chase. He's listed on the electoral roll as the only resident.'

'He *was*. The man they've taken to the hospital is his son. I saw him a few hours ago. He only drove down here because I had to ring him and tell him his father had died.'

'Poor bugger. Not his night, eh?' The penny drops with Bentley. 'Was that the professor chap who shot himself?'

'The same.'

'At any rate, two officers turned out, PCs Robin Featherby and Alan Jones. Jones is getting treated for neck injuries and Featherby asked me to call and let you know. Said to say sorry for ringing late but figured best to tell you now than get shouted at tomorrow.'

'He figured right. Thanks Jack. Have a good night.'

She turns her phone off just as her mother slips into the bedroom to check on Sammy. They're going to have a row. She just knows they are. Rather than do that, she slopes off downstairs to make a cup of tea.

As the kettle boils, Megan recalls her brief meeting with Gideon and the strangely disturbing letter from his father. There's no way this incident at Tollard Royal is just a burglary gone wrong.

No way on earth.

13

TUESDAY 15 JUNE
SALISBURY

When Gideon opens his eyes it's morning and he thinks he's back at home in his own bed. In a blink he realizes how wrong he is. He's in a hospital. There'd been a fire and a burglary at his dead father's house and the doctors at Salisbury District had insisted he'd stayed the night, 'for observation'.

He's straining to sit up when the matronly form of ward sister Suzie Willoughby appears. 'You're awake, then. How are you feeling?'

He touches his head, now throbbing in protest. 'Sore.'

She lifts a chart off the bottom rail of the bed, glances at it and inspects him more closely. 'You got a bump on the head, a split lip and a nasty cut to your left cheek, but the X-rays say nothing's broken.'

'I should be thankful for small mercies.'

'Something like that.' She looks at his cut face. 'It's less angry than it was, but maybe we should put a couple of stitches in there.'

'It'll be okay, I'm a quick healer.'

She can see he's squeamish. 'They don't hurt. Not like they used to. Have you had a recent tetanus injection?'

'Not since I was a kid.'

'We'll give you one then and just check your blood for infection, better safe than sorry. How's your throat?'

He feels as though he's back in boarding school, being checked over by Sister to see if he's trying to skive lessons. 'It's a bit rough, but I'm okay. Actually, I think I'm fine to go home, if that's all right.'

She gives him a look that says it isn't. 'Doctor will be around in about twenty minutes. He'll give you the once-over and if everything's fine, then we'll discharge you.' She fusses with the thin blankets. 'I'll get you something for the headache and some water for the throat. Best you drink *lots* of water. Flush the system. The fire you got caught in gave off a lot of smoke and you sucked it down into your lungs. You'll probably be very sore and coughy for a few days.'

He nods gratefully. 'Thanks.'

As she waddles off, he thinks about what she said. *The fire.* He remembers everything now: the intruder in his father's study, the blazing curtains, the fight in the hallway.

The nurse returns with a plastic cup of water and a couple of small tubs of pills. 'Do you have allergic reactions to paracetamol or ibuprofen?'

'No.'

She shakes out two paracetamol pills. 'Take these and if they don't work, the doctor will give you something stronger.'

He has to drink all the water to swallow them. Vicky – his ex – used to be able to pop pills, *any* kind, without even a sip of water, but he has to empty half the Thames down his neck to swallow just one.

Funny he's thinking about her today. It must be the whack to the head. It's more than a year since they broke up. Queen Vic went back to Edinburgh after completing her doctorate, as she'd always threatened to do, and the separation made them both realize that it was the right time to move on. *Shame*, Gideon thinks, there are times when he still misses her. Like now.

Sister Willoughby is hovering.

'Do you think you're up to visitors?' She sounds almost apologetic.

Gideon's not sure how to answer. 'What kind?'

'The police. There's a lady Detective Inspector just arrived in reception.' A hint of mischief twinkles in her eyes. 'You don't have to see her if you don't feel up to it. I can have her sent away.'

'It's fine. I'll see her. Thanks.' His head throbs out a protest. Megan Baker is emphatically not the kind of company he wants right now.

14

The Inner Circle assembles in one of the outer chambers of the Sanctuary. A waist-high ring of purest beeswax candles casts a spectral glow over the emergency gathering convened by the Keeper.

Musca stands in the center, disgrace hanging like a stone around his neck.

'You have failed.' Draco's voice cannons off the cavernous stone walls. 'Failed your brothers, failed our Craft and endangered all we stand for.'

Musca knows better than to protest.

Draco's voice grows cruel. 'For the sake of us all, summarize the list of "gifts" you left for the police.'

Musca recites them blankly. 'A tool bag. There was a crowbar, screwdriver, hammer, duct tape, wire cutters—'

Draco interrupts: 'And enough DNA to convict you for burglary, arson and perhaps attempted murder.'

'It's not traceable to me.'

'As yet.'

'I have no criminal record,' protests Musca. 'My fingerprints or genetic fingerprints are not on file anywhere.'

Draco slaps him across the face. 'Don't add insolence to incompetence. Afford me the respect I deserve as Keeper of the Inner Circle.'

Musca puts a hand to his stinging cheek. 'I apologize.'

Draco looks across the darkened room. 'Grus, can we make this evidence go away?'

'Have it lost?'

Draco nods.

'Not yet. There is the small matter of the policeman he assaulted as well. But later, yes. I'm confident that can be done.'

'Good.' He turns back to Musca. 'Did anyone see your face?'

'Not the policeman, it was dark. But the son. I am certain he saw me.'

Draco bounces a question across the chamber: 'Do we know *how* he is, *where* he is?'

The smallest among them, a red-haired brother known as Fornax, answers. 'He's in hospital in Salisbury, detained overnight, no serious injuries. He'll be discharged tomorrow, perhaps even later today.'

Grus speaks out, his voice calm and mature: 'The Lookers will keep tabs on him as he leaves.'

'Good.' Draco has another question for Musca. 'To be clear, you found nothing inside the house that would alert the world to us?'

'Nothing. I searched all the rooms. Upstairs and downstairs. There were hundreds – perhaps thousands – of books, but no records, no documentation and no letters that in any way mentioned the Sacreds or our Craft.'

Grus speaks again. 'Perhaps he remained loyal until the end.'

Draco doesn't think so. 'We know of your affection for our lost brother, but it is misplaced. His suicide is more than untimely; it's selfish and potentially disastrous. He knew what was planned and what was expected of him.'

The Keeper switches his attention back to Musca. 'You are

absolutely certain that there was nothing in that house that referred to us and our Craft?'

'If there was, there isn't now. I'm sure the fire destroyed the entire contents of the study.'

Draco's anger and anxiety subside. Perhaps the mistake with the forgotten bag is the price that has to be paid for a cleansing fire that safeguards the secrecy of the Craft. But a bigger problem remains. Nathaniel Chase had a vital role to play in the Craft's destiny. A key position in the second phase of the ceremony.

Now he's gone, that role has to be filled.

And quickly.

15

Megan Baker smoothes out her charcoal-gray mid-length suit skirt and sits on the hard chair next to Gideon's bed. 'So, what on earth happened to you?'

'I'm afraid I don't remember much.'

She glances to the nurse now at her side. 'Is there somewhere more private than this? A place he and I can talk?'

The nurse has to think for a second. 'There's an examination room down the corridor.' She points. 'Use that. Flip the sign on the door so you don't get disturbed.'

Megan looks back towards Gideon. 'Are you good to walk?'

'Sure. I'm fine.' He slowly swings his legs out of bed, taking care the ill-fitting pajamas don't reveal more of him than is acceptable. 'Forgive my appearance.' He gestures to the striped and faded flannels that finish way above his ankles.

They enter the room and the nurse leaves them.

Megan flips the sign to 'Engaged', shuts the door and pulls out two chairs, one from behind a desk. 'So what happened after you left the police station?'

He feels stupid. 'I hadn't really thought things through. After I left you, I realized I didn't have anywhere to stay. It seemed like a good idea to go to my father's and sleep there. I suppose deep down I felt drawn to it.'

'That's natural enough.'

'Maybe. Anyway, the back door had been broken open so I called 999 and went to have a look around.'

She laces one leg over the other. 'You should have waited until the patrol car arrived. Didn't they tell you to wait?'

He can't remember if they did, but he doesn't want to get anyone in trouble. 'I suspect so. I just wanted to have a look inside and make sure I hadn't raised a false alarm.'

'Which you clearly hadn't.'

'No. I hadn't. I saw this man in my father's study. He was setting it on fire.'

'How? What exactly was he doing?'

The image is clear in the archaeologist's head. 'He had one hand – his left – full of papers and he lit them with a cigarette lighter, one of those cheap little ones.'

'Disposable. A BIC?'

'Something like that. He lit the papers, then set the curtains on fire and was about to do the same with my father's desk.'

'When you confronted him?'

'No, not exactly. At first I just pulled the door shut and locked him in. Then I realized I had to let him out, otherwise he'd have probably died.'

'Some people might have been tempted to leave him in there.'

'I was.'

'Good job you didn't. I'd be charging you with a criminal offense this morning if you had done.'

'I know.'

She studies him. He's an academic, not a fighter. One of those men who looks tall enough and fit enough to handle himself but evidently never learned how.

'So you opened the door and he just starts laying into you?'

'Virtually. He pushed me out of the way and I grabbed him around the waist, rugby-style. Only I didn't take him down and he started punching and kicking me.'

She looks at the bruising. It's unusual. 'He cut your cheek quite badly. From the mark, I'd say he was wearing some jewelry on his right hand, maybe a signet ring.'

'I didn't notice. Just the pain.'

'I imagine.' She lifts her handbag from the floor. 'You mind if I take a shot of this, the outline is really clear?'

'I suppose not.'

She slides back the cover on the tiny Cyber-shot that she carries, then virtually blinds him with a camera flash. 'Sorry,' she says from behind the lens, 'just one more.'

Another flash and she clicks it closed. 'We may want SOCO to look at that.' She drops the camera back in her bag. 'If we can catch the guy that laid that ring on you, he should go down for assault, burglary and arson. A nice trio, he could get a good stretch for that.'

'Could?'

'Afraid so. The English judiciary will listen to any sob stories about him wetting the bed as a child, his father being an alcoholic or such like. They call it mitigating circumstances. Did you get a good look at him?'

Disappointment shows on Gideon's face. 'No, I'm afraid not. It all happened so quickly and it was really dark.'

Megan has a degree in psychology and spent two years working on secondment to one of Britain's top profilers. She can see a lie coming before it's even crossed a guy's lips. She frowns and tries to look confused. 'I don't quite get it. You clearly noticed the lighter in his hand – the BIC. But you didn't see his face.'

Gideon feels uncomfortable. 'I don't know. I guess my eyes were drawn to the flame.'

'I can understand that. But despite all the light from the fire – from the papers in his hand and from the blazing curtains – you didn't get at least enough of a look at him to give a rough description?'

He shrugs. 'Sorry.'

'Mr. Chase, I want to help you. But you're going to have to trust me.'

He looks surprised. 'I do. Why wouldn't I?'

She ignores the question. 'Are you sure you can't tell us anything about the man. His size? Weight? Hair color? Clothing? Anything?'

He can feel her eyes boring through him but he's staying silent. He has a photograph of the man, snapped on his mobile phone, just before he'd shut the door. The burglar must have been there in connection with his father's secrets, and he intends to discover precisely what they are long before the police do.

Megan is still waiting for an answer.

He shakes his head. 'I'm sorry. I just can't help you.'

She flashes him a smile so bright he nearly flinches. 'You will,' she says with an icy coldness. 'Believe me, you will.'

16

STONEHENGE

Protecting the precious stones principally means stopping people from climbing on them or defacing them. To that end, English Heritage has erected fences, traffic barriers and ropes, and only allows people into the roped-off relics on special occasions or with written permission.

The government-funded body is good at its job but has no idea just how devoted some of its subcontracted security staff are. The likes of Sean Grabb are devout members of the Followers of the Sacreds. Long after their paid shifts have finished, they still watch the precious site.

Thirty-five-year-old Grabb is one of those sleeves-rolled-up, slightly overweight guys who always gets a job done and is never short of a good word for those who work for him. He heads up a team of Lookers who keep Stonehenge under constant vigil. Three hundred and sixty degrees. Twenty-four hours a day. Seven days a week. Three hundred and sixty-five days a year.

He and his Lookers never stop looking. Some of it is done openly during the Heritage-paid shifts, some covertly by tiny remote cameras strategically placed across the landscape.

Grabb has been a Looker for ten years. Known inside the Craft as Serpens, he is following in the deep footsteps of his father, grandfather and every other traceable male in the paternal line. With him today is twenty-five-year-old Lee Johns, a relatively new recruit, yet to be formally admitted into the Craft's hallowed ranks. He's tall and thin with pimply, undernourished skin and, outside of his work uniform, lives in unwashed denims and rock band T-shirts. He's not too bright and has weathered his share of problems, including drugs and homelessness. By his early twenties, society had written him off as an eco-hippie troublemaker. For a while he sought solace in the company of other protestors and agitators. He never totally fitted in.

His life started to have meaning only when he drifted down to Stonehenge en route to Glastonbury, where he'd hoped to score some cheap gear and maybe string together a bit of money from low-level dealing. But he never made it to the music gathering. The solstice was so breathtaking he felt unable to even move from the henge. He stayed, helping clear up and volunteering for any kind of work in relation to the magical stones.

He's been working with Sean for close on three years now and they have something of a master and apprentice relationship. Sean is his sponsor and dispenses wisdom as regularly as he does the sludgy brown tea from his trusty flask. Every watch he quizzes his protégé in the effort to ensure he's fit to be admitted into the closed circle of the Followers.

'Question one.' Grabb gives his pupil a pay-attention stare. 'What are the stones and what do they mean to those of us in the Craft?'

Johns grins – an easy one. 'The stones are our Sacreds. They are the source of all our earthly energy. They are our protectors, our guardians and our life force.'

Grabb splashes a reward of tea into Lee's brown-ringed mug. 'Good. And *why* do the Sacreds bestow such blessings on us?'

Johns cradles the dark elixir as they stand by the traffic barrier in the parking lot. 'We are the Followers of the Sacreds, descendants of those who placed the great ones here thousands of years ago. The bones and blood of our ancestors nourish the Sacreds in their resting places, just as one day our remains will follow them and complete the circle.'

Steam wafts from the top of Grabb's steel thermos cup. He sips the hot tea and asks, 'And *how* do the Sacreds bless us?'

'With their spiritual energy. They transfer it through the stones to us and their blessing protects us from the ravages of illness and the humiliation of poverty.'

Grabb is pleased. His pupil is learning his catechism well and that can only reflect kindly on him. He pours more tea into Lee's mug. 'And what do the Sacreds expect in return?'

'Respect.' He pronounces the word with sincerity. 'We must recognize them, respect them, have faith in them and follow their teachings through their appointed oracle, the Henge Master.'

'That's right, Lee. Remember those who would steal our heritage. Remember the Catholics and their commandments written in stone supposedly passed down from God. They cooked up that story two thousand years after the Sacreds had been established here in England.'

Lee nods. He understands. He must not be sidetracked or seduced by other religions, false-belief systems that have big gold glittering palaces for adoration, that collect money each week from congregations and create their own banks and states. 'Sean,' he starts, thirsty for reassurance. 'I know you can trace your bloodline all the way back to the greats who carried the bluestones and the sarsens. I understand why that makes you worthy for the blessing and protection of the Sacreds, but what about people like me? We're outsiders. We don't come from around here.'

Grabb recognizes the insecurity; it's a regular thing with Lee. 'We are all from *around here*, my friend. Five thousand years ago the population of Britain was tiny. Way back then, you and I were probably brothers, or cousins at worst.'

Johns likes that idea. And it makes sense too. Even the Christians believe in Adam and Eve and how one moment of sex somehow spawned all of mankind. Or something like that, he can't quite remember. Brothers – him and Sean.

'You're doing real well, Lee.' Grabb puts a broad arm around the kid's near-skeletal shoulders and shows him how proud he is.

But in reality he's worried – worried about how his protégé will face up to the horrors of the challenge that awaits.

17

After a tetanus shot and what he viewed as a completely unnecessary taking of blood, Gideon is discharged from hospital in the late afternoon. The only good thing is that the DI was able to get the keys to his father's house biked over before the discharge was completed.

Approaching the grand house in a taxi from the hospital, he can see that the damage is considerable. The lawns have been churned up by fire engines and the side of the building is shrouded in the remnants of black smoke. Windows are blown in and boarded up, brickwork cracked.

Right now he doesn't care. The place is still just bricks and mortar to him. Only when he lets himself in through the colossal front door does he feel any emotion.

When his mother died, Gideon was distraught. He went from being confident and extroverted, trusting in the world and his place in it, to being disturbingly introverted and wary of people. The death of his father is bringing on another change. He is uncertain of what but he feels it. Inside him is a volatile mix of anger, frustration, resentment and a residue of unfairness. A swirling blend of components that he knows is going to alter the DNA of his personality irrevocably.

He wanders the big empty house and feels acutely alone. He has no brothers or sisters, no grandparents. No children. He is the end of the Chase line. What he does with the remainder of his life will determine not only what the world thinks of him but the whole Chase lineage.

He drops his jacket in the hall. Climbs the grand staircase to a long open first-floor landing and searches for a place to wash and crash for a while.

The house is plainly not equipped for life four hundred years after it was built. The big rooms with their high ceilings must cost a fortune to heat. No wonder his father appears to have lived in only a couple. The windows are draughty and need replacing. Most of the walls are flaked with damp. Floors creak worse than the planks of an old sailing ship in a storm and it must be fifty years since the place saw a decent lick of paint.

His father's bedroom is the smallest of all and gives him the strangest of feelings. It's crammed with emptiness. The old man's things are everywhere but they have become depersonalized, as though blasted with some radioactivity that eradicated all trace of him.

A pile of books towers by the bed. Near them is a white mug, an inch of tea still in it, a crust of mold on the surface. He guesses it was the last morning cuppa or late-night drink his father tasted.

The quilt is pulled back on one side of the high, wooden-framed double bed. The indent in the old spring mattress, gray base sheet and crumpled feather pillow show exactly where Nathaniel slept. The other side of the bed is pristine. Gideon feels himself frown. For all Nathaniel's legendary brilliance and inarguable wealth, his father lived like a squatter and died lonely.

He casts a last look around the little bedroom and notices the remains of an old bell circuit above the door, a hangover from the time a nanny or butler slept here waiting to be called by the master of the house. He is reminded of a boyhood visit one wet weekend to a National Trust home and the single interesting comment from the tour guide: the property, he'd said, was veined with secret passages so servants could pass quickly and discreetly from upstairs to downstairs.

Gideon wonders if his father's place is the same. He steps out into the corridor, kicking up a swirl of dust motes. He ponders if there's another room behind Nathaniel's tiny bedroom.

There isn't.

The landing runs down to a casement window overlooking the garden. He walks down and to his right sees an odd join in the wallpaper. He taps the wall. It sounds like plasterboard. He knocks a meter to the left and then a meter to the right.

Stone.

He taps again on the board. All over and around it. The plasterboard area is big enough to be a door. There's no visible handle or hinges, but he's sure it is. He gets down on his knees and digs, just as he would in an archaeological trench. His fingers find the edge where the skirting board meets the landing floor. He tries to pull it open but it is jammed tight. Out of frustration he pushes rather than pulls.

It bursts open, belching out a breath of musty air.

Gideon bolts upright. A sliver of darkness is cut into the wall. He reaches inside and finds a light switch. He is astonished by what he sees: a narrow room like a very long cupboard. One wall is stacked floor to ceiling with books. Another contains old VHS tapes, some DVDs. Set into the far wall is an old pre-HD plasma TV.

His mind trips into overdrive. Why did his father have a hidden room? What's on the tapes – and why are they in this place? Why are dozens of books in here and not on show downstairs?

Why was his father so determined to keep all this secret?

PART TWO

18

WEDNESDAY 16 JUNE
SOHO, LONDON

Jake Timberland is thirty-one but tells anyone who doesn't know better that he's twenty-seven. There's something about thirty or over that he simply isn't ready to have pinned on him. In Jake's circle of friends, age is like the big birthday badge fastened on your chest when you are a kid, proclaiming 'I AM 5'. Only at thirty it might as well say 'I AM Slippers. Carpets. Dogs. Families. Volvos. I AM DULL.'

And dull sure ain't Jake. Especially on a night when he's done more chemicals than Pete Doherty and Amy Winehouse put together.

He's not rich. But his father is. Banker bonus rich. The kind that comes from so far back in the family tree that the damn thing must have been a sapling in the garden of Eden when Adam was still pawing around. One day Jake will cop for the lot, but until then he has to make do with a five-million-pound pied-à-terre in Marylebone and an allowance that's just enough to run the Aston, pay his club bills, make the occasional investment and enjoy the odd night on the town.

Jake is the only son and heir of Lord Joseph Timberland and he's been papped with some of society's hottest models, page-three girls and wild-child daughters of ageing rock stars. Sure it helps that your best buddy is a lensman at *Heat* magazine, but then what are friends for?

Tonight he is dressed to kill. A shimmering silk and cotton blue suit with a plain saturated-blue shirt and new black Italian leather shoes.

He already has his sights set on a real hottie. A lithe piece who's breezed into the VIP area at Chinawhite's and is acting like she owns the place. Her perfect teeth say she's American long before you hear her laugh and chat over-loudly to her entourage. Soaring cheekbones, warm brown eyes, carefully scrunched long dark hair and fabulous legs that stretch from a retro dashiki-style miniskirt in green, hot pink and coral. She looks like a film star hippie.

Just watching her sends a rush of blood to his head.

Then she glances his way.

Oh, man. Jake thinks he's going to blow like an oil well. He floats across the floor, pulled by her sheer sexual gravity. The lithe one is surrounded by lots of pretty young things, boys and girls, but it seems she has eyes only for him.

'Whoa, fella. Hold up.'

The voice and a big black hand on his chest come out of nowhere.

'Excuse me.' Jake peers disdainfully at the big fingers spread like the jaw of a crocodile near his puny white neck. 'Do you mind?'

He's speaking polite and perfect English into the face of a man so large he can't see beyond his shoulder-span. 'You need to back up a little, sir. The lady over there is having a party and there are no strangers allowed.'

Jake gives in to a nervous laugh. 'A party without strangers? Just let me introduce myself to the young lady, I'm—'

The crocodile snaps. The finger-jaws grab Jake's throat and have him walking breathlessly backward all the way to a seat in the far corner of the VIP lounge.

As he struggles for breath, an older man with short white hair squats on his heels and looks deep into Jake's eyes. 'Son, we're sorry to have had to do that. Now we're going to order you a complimentary bottle of whatever you like and you're going to stay right over here and drink it. Okay?'

'This is my club,' protests Jake, his voice raspy. He surprises himself by standing up. But once on his feet he has no real idea what he should do next. His way forward is blocked by crocodile man and another black-suited animal. He'd need ladders to climb over them.

Beyond the mountain range of their muscles, his eye again catches that of the beautiful young American. She murmurs to a blonde beside her – and, to Jake's amazement, starts to walk his way.

There is no mistaking her intention. Her eyes never lose contact with his. Whoever she is, she's coming over to talk to him.

The mountains shift menacingly toward him but he doesn't care. They say love hurts. Jake guesses he's just about to find out precisely how much.

19

Gideon's mobile is chirping downstairs like a bird trapped in a flue.

He knows he won't get to it before it trips to his message service but hurries out of his father's hidden room and tries anyway.

He misses it by seconds.

The voicemail kicks in as he scours the worktops for pen and paper. He finds a rip-and-stick pad by the fridge. The front page bears a rough shopping list – cheese, biscuits, fruit, chocolate – the last supper his father never had.

He plays back the missed call, scribbles down the number and punches it in once the message has ended.

The voice at the other end is a woman's. 'CID. DI Baker.'

His hopes drop. 'This is Gideon Chase, you just called my mobile.'

'Mr. Chase, thanks for ringing. I called to fix a time for you to see your father's body.'

The words stun him. He'd been fearing this. She'd even asked him about it. But now it's come he feels totally unprepared. 'Right. Thank you.'

'The funeral director is Abrahams and Cunningham on Bleke Street in Shaftesbury. Do you know where I mean?'

'No. I'm not local, I don't know the area at all.'

'Well, it's easy to find. It's on the right, not far down from the Ivy

Cross roundabout. They've suggested ten a.m. tomorrow. If that's not suitable, I can give you a number and you can make your own arrangements.'

There isn't a time on the clock face that seems *suitable* to see the semi-obliterated body of your father. In true English fashion, Gideon says the opposite of what he's thinking. 'Yes, that would be fine.'

'Good. I'll confirm with them.'

'Thanks.'

Megan senses his tension. 'If you'd like I could get an officer to accompany you. Would that help?'

'I'll be okay on my own.'

'I understand.' She sounds sympathetic. 'Call me if you change your mind.'

Gideon hangs up and heads back upstairs.

He re-enters the secret room with a degree of trepidation, worried that the tapes are going to turn out to be pornographic. He tells himself he can live with it. Because it may be worse. It may relate to Nathaniel's grave-robbing, his tomb-raiding, his highly questionable 'trade' in prized artifacts.

He stands for a moment and surveys the room. Years of training have taught him to take in the landscape before you start digging it up. The old saying about needing to know the lie of the land is true in archaeology – the terrain can lie like a faithless lover and lose you years of your life.

He knows that his father was the last person in here before him. The way it is, is how *he* left it. Generally tidy. Neat, except for a couple of open DVD cases. Orderly. There is a leather desk chair positioned in front of the wall-mounted TV and a low coffee table in the middle of the room. It's marked with shoe polish on the near side, from where his father must have put his feet while watching the screen. There's a crystal glass that smells of whisky, but no sign of a decanter or bottle. He suspects the liquor is stashed in one of the built-in cupboards at the bottom of the shelving that fills the room. There are boxes on the back shelves. He wonders how much his father was drinking at the end. Next to the glass is an ancient laptop computer – the type that still takes floppy disks – a notepad and a small and ugly clay pencil holder that he recognizes instantly. He made it at school and brought it home for Father's Day.

He can tell that the room has been used for logging, reviewing and filing. But what? He finds the TV remote control within reaching distance of the chair and turns the set on. Built into the wall beneath it are three shelves, one holding a chunky, near-industrial VHS player, one for a DVD machine and a bottom one that looks like a place to throw junk – cables, open tape boxes and loose coins.

The TV throws up a haze of broken white and black fuzz as it stirs itself. The DVD whirrs into life and fights for channel supremacy. Up on to the screen comes an out-of-focus, grainy picture. It's a digital copy of old Super 16mm film by the look of it. It sharpens and shows his father reincarnated as a more youthful man, speaking confidently from the stage of a lecture theater: 'Stonehenge is a miracle of the ancient world. To build it today, with all of our machinery and mathematical know-how would be impressive. To have begun building it five thousand years ago, without computers, CAD packages, cranes and trucks and barges to carry those monoliths is beyond wonder.'

Gideon is bored already. His childhood had been littered with nonsensical theories about Stonehenge being a temple, a burial place for ancient kings, the world's first astronomical observatory, a cosmic link to the pyramids in Egypt. And most ignorantly of all, the birthplace of the druids.

His father's face is up close to the camera, so close Gideon can see the pores of his skin, the stubble, the blemishes, the marks life has made on him. His eyes are glazed with that insane enthusiasm that glistened only when he spoke about prehistoric things. The clock has suddenly been turned back. He's espousing his theories again, waving his arms and linking Stonehenge to other megalithic sites across Western Europe.

'This creation - this *wonder* - behind me is not singular, far from it.

Walk the fields of France and you'll begin to understand that the ancients had a *collective master plan* - one that stretched across the world as they knew it. The thousands of *minhirs*, the long standing stones spread from Brittany to the south of France are clues to the connections they were constructing – as are the *dolmens*, the portal tombs and graves in the Loire. And then there is *Carnac*!' The emphasis brings a smile to Nathaniel's face as wide and happy as Gideon can ever remember. The old film camera zooms out and his father turns toward the widening shots of the stones behind him, 'Archaeologists often call Carnac the French Stonehenge. It bares the same name as Karnac, the famed Egyptian temple complex that makes up the largest ancient religious site in the world. Carnac dates back four and a half thousand years before Christ's birth. Like Stonehenge it was built in two distinct stages and – fascinatingly –it is positioned at the unique latitude on the Earth at which the solstice sun - both summer and winter - forms a perfect Pythagorean triangle relative to the parallel of latitude. This archaeoastronomical marvel is no accident of design; this is the stuff of global visionaries - the work of the gods.'

Gideon turns off the film and fires up the old VHS machine. It clicks and clunks as the mechanical heads shuffle around and lock on a tape that has been left in there. A big close-up of a beautiful woman's face appears on screen. Beautiful enough to suck the air from his lungs.

It's his mother.

She is laughing. Holding her hand up to the camera and looking embarrassed that she's being filmed. He finds the volume. 'Turn it off, Nate. I hate that thing, *please* turn it off.'

Her voice makes him tremble. He can't help but step forward and put his fingers to the screen.

'Nate. Enough now!'

The shot pulls wider. Marie Chase sits on a gondola in Venice against a cornflower blue sky. She turns her head from the camera faking annoyance with her husband. Her hair is dark, long and thick – exactly the same texture as Gideon's – and it is being made to dance on her shoulders by a light summer's wind. In the background, St.

Mark's bobs away as a stripe-shirted boatman punts them across the lagoon. The shot is wide enough now for Gideon to tell that she's pregnant.

He stops the tape and looks away wet-eyed to the stacked shelves. They're not all full of home movies, of that he's sure. The last thing his father watched was his mother because he was reconnecting with happier times, probably the happiest of his life. It's the kind of thing people do when they're experiencing the worst of times, the worst of their lives.

Everything on the shelves was important to his father. Important enough to classify and to protect. But not as important as this precious memory of the only woman he really loved.

Gideon walks to the books. They are all red, leather-bound journals, the lineless type favored by artists and writers. He tries to pull down a volume from the top left-hand corner but the covers are stuck together. He prises them apart.

He opens the book on the first page and reels from another emotional blow. It's dated the day of his father's eighteenth birthday.

The handwriting is the same but somehow hesitant:

> My name is Nathaniel Chase and today is my eighteenth birthday, the day I come of age. I have made a promise to myself that from this instant onwards I will keep a meticulous record of what I hope will be a long, eventful, happy and successful life. I will record the good and the bad, the honourable and the dishonourable, the things that stir the soul and those that leave me indifferent. My tutors say that much can be learned from history, so perhaps as the years unfold I shall learn much about myself by keeping an honest record of the passing years. No doubt, if I am famous I will publish these small literary missives, and should I be a nonentity then at least in my winter years I shall gain some warmth from looking back and reflecting in the hot optimism of my youth. I am eighteen. A great adventure awaits me.

Gideon finds it too painful to read on. He glances along the rows. Is this stuff in all of them? Every event, emotion and detail of Nathaniel Chase's great adventure?

He runs a finger along the red spines and counts off the years: his father's twentieth birthday, his twenty-first, his twenty-sixth – the year he met his wife; his twenty-eighth – the same as Gideon is now; his thirtieth – the year Nathaniel Gregory Chase and Marie Isabel Pritchard married in Cambridge; and his thirty-second – when Gideon was born.

The fluttering fingers stop. He has entered his own space. His eyes drift down to the thirty-eighth year. The year Marie died.

His hands stretch to the slim volume and he begins to lever it out of the vice-like grip of those either side, but he cannot bring himself to remove it. Instead, he jumps on two years. To the fortieth of his father's life.

He withdraws the diary. Two years after his mother's death. He feels prepared for whatever the eighth year of his own life has to offer.

Only he isn't.

It's not written in English. It's not written in any recognizable language.

It's in code.

Gideon pulls out the following year's book.

Code.

And the year after.

Code.

He rushes to the end of the room and stoops for the final volume. Again he freezes – this book will bear the last entries of Nathaniel Chase's life.

His heart is like a raging bull butting his rib cage. He swallows hard, lifts the volume from its shelf and opens it.

20

SOHO, LONDON

She smells like cinnamon. And she's high as a kite.

Jake Timberland notes these things as the beautiful American kisses him goodbye on the pavement. She's maybe twenty-two at most. And it's not a peck on the cheek. It's a proper smacker. She holds his face between her manicured fingers and her lips gently touch his. But he lets her make the running.

And she does. A little brush of the tongue – just a glance against the underside of his upper lip. His eyes dance beneath closed lids. She moves back. 'Bye.' A smile and she steps away.

'Wait.'

She smiles again as she folds herself daintily into the backseat of the limo. The black guy with the crocodile hands slams the door shut and shoots him a look that's more than just a warning; it's a declaration of war.

Fuck it. Jake squares his shoulders and approaches the tinted rear window. For the second time that evening, a massive hand explodes like a grenade in the middle of his chest, sending him sprawling. The bodyguard slips into the passenger seat and the limo is gone before Jake's anywhere near getting to his feet. The most beautiful woman he's ever met has just watched him fall on his butt. Not a good way to end the evening.

He gets a few strange glances as several couples slalom past into the depths of Soho. The pavement is soaked from an earlier downpour and his clothes are now wet. He brushes himself down and digs in his pocket for a handkerchief to wipe the mud and grit from his hands.

Something flutters to the floor. He bends and picks it up. It's a bar mat, the advertising ripped off, and there's a message in pen on it: 'Call me tomorrow on number below x.' Next to the kiss is a small squiggle of a padlock.

Jake stares at the doodle. He knows it. *Jesus*. Now he understands what all the security was about.

21

Gideon holds the diary in shaking hands. He sits on the room's hard floor, rests his back against the shelving, afraid to read. He feels beaten – as though assaulted and battered by some invisible enemy. Floored by the ghost of his father.

He looks up at all the handwritten journals around him – a complete personal history of the father he never knew. And the man wrote more than twenty years of it in code.

Why?

He shakes his head and blinks. Darkness presses like shoveled earth against every pane of glass in the house. He feels entombed. Carefully, he opens the cover and on the right-hand inside page is the inscription: ΓΚΝΔΜΥ ΚΛΥ.

It makes him smile. He runs his fingers over the top of the page and feels himself slipping back to childhood. His father never kicked a football with him, never swung a cricket bat, never took him swimming. But he played mind games with him. Nathaniel spent hours devising puzzles, teasers, problems and games that imbued in him powers of logic and the roots of classical learning.

The letters ΓΚΝΔΜΥ ΚΛΥ are ancient Greek, which his father considered the first true alphabet, the source of European, Latin and Middle Eastern alphabets. And he recognized its importance in mathematics, physics and astronomy. His son was made to learn every letter. To test the boy, and to break the boredom, the professor devised a simple code. The twenty-four letters of the Greek alphabet assumed reverse values to their English equivalents, so Omega represented A and so on until Alpha represented X. The obsolete Greek letters Digamma and Qoppa represented the final English letters Y and Z. For years Nathaniel would leave his son coded notes around the house – until the relationship became too strained for any form of communication.

Gideon struggles to remember the code. It's been more than fifteen years. Then it comes to him. ΓΚΝΔΜΥ ΚΛΥ means VOLUME ONE. He glances up again at the dozens of books and wonders how many coded words have been written. It could take a lifetime to decipher them all.

A lifetime to translate a lifetime.

He turns another page, and feels queasy. The handwriting is a savage reminder of the suicide note. He tries to make sense of the first paragraph but he is too rusty to get further than a few words. From the low coffee table he picks up some paper and a couple of pens – black and red. He constructs a table, writing the Greek letters on the left and to the right, the English.

Ϙ	Qoppa	Z	Μ	Mu	M
F	Digamma	Y	Ν	Nu	L
Α	Alpha	X	Ξ	Xi	K
Β	Beta	W	Ο	Omicron	J
Γ	Gamma	V	Π	Pi	I
Δ	Delta	U	Ρ	Rho	H
Ε	Epsilon	T	Σ	Sigma	G
Ζ	Zeta	S	Τ	Tau	F
Η	Eta	R	Υ	Upsilon	E
Θ	Theta	Q	Φ	Phi	D
Ι	Iota	P	Χ	Chi	C
Κ	Kappa	O	Ψ	Psi	B
Λ	Lambda	N	Ω	Omega	A

Using the table, he scans the opening page and quickly translates ΛΩΕΡΩΛΠΥΝ into NATHANIEL and ΧΡΩΖΥ into CHASE. The journal is written in the first person and contains his father's day-to-day thoughts.

He flicks through a dozen or so more pages, not looking for anything in particular, fascinated that he can travel backward or forward through days, months or years of his father's life. Halfway through the journal, the writing becomes bolder. The passages look as though they've been written with vigor and excitement. Years of speed-reading have trained Gideon's eyes to hop diagonally down a document in search of key words.

ΖΕΚΛΥΡΥΛΣΥ, ΨΝΚΚΦ and ΖΩΧΗΠΤΠΧΥ leap out at him.

He hopes he's made a mistake. Prays that tiredness has made him jump to the wrong conclusion. On its own, ΖΕΚΛΥΡΥΛΣΥ may be innocuous enough; he'd expect his father to mention it. It means STONEHENGE.

It's the other two words that are chilling his soul.

ΨΝΚΚΦ is BLOOD.

And ΖΩΧΗΠΤΠΧΥ is SACRIFICE.

22

MARYLEBONE, LONDON

Jake Timberland flings his suit in a corner and sits on the edge of his giant black leather bed with built-in fifty-inch plasma and room dimmers. He's too wired to get any sleep and strangely enough not in the mood to go hunting cute-ass-would-be-wags for the rest of the night. In any case, the date isn't over. Thanks to his mobile phone, it's about to go virtual. The beauty of technology.

In his left hand is his iPhone and in his right the piece of paper with the padlock doodle that the American lovely gave him. Caitlyn to be more precise. Caitlyn Lock.

Just being seen within touching distance of 'The Lock,' as she's known, could make him an 'A-Lister.' He reckons that right now she'll be doing one of three things. She could still be partying, which he doubts because the gorillas probably wouldn't allow her that much freedom. She could be having a drink with some of the other clean-cut cuties she was hanging with. Possible. Or she could be a good little girl and already in bed. Probable. Whichever it is, she'll be thinking about him. You don't kiss someone like she did and then not think about it later.

What he has to do is tap into that. Tap in and stretch it while it's still fresh. Give himself something to build a little romance on. And the perfect tool to pull off that little trick is sexy texting. Nothing hard core. Just a couple of short notes to say that he can't stop thinking about her. Start off casual and polite then feel his way in, reveal a little more of his emotions. No point simply gushing it all out on the first message. If you do that, the girl won't reply, she'll just leave you hanging on until you try again.

Jake gets typing. *Hope you got home ok. It was great to meet you tonight. Jake.* No, that's not good. He rewrites: *Hope you got home ok. It was GREAT to meet you tonight. Jake.*

Still not right.

He remembers her age. Considerably younger than him. He adjusts again: *Hope u r ok. Gr8 2 meet u! Jake x.*

He allows himself a satisfied smile and hits send. Phones are terrific. He watches the little virtual envelope on the screen fold itself up, develop wings and then fly off, straight to the heart of the woman he loves. Well yeah, maybe. For now it's lust, pure and simple. But let's face it, without that, love probably doesn't have a chance.

The phone beeps. Wow, she's replied quickly. Good sign.

U can ring if u want x.

Not what he expected. Not what he wanted either. A little text flirting before turning in for the night was a perfect idea, but a conversation right now could blow things. He thinks. When a girl says you can ring *if you want,* that's not a request, it's an instruction.

Jake pulls off his socks and shirt, grabs a glass of water from the bathroom and climbs in bed. He feels almost panicky as he calls her.

'It's Jake. Hi.'

'Hi there.' Her voice is soft and a little sleepy. 'I wondered if you'd ring or text.'

'Even after you saw me sit down in a puddle?'

She laughs a little. 'Especially after you dumped your ass in a puddle.'

'Actually, *I* didn't dump my ass – one of your apes did.'

'That would be Eric. He has a thing for me. I've seen him rough guys up much worse. Much, much worse than you got and I didn't even kiss them.'

'Remind me not to put Eric on my Christmas card list.'

'He's just protective.'

'So I noticed. Why did you do that?'

'Do what?'

'Kiss me.'

'Ah, that would be because I wanted to.' Her voice is almost sleepy. 'And let's face it, *you* wanted me to.'

'I did?'

'I've never seen a man aching so badly to be kissed.'

He laughs. 'You've *no idea* how much.'

'Oh, I've an idea all right. You were sticking it in my hip. Pretty big clue.'

He feigns shock. 'Oh my God, was I?'

'Yeah right, like you didn't know.'

'Let's change the subject before one of us gets embarrassed.'

'It won't be me.'

'I believe you. How do I get to see you again?'

'Good question.'

'And?'

'*And* you have to be patient. You can use this phone to call me, it's my own pay-as-you-go, but it may be awhile before we can meet up.'

'What about my aching?'

'Be inventive. Goodnight.'

The phone goes dead.

He's left staring at it. Wondering how he's going to cope with his pounding heart and a hard-on so big he could spin a plate on it.

23

After yesterday's sleepless night, Megan is relieved to have her daughter tucked up and sound asleep in her own bed tonight. Loathe him as she does, Adam had a point. She switches off the bedroom light, closes the door on her already snoring angel and the army of soft toys surrounding her. Sammy's temperature's down, she's less clammy and feverish. Come the morning her little angel may be back to her normal self.

Megan wanders into the open-plan kitchen-lounge of her small cottage and empties the last of a bottle of Chianti into a glass. Maybe she'll turn on the TV and watch something dull, clear her head of the worries about Sammy, money and the ever-present problem of balancing motherhood and her job.

But the Chase case is bugging her like a wasp. Suicides usually put a gun to their head and mess up the walls for one of three reasons: they can't live with the guilt and shame of something they've done, they're afraid of something they've done being exposed and their personal or private reputation ruined, or they're desperately ill, either physically or mentally.

Nathaniel Chase doesn't seem to fit any of those categories. She's pulled all the background intelligence she can. Bank records, mortgage accounts, stockbroker dealings, everything financial and personal on both father and son. But there are no real clues. Fascinating family – and deceptively wealthy. Or at least now the son is. He's getting it all, the solicitors told her. From what she can see, that turns out to be more than £20m in property, cars, stocks and savings. As well as the estate and the two cars garaged in it – a seven-year-old Range Rover and a vintage Rolls valued at more than a million – there are paintings and antiques held in vaults, collectively worth in excess of five million. There is Nathaniel Chase's portfolio of personal investments and private banking matters, all routed through UBS in Switzerland. Another six million. Strangely, UBS didn't handle his company activities. He left that to Credit Suisse and this year's figures show a bottom-line profit of more than a million. The old professor owned land across the county too, no doubt of obscure archaeological worth.

Now it's all Gideon's.

She looks again at the money trail. If in doubt, follow the cash. If it's not about sex, it's about money. If there's no other explanation, then it's money. Always money.

Could the son have faked his father's suicide? He had so much to gain and she knows he's lying to her. Might explain why he didn't identify the man who attacked him in his father's study. Maybe the attacker was an accomplice. Perhaps Gideon Chase is really a murderer and a fraudster?

Then again she could just be very tired and not thinking straight. She gives in and switches on the TV. *The X Factor*. Fantastic. Utter drivel. Just what she needs to forget about work.

24

It's the middle of the night and Sean Grabb can't sleep.

He knows a good rest is a long way off. Years away. He pulls a fresh bottle of vodka from his fridge, unscrews the top and swallows almost a quarter without even getting a glass. He's not so dumb that he doesn't understand what's happening. If any sane man had done half the things he has, they'd be hitting the bottle as well.

That's how he rationalizes it, as he finally gets a tumbler from the loose-hinged cupboard in the tatty kitchen of his terraced home. Some nights the memories are just too much to bear. They hit the back of his retinal screen like the flash frames of a horror film. Tonight is one of those nights. The image of the sacrifice's smashed skull won't go away. Nor that of his dull empty eyes or his moon-white, bled-out flesh.

Grabb downs another blast of vodka. It was done for the greater good. He gets that. But it doesn't stop the horror show rerunning in his head. One blink and he's back there dealing with the corpse. Dead meat, that's what Musca had called it. Told him to treat the kid that way. Imagine the body was a rack of lamb, a leg of pork.

They threw the mutilated corpse into the back of Musca's van and drove out to the abattoir, for which he had keys. The kid weighed a ton as they hoisted him up on to the processing line. Musca dangled him upside down, like a stunned cow, then he slit his throat and drained the last of the blood into a run-off grid.

Grabb can still hear the clank of the chains, the buzz of the electric motor and the ghostly echoes of equipment clunking into life and towing the dead body along the line. Then the monstrous mangling. The decapitation. The organ removal. The skin peeled off by hydraulic pullers. He almost threw up when Musca had to free flesh clogged from the claws of their automated accomplices.

He takes another hit of vodka. But the images stick. They're clogged in his memory. Stuck as doggedly as the awful clumps of flesh that jammed the process line. He tells himself that the visions will fade but deep down he knows they won't. They'll always be there. Now the soft, warm wave is coming. Not fast enough, but it's coming. He can feel it rolling in. But it won't wash away the guilt. Or the fear of being caught.

The line stripped the kid's bones clear of any shred of flesh or evidence that could be used against them or anyone. The advanced meat recovery system at the plant reduced it all to mechanically recovered meat – ready for human or animal consumption. It was so damned efficient it even produced neat packages of bone, lard and tallow. The blood and fecal matter just got dumped, washed away like sewage.

'No need to worry,' Musca kept saying. 'No need to fret.'

But he *was* worried. *Is* fretting. Not just about the nightmares. Or the guilt. But that it's all got to be done again.

Soon.

25

THURSDAY 17 JUNE

LONDON

Caitlyn Lock squints through the morning's bitter yellow haze across the shimmering water of the Thames. She is lying in the warm soft bed at her father's apartment, just one of his many properties. There is a house in Rome. Another in Paris. And two or maybe three more in Spain and

Switzerland. So many she can't remember. Then there are the places back home: LA, New York, Washington. Pop is famous and loaded. And Caitlyn is on track to become more famous and loaded than he is. Or her mom.

She will talk about her father at the drop of a hat, but not her mother. Oh, no. Mom is out of bounds. Kylie Lock is a minor Hollywood star who walked out on them to set up with her toy boy co-star. Caitlyn can barely give her the time of day, let alone free publicity. If she was honest, maybe she'd admit understanding what she sees in François, a dark-eyed Frenchman who tops six feet and looks like he could model swim shorts.

She gives up hugging the quilt and slips naked out of bed. Hands on hips, she admires herself in the long mirror next to the giant picture window overlooking the London Eye. She turns. Strikes a coy look over her shoulder and completes a three-sixty. Her mom would kill to have a body like this.

She turns sideways, studies the Union Jack tattoo on her behind. No one but her and the tattooist who put it there has seen it yet. She pads over the cream shag pile carpet to the low table with her cellphone on it. She laughs and picks it up. It's untraceable. Packed with pay-as-you-go credit that no one but she and her girlfriends know about. She turns it on and taps in the pin. While waiting for it to find a network, she looks at her ass again, thinking how hard her pop will kick it if he ever finds out what she's about to do.

The phone finds a signal and she thumbs her way through to the camera function. It takes a while for her to stop giggling and shoot some pictures. Most are hazy and badly framed – finally she takes one that will do just fine.

She sits on the edge of the bed, brings up Jake's number and adds a brief message. She hits *send* and collapses with laughter.

26

Chepstow, Chepstow and Hawks looks more like an antique auctioneers than a law office. A legal professor at Cambridge once told Gideon you can classify the client according to the lawyer he engages and Chepstow and Co. seems to prove his point. Traditional and reliable no doubt, but old-fashioned and dusty. The place fits Nathaniel to a T.

A gray-haired, bespectacled woman in her fifties tells him politely that Mr. Chepstow is ready to see him and leads the way to a mahogany-paneled door bearing its occupiers' brass nameplate. The man rises from behind a squat walnut pedestal desk in the corner, framed by a curtainless sash window. 'Lucian Chepstow.' He thrusts a Rolex-wristed hand from the cuff of a blue pin-striped suit.

'Gideon Chase. Pleased to meet you.' He silently curses his automatic politeness.

'I'm very sorry about your father. Please take a seat.'

Gideon occupies one of two leather library chairs positioned on the near side of the grand desk, while the lawyer, a man in his early forties with gray-white hair, returns to his seat, smoothes down his jacket and sits.

'Have you been offered tea? Or water?'

'I'm fine, thanks.'

Chepstow places his hand on the desk phone. 'Are you sure?'

Gideon's irritated to be asked twice. He puts his uncharacteristic edginess down to unfamiliarity, the unpleasant circumstances. 'Thanks, but really I'm fine.'

The door opens. A worn old man lumbers in – shoulders slightly rounded. Unmistakably Lucian's father, the practice's founder. 'Cedric Chepstow,' he mumbles, almost as though answering a question. Without offering his hand, he takes the chair beside Gideon. 'I hope you don't mind my coming in. I want to offer my condolences. I knew your father very well. Splendid fellow. I've been his solicitor for twenty years.'

Gideon considers pointing out that Nathaniel never qualified for the title 'splendid' but lets it slide. 'No, not at all. Thank you.' He adds, almost surprising himself, '*How* well did you know him? What *exactly* did you do for him?'

The Chepstows exchange glances. The question has clearly thrown them, and that interests Gideon.

'More professional than personal,' concedes the old man. 'We handled all the legal paperwork connected with his businesses – deal memos, contracts, agreements, some import and export documentation, those kind of things. He was one of our major clients.'

'I'm sure he was.' It comes out with a little more acid than Gideon intended.

Lucian feels obliged to chip in. 'Your father was very driven. Very successful, Mr. Chase. He was a pleasure to work with.'

Gideon stays focused on Chepstow senior. 'And personally?'

He purses his dry old lips. 'I'd like to think we were friends. We shared the same love of history, same respect of generations gone.'

Lucian withdraws an envelope from a drawer in the desk, keen to get on with the business side of the meeting. Gideon isn't. 'My father left me a letter.'

The old lawyer flinches.

'A suicide note. Do you know of anything that would make him take his own life?'

Cedric's eyes widen.

Gideon looks from one to the other. 'Can either of you tell me what he might have done, what he was ashamed of that made him feel so desperate and so depressed?'

Chepstow senior plays with a fold of wrinkled flab beneath his double chin. 'No, I don't think we can. There isn't anything. Certainly not legally. Nor could we share such information, even if we knew, because of client confidentiality.'

Now Gideon can't hide his annoyance. 'He's dead. So I presume such confidentiality doesn't apply.'

The old man shakes his head like a professor about to point out an elementary mistake. 'That's not how we work. We respect our bonds to our clients – forever.' He looks Gideon up and down. 'Mr. Chase, let me assure you, to the very best of my knowledge – personally and professionally – there is nothing your father should be ashamed of. No skeletons in his closet.'

'Skeletons?' Gideon laughs. 'My father was a grave-robber. He stripped tombs in Syria, Libya, Mexico and God knows where else. He sold historic and irreplaceable objects to foreign governments or private collectors who had no right to them. I'm sure he had a whole necropolis of skeletons to hide.'

Years of experience have taught Cedric Chepstow to know when arguments are winnable and when they are not. 'Lucian, please inform Mr. Chase of his father's will and ensure he has a copy.' He creaks his way out of the chair. 'Good day to you, sir.'

Lucian Chepstow doesn't speak until his father has left and shut the door behind him. 'They were close,' he says. 'Your father was one of the few mine spent time with.'

Gideon's still annoyed. 'Seem like a good pair.'

The timid lawyer doesn't respond. He passes a sealed letter over the desk and pulls another copy across his red, leather-edged blotter. 'This is the Last Will and Testament of Nathaniel Chase. It's witnessed and fully in accordance with English law. Would you like me to talk you through it?'

Gideon takes the envelope in both hands. His mind still on Cedric Chepstow. The old man probably knew what his father was hiding. Why else react like that? Why the resort to 'confidentiality', covering himself with the pathetic 'to the best of my knowledge'?

'Mr. Chase. Would you like me to talk you through the will?'

He looks up and nods.

'I should warn you that one of his requests is unusual. Your father made pre-death arrangements at the West Wiltshire Crematorium.'

Gideon frowns. 'That's unusual?'

'Not in itself. Many people prepay and prearrange their own funeral requirements. But after cremation at West Wiltshire he wished his ashes to be scattered at Stonehenge.'

27

LONDON

Jake Timberland saw himself stepping out of the shower this morning and almost died. He dragged the scale from beneath the sink and stepped up to be judged. Fourteen stone. Holy fuck. He stepped off and back on again. It wasn't a malfunction. At five foot eleven he could carry thirteen but at fourteen, before you know it you look like a fat man's body double.

His misery morphed into determination. Fifty sit-ups later he could see his six-pack rising through the flab again and felt better.

Now he's sitting in a winged chair in his club downing the third cappuccino of a breakfast meeting. He's listening to his guest, Maxwell Dalton, talk about cash-flow problems, the downturn in the economy, a slide in ad revenue and how he needs investment or he could go out of business. Dalton is chubby with big glasses as black as his hair and baggy suit. He runs a website that showcases short films made by the kind of people who can't get proper jobs in TV.

'How much do you want and how much do I get in return?'

Dalton laughs nervously. 'A hundred thousand for 10 percent?'

Jake's expression makes it clear that's not going to work.

'Twenty percent?'

He says nothing. His attention is focused on the fried egg on Dalton's plate.

'Twenty-five?' Dalton pleads, then adds, 'At a push I could go to thirty.'

Jake quite likes the idea of saying he's in media. No doubt it would increase his pulling power. At a stretch, he could even describe himself as a film producer cum distributor. 'Maybe we can do a deal. But not at a hundred k and not for thirty percent.'

Dalton looks disappointed.

A hundred thousand is nothing to Jake. He could even get his old man to stand the whole stash. If not, he could raise it if he cut down on the Cristal, skipped the winter skiing and tanked the overdraft. 'Listen, Max. I'll put fifty thousand into your company but for that I want fifty-one percent of it.'

'Controlling interest?'

'Exactly.'

Finally, a glum Dalton spits out a reply, 'I'm sorry. Forty-nine is really all I'm prepared to go to in terms of equity and for that I'd want seventy-five thousand.'

Jake smiles. 'I want to help you, not fuck you. But that slice is not worth seventy-five. I'll go to fifty k for forty-nine percent. Final offer.'

Dalton is in a bad place. With the landlord banging on the door for the rent. 'All right.'

As Jake stands to shake on the deal, his iPhone buzzes. 'Excuse me.' It's Caitlyn – he instantly recognizes her number. He opens the text and when he unzips the picture attachment his eyes nearly pop. Beneath the Union Jack tattoo is: *I have the flag. Do you have a pole big enough for it? ☺ Call me x.*

Jake smiles across the table at Dalton and offers a hand. Could be that he gets to screw two people in one day.

28

Sammy is well enough to go to nursery but Megan's mum Gloria insists on coming round to look after her granddaughter. For once the DI gets away without a lecture. She's grateful. After the short drive to Devizes police station, she is at her desk sipping a cup of black tea in the open-plan CID room, reading the full statements of PCs Featherby and Jones.

Gideon Chase is lucky. Very lucky. If the two plods had been more than a village away when the 999 came in, they probably would have arrived too late. Featherby found him unconscious in the hall and managed to drag him outside, before calling the paramedics and fire brigade.

She studies the crime scene photographs, shots of flame-blackened brick walls and burned-out windows. The fire team's report seems consistent with Chase's account. No doubt the seat of the blaze was the curtain area of the downstairs study on the west side of the house. No doubt at all. That room and most of the corridor and the adjoining reception area have been gutted. It'll cost a pretty penny to sort out.

The incident report in her hands says Chase slipped in and out of consciousness until the medics got him into the ambulance and cleared his lungs with pure oxygen. Seems to shoot down her theory that he might have been involved in his father's death and got an accomplice to fake the attack. Unless of course the accomplice got greedy. In that case, an attempt to kill him would make sense.

But it doesn't. None of it makes sense.

She puts down the papers and wonders again why Gideon lied to her. He seems decent enough. Intelligent, well turned-out, polite, maybe a bit quirky. But then academics are.

So why lie?

Does he know the man he surprised? Unlikely. Her info says Chase spent most of his childhood at boarding school and his father only moved to Tollard Royal in recent years. Until then they'd lived in more modest accommodation either in the east of Wiltshire or over in Cambridge where Nathaniel was a don.

So why? There are only a few other possibilities. Maybe he's afraid. Many victims of crime are frightened to identify attackers in case they come back. Or someone else comes back. Fear of being victimized. Makes some sense.

Chase certainly isn't fearless. Then again, he doesn't strike her as being particularly afraid either. Not what her mum used to call cowardly custard. There's another possibility. Maybe he knew the old man was involved in something and it was connected to the intruder at the house. Perhaps Gideon arranged to meet him there, they'd argued, the man threatened or assaulted him, Chase called the police.

It doesn't fit. She glances down at the report again. There's no doubt that he was unconscious and left for dead. The man who made the emergency call was calm and composed – not groggy from an assault and with a chest full of smoke.

But she feels close to the truth. Nathaniel Chase was up to something bad. She's sure of it.

'Baker!'

Megan looks up from her desk and her heart sinks. DCI Jude Tompkins is heading her way. These days the forty-year-old blonde is certifiably insane. Jumpier than a box of frogs. Her upcoming marriage – her second – is the cause of the manic personality shift.

'Are you done with that suicide yet, Baker?' She settles her crash-dieting-behind on the edge of Megan's desk.

'No, ma'am.' Megan fans out the PC statements. 'I'm just going through the reports. There was a fire at the dead man's house.'

'I heard. What are we talking, burglars? Squatters?'

The DI explains. 'The son went back there after we asked him in to talk to us. He found an intruder in the study about ready to torch the place.'

'What was he, some kind of a junkie?'

'We don't know. He knocked our man unconscious and left him for dead. If a local patrol hadn't been around the corner, the Chase family line would have come to a complete end in just forty-eight hours.'

Tompkins takes it in. Unsolved burglary, arson and attempted murder are not what she wants on her crime sheets. The whole division is under pressure to improve the figures. 'I get that it's more complicated than I thought. Can you juggle another case as well as this one?'

It's not really a question. The DCI drops the file on Megan's desk. 'Sorry. It's a missing person. Give it a look over for me.'

She watches the DCI turn and leave. Delegation is a wonderful thing. You just shift your garbage to someone else's bin and leave them to jump on the lid until they get it to fit. 'Boss, any chance of an extra pair of hands?' she calls.

Tompkins stops and turns. A smile on her big round face.

Megan knows it's hard to turn down a plea for help in an open office. She gives the DCI a desperate look. 'Just for a day or two?'

Tompkins beams. 'Jimmy Dockery. You can have Sergeant Dockery for forty-eight hours, then he's back on vice.'

Megan shuts her eyes. Jimmy Dockery? She puts her hands over her ears, but it makes no difference. She can still hear the whole office laughing.

29

The Henge Master has been expecting the call.

It was simply a matter of when. He excuses himself and steps away from the highly distinguished company. He has two phones in his pocket. A BlackBerry that he uses publicly and a cheap Nokia that is a 'burner,' a no-contract, nontraceable phone with credit he can purchase almost anywhere. He takes out the Nokia. It's Cetus.

'Can you speak?'

'Wait a moment.' The Master walks into an open courtyard. 'Go on.'

'The Chase boy has just come in for his father's will.'

The Master searches a jacket pocket for his cigarettes. 'And?'

'He was asking what Nathaniel might have been ashamed of.'

'He used that word, did he? Or is it your interpretation of what he said?'

'He used it. He told Lupus that he'd been left some kind of letter. Apparently, the police recovered it from the scene.'

The Master lights a Dunhill with a gold monogrammed lighter. 'What's in it? Some form of accusations or confession?'

Cetus tries to allay his fears. 'Nothing so drastic. If there had been anything explicit in there, no doubt the gentlemen of the constabulary would be camped in my office asking awkward questions.'

The Master blows out smoke and looks across the courtyard. 'But they have been in touch. You said so and Grus says some DI thinks she's got herself something of a case.'

'That's true but it's routine. They found invoices in Nathaniel's study and wanted to know if we still acted for him. And don't worry about the DI.'

'I shan't.' The Master paces a little. 'From what Nathaniel told me, they had a fractured relationship. Unfortunately, his son is unlikely to be our friend.'

'That would fit with his behavior at my office.'

The Master thinks for a few moments. 'A shame. Given his father's contribution to the Craft, he'd have been an asset. Did the police ask about the will?'

'Of course.'

'And presumably he gets everything?'

'Everything.'

'You must have done well out of this fee-wise.'

Cetus is offended. 'I treated Nathaniel well. He was a friend, remember.'

The Master berates himself. A crass remark. 'Forgive me, I shouldn't have made light of the situation.' He looks to a junior colleague at the edge of the courtyard pointing to his watch. 'I'm going to have to go.'

'Are you thinking of postponing?'

'We can't.' The Master takes a final draw on the cigarette before dropping it and grinding it into the gravel. 'The divination is clear. The completion must be at midpoint between evening twilight on *solstitium* and morning twilight of the day after, or it has no meaning.'

Cetus is quiet and the Master senses something. 'We will be ready with the second offering, won't we?'

'We will. All will go as planned. But what of Chase the Younger?'

The Master nods at the colleague hovering not far away. He silently mouths that he'll only be another minute. After the man is gone, he concludes the call: 'I will have the son taken care of. Just make sure the other arrangements go as planned.'

30

Caitlyn's instructions were clear. Rent a room. Chill a bottle of champagne. Put two tubs of Ben & Jerry's in the minibar – any flavor except Cake Batter. Run a bath – three quarters full. No smelly stuff – just water, hot water. Bring protection. Nonflavored and ribbed. At least five. Make sure there's plenty of dope and ecstasy.

Caitlyn is plainly used to getting whatever she wants. Fine by him. At least there's no mistaking what this get-together is going to be about. No need for small talk, no painful progressing from kiss to fumble to hopefully much more. He has canceled everything he had planned for the rest of the day. Which wasn't that much.

He has little problem getting the stuff. He already has a block of Lebanese Black and a few days' worth of Es and he picks up the ice cream and a couple of bottles of Louis Roederer Cristal in the Food Hall at Selfridge's. Then he drives over to Hyde Park and books a suite at Été, a discreet boutique hotel noted for its French cuisine. Even he considers arguing over the thousand-pound room tariff – then he remembers that he's now in the media and is about to bed a celebutante.

The suite turns out to be almost worth it: a king-size bed draped in a golden quilt, heavy matching window curtains lined in burnt orange and tied back to reveal a small terrace and some white metal seating. He draws the curtains and lights the Egyptian-style pot lamps either side of the bed.

He plugs his iPod into a docking station. What to put on? The sudden question scares him. You can tell a lot about a person from their choice of music. He wheels through some of his later downloads and settles on Plan B's *The Defamation of Strickland Banks*. 'Love Goes Down' is coming to an end when there's a rap on the door.

It's smack on two p.m. He was sure she was going to be late. He was wrong. He opens the door. She's carrying a light-cream coat over her arm and wearing a near-translucent gathered-sleeve tea dress. 'Don't just stare, let me in!'

He steps aside. 'Sorry, you just look so . . .' He realizes she's worried about being seen and shuts the door quickly. '. . . beautiful.' As he turns she's right next to him. She drops the coat and a small matching handbag and kisses him. It's like being gently electrified. Flows all the way through him. This is already about more than the great sex he knows is going to follow.

Caitlyn breaks for air and smiles. 'I have an hour. That's all. Sixty minutes. Let's get started.'

31

DEVIZES

Detective Sergeant Jimmy Dockery is Wiltshire's Horatio Caine. Or so he thinks. He speaks slower than a dying man with asthma and even on the dullest days wears sunglasses. The kind that went out of fashion with *Top Gun*.

Bullied as a kid, the ginger whinger got his own back by becoming a cop. The only problem is, unlike the *CSI: Miami* lieutenant, he's not a hot shot. He's not even a lukewarm shot. But he is the Deputy Chief Constable's son and everything pales into a ginger fuzz after that single fact.

'I heard you need help, Detective Inspector.' He hovers over her shoulder, then slides into a seat alongside and flashes his best smile. 'Glad to be of service.'

Megan feels a shiver of revulsion. 'Thanks, Jimmy.' She pulls over some stapled statements and a thick file. 'This is background on the Chase suicide. You know about that, don't you?'

He looks blank.

She resists screaming. 'Professor Nathaniel Chase, international author, archaeologist, antiquities trader, has a place out on Cranborne Chase, at Tollard Royal where the rich folk live.'

'Oh, yeah, I know who you mean.'

She knows he doesn't but ploughs on. 'Google him, and there's background on him in here, as well as the suicide.' She opens the file and points out a list of contact numbers. 'This is the mobile number of Gideon Chase, Nathaniel's son. He has asked to see the body. Would you mind making sure he's dealt with sympathetically?' She wonders if Jimmy's repertoire stretches that far.

'Consider it done.' He smiles broadly and widens his eyes. It's a little trick he's picked up. A dead certain way of letting her know that he is more than just willing to do his duty at work.

She can't believe he's hitting on her. 'What are you waiting for, Jimmy?' She tilts her head. Much as she might study a strange insect that's appeared from beneath a rock. 'Apparently, I only have the pleasure of your company for two days, so now is a really good time to get started.'

He takes the hint, walks away with a backhanded wave. 'Later, boss.'

Megan unclenches her fists. She has to learn to relax. Not suffering fools is one thing, wanting to crack them in the nose is another. She makes black tea in the small kitchen area off the main office and comes back to her desk just in time to catch the phone ringing. She spills some of the hot drink on the paperwork in the rush to grab it. 'DI Baker. Damn.'

There's a hesitation on the line before the caller answers. 'This is PC Rob Featherby from Shaftesbury. My sergeant said I should call.'

'Sorry, Rob, I just spilled something. Give me a sec.' She shifts the paperwork away from the spreading dark puddle and blots it with tissues from her bag. 'Back with you. Apologies again, what were you saying?'

'Myself and PC Jones turned out to that burglary over in Tollard. I had the control room call you – they did, didn't they?'

'They did. Many thanks. How's your colleague?'

'He's fine. Lost his voice for a bit. Which was no bad thing.'

She laughs. Like most coppers, black humor is what keeps her sane.

'I just read your report. Very thorough. If we ever get this on *Crimewatch*, they should book you.'

He's flattered. 'Thanks. I try to remember as much as possible.'

'How can I help?'

'Are you still interested in the case? The break-in I mean, I know you're investigating the suicide.'

'What have you got?'

'Well, the scenes of crimes mob lifted some good sets of footprints from the lawn and soil beds this morning and they match prints inside the house.'

'Excellent.' Her optimism gets the better of her. 'Have you got a suspect?'

He laughs. 'We wish. It gets better though. The offender left behind a canvas bag, a sort of break-in kit. It's filled with tools.'

'Rob, I'm about forty miles from the Chase estate. Do you think you could meet me over there in, say, two hours' time? I'd really like you to walk me through where things were found, what you think happened.'

'I'll have to check with my sergeant but I don't see why not. If there's a problem, I'll call you back. Okay?'

'Fine. Thanks.' She hangs up. She's glad of the chance to see Gideon Chase again – the opportunity to find out why he's lying.

32

HYDE PARK, LONDON

The hour is up. Caitlyn is dressed and at the door ready to leave.

She got everything she wanted. The guy is cute. Obedient. A pretty good lay. Granted, he could learn to be a bit more patient but that's a lesson all men could do with attending a few boot camps on.

Jake hasn't bothered getting dressed. He's slung on a white toweling robe. He'll step in the shower when she's gone. Or maybe he'll keep the smell of her on him all day. He approaches her, his eyes still hungry. 'Do I get a kiss goodbye?' He pops an ecstasy tablet on to the tip of his tongue.

She steps forward and smooches it off him, a reward for his attentiveness. She swallows and steps back a pace. 'If only they made Es that tasted like Ben & Jerry's.'

'Everyone would be high all the time.'

'*Exactly*.'

'So you liked the Cherry—'

She interrupts. 'What wasn't there to like. You did well.'

He smiles. 'And when might I get the chance to do well again?'

'Don't get clingy. I can't do clingy.'

He looks taken aback.

'Same time, same place, next week. You book. Get everything the same again, only I'll pay. Okay?'

Now he feels cheap. 'That's not necessary. What about a more regular date? A movie, a club, dinner. You do that kind of shit, don't you?'

She breaks up laughing. 'Man, you've no idea the hell my father would put you through before you even got to buy me coffee.'

He goes silent on her.

She buttons her coat. 'Look, I have to go. Same time next week?'

He nods.

'For what it's worth, I like you. Let's see how next week goes. Then we can talk about whether we risk the wrath of Daddy for the sake of dinner or a cup of coffee.'

He has nice crinkly lines in the corner of his eyes and a really friendly smile. She gives in to a moment of softness and puts her hands around the back of his neck, kisses him in a way she hasn't kissed another man. Relaxed. Nonurgent, nondemanding. Intimate.

It shocks her. 'I have to go.'

Jake barely has time to open his eyes before she's clicked open the door and is down the corridor. 'Hey!'

She turns her head.

'I'm going to surprise you.' He makes a pretend phone out of his thumb and little finger and holds it to his right ear. 'Listen for your mobile. Be ready for my message.'

33

Megan draws her Ford alongside the patrol car parked outside the gates of the Chase estate and winds down the passenger window. 'I guess you're Rob Featherby?'

A good looking dark-haired man in his early twenties smiles across at her. 'I am. I just arrived myself. Shall we drive on up?'

She gestures towards the house. 'Lead the way.'

The PC gives her a playful look, starts the engine and heads off.

They park behind an Audi in the drive and step out into warm sunshine. Featherby brings a thick envelope with him packed with photographs of evidence recovered from the scene.

Megan presses the buzzer and raps the heavy door-knocker for good measure. After close to a minute, she looks toward the A4. 'He must be in, that's his vehicle.'

The PC gives the bell another long ring. As he takes his finger off the button, the door opens. Gideon Chase holds it and peers through a foot-wide gap. He looks pale, shaken.

'Sorry to have to trouble you,' Megan says. 'We need to ask a few more questions.'

Gideon can't face it. 'It's not convenient.' He starts to shut the door.

She puts her foot against it. 'This is PC Featherby. You have met, though you don't remember it. He dragged you out of the fire the other night.'

The revelation pulls Gideon up short. He marshals his manners and extends a hand. 'Thank you. I'm most grateful.' He glances at her and reluctantly opens the door wide. 'Best go right through to the back. The kitchen's the only place I've got to know so far.'

They head in as he closes the door. His head is screaming from decoding several diaries and he really doesn't want them here.

'Big kitchen!' Megan shouts, trying to alter the mood. She runs a hand over an old Aga. The only thing missing is femininity. There are no curtains, vases, casserole pots or stacks of spices. It's been reduced to the worst thing she can think of – functional masculinity.

Gideon joins them. 'I'm a little embarrassed.' He looks toward Featherby. 'You should at least be able to offer the man who saved your life a cup of tea or coffee but I'm afraid there's no milk. I can do black, if that's any good?'

'I'm okay, thanks,' says the PC.

'I'm fine as well,' Megan adds.

Gideon folds his arms defensively. He leans against the cupboards and tries to look bright. 'So how can I help you?'

She notices his red eyes and presumes stress is starting to take its toll. 'Forensics from Rob's station found quite a bit of evidence in relation to the break-in. I've asked him to walk me through it, so I can best assemble a profile of the offender. Is it okay with you if we do that?'

He looks helpless. 'Of course. What do you want me to do?'

'Nothing.' She tries to be gentle. 'We just need access to the study, that side of the house and the gardens. Do we have your permission to do that?'

He'd rather they didn't but doesn't feel like he can object. 'Sure. I'm just sorting some of my father's things upstairs; please shout if you need me.'

She nods. 'Thanks. We will.'

He wanders off, feeling like he's being banished.

Featherby leads the way to the burned-out study. Megan looks at the blackened walls, ceiling and floor. 'What a mess.' The place stinks of the fire. 'You say the source of the blaze was around the curtains and desk?'

He circles a hand around a coal-black spot on the floor. 'Right about here. That's what the chief fire investigator said.'

She makes mental notes. The offender did this in the study, not the lounge. It was premeditated. He was searching for something and either found it and burned it, or ran out of time. If the latter, he wanted to make sure no one else discovered what he couldn't. 'Any accelerant used? Any petrol or oil from the kitchen?'

Featherby shakes his head. 'Not that I was told of.'

She steps into the corridor and shouts up the stairs. 'Gideon! Do you have a minute?'

The archaeologist hangs his head over the banister.

'Was your father a smoker?'

He thinks for a second. 'No. I don't think so. From what I can remember he was strongly against.' He gives a resigned look. 'It's possible he started in the last few years, after I lost touch, but I think that's unlikely. Anything else?'

She smiles up at him. 'No, not for now.'

He disappears and she returns to the study. The constable looks at her for an explanation. She takes time out to educate him. 'The offender is a smoker. He used his own lighter, a disposable BIC. The son said he saw one in the intruder's hand before he accosted him in here. This person's not an arsonist, has never committed arson before. Had he been, he'd have used an accelerant. He's also unlikely to have a criminal record but given the way he disabled your partner, he may well be ex-services.'

Featherby is fascinated. 'How can you be sure?'

'I can't. That's why I said not likely. Use your common sense though. This is what in profiling is called a mixed scene – some of the job was highly professional and some total bungle. You go breaking the law and you need an element of luck to keep things as you planned, otherwise you're off script and then anything goes. This offender didn't get any good luck. The householder came back while he was torching the place, caught him unawares, called the cops and almost trapped him in a burning room. At that point the guy acted off script and was thinking only about survival and escape, hence why he disabled but didn't kill PC Jones and forgot the tool bag.'

Featherby's seen enough burglaries and car break-ins to know she's making sense.

Megan's not finished. 'Arson wasn't the original intention. It was an afterthought. He was looking for something, something that presumably he didn't find.'

'So why set the fire?'

She thinks. 'So no one else could find it. Meaning whatever it is, threatens him or whoever he's working with.'

Featherby nods toward the hall and staircase. 'Did he give you a description?'

She screws up her face. 'Don't even go there. He couldn't remember a thing about the way the man looked.'

'Pity.'

'Forget it for now. Concentrate on the offender. As well as not having a criminal record, he's not too bright. But he is bold. It takes balls to break into a house, especially one where someone's just died. So let's presume our individual is confident, strong and relatively mature. I guess he's thirty to forty-five years old, works doing some kind of physical labor. Given that only about six percent of Wiltshire is ethnically diverse, we can assume he's white.'

The PC puts it together. 'White male, manual worker, thirty to forty-five, smoker, no criminal record. That's amazing, given that you're just looking at a burned-out room.'

She almost starts explaining that the room is the last thing she's looking at. What she's really studying is the invisible clues that all offenders leave about their behavior.

'What do you think is the guy's connection to the deceased?'

She takes a beat. 'Smart question. And if we crack it, we solve all the mysteries of this case.'

'But there *is* a connection, right?'

'At least one. Probably several.'

He looks confused.

Megan explains. 'The intruder may have professional links to the deceased. He might be a gardener, window cleaner, car mechanic. He probably knew the professor because he regularly did jobs for him or delivered to his house. That would also make him more confident about coming up here and breaking in. But I think he may also have known Nathaniel Chase because he was mixed up in whatever the old man was.'

'I don't get it.'

She expands. 'Chase had a lot of money. Too much for a man like him. He was dirty, I'm sure of it. The only question is, what kind of dirt?'

Sitting at the top of the stairs, Gideon feels like someone's stabbed a pin in his heart. But deep down he knows she's right. His father was involved in something bad. Bad enough to keep secret.

34

Just before midnight they come for him.

They move quickly and don't speak. There's no going back now. Lee Johns will soon be known only as Lacerta. But the change of name is going to be painful. He's been blindfolded and driven for miles in preparation. He's about to be initiated.

He has earned the right to know of the Sanctuary's existence but it will be some time before he is entrusted with its location. The strong hands of unseen men lead him through the Descending Passage and into an antechamber. Still blindfolded, he is stripped and washed, led naked to the Great Room. It is vast. Cavernous. More than a hundred square meters. So high, the ceiling is invisible, a black shroud somewhere up above.

The smell of hundreds of burning candles fills the cool air. Fear and nakedness heighten his senses. The stone slabs beneath his feet feel as hard and cold as ice.

The Henge Master raises a hammer, a symbol of the craft of the ancients who created the resting place of the Sacreds and the

Sanctuary. He looks across the congregation and lets it fall. A gigantic marble block is pushed across the single entrance and seals the chamber.

'Let the eyes of the child be opened.'

The blindfold is removed. The initiation has begun.

Lee's heart pounds. He is in an entirely circular room. Through blinking eyes he sees in front of him a life-size replica of Stonehenge. It is complete. As perfect as it was on the day it was finished. At the center is a cloaked and hooded figure, his face covered in shade and unrecognizable.

The Henge Master speaks: 'Behold the embodiment of the Sacreds. The divinities rested here centuries ago, when our forefathers, the founding Followers, built this cosmic circle and this Sanctuary. In here, you are in their presence. Out of respect, once initiated, you will ensure your head is always covered and your eyes always lowered. Do you understand?'

He knows how to respond. 'Yes, Master.'

'You are brought before us because you are deemed fit by members of our Craft to become a lifelong Follower. Is that your will?'

'Yes, Master.'

'And are you ready to pledge your life, your soul and your loyalty to the Sacreds and to those who protect them?'

'Yes, Master.'

'The Sacreds renew us only as long as we renew them. We honor them with our flesh and blood and in return they protect and renew our flesh and blood. Do you pledge your flesh and blood to their immortal holiness?'

'Yes, Master.'

From behind him, incense begins to burn inside handheld copper thuribles swung on heavy chains. The air fills with the smells of sweet spices, onycha and galbanum. The Henge Master spreads his arms wide. 'Bring he who wishes to Follow to the Slaughter Stone.'

Lee Johns is led through the circle to the stone. He feels an urge to look at those around him. Sean warned that he must not do this, must not look into the face of any of those inside the Great Room, especially that of the Master.

A voice in his ear tells him to kneel. The floor is bone hard. Hands force him flat. Four Followers fasten his ankles and wrists, spread-eagling him across the mottled Slaughter Stone. The Henge Master moves close, followed by five incense swingers, all members of the Inner Circle. 'Do you believe in the power of the Sacreds and all who follow them?'

'Yes, Master.'

'Do you trust unquestionably and unhesitatingly in their power to protect, to sustain and to heal?'

'Yes, Master.'

'Do you dedicate your life to their service?'

'Yes, Master.'

'And do you swear upon your life and the lives of all members of your family and those you hold dear never to speak of the Craft outside of your brotherhood unless given permission to do so?'

'Yes, Master.'

The incense burners swing their thuribles in a series of circles over his tethered limbs and torso, then step away. The Henge Master holds a long dark blade fashioned from razor-sharp stone cut from the first trilithon of the henge. 'I draw this human blood, flesh and bone in the hope that you will accept him as one of your servants and will afford him your protection and blessings. Sacred Gods, I humbly beg you to find a space in your affections for our brother.' He moves to the Slaughter Stone and slashes cuts from wrist to shoulder, from ankle to top of the leg, and from neck to the base of the spine.

Lee tenses. The wave of shock hits him. He fights not to scream. A blast of adrenaline overwhelms the pain. He feels a hot scratch that becomes a burn, then an ache as the mutilation progresses across his body.

The bleeding lines of flesh create a star shape beneath the eyes of those looking on. They've endured the same ritual, the same naked humiliation. They know the pain that he is about to endure.

The Henge Master kneels. From beneath his cloak he recovers the ceremonial hammer. He puts the stone blade to the initiate's skull.

'With the blood we shed for you, we add the flesh and bone that proves our loyalty and devotion.'

The Henge Master swings the heavy hammer and sees it connect with the knife's butt. The blade slices free a piece of scalp and skull.

Now he screams.

Darkness grabs him and holds him tight.

By the time Lee Johns recovers consciousness, the Great Room is empty. He lies where he was, still tied, face down. The marble block has once more sealed the chamber. He knows his fate.

35

FRIDAY 18 JUNE

It's a cloudless morning, the start of what weathermen predict will be the warmest day of the year so far. Megan smothers Sammy in factor-thirty, puts the tube in her lunch bag, drives her to nursery.

She's keen to get to work and draw up an offender profile of the burglar at Tollard Royal. The trip there yesterday provided a rich source of psychological clues – most based on the physical evidence Rob Featherby and the Shaftesbury crime team had gathered from the scene.

The first thing she does when she reaches her desk is review the evidence list: (1) Bag of tools discovered near back wall of garden. (2) Blood found on broken glass of greenhouse. (3) Small piece of cloth found on wild rose bushes. (4) Disposable cigarette lighter recovered from ground near molehills. (5) Footprints taken from soil beds, lawn and house.

Megan takes it in reverse order. The footprints are a size-ten trainer, brand to be determined. That's a full size larger than the average UK male, giving an indication – though no *guarantee* – that the owner is above the average male height of five feet nine inches. She guesses he's around five-eleven. There's also the indentation in the soil beds. In several places he'd been on the flat of his feet, as well as on his heels. These were deep impressions, signs of slipping or being off balance. Likely he was having difficulty because of how dark it was. Or maybe he was carrying a little too much weight to make a perfectly agile burglar. At five-eleven the average male weighs about thirteen stone. She hedges her bets and puts the intruder at around thirteen and a half. That kind of weight and height mean he'll probably have a forty-two-inch chest and thirty-six or thirty-seven-inch waist. The size is important because he may well have thrown away the clothes or even given them to a charity shop as many offenders do.

Megan considers the disposable lighter. Highly likely it's the one the man had. She has got to trust Gideon Chase's vision on this point at least. No mileage in not doing so. It's a multicolored Christmas edition BIC. Given it's now June, it might indicate that the guy is only an occasional smoker. Or it could be that he bought it in a multipack, these things often come in threes. That would make him more regular. She hopes his fingerprints are on it. Even if he used gloves in the house, the wheel and other parts of it could produce latents.

Third on the list is a small piece of fabric recovered from the rose climber. It's 100 percent black cotton but according to PC Featherby, forensics got excited because the color is so strong. They believe it's new or at worst has been washed only a couple of times. Megan's more cautious. It could have been bought months ago and left in a drawer. Still, there was a good chance of tracing the owner if it had been bought new.

The blood on the greenhouse is being analyzed, but already she knows from the lab that it's Rh (D) O+, the same as almost forty percent of the country. Tox tests may provide clues to drug addiction or undue alcohol consumption.

She takes a hungry chew of an energy bar and wonders what it's supposed to taste of. She guesses chalk and soot. Amazingly the label purports it to be Chocolatey Bliss. She wolfs it and moves on to consider the most impressive of the physical finds. The bag of tools.

Megan has seen several burglary kits in her time. Usually they contain glass breakers, tape and lightweight blankets to help get through windows without too much noise or injury. Often there are extra sacks in which to stow stolen goods and spare surgical gloves to prevent fingerprints. Heavier mobs bring along bolt-cutters, lump hammers and steel chisels to get through safes. Some carry blowtorches and even plastic explosives.

Not this guy. He brought a crowbar, screwdrivers, a lump hammer, some kind of metal spike with a handle on it, duct tape and a lethal-looking ax. It confirms her suspicions that he's not a professional. It also tells her that he probably didn't have long to plan for the job, he just grabbed what he had in his tool shed or garage.

She wonders what the urgency was. Why move so quickly, so recklessly? Because someone had told him to? Forced him to? The absence of other bags indicates that he didn't go with the intention of stealing multiple items. He was after one or maybe two specific things.

She looks again at the photographs Rob Featherby gave her. The ax is the most interesting. It's not for chopping wood, that's for sure. It looks like an expensive piece of kitchen equipment. She can't tell without seeing it for real but it could be a boning cleaver. Maybe the guy works in a kitchen.

She turns her thoughts to how he escaped. Greenhouse racking was found up against a back wall that led to a scrub of public land and then a B-road. The thick overgrown grass had been trampled. Mud in the road showed several sets of tire tracks. It all means he had good local knowledge. He knew where to park out of sight and was comfortable that the road didn't have a high volume of passing traffic.

Megan nails him down as ex-military, moderately intelligent, not university material. A mixed offender: one who showed signs of organization and planning but also a serious lack of ability to carry them through. She summarizes the profile:

- White male.
- 30–45.
- Manual worker – possibly in catering business, local pub, restaurant.
- Former armed services, probably army, lower rank.
- Lives locally.
- Drives car or van.
- 5 ft 11 inches.
- 13½–14 stone.
- 42-inch chest min.
- 36-inch waist min.
- No previous criminal record.

Megan hesitates before adding another line, a final word: 'Ruthless.'

She's sure the offender isn't a regular burglar or robber, but he didn't hesitate to choke a policeman unconscious and left Gideon Chase to die in a fire.

Whoever he is, he'll kill rather than be caught.

36

TOLLARD ROYAL

The screech of wild geese wakes Gideon.

He's groggy and his whole body aches as he makes his way to the bathroom. Through a window he watches four of the birds fighting for territory around the garden's small lake. Flapping and flying at each other in full beak-to-beak combat. After an ear-piercing cry, the loser and its mate flutter away low over the surrounding fields.

He investigates the old showerhead over the rust-stained enamel bath. It is coked up with limescale, yet although the pipes cough and wheeze, it runs surprisingly fast. No shampoo, but there is a bar of soap on the sink. He takes it, climbs into the tub and pulls the flimsy plastic curtain around him to catch the erratic spray.

The hot water feels good. It eases some of the tension in his shoulders as he remembers what he'd discovered in the journals he'd read late last night.

Thirteen months after the death of his mother, his father joined the Followers of the Sacreds. At first Gideon thought this was some kind of local historic society. Only it wasn't. It turned out to be something very different. He reasoned his father took some desperate spiritual comfort from the stones, much in the way that many grieving people do from the church. Nathaniel called them 'Sacreds' and came to regard each rock as a touchstone, a source of help. His writings detailed how one stone could give spiritual renewal and banish depression, while another could provide physical strength and resilience. And there were others.

Gideon's amused at the thought of Stonehenge as some kind of magical aromatherapy circle. Who'd have thought that his much-published brilliant father would have believed such a thing? Marie's death must have driven him off the rails. That would explain things.

The hot water suddenly runs cold. He clambers out of the tub and grabs a hard gray towel. He dries and puts his old clothes back on. They smell of smoke from the fire but he can't bring himself to go through his dead father's wardrobes and drawers, not even for underwear.

Downstairs, he finds an opened box of Bran Flakes but no milk. He pours a handful into a cup and dry chews his way through them while looking out the kitchen window. Several pheasants strut by as though they own the place, glancing at him as they go about their business. He finishes the meager breakfast, grabs a glass of tap water and takes it back upstairs.

Books are strewn all over the place but he's in no mood to tidy. All he wants to do is read. Devour the text until he can make some sense of it all. He picks up last night's final volume and follows the decoded notes he made in pencil above his father's writing:

The ways of the Craft are wonderfully simple. Divinely pure. Our ancestors were right. There is not one single god. There are many. No wonder the leaders and followers of every religion fervently believe that they alone have discovered the Messiah. They have merely discovered *one* Messiah. They have stumbled upon spiritual trace evidence of the Sacreds – of lives the Sacreds have touched – of gifts they have given.

It is a shame that these followers pray so indiscriminately to their particular gods. If only they knew their deity was capable of delivering a single specific blessing alone. Man's desire to monopolize religion has closed his mind to its multifarious benevolence.

Gideon tries to stay open-minded. Evidently, his father believed that the stones were vessels. Houses for the Gods. Was it so mad? Billions of people have believed similar things: that gods live in their places of worship, that they hover mysteriously in golden tabernacles on high altars, or that they can be conjured up by ritualized gestures or mass prayers. He guesses his father's beliefs are no more ridiculous.

He looks down at the book in his hands and the dark ink from his father's pen. The page has physically absorbed the man's inner thoughts. Even decades after they were written, the words convey something that he can't quite grasp – an emotional contact with his father. It's almost like he's touching him.

Gideon wonders if that's what happens when you touch the stones? Do you absorb thoughts and feelings, wisdom, from people who lived long before you – the wisest of the ancients – people so great that they were considered to be gods?

Only now when the notion of the Sacreds doesn't seem so insane, does he return to the words that troubled him.

ΨΝΚΚΦ.

Blood.

ΖΩΧΗΠΤΠΧΥ

Sacrifice.

Only now does he dare read the entry in full:

The Sacreds need renewal. It needs to be constant or else their decay and decline will be accelerated. The evidence is already there. How foolish it is to think that we may draw from them but not replenish them. The divinities are rooted in the blood and bone of our ancestors. They gave themselves for us. And we must give ourselves to them.

There must be sacrifice. There must be blood. Blood for the sake of future generations, for the sake of all, and especially that of my darling son.

Gideon's shocked to see himself mentioned. But not as shocked as when he reads on:

I will willingly give my own blood, my own life. I only hope it is worthy. Worthy enough to change things. To alter the fate that I know awaits my poor, motherless son.

37

'Have you found my missing person, yet?' DCI Jude Tompkins bowls the question down the corridor to Megan Baker, who is skittled while carrying a cup of tea from the pantry area back to her desk.

'No, ma'am. Not yet.'

'But you're doing it, right? You've been through the file I gave you and you have some leads?' She gestures grandly in the air. 'And I'm absolutely sure that you've also already contacted his family and got your hands on at least one photograph.'

Megan ignores the sarcasm. 'Ma'am, I'm still working the Nathaniel Chase case.'

'I know. I'm not Alzheimic. I recall with total clarity that you're also working the missing person case I gave you – so work it.' She gives a caustic stare and veers off toward her own office.

Megan curses. She walks to her desk, slops hot tea from the flimsy plastic cup on to her fingers, and curses again. She wipes her hands on a tissue and flips open the MP file her boss dumped on her. She'd been hoping to *sub*-dump it on Jimmy Dockery but he's gone AWOL.

She reads through the summary: the twin sister of some twenty-five-year-old bum called Tony Naylor has reported him missing. Several times by the look of things. Naylor is unemployed, has an alcohol dependency problem and appears to make a bit of cash-in-hand laboring on building sites.

He's a typical drifter, the hand-to-mouth kind. No mum and dad. No fixed abode. Just wanders around drawing benefits and working on the quiet. A ghost in the machine. She reads on. The only regular contact he seems to have is with the sister, Nathalie. He calls her – reverse charge – once a week.

Megan looks for a number, dials it and lets it ring.

'Hello.' The voice is hesitant.

'Miss Naylor?'

'Who is it?'

'This is DI Baker from Wiltshire Police. I'm following up on reports you made about your missing brother.'

'Have you found him?'

'I'm afraid not. That's *not* why I'm calling. Do you have a few minutes to talk?'

The young woman lets out a frustrated sigh. 'I've already gone through everything. I've given all the details to the policemen at my local station. Why don't you talk to them?'

'I'm from CID, Miss Naylor, you spoke to uniformed officers.'

'Oh, I see.' She seems to understand the distinction. 'All right then. What do you want to know?'

'When did you last talk to him?'

'Three weeks ago.'

Megan checks her notes. 'I'm told he usually rings you every week.'

Nathalie corrects her. 'Not usually. *Always*. He never forgets to ring me.'

'Do you know where he was and what he was doing work-wise when he last called you?'

Nathalie hesitates. 'Listen, I don't want to get Tony in trouble. Can I tell you something without it affecting his benefits?'

Megan knows better than to make deals. 'Miss Naylor, you called us because you were worried. I can't help find your brother unless you're honest with me.'

There's a pause, then Nathalie opens up: 'When I last spoke to him he said he'd been in Swindon. Helping out some Paddies, I think. Digging and cementing and such like. He said it was a job somewhere over near Stonehenge. He fancied going, he said, because he'd never seen the place.'

'And you've heard nothing since?'

'Nothing at all.'

'Any names for these Irish guys?'

'No. He talked about a Mick, but I'm not sure if he meant Mick as in Michael or as in the Micks, you know, the Irish.'

'And you don't have any contact numbers for him?'

'None other than his mobile and that's dead. Sorry.'

Megan moves on. 'The last time you spoke, did you and he argue about anything?'

'*No!*' She sounds almost offended.

'Miss Naylor, if there is any bad blood, recent or previous, between you and your brother, I need to know.'

The sister gives an ironic laugh. 'Tony and me are like chalk and cheese but we never fall out. We've never had a cross word in our lives.'

Megan sees no reason why she should lie. 'Okay. Does he have any other friends, particularly any *lady* friends that you know of?'

'No, no special ones. He's a bit of a lad, given the chance, but . . .' she dries up. 'Put it this way, Tony isn't the kind of guy that a woman wants to spend a lot of time with.'

'Why's that?'

She blows out a long breath. 'Where to start? He's not so hot on his hygiene. A shower once a week is more than enough for our Tony. And he's not romantic. Tony probably can't even spell romantic.'

Megan finishes writing. 'If I send a PC round, could you give him some photographs, recent ones of Tony?'

She thinks for a minute. 'Latest I've got is one of them passport ones, you know, the type you have done at the train station.'

'How old is it?'

'About five years. It wasn't even *for* a passport, we was just messing about after a few drinks. I made him have his picture taken with me.'

'Should be fine. You give it to the bobby I send round and I'll start chasing things up and we'll see if we can find him. All right?'

'Yeah. Thanks.'

Megan hangs up and finishes the last of her tea. She has a bad feeling about Tony Naylor. His sister was his only anchor and without a falling out, there's no reason why he'd set himself adrift. Which means he's going to be easy to find.

He's either in jail, or in the morgue.

38

It's a fifteen-minute drive from Tollard Royal to Shaftesbury. But Gideon Chase makes the journey last twice as long. He checks and rechecks the map and goes at a snail's pace in Ashmore and East Melbury.

In Cann Common he glides the old Audi off the road near Ash Tree Lane, bangs shut the door and just walks for five minutes. There's not much to see. Retirement bungalows. A whitewashed cottage. Black smoke billowing from a garden fire. Endless green fields.

Gideon doesn't really care what's around him. He's thinking about what he doesn't want to see. His father. Dead. Laid out in a funeral parlor only minutes away. Some mortician no doubt hoping his reconstruction disguises the fact that a bullet blew the man's brain away.

Gideon suddenly throws up. It splatters the pavement in the quiet cul-de-sac. He retches again and feels bad that he didn't make it to the verge or a drain. If anyone is watching, he knows what they'll think. He's a drunk with a monstrous hangover. Fat chance.

Embarrassingly, he doesn't even have a handkerchief to wipe his mouth. He uses a hand and then rubs it on the grass. Thank you Mother Nature. He turns and sees a sour-faced granny in a doorway glaring at him. There and then he decides on a course of action that will make him late. So be it.

He climbs back into the car with a sense of purpose and drives quickly through Cann Common. He comes to a roundabout and spots a Tesco.

Inside, he feels like he is in *Supermarket Sweep*, rushing the trolley down the aisles, throwing in milk, bread, beans, pot noodles, orange juice, anything he can think of. Then, most importantly, toothpaste, shampoo, shaving foam, razor and blades. He grabs packs of underwear, socks, deodorant and even a hairbrush.

Straight after checkout, he rushes to the washroom to clean up. It's such a luxury to use his own toothbrush, not one left by some anonymous guest of his father. He remembers something and goes back into the store and picks up cheddar, a packet of biscuits, some chocolate and a selection of fruit – the items from his father's shopping list pinned to the fridge. The ones he never lived to buy.

On the way out Gideon casts a greedy eye at a small café. He's been dreaming of eating a full English breakfast. Maybe later. He asks an old guy walking a Labrador how to get to Bleke Street.

A couple of minutes later he's there – literally at Death's door.

Abrahams and Cunningham is to funeral directors what Chepstow, Chepstow and Hawks is to solicitors. Traditional. Old-fashioned. Grim. For a split second, he's taken in by the illusion that he's wandered into some old aunt's quaint hallway. The brushed-velvet striped wallpaper and thick dark-green carpets guide him into a dowdy reception area.

It's empty. A discreet sign is pinned to the wall: 'Please ring for attention,' below it is a polished brass plate with a white marble button. He doesn't ring. Instead, he wanders. Down the corridor he goes. He doesn't really know why. It's a compulsion. He wants to see beyond the dull and easy façade. Understand a bit more before he steps into the black business of burials and cremations.

Behind the first door, the room is filled with caskets. A showroom. Where the gentle persuasion no doubt begins. Oak or cedar instead of cheaper pine or chipboard. Next door is a staff room. A few chairs, a big table, microwave oven, sink and coffee machine. Life goes on, even around death.

The third room shocks him. First the smell. Embalming fluid. Then the metal. Too much of it. Steel sinks, trolleys, implements. A young man in a white coat looks up from a slab of gray flesh. 'Excuse me, you shouldn't be in here.' He hesitates, walks around the lifeless form laid out on its trolley. 'Are you a relative? Can I help you?' The man comes toward him, trying to block Gideon's view as he advances. 'If you go back to the reception area, I'll call through and have someone help you, okay?'

Gideon nods. He notices the man has put his hands behind his back, hiding the red mess on his white rubber gloves.

'Sorry,' Gideon says as he exits and heads back to the bell. This time he pushes it. Within a minute, a stout man in his midforties with curly hair and brown rectangular glasses appears, straightening his dark suit jacket as he approaches. 'Craig Abrahams. Mr. Chase?'

He extends a hand. 'Gideon Chase.'

'I'm very sorry for your loss, Mr. Chase. Would you like to see your father straight away or would you like to sit down first and talk about the arrangements?'

'I'd just like to see him please.'

'As you wish. Please follow me.'

He trails the man down a river of old blue Axminster and through a door at the far end into another corridor, less well lit. Abrahams stops outside a room marked 'Chapel of Rest.' He coughs, covering his mouth respectfully. 'Before we go in, there are two things I'd like to mention. We took the liberty of dressing your father in clothes that the police gave to us. If they are not appropriate, we will of course be happy to change them for any that you prefer.'

'Thank you.'

He gives Gideon a serious look. 'Secondly, our cosmetic artist has done considerable work, but I'm afraid you may still be a little shocked when you see him.'

'I understand.'

'Many clients expect their loved ones to be exactly as they remembered them. I'm afraid that simply isn't possible. I just want to prepare you for this eventuality.'

Abrahams smiles sympathetically and opens the door. The smell of fresh flowers hits Gideon. The curtains are drawn and large candles flicker everywhere the eye falls. Nathaniel Chase is laid out in a mahogany coffin with a crêpe interior, the top of the casket hinged open so his head is visible. Gideon approaches the body and he can tell the artist has done a good job. At first glance there is nothing to suggest that his father put a gun to his temple and pulled the trigger.

Slowly he notices things. The skin is too orange. The hair combed in odd directions. His father's head is misshapen near the left ear – the point the bullet would have exited.

Abrahams touches his arm gently. 'Would you like me to leave you alone for a while?'

Gideon doesn't respond. He feels like his emotions are being fast-blended. Regret. Love. Anger. Churned up into a curdled and sickening shake. Fleetingly, he remembers his mother's funeral. The tears. The black clothes. The men with the long, strange car. Standing at the graveside gripping his father's hand so tightly because he felt like he was falling off the edge of the earth. It all comes back to him.

'I've seen enough, thanks.' He smiles at his father, kisses the tip of the fingers and places them on the misshapen head. The brief contact isn't enough. He can't just leave it at that. He leans over the casket and puts his lips to his father's head. Something he can't ever remember doing before now. Walls in his subconscious collapse. Tears flood his eyes. Gideon wraps his arms around the man who made him, and he sobs.

Craig Abrahams slips silently out of the room. Not out of discretion. He has a phone call to make. A very important one.

39

Nine days to go.

The Henge Master is reminded of the fact wherever he looks. It's staring at him right now from the calendar on his grand antique desk at work. On the front page of *The Times* folded neatly for him by one of his assistants. It is everywhere.

In just over a week he must complete the second part of the renewal ritual. He has to prepare the Followers for the nexus. And they are nowhere near ready. If only Chase hadn't ruined everything. Had he held his nerve and done what had been expected of him, all would have been well. But it isn't.

The Master's eyes stray to a gold frame and the gentle face of his wife. Today is their wedding anniversary. Their thirtieth. But it could have been so different, had she not defied the medics and their so-called expert opinions. Their high-tech 'no-mistake' diagnosis: PH. Two letters that twenty years ago meant nothing to either of them. They'd both stared at the consultant in disbelief as he said it. Only the twitch in his eye gave away the fact that it meant anything serious.

It was terminally serious.

PH.

Pulmonary Hypertension.

They'd put down the shortness of breath and dizziness to her being tired. Doing too much. Burning the candle at both ends. No proper job–life balance. It was bound to take its toll.

PH.

'Uncurable.'

He'd almost corrected the consultant, Mr. Sanjay. He wasn't disputing what the earnest medic meant, just his poor English. He wanted to point out that it was 'incurable' not 'uncurable.' A man of Sanjay's standing, regardless of his origins, should have known that there was no such word. But suddenly there was. And his sweet, gorgeous wife kept repeating it to herself.

'Uncurable.'

PH.

Then he found the miracle. The Sacreds. Within weeks of embracing the Craft, 'uncurable' didn't exist any more. PH was gone. It vanished as quickly and mysteriously as it had materialized. The hospital ran three months of exhaustive diagnostics before they finally admitted it and almost grudgingly gave her a clean bill of health.

It had baffled them. They had come to hold their cold stethoscopes to her precious breasts, to inspect her blood and peer at charts and notes. They all agreed – there had been no misdiagnosis – and yet the PH had gone. She was cured.

The mobile phone lying on the leather blotter on his desk rings. He looks at it for a moment before answering. 'Yes.'

'It's Draco. The son is at the funeral parlor.'

'Anything unusual happen?'

'No. I'm told he became emotional when he saw his father.'

The Henge Master drums his fingers on the desk. 'Maybe time has healed whatever rift there was between them.'

'Maybe.'

'Go easy on him. Be open to all possibilities.'

'I always am.'

'And of the other matter?'

'Yes.'

'The Sacreds will decide.'

Draco is worried. 'Are you sure there is time?'

'The Sacreds are sure. Inform the Lookers.'

40

It's early afternoon when Gideon gets back to the house. He is emotionally drained but he knows it would be unnatural to feel any different. Not after seeing your dead father laid out in a coffin, cosmetics barely disguising his bullet-blasted head. But he won't wallow, it's not his nature. Life knocks you down, you get up and get on with things.

He realizes he is repeating advice his father gave to him. For so long he has tried to deny the man. It comes as a shock. The old man had a much bigger impact than he appreciated. Gideon makes himself a cup of black coffee and sits in the lounge looking absentmindedly out on to the tumbling lawns. He never had his father down as a gardener. Most probably their shape and maintenance has been done by hired help.

He is close to falling asleep when the front doorbell shocks him with its alien jangle. He goes to the door, opens it, the chain still on. A stocky bald man of around forty stands there in jeans and a blue T-shirt.

'Afternoon, I'm Dave Smithsen.' He nods to a big white box van parked by the Audi, his name proudly stenciled in black down the side. 'I own a building company. I heard from someone in town that you'd had a fire. Thought you might need some help.'

Gideon flips the chain. 'I do, but in all honesty, I'm not sure now is the right time. My father very recently died.'

Smithsen sticks a hand through the gap. 'I know, my condolences. I was due to do some work for him.' They shake and the builder pulls a wad of notes from his pocket. 'Mr. Chase paid me to repair some old iron guttering around the back and fix a broken tile. You best have it back. I'm very sorry.'

Gideon takes the money. He looks at it, about two hundred pounds, and returns it. 'You keep it. Maybe you can fix the roof when you repair the fire damage?'

'Thanks.' The man pockets the cash and smiles sympathetically. 'Let me get you a card from the van. You can give me a ring when you feel like it. My old man died just over a year ago, I know what it's like. Parents are funny – they drive you mad while they're around, then when they're gone, you feel like your world exploded.'

Gideon starts to think that putting off the work isn't a good idea. Nothing to be gained from delaying. 'I'm sorry, I'm just being daft. If you'd like to take a look at the damage and give me an estimate, I'd be grateful to get the job done.'

Smithsen weighs him up. 'You sure? It's no trouble to come back.'

'No. Go ahead.' He steps outside. 'I'll let you in from the back. Do you want a drink? I've just put the kettle on.'

'That'd be great. Tea, two sugars, please.'

Gideon pads through the house. It feels strangely reassuring to have the mundane distraction of a workman around the place. Normality. An acceptance that life goes on. He unlocks the back door.

It doesn't take the builder long to size up the job. The walls are made from heavy stone, little real damage done. They'll need pressure washing inside and out and probably repointing in places. Gideon puts down a mug of tea for him. Smithsen thanks him and carries on making pencil notes on a sheet of folded paper.

The inside of the study is a big mess. The parquet flooring is ruined and will need to be relaid. The window will have to be replaced. The ceiling plaster has all cracked off and the beams and joists are exposed and blackened by smoke. He wanders through to the kitchen where Gideon is standing sorting through the morning's post. 'Sorry to interrupt. Do you mind if I take a look upstairs, over the study? I think the floor may have been made unsafe because of the fire.'

'Sure, go ahead.'

'Thanks.'

Gideon wonders how many more letters are going to arrive in his father's name and how long he'll feel a stab of loss every time they do. Another thought hits him. One more disturbing. The door to the room is open. He drops the post and runs up the stairs.

The man is nowhere to be seen.

He rushes into the bedroom. Smithsen is not there.

Gideon dashes into the corridor and into the little room. The builder is on his knees in the corner. He looks up with half a smile on his face. 'There's a bit of a creak in the middle but it's probably all right. Is it okay to take this carpet up and do some proper stress checks?'

'No. No, it's not okay.' He can't help but look and sound flustered. 'Look, this is a mistake. I'm sorry. It's too soon. I'm going to have to ask you to leave.'

Smithsen stands up. 'I understand. No problem. But I wouldn't spend time in here until you've had the place checked out. The fire has probably damaged the beams and you might have a bad accident if the floor is unsafe.'

'Thanks. But right now I need you to go.'

The man gives him another sympathetic look. 'Sure. I'll put that card through your letterbox. Ring me when you're really sure that you're ready to have things done.'

Gideon follows him down and says goodbye at the back door. His heart is hammering. Maybe he's paranoid. Spooked by nothing. The guy seemed honest enough, even nice. He was just trying to help out.

But something is nagging him. He watches the builder's van drive off and then he returns to the room.

His father's books have been moved.

41

Caitlyn Lock has a simple rule about men – one date, one goodbye. Simple as that.

Sitting in her father's apartment, she is reminding herself of all the reasons to stick to it. But there is something about Jake Timberland that makes her want to throw caution to the wind.

It's not just that he is good-looking. They always are. Or that he is wealthy. They all have to be. It's that he's . . . well . . . so . . . British. Which after all is why she is in the damned country in the first place. To get a slice of Britain. See something older than her grandmother's house. A culture that shaped the world, a people that dominated half the globe. Queen and Empire and all that weird stuff.

And deep down, yes, she had even thought about meeting a man like him. The kind who is exotically unusual and *deep*. Awkward even. She knows that there's more to Jake than meets the eye. Maybe even romance. Her parents' split had pretty much drop-kicked that thought out of her, but now it's back, prompted by the text he's just sent. A picture message of a beautiful sunrise. Below it the words, 'Sit with me through this. Drive with me through the night to a place full of ancient magic. Be with me through a cherry-colored sunrise and laugh with me until sunset.'

The proposition is a delicious one. No nightclubs and paparazzi wolves. No prying eyes of her father's security team. Pure escapism. The message appeals to her spirit, one starved of the taste of freedom. She types in a simple reply: 'Yes!'

She doesn't know how she'll get past the men in suits who are always watching, with their radios and surveillance logs, but she will. Tonight she'll escape the golden cage and fly.

42

The builder's surprise visit and nosing around has made Gideon feel vulnerable. The big old house is isolated. He's been attacked once already and doesn't want it to happen again. He certainly doesn't want to lose the books and the secrets they contain about his father. He needs to take precautions. Lock the gates. Put the alarm on.

It takes several calls and more than an hour to convince the security company that he isn't a burglar. Finally they tell him how to reset the system and he's pleasantly shocked at how noisy it is. Not that it matters. You could let off a small nuclear explosion and it would probably go unnoticed around here.

Which is why he searches the place for things to defend himself with. He finds an ax in the shed and takes a large knife from a wooden block in the kitchen. The best he can muster. Makes him feel slightly deranged, carrying them around while making beans on toast for a late lunch but deranged is better than scared.

Afterward, he finds a handheld controller to lock the garden gates. He activates them, then sets the alarm to cover the downstairs and retires to his father's hidden room with a cup of tea, bottle of water and his knife and ax. He knows life can't go on like this. But right now he needs to feel secure not scared rigid. He remembers the builder's comments about the floor being unsafe. What if he's right? What if the fire has burned the support timbers and any second now they give way. He'll fall through, break his back probably. Gideon feels like he's going mad. Fear is spreading through him like a virus. He's got to kill it off.

Methodically and unemotionally, he clears his head by deciphering the journals. By late evening finds he's able to translate automatically, rather than writing out the symbols first. He reads how Nathaniel believed followers of the Sacreds were saved from the outbreak of Asiatic Flu, Russian Flu, in 1889, when a million people were killed. Similarly, how they avoided the 1918 Spanish Flu outbreak – a virus that went on to claim the lives of almost fifty million people. It was the same in 1957, when Asian Flu swept the world and wiped out almost two million people. And in 1968, when Hong Kong Flu killed a million and again in 2009, during the deadly outbreak of Swine Flu, the H1N1 virus. None of the Followers perished.

Gideon is skeptical but fascinated by the claims. He guesses it's possible. A psychosomatic reaction to the stones brought on by powerful beliefs. Lourdes springs to mind. From what he can recall, more than two hundred million people have made pilgrimages there. His atheist's mind equates the two. The healing powers of the stones versus those of the waters of a grotto in the foothills of the Pyrenees. Both as equally incredible as each other.

He looks at his watch. It's almost one a.m. He's hungry and exhausted. Too tired and anxious to go downstairs or make anything to eat. He vows to look over just one more page and then turn in for the night.

He wishes he hadn't. The passage he's focused on makes his blood run cold:

> Gideon knows only that his mother had a fatal illness. The single good thing about the word 'cancer' is that it scares off further interrogation, especially in a child. I hope he goes through his entire life not knowing that it was CLL, never realizing that it was hereditary. I put my trust in the Sacreds, in the bond I make with them, in the clear blood of mine that I pledge to purify that of my child.

He reads it again. His brain pounds as he tries to take it in. Only the key words – cancer, hereditary, CLL – stay sharp in his mind.

CLL.

What is it? Does he have it?

Will it kill him?

43

The Henge Master walks in the comforting dark circle of the Sacreds, his eyes turned to the pin-prick stars. The night sky is an avalanche of black soot, a limitless mystery, a dark hurricane hurtling toward the sleeping heads of the ignorant. It is his duty to look for them. To understand for them. To save them from their own folly.

In the unseen currents and dark streams above, he senses the shift, the wheeling constellations, the lethargy of the Lyrids, the impatience of the coming and deadly Delta Aquarids. He feels the pull of the tides, the shift of winds across oceans, the growing cracks in the core of the earth.

As always the innocent will come running to the summer solstice, their heads beaded, their hands clasped. Their vaunted hopes of wild lovemaking and drug-induced euphoria. They will choke on their own naïveté. Every last one of them. Even those who think they are wise have no idea, no understanding that the important thing is not the solstice and the sun. It is the full moon that follows.

Balance. Always balance. So many only ever see the obvious. Just as the greatest magicians fool us by distraction, so do the gods. Only the chosen can see beyond the cosmic illusions. Let the blind prostrate themselves and pose in the dazzling show of light at the equinox. Redemption lies in the twilight. The moon is rising to its most powerful apex.

The Master knows the importance of the unseen. Farmers since time began have learned this primary lesson. The crop we see depends on what we cannot see. The darkness in the earth must be respected, it must be loved as much as the brightness in the sky. The ancients knew – and their children know – the earth's unseen powers of growth need to be nourished. They need blood meal, the richness of bone, the coolness of the grave. Scientists say blood on soil provides vital nitrogen, but it obliges with much more than just chemicals. Blood contains something else. Soul. And the more the soil has, the more it wants.

In forty-eight hours the summer solstice will bring tens of thousands to Stonehenge. The ignorant will jibber-jabber like baboons. They will clamber like cavemen on the stones. They will claim to be touched spiritually by an energy they have yearned to feel.

If only they knew the truth. The brutal truth. Because by then the circle will be empty. The Sacreds will be in the Sanctuary.

The Master smiles as he walks away. Tomorrow he will return and begin his pilgrimage. He will supplicate himself before each and every god and absorb their divine spirits. He will be their vessel, their portal through the black earth to the ancient temple below.

44

Eric Denver has been head of security for the Lock family for almost twenty years. Husband, wife and now daughter. Guardian angel to them all. Thom Lock is a self-made multimillionaire. When he was made Vice President of the United States, he had no choice but to accept Secret Service protection for himself. But he put his foot down when it came to Caitlyn. He was determined that his only child would have something more personal and *private*. Hence Eric. Given her wild behavior, it's a good job he signed him up. Tongues would certainly wag in Washington if the smileless ones in the corridors of power knew half the things she gets up to under cover of completing her studies in the UK.

Eric gives the VP daily reports, but he leaves stuff out. The kid's got to have room to breathe. Even he can see that all the attention and private scrutiny suffocate her sometimes. So occasionally, like now, he turns a blind eye when things get a bit loose.

Just before midnight, six of Caitlyn's girlfriends roll in and all but fall down the corridor outside her apartment. They're clutching handbags and bottles of champagne. On their slim faked-tan arms are six muscled youths straight out of an army poster. Big, brawny heads, biceps like rugby balls, eyes glazed from booze and dope.

Eric and Leon, his number-two, step forward and block the march of the dirty drunken dozen. 'Homework club's canceled, kids,' he says, recognizing a couple of the girls' faces. 'You need to be getting off now.'

The tallest of the youths – blond-haired with the kind of physique few would want to test – swaggers forward. 'Hey, we don't want no trouble, brother. We just come to party with Caitlyn.'

Eric raises an eyebrow. 'Brother' is not a term he takes easily from a white kid. 'No partying tonight, my friend. Miss Lock already has an important date – with a cup of cocoa and a TV show.'

Blondie's about to push his luck when Caitlyn opens the front door. Four of the girls scream with drunken excitement and rush her. The guys start to follow but the two bodyguards block the door. Music explodes from a Bose system rigged into the walls. Black Eyed Peas' 'Rock that Body.'

The guys are having a stare-out when two of the women briefly reappear from the apartment. One of them jumps into Eric's arms and tries hard to kiss him. He pulls her away and puts her down. She smooths out her sparkling blue cocktail dress. 'Please let us all in Eric, pleeeze. You can't keep Caitlyn cooped up like this. She needs some fun.'

The girl smells of booze and perfume, mouth-fresheners and spray-on deodorant. 'C'mon Janie, you and these friends of yours need to go home, you know the score. Caitlyn had her fun the other night.'

The situation changes in a second. One of the youths spins and shouts, 'Fuck him, Janie, we're outta here.' He and his friends tow a couple of the girls back to the elevators. 'C'mon, let's go to China's.' The call brings the others from the apartment. One of them giggles then stumbles and breaks a heel. Leon helps her up and she hobbles off holding the shoe in a hand.

As the apartment door bangs shut, Caitlyn's voice screams through the wood: 'Thanks a-friggin *lot*.'

Eric smiles and listens to the elevator ding, then goes back to the apartment door and knocks lightly. 'Caitlyn, we're just looking out for you.'

'Screw you. I'm going to bed.' Another door slams deep inside the apartment. He looks at Leon. 'Could be worse.'

'How so?'

Eric grins again. 'We could have let them in. Then we really would have had trouble.'

45

They hail taxis in the road outside Caitlyn's apartment and head north of the river into the frothy wash of endless partyland. Eric and Leon make coffee in their adjoining apartment and watch a TV among a bank of monitors linked to security cameras on the landing, elevators, stairways and outside areas. They relax now that Caitlyn's sulking in her room and they're not traipsing around Soho or the West End watching her back. Neither really fancied another late night. Tomorrow they'll think differently. Tomorrow they will know that amid all the shouting, kissing, comings and goings, they both missed something. Something significant.

Caitlyn.

The angry voice from inside the apartment wasn't her voice. It was Abbie Richter's. The young American is now snuggled up in Caitlyn's king-size bed, ready for a good night's sleep and no doubt a tongue-lashing from Eric in the morning when he finds out they switched.

Caitlyn is in the front seat of the VW Campervan Jake Timberland has hired for this very special occasion. He looks across from the well-worn steering wheel. 'Vintage Type 2,' he brags, adding ironically, '*Whopping* 1.4-liter engine that will whisk you to your secret destination at a dizzying sixty miles an hour. Check out the rock 'n' roll rear seat.'

Like a small child, she scurries from the front to explore the back of the van. She finds cupboards stacked with snacks, a DVD player, flatscreen TV, fitted oven and fridge full of champagne, strawberries and three different types of ice cream. 'Yay!' she shouts as she inspects the flavors and eyes up a backseat that converts into a double bed.

Caitlyn returns to the front and pecks him on the cheek before sitting back down. 'I love it. Love it, *love* it.'

'Glad I could please.'

'I'm so sparked up! So, where are we going?'

'Somewhere you've never been. Where few have trod but many have dreamed.'

She play-punches him on the arm. 'Cut it out. Tell me.'

He laughs. 'No. It's a surprise.'

They cross the river and head west out to Hammersmith, past Brentford, north of Heathrow then south down a river of endless black tarmac. They stretch their legs at a service station near Fleet, then climb back in and Caitlyn soon falls asleep.

Jake drives for another hour, fighting off tiredness by listening to the radio and taking occasional glances at the sleeping beauty in the passenger seat. Sometimes he lifts her hand. Just to hold it. His mind running away with him. Imagining their relationship is already more than it actually is. Finally he sees the sign he's been looking for and pulls off the road. He parks up, kills the engine and retreats into the back to pull out the bed.

The sudden stillness causes Caitlyn to stir. He leans close and strokes her hair as he whispers, 'We're here.'

She murmurs. Her eyes flicker open but she's having trouble fighting the pull of sleep.

'Come and lie down in the back. You can sleep better for a while.'

She gets it together enough to stumble through to the bed he's laid out. She curls up quickly and he lies next to her and pulls the quilt over them. Her eyes closed, she asks, 'Where are we?'

'Wait until sunrise,' he says, kissing her lightly.

46

Lee Johns has lost track of time. He doesn't know how long he's been slipping in and out of consciousness. It could be hours or days. He's only aware of those long moments when pain is clamping his limbs and screams are climbing his throat.

Left naked face-down on the floor of the Great Room, he's been close to death and has lost several pints of blood. The icy Slaughter Stone under him has chilled his body to hypothermic levels.

He wakes. Feels a deep, rhythmical bludgeoning in his head. But is glad to be alive. He can move a hand. The bindings have been cut. Two robed and hooded Helpers see him stirring and step forward. They carefully lift him from the floor and wrap blankets around him.

It's over.

Johns is stiff and barely able to walk. His senses are peculiarly heightened. He has no feeling in his feet but can hear loud echoes from his own footsteps like he's walking on the surface of a giant drum. The Helpers support him as he sways unsteadily down the cold, shadowy passageways. 'We are taking you to the cleansing area,' says a distant voice. 'You'll be washed and dressed, then instructed.'

The words seem to leave an imprint in the air, like a sound wave on a recording screen. Johns strains over his shoulder and sees the syllables trailing behind him like the fluttering tail of a multicolored kite.

They must have drugged him. He's hallucinating, that's all.

They take him to a deep stone trench being filled by a roaring waterfall. It's red. Blood red. And it's steaming on the floor like a pan of spilled tomato soup. Johns stands naked, terrified, frozen to the spot.

'It's all right, *trust* us.' A Helper holds his own hand under the cascading blood and as it touches his skin it becomes transparent. Crystal clear. As pure as a mountain stream.

Johns steps in and closes his eyes. The steam from the shower smells like rusty iron. It feels like a thousand needles are being jabbed into his scalp. His heart bucks hard as the hot spray spikes into his head like thorns.

Slowly his cold-numbed nerves come tingling to life beneath the warm downpour. Finally, he opens his eyes. He looks at his hands and body. The water is running clean. No blood. Everything's normal.

The Helpers stand at the edge of the trench, holding towels for him. He steps out, leaving wet footprints as he pads across the slate floor, mist drifting from the cleansing area. In front of him are his own clothes and a rough sack robe. It is his. He is a member of the Craft. He's been accepted.

There's a full-length mirror in the corner. He twists his body to see the extent of the wounds caused by the Master. *Strange.* He twists his right forearm and then his left arm to inspect the initiation cuts. He checks the mirror again.

'What's going on?'

Those around him say nothing.

'I was bleeding. But I can't see any scars.' He angles his body again in front of the mirror. 'There's nothing. Not a mark.'

A cloaked shape fills the doorway.

Johns looks across and recognizes the rugged face beneath the hood. Sean Grabb, Serpens, his Craft brother.

Proud mentor smiles at protégé. 'Get dressed, Lacerta. There are important duties to be done.'

47

SATURDAY 19 JUNE

Just after four a.m. the sky begins to lighten. Jake gently wakes Caitlyn.

She is jelly-legged as he helps her from the Campervan and starts to shiver in the cool morning air. He rushes back for a couple of blankets and the bag of goodies he's packed up from the fridge.

'Where are we?' she mutters as he snuggles her beneath his arm and the warm wrap. 'I still can't see anything.'

'You will in a minute. It's a piece of old England. Tomorrow, it will be flooded with thousands of hippies like you, but this morning, right now, it's ours. Just yours and mine. I booked it.'

'Booked it?'

'Everything is buyable these days. Others had paid to tour the site but I paid them off. Bought them out. Just for you.'

She's too touched and tired to say anything.

They shuffle across the damp grass in the receding darkness and gradually she starts to see it. Something huge. Rising out of the rosy warmth of the breaking dawn. Her pupils pulse wide as she stares at the monumental shape. '*Jesus*, what is it? It's like some weird space ship.'

And it is. It's just like a massive stone UFO crashed into the ground. Jake throws open his arms in a grand gesture. 'Welcome to Stonehenge.'

'It's . . . awesome.' She skips and takes in the heady scene, then wanders back into his arms and kisses him deeply. They hold each other beneath the fading constellations and block out everything that exists except themselves.

'Come on.' He takes her by the hand. 'Let's go to the center.'

They run together and she can't remember when she last felt like this. So free. So energized.

Jake stands back to take photographs. Snaps on an old pocket Nikon and knows he's going to keep the images forever. One day when they're both old, he'll dig them out and they'll remember today. History in the making.

Caitlyn pauses, breathless, wraps her arms around one of the sarsens. She looks like a child clinging to the leg of a giant. She laughs and poses for him.

Click.

She scoops a hand behind her hair and pouts.

Click.

She kisses the stone and strokes it.

Click. Click. Click.

'One more!' he shouts and she obliges, leaning against the stone and blowing a kiss right down the lens.

Click.

He stops shooting and gives in to another urge to kiss her.

They lock together. Her back against the giant stone, him pressed hard against her soft warm body. Raw sexual energy rushes through them both.

She closes her eyes and goes with it. Rises like a bird on the hot thermals of his passion. She yields to the invasion of his hands beneath her clothes, the conquering of her flesh. The mystery and magic of his romantic surprise have overwhelmed her.

He spasms against her. It's not as passionate as she hoped. In fact it's off-putting and embarrassing. Less of an orgasmic peak, more a sudden and awkward crash of his forehead against hers. Caitlyn flinches and grabs her bruised head. Jake pulls away from her.

'Ow!' she exclaims, mad that the moment has been ruined.

A hand slaps across her mouth. A stranger's hand.

She manages a brief panicking glance at her unconscious lover before a hood is pulled over her head and duct tape wrapped around her mouth.

Within sixty seconds the fields are empty and silent, save the first birdsong of a new day. The sun finishes its slow upward arc into the bruised sky above the henge.

48

Serpens drives the Campervan. On the floor in the back is the blindfolded and bound form of Jake Timberland. Lacerta follows in his friend's old Mitsubishi Warrior. Caitlyn Lock is tied up and tightly gagged in the rear.

The instructions to the Lookers had been clear. Keep surveillance on the site and wait until the Sacreds choose. Be patient. Like the last victim, it would be *their* will. And it was. The couple arrived in twilight. They invaded the circle. They touched the stone that the Master said would be touched. They had been drawn to it. Just as the Master said.

The Followers call that particular trilithon the Seeking Stone and there's no doubt in Serpens' mind these two lovers sought it. They chose their destiny. Draco will be pleased. All of the Inner Circle will be. He and Lacerta have done a good job.

Ordinarily, Serpens doesn't take them at the circle itself. Once chosen, they are followed. Sometimes for weeks. Sometimes months. Greater care is usually shown before any abduction is executed. But time is against them. The stars are shifting. There is only a week to go to the change of the moon phase. The renewal must be completed. There is barely time to cleanse the sacrifices, to make them pure.

The lad in the back has suddenly started banging his feet on the wooden floor like a toddler having a tantrum. He will learn to be quiet. He'll soon know to be silent. Serpens turns up the radio. Before long he takes the van offroad, through land that the Craft own, through woods and vales once home to Mesolithic, Neolithic and Bronze Age tribes.

Serpens pulls over in a quiet place not far from the isolated track that leads to the hidden entrance of the Sanctuary.

Lacerta tucks the Warrior behind the Campervan and waits for his mentor to make the next move. All he knows is that they are going to leave the sacrifices there and drive the van to a barn, where it will be kept until dark. Later it'll no doubt be taken to a scrapyard and crushed.

Serpens kills the engine and climbs into the back. At least the guy's stopped kicking. Learned his lesson. Best not to fight it. Best not to resist what's going to happen next.

49

Lacerta wanders toward the parked Camper. He wonders why Serpens is still in there. Nothing is happening. Through the window he sees him crouched in the back. He opens the door and sticks his head in, 'Everything okay?'

'No, it's not.' Serpens turns. 'Everything's very much not okay.'

Lacerta climbs in and shuts the door. 'Why, what's wrong?'

Serpens moves back and reveals the body on the floor. 'He's dead.'

'*Dead?*'

It's one of those words that you just have to repeat. 'Dead.'

He emphasizes the point by picking up Jake Timberland's arm and letting it fall.

'Fuck.'

'Fuck indeed.'

Lacerta is in shock. He steps closer and peers at the crumpled form on the floor. 'What's wrong with him?'

'You mean, apart from the fact his heart's stopped and he has no pulse?'

'I mean, what killed him?'

Serpens shakes his head. 'I don't know. Maybe I hit him too hard. Maybe you tied him up too tight and he suffocated.'

For almost a minute they both stare guiltily at the corpse and wonder which of them was responsible.

Both are aware of the fate that awaited the couple. Sacrifice.

That would have been much worse for the guy. But it would have been done under the eyes of the Gods. Done with their blessing, in their honor and with their protection. Under controlled circumstances. Carefully planned procedures to protect everyone concerned. Nothing like this. This is a screw-up.

Lacerta breaks the silence. 'What are we going to do?'

The older man sits back and puts his head in his hands. 'I'm trying to think, trying to work something out.'

'We could just dump them both.' He nods toward the pickup. 'No one knows about the girl or him. We could drive them somewhere away from here and just leave them.'

Serpens thinks about it. 'Did she see your face?'

'No. I don't reckon so.' He reconsiders. 'Maybe. But even if she did, it was only for half a second.'

Serpens grimaces. 'That's all it takes. You see a lot in half a second.' He has another thought. 'She'll know where she was, what time. It's too risky.'

'Then we kill her.' Lacerta shrugs. 'She was going to die anyway. We can make it look like the boyfriend got rough. He was almost humping her back there at the stones. I bet he's given her one earlier in the night. His DNA will be all over her. The police are bound to think he did it.'

His mentor shakes his head. 'She's been chosen. She touched the Sacreds and it's our duty to supply her to them.'

Lacerta is panicking: 'It's *our duty* to stay out of fucking prison.'

Serpens stays calm, gets his head together. 'We need to drive this Camper somewhere, get it out of sight. Then I'll call my contact in the Inner Circle. It's up to the Master to decide.'

'What about the girl?'

He nods. 'You stay here with *him*. I'll take her into the Sanctuary.'

Lacerta is not happy. Even in this remote location, far from any road or house, he doesn't want to be left alone with a dead body. 'Hurry up.'

Serpens runs to the Warrior. The girl is red-faced and struggling in the back of the cab. At least she's alive.

Caitlyn sees the panic on his face. The fear is contagious. It makes her kick and thrash against the bonds.

Serpens considers taking the duct tape from around her mouth and trying to calm her down but decides against it. Best get her inside as quickly as possible. Get her locked up. Call Draco and tell him about the awful mess they're in.

50

Yesterday's personal discovery gave Gideon a restless night.

CLL.

It stands for chronic lymphocytic leukemia and is a dreadful disease that occurs when the DNA of the lymphocyte cell mutates. As years pass, damaged cells multiply and the mutant army kills off normal cells in the lymph nodes and bone marrow. Blood-forming cells are eventually overwhelmed and the body's immune system surrenders – it no longer has the ability to fight off infection.

It is how his mother died.

He knows all this because he spent all night reading about it online. He also found out that the disease is hereditary. But not always. CLL inheritance is a game of medical roulette. Maybe he has it, maybe he hasn't. Only time will tell.

Deep in his memory something stirs. Rises from the sands of forgotten nightmares. He wasn't a healthy child – he was plagued by colds and hay fever, coughs and dizzy spells. One time he fell really sick. A raging fever and heavy sweats. It was so bad his father took him out of school. Had him hospitalized and seen by specialists. There were machines and monitors, needles in his arms, stern faces and long adult conversations just out of earshot. Then they let him go home. His father had red eyes, like he'd been crying.

And he remembers something else. For a second, he has to stop himself. Needs to make sure his mind isn't playing tricks. The diaries have churned him up, left him exhausted and emotional. He could be suffering from false memory syndrome, implanting things into the past that hadn't happened.

But he doesn't think so.

His father made him lie down in the cold metal bath in their old house. He remembers it distinctly because he was embarrassed. He was naked and the bath was empty. Then Nathaniel poured cold gray water all over him. Doused him from head to toe, told him to splash it over his face and in his hair. Urged him not to waste a drop.

He was shaking from cold and fear when he got out. His father wrapped him in a towel and held him tight, told him not to worry, said the water was special and would take the sickness away. And it had. Almost instantly. He went back to school days later and felt perfectly well.

Another piece of his childhood jigsaw falls into place. He's never been ill since that day. Not even a sniffle. Whenever he has cut himself, it has healed quickly.

Gideon walks to his father's old bedroom and looks in the mirror on the dressing table. The injuries he sustained in the fight with the intruder downstairs have gone. He puts a hand to his face. The skin is unblemished. There's no trace of the split lip or cut cheek. It's like it never happened.

51

Black carrion crows settle on the jagged ridge of an old barn that has seen little care in the last twenty years. Draco points at the avian army as he walks through the long grass with Musca.

He bangs on the dark twisted wood of the barn door and the birds scatter skyward, then swoop and settle into treetops edging the vast field.

From inside there comes the noise of urgency. Metal against metal. Things being moved. Serpens has already seen them through cracks in the barn boards and opens up. He looks embarrassed. 'Sorry about all this.'

Draco says nothing. He is sorry too. Sorry about the screw-up. Sorry he has to come and sort out the mess. The two men slide past Serpens. He locks the door again. Rolls a broken scarifier back behind it, positions the long metal arm that connects to a tractor so it jams against one of the door beams. 'Thanks for coming.'

Draco looks quickly around. 'Are we are alone?'

Serpens nods. 'I have sent Lacerta home.'

'Good,' says Musca. 'At least you've done one thing properly.'

Draco gets straight to the point. 'Where is the body?'

Sean points across the barn at the Campervan. 'He's in there.'

'And the woman?'

'Safe at the Sanctuary. In one of the meditation rooms.' It is a euphemism. They are merely spaces chiseled in the thick stone walls, no bigger than a broom cupboard. The supplicant can't kneel, let alone sit or lay down. Air dribbles through letterbox-sized slits by the feet and head. 'Did she say anything?'

'Nothing you could make any sense of. Just screamed.'

Musca smiles. 'She'll stop after an hour or two.'

Serpens slides open the Camper door and they climb in. Draco leans over the corpse. 'Have you searched him?'

Serpens shakes his head. Musca opens up the glovebox and pulls out hire documents, a driving license and a bag of something. He holds it up to the windscreen. 'Ecstasy. A nice little stash.' He drops it on the driver's seat. 'There's a name here.' He flicks through the agreement. 'Edward Jacob Timberland, address New Cavendish Street, Marylebone.' He picks up the driving license and looks at the photograph. 'Yep, that's our guy. Thirty-one years old.' He flips it over. 'And six points to his name.'

'He won't be worrying about those any more,' says Draco. He takes a deep breath. 'So he and his girlfriend hire the VW for a hippie trip to Stonehenge. That means they won't be missed for a day or two.' He gives them a smile. 'Not as bad as you thought. The Sacreds picked the perfect sacrifices, free souls who can take time off and play at being children of the sixties.'

Serpens looks relieved. 'So what do you want me to do with him?'

'Nothing. We'll keep the van here until after the ceremony and then we'll dispose of the bodies together. Go get yourself a decent breakfast. And relax. You can leave the girl to us now.'

52

DCI Jude Tompkins stomps into the CID office with a face like thunder. 'Baker, Dockery, conference room, five minutes. *Don't* be late.'

She's gone as quickly as she appeared. Jimmy looks across desks to Megan. 'What's all that about? I have to see an informant in ten minutes.'

'I think this is more important, Jim. You'd better ring your man and stand him down.'

'Shit.' He rips the desk phone from its cradle and punches in a number.

Megan calmly finishes reviewing the document she was working on, saves it and locks her computer. She grabs a plastic cup of water from a dispenser in the pantry and wanders down the corridor to the meeting room.

It's crowded. Full of bigwigs. She tries to put ranks and names to faces. There are five or six sergeants, at least three inspectors, two DCIs, the Detective Chief Super, John Rowlands, and there at the top of the table is Jimmy's old man, the Deputy Chief Constable, Greg Dockery. He's flanked by two smartly dressed civilians she doesn't recognize.

'What's the score?' asks Charlie Lanning, a uniform inspector, taking a seat next to her. 'Something to do with the solstice? Bloody hedgerows are already full of dopeheads. It's going to be worse than ever.'

'Your guess is as good as mine.' Megan gestures to the end of the conference table. 'The suits look too serious for solstice ops. Too official. Could be a Home Office review. Or maybe more cutbacks.'

'Nothing left to cut in my unit. We're not down to the bone, we're into it and almost out the other side.'

They don't have to wait long.

The Deputy Chief raises his voice. 'Your attention please.' He waits a beat for the noise to die down. 'You have been gathered for a matter of urgency. To my left is Drew Blake of the American Embassy and to my right Sebastian Ingram of the Home Office.' He picks up a large photograph that has been facedown on the table. 'This is Caitlyn Lock. She is twenty-two years old. She is an American citizen at university in London and she is missing.' He turns the photograph left and right for all the room to see. 'Some of you may recognize this young lady. Miss Lock is something of a celebrity. She won the US reality television show *Survivor* and is the daughter of Hollywood film star Kylie Lock and of course the Vice President of the United States, Thom Lock.' Most in the room are taking notes and Dockery pauses briefly before continuing: 'At this stage we have no reason to believe any harm has come to Caitlyn. There has been no ransom demand. She is known to be something of a free spirit, so this may simply be an innocent disappearance with a new boyfriend. However, she has not been seen since midnight last night so it is extremely important that we find her.' He scans the faces around the table, lets the point sink in, then gestures to his Detective Chief Superintendent.

John Rowlands stands. The head of CID is lean, a little over fifty and serious looking. He's the only officer in the county who's also worked in the Met on homicide, abduction and terrorism cases. 'Just before midnight Caitlyn Lock tricked her private security team into believing she was in bed when in fact she had slipped out of her father's apartment in central London, just south of the river, to be with a man known to her friends only as Jake. She later telephoned one of these friends from a service station in Fleet, heading west, and said she didn't know where she was going – she was being treated to some kind of surprise. The friend said she sounded happy and excited and mentioned an old Campervan but gave no description, no make or color.' He lets them process what he has given them. 'Given the solstice, the van and the timing, this young woman could well be on our patch. If she is, I want her found and returned to London before the maids have changed the sheets on her bed.' He turns to his left. 'I will head the inquiry, DCI Tompkins will be my number-two. She will give you the operational details and your duties straight after this meeting. Surrounding forces are setting up their own investigations and the national press is being informed of Caitlyn's disappearance.'

He hears groans around the room.

'Be smart, people. The public and the press have the power to find this girl much quicker than we can. They are our eyes and ears. Use them, don't abuse them. And don't be stupid. All press inquiries have to be channeled through the communications office. Now go and get something to eat. It will be your last opportunity for quite awhile.'

53

Draco catches it on the radio. Not all of it but enough. Something about the daughter of a Hollywood actress and an American politician going missing with her boyfriend. In a Campervan. He pulls out his burner and calls Musca. 'Have you listened to the news in the last hour?'

'No. Not been near a TV or radio.'

Draco starts to think. 'Wait.' He opens the browser on his phone and pulls up the BBC News page. It's the lead story. Beneath a picture of the girl. 'Listen to this.' He reads aloud: 'US reality star Caitlyn Lock, daughter of Vice President Thom Lock and actress Kylie Lock has disappeared from her father's home in south London with an unnamed man. Miss Lock, twenty-two years old, is thought to be in the southwest of the country and police have issued an appeal for anyone who sees her to call them immediately on the number below. She is of athletic build, five feet nine inches tall, has dark shoulder-length hair, brown eyes.' He pockets the phone. 'You went to the Sanctuary after we split up this morning, does it sound like the girl?'

Musca can hardly answer. 'I think so.'

Draco winces. 'Why? Why do you think so?'

'She's American. There's no doubt about that. She looks athletic and young as well.'

Draco shuts his eyes and wishes it wasn't so. 'Get over there now. I'll call the Master.' He hangs up, unsure what to do. If the girl *is* the daughter of the US Vice President the Americans will be going crazy to get her back. They might be using spy technology for all he knows, listening in to phone calls from all over the world.

He glances up at the sky, almost expecting to see a drone hovering above him. If they can do that, he's said too much already. He calls the number. 'It's Draco. I have to see you. It's urgent.'

'I understand. I'll be there as soon as I can.'

They both know where for such an emergency. Draco has little time for courtesy: 'When you hang up, dump your burner somewhere public. We may be compromised.'

The line goes dead. He breaks open the back of his phone and pulls out the battery and the sim card in order to discard them and the hardware separately. Without wasting time, he gets in his car and drives quickly but within the speed limit to the Sanctuary. He takes three detours en route to dispose of the phone. Each time he looks up and wonders whether he is being watched.

54

The Henge Master comes and goes unseen through his own entrance to the Sanctuary, one that only he knows, one disclosed in the sacred books that he inherited.

He walks the unprotected passageway to his chamber and waits for Draco. Before long there's a knock on the heavy door and he shouts, 'Come.'

Draco enters hesitantly.

'Sit.' The Master's voice gives away his irritation at being summoned at such short notice. He gestures to the semicircle of stone benching opposite him.

Draco adjusts his cloak as he settles. His voice is low and apologetic.

'The girl chosen by the Sacreds turns out to be the daughter of the American Vice President. It's on the news.'

Shock registers on the Master's face, then disappears. 'That may well be, but as you just said, she has been chosen.'

Fear glistens in Draco's eyes. 'Master, do we not need to distance ourselves from her? The US security services and every police officer in Britain are going to be searching for her.'

'And they are more important than those we follow?'

'No, Master.'

'I repeat – she has been chosen. Has she not?'

'Yes, Master, but—'

'Enough.' The Master's sharp tone cuts right through him. 'Our beliefs, our activities have gone uninterrupted by the police for centuries. Our existence has been kept secret for thousands of years. That is not due to luck. We are guided by the will of the Sacreds and that is a greater force than any police constabulary or government in existence.'

Draco understands. 'I am sorry. I believed caution would be prudent.'

The Master nods. 'You have done well to consider it and are right to alert me.' He looks over his steepled fingers. 'The girl is the one on the radio, Caitlyn Lock?'

'Yes.'

'And her boyfriend – what of him?'

Draco swallows. He fears the blunder could somehow be seen as his fault. 'The boyfriend is dead. He died when he and the girl were taken by the Lookers. It was an accident.'

The Master doesn't look concerned. 'Or it was the will of the Sacreds. Perhaps the male was not worthy. What of his body and the vehicle the press are speaking of?'

'In a barn not far from here on land we control.'

'Dispose of both, quickly.' The Master rises from the stone seat. 'We are done. I am expected back. Call the Inner Circle and inform them of our meeting and my wishes. The stars are aligning, the moon is changing. We go ahead as planned.'

55

Megan is assigned to run actions on the Campervan and report directly to Tompkins. In addition to Jimmy Dockery, she's been given two other detective sergeants – Tina Warren and Jack Jenkins. Warren is a waster. She can tell that already. Fit to make tea, run errands and put petrol in a car. Jenkins is more promising. Newly promoted, a little green but bright.

Megan divides the work. 'Jack, get a statement from this friend of Caitlyn's, the one she last spoke to. Ask her again about the vehicle. I know she didn't get a description but ask. She may remember something.

'Jim, take a team to the Fleet service station on the M3. We are looking for CCTV footage from the garage forecourt, also from the parking lot – it's likely they used the toilets as well. Ask in the shops and restaurants, hand out photographs, jog memories. They probably bought something out there. Find out what – and who sold it to them. If we're lucky, they asked for a guide map or even directions. Check with all the security. They may have images of the couple on a camera here or there. Tina, get interview teams at the services before and after Fleet. See if they stopped there.'

They all look at her for further instructions.

'*Now*, please. Treat this as though the girl's life depends upon it.'

Even before they've gone, Megan rings a friend in traffic and asks for a list of Campervans. While she waits, she goes online and sets up a vehicle search. There are dozens of campers: Fiat Cheyennes, Ducatos and Komets, Ford Transit Auto-Sleepers, Winnebagos, VW Transporters, Toyota Hiaces, Hymers, Bedfords, Mercs. Then she stops. Her profiling instincts kick in and she starts to think. Not about the vehicle. About the people in it. Impulsive people. Rich people. Caitlyn is hardly likely to move in the circle of paupers. Her lover will have money. He will want to impress her. Surprise her.

None of the vans on her screen do that. She types 'Celebrity Camper vans' and fifty-three thousand entries appear in a third of a second. Over fifty pages of results. The one topping her lists is the VW. She hits a link: 'VW Campervans for hire.'

It brings a smile to her face. It's the Mystery Machine. The van Scooby-Doo and Shaggy drove around in. She types in 'VW Camper vans to hire *in London*.' Her heart sinks. Half a million results. She browses and it turns out not to be as bad as she thought. The keyword search is too loose, it's inaccurate – she should have written 'Campervans' not 'Camper vans.' She finds a number for a VW Campervan Association and soon assembles a shortlist of dealers in the London area.

After a couple of hours the list is even shorter. Several people hired Campervans within the last twenty-four hours but only one stands out. He paid on an Amex Gold card and his name is Jake Timberland. Her heart jumps – the way it always does when she knows she's got her man. Before telling the DCI, she has one more call to make. One she's dreading. Sammy is going to need looking after again.

56

Caitlyn can't move. She can't see and can't breathe properly.

She feels like she's been buried, standing up. Entombed in stone. There's barely enough room to raise her hands to her face and feel the sweat of fear pouring off her.

'*Jake!*' She screams his name but knows he's not going to answer.

Emblazoned in her memory is an image of him slumped on the ground inside the strange stone circle. There was something about the way he didn't move that made her feel sick. '*Jake!*' Somehow shouting his name keeps him alive. At least in her mind.

Her fingers feel the rough stone in front of her. They find a tiny slit and the thin stream of air that's keeping her alive. She just hopes whoever took her captive are professionals – seasoned kidnappers who know what they're doing and not weirdo rapists or serial killers. If it's a pro kidnap gang, they're after money and her life is not in danger. Well, not immediately. Soon they'll come and clean her up, feed her, make the film, a message to her parents most likely, and the game will start. She's been trained for this. Eric Denver has run her through it dozens of times and her father has run her through it. Even her damned mother has gone over the possibility with her that this might happen.

She sees now that she was crazy to go with Jake. To slip out of the safety of her own security net. A bad thought hits her. One that saps what little remains of her esteem. Maybe Jake helped set her up. Perhaps he'd been thinking about it right from the first moment he met her. The alternative is almost as bad. If he wasn't, then where is he? She knows kidnappers rarely take two hostages at a time. It's too complicated, too much of a struggle. She feels the sickness rise again.

'*Jake!*' Her scream tails off into a whimper. It's been hours since they locked her in, since anyone talked to her. Her spine is hurting. Her shoulders, the back of her head and her knees are raw from rubbing against the stone walls. And unless she's mistaken, and she's pretty certain she isn't, she's soiled herself.

Despite the pain, the cramp and the humiliation Caitlyn keeps falling asleep. Deprived of stimulation, her crazy overactive brain simply shuts down and she drifts off, drifts to some faraway place that bears no resemblance to this dank dungeon. She is in one of those fitful dozes when the cell wall slides back and she slumps forward. Men in brown robes and balaclavas beneath their hoods catch her and lower her to the ground.

She comes round on her back. Dizzy and glassy-eyed, staring at a high black ceiling and a huge cast-iron chandelier ringed with thick burning candles.

Four hooded faces appear in Caitlyn's line of vision and a low rasping voice issues a chilling instruction. 'Strip and wash her. The ceremony goes ahead.'

57

For once, Megan's ex seems happy to have Sammy for the night. He even promises home-cooked food and not a Happy Meal. A weight off the working mum's mind.

She returns to the Campervan case filling her desk and the Facebook photographs of Jake Timberland she tracked down by following the lead the Amex bill gave her. Things happen quick when there's a break. Over in London a Met team has confirmed that the young Englishman isn't at home in Marylebone, another is showing his picture to Caitlyn's minders and a third is visiting Jake's parents, Lord and Lady Timberland. Meanwhile, itemized mobile and landline phone records are being studied along with Switch and credit card bills. The wheels of investigation are turning fast.

Megan places photos of Timberland and Lock side by side. They make a good couple. The press are going to go crazy on this one. There'll be enough pressure to squash a battleship. She looks at their faces and figures the romance – if that's what it is – must be recent. If they'd been an item for any length of time, they would already have been splashed across the gossip mags.

Then comes a moment of doubt. Perhaps she's got the wrong guy. Maybe there's no connection between Jake and Caitlyn. Could be that he just happened to take a three-day minimum hire on a cornflower blue Camper on the same day she did her vanishing trick. Perhaps she's up a hill in a Winnebago with someone else and doesn't even know Edward Jacob Timberland exists.

It could all be coincidence.

Megan hates coincidences. Coincidences are God's way of seeing if police officers can do their job. She hopes the motorway teams come back with video of the couple with the Camper that will prove there's a link between everything.

She looks again at Caitlyn's photograph and then checks the girl's Facebook page. Obviously handled by a publicist and vetted by her father. There is nothing too personal on there – just fashion, music and girly gossip. Bland stuff.

She tries Twitter. Even more disappointing. Then she checks Jake's Twitter account. Dating Caitlyn Lock would be the kind of thing any man would find difficult to keep quiet about. She draws a blank. There's nothing from the last day – no hint of the journey to Wiltshire. She scrolls back twenty-four hours and feels her heart leap. Her eyes hook on a coded piece of male bragging: 'I have a plan to win my new muse, to unlock her chains and make her mine.'

Encouraging. Even tantalizing. But not quite enough. She trawls back further and finds another gem: 'I have met this American and I'm smitten. She is everything I dreamed of.'

The remarks all point to him running off to Stonehenge with Caitlyn for some quality time out of view of her security. Lust makes everyone go crazy – even sons of English lords and daughters of American film stars. Come to think of it, especially them. They must have run off together. Gone off radar. Maybe even eloped.

No. She's getting carried away. They certainly did not get married. The Camper was hired for three days only. Off radar is right though. They must have conspired to trick the girl's security and grab some time together.

But something doesn't make sense. Something she can't quite put her finger on. Then the penny drops. Caitlyn must have planned to call in to her minder *before* the alarm was raised and everyone went crazy. Why didn't she? It's the kind of protocol her father and everyone would have drummed into her. *Always call in, whatever you do, always call in.* And she would have. Of course she would.

But she hasn't. That means something is wrong. Terribly wrong.

58

Fear stabs Caitlyn like a hot spike in the heart. A group of hooded men have her pinned to the floor. She's going to be raped. She's sure of it. Well, she'll bite their throats out rather than let that happen.

One grabs her left wrist, another her right. She kicks out. Feels her foot connect with soft flesh. 'Leave me the fuck alone!' Deep down she knows shouting and fighting is pointless but she sure as hell isn't going to give in peacefully. 'Get the *fuck* off me!'

Unseen hands clasp her ankles. They pull open her blouse and tug down her jeans. They turn her over, unclip her bra and pull off her panties. She thrashes and screams until her throat burns and her energy is spent. She's done. She has no more resistance.

They're going to take it in turns to debase her – she just knows they are.

Someone pulls her hair and slides a hood over her head. They haul her to her feet and cuff her hands. She's unsure what's happening but is relieved she's not been molested. Firm fingers grip her arms and shoulders. They push her in the back – force her to walk. Caitlyn's heart is beating so fast she feels like she is going to die. *Don't panic. Stay calm.* She mentally repeats the instructions Eric gave her. *Whatever happens, you deal with it. One second at a time you deal with it – or you die.*

They walk her down dark mazy passageways, then make her step into some kind of pit. They pull the hood from her head and from the blackness above a waterfall of steaming hot water is unleashed. The shock makes her gasp for breath. She's in some kind of step-down shower. Isn't she?

Then Caitlyn realizes. It's not water. It's blood.

They're showering her in blood.

59

When Draco and Musca pull into the parking lot at Stonehenge, it's crowded with staff busying themselves for the solstice. People are everywhere. Extra toilets are being set up and bins slotted on poles, ready for the avalanche of litter that will inevitably come.

Serpens wanders away from the group he's been supervising and slips in the back door of the Merc. Draco doesn't even wait for him to settle. 'We have to get rid of the Camper and the body tonight.'

The Looker's instinct for survival kicks in. 'I'm not driving it. There are police on every major road.'

'What about your boy?' asks Musca. 'Would he do it?'

'Lacerta is young but not stupid. He'll get stopped. You know he will.'

'Sooner or later the police will find the vehicle,' says Draco. 'They are checking all roads, parking lots, anywhere the dopeheads can hide. It is only a matter of time.'

'What if we use the Ecstasy we found in the glovebox?' says Musca. 'Make it look like he and his girl overdosed.'

Draco shakes his head. 'You can't just cram drugs down his throat. He won't be able to swallow and digest, none of the chemicals will be absorbed. The autopsy will show you did it after he'd died.'

'What if there's nothing of him to autopsy?' presses Musca. 'We torch the van and him in it, make it look like they had an accident.'

Draco's interest is awakened. 'How so?'

'Well, they were tired, pulled off the road, parked up in the field for the night.' Musca struggles to complete the picture, then adds: 'Maybe the guy was making a cup of tea and the stove blew. The cooking gas canister went up. You should get a good explosion from one that size.'

'Can you rig something like that?'

Serpens nods. 'It can be done. But they'll only find the man's body. They'll wonder what happened to the girl.'

Musca tries to fill in the gap. 'They had a row. She walked off. Hitched a ride. Got dropped at the train station and is now out of the area.' It's the best he can manage. 'If she's out of the county, she's someone else's missing person and the police will slacken off.'

'Can you deal with the body?' Draco looks deep into Serpens's eyes. 'We need you to do this.'

He feels like he doesn't have a choice. It was his blow that killed the guy. He wants a drink. Needs one badly. Finally he nods.

'I'll help you,' volunteers Musca. 'You don't have to do this alone.'

60

Caitlyn opens her eyes and gasps. Blackness. She's upright and back in the mind-numbing void that's become her personal prison. She has no recollection of them returning her to this hell hole. She must have passed out in the shower. The shower of blood.

Slivers of light are bleeding through what must be a panel right in front of her eyes. One that can be removed so they can see her. Feed her maybe. She realizes now that it's not the same hole as she was in. It's slightly different. The space is bigger. Not much, but still bigger.

Gradually she notices other differences. The handcuffs are gone. She can lift her arms from her sides. She feels the walls that enclose her. Stone to the front, the sides and the back. She is certainly in another crevice, no change there. She stretches her arms as wide as she can. Probably less than a meter. She can't raise her hands beyond her elbows.

There's something touching the back of her legs, at knee-level. A ledge? She tries to sit and finds it takes her weight. It feels like a blessing. She's still barefoot but has been dressed in some sort of robe with a hood. She moves her head, shoulders and hips, lets the fabric rub against her. It's rough. Feels like sandpaper against her breasts.

She starts to piece together the missing parts of the night before. They stripped her of her clothes. Showered her in blood. Dressed her in their robes. Words come back too. There weren't many to analyze. But one was enough.

Ceremony.

That's what someone had said. '*The ceremony goes ahead.*'

But what kind of ceremony? And what in God's name are they going to do to her?

61

DCS John Rowlands already feels like he's gone a week without sleep. The clock is ticking fast and the leads are coming slower than he hoped. The pressure is relentless. The Chief Constable, the Home Office, the Deputy Chief Constable and the Vice President's private secretary are all on his back.

Teams of DCIs and DIs shuttle in and out of his office, tossing what bits of information they have on to his wrecked desk. Jude Tompkins and Megan Baker are the latest to take their turn. He greets them with what's left of his charm. 'Ladies, welcome to the pleasure dome. What have you got for me?'

'Some good news.' Tompkins clears a plate and a crust of pizza from a seat. 'DI Baker has a positive on the vehicle. And the boyfriend.'

His blue eyes widen. 'Tell me.'

Megan puts a ripped DVD on his desk. 'A compilation of CCTV footage, sir. The first clip is from the petrol pumps at Fleet. It's in color and you can clearly see Lock and Jake Timberland, the man who paid for the Campervan rental.'

Rowlands doesn't need his notes. 'Son of Lord Joseph Timberland.'

'That's right.'

He picks up the disk and slides it into a player on a shelf beneath a TV behind him. Megan talks as he fiddles with a remote control to find the channel. 'The vehicle you are about to see, sir, is an imported right-hand-drive Type 2 Vintage in cornflower blue with chrome wheel hubs and refurbished interior.' A picture of the van comes up on-screen. The Camper pulls up at the pump. Two figures get out. And then they become clear. Jake shows Caitlyn the pump and starts her off. Leaves her to fill up and walks toward the shop to pay.

'Freeze it please, sir.'

Rowlands stops the picture with the remote.

'Look in his right hand.' Megan smiles. 'A gold credit card. Amex. It's the one he used to pay for the rental.'

Rowlands nods and turns off the DVD and TV. 'Good enough for me. Jude, get someone to make copies of the footage for the investigation teams and the press. Talk to the communications office and call a conference for eight in the morning.' He turns to Megan. 'Well done. Make sure your team know we think they're doing a first-class job.'

'I will. Thank you, sir.' She gets up to leave but pauses.

Rowlands glances at her. 'Is there something else?'

'Sir, if there *is* a press conference in the morning, I'd like to be part of it. I'd like the experience, sir.'

He smiles and turns to the DCI. 'My, you have got an ambitious DI here.'

Tompkins nods. 'She's aching with it.'

He looks back to Megan. 'No, Detective Inspector, you may not.'

'Why not, sir?'

It's Tompkins' turn to smile now. 'Two reasons, Megan,' she says. 'Firstly, you're doing too good a job on the inquiry to be wasted posing about in front of cameras. Secondly, you're too inexperienced to be put in front of those dogs. Not enough gravitas for the press pack, do you see? It's late, so why don't you go home, get some well-earned rest and see your kid.'

Megan has to fight not to show her anger at the put-down. 'Thank you ma'am – for your kindness and concern – but my daughter is being well looked after by her father, so if it's okay with you, I'll go back to my team and resume the job. The one the Detective Chief Super says I'm very good at.'

Point made, she wheels around and walks away before they can get in the final word.

62

Serpens checks his watch. Midnight. The time has come.

He stands and waits outside the old barn, his thoughts as black as the night sky. Psychologically things are piling up. Crushing him. Pressing him down. Not giving him a moment's relief.

The disposal of the sacrifice earlier in the month had got to him. He'd been involved in selections before but never afterward. Never the bloody carnage of it all. And now he's crossed the line even further. He's taken someone's life.

The realization that he'd killed the man in the Camper is eating him. He's a tough guy, been involved in plenty of fights in his time, even got a criminal record, but not for anything like murder.

Maybe if he went to the police he'd get away with a charge of 'accidental murder.' If he came clean now and told them everything he knew, there'd be some deal to be done. Possibly even immunity from prosecution. But the Craft would get to him. They'd find him and they'd kill him. He knows they would. They have brothers in the police – in the courts – in the prisons. They'd get to him all right.

Serpens hangs his head. It's a crisis of faith. That's all it is. Everyone has one. He's sure they do. Musca appears out of the clouded moonlight, a white plastic carrier bag in his right hand. 'All right?' he says and puts an arm around Serpens' shoulder as they head inside. 'Don't worry, all this will be over in half an hour. We'll go straight to Octans' afterwards. He'll alibi us. Say we've been there all night playing cards. Everything's going to be fine.'

Musca always says *everything will be fine*. Draco too. And for them it always is. Fine lives with fine consciences, not a guilty thought in their fine heads.

The barn is lit by a paraffin lamp on an overturned wooden crate a couple of meters from the Camper. It casts a yellow delta of light into the cobwebbed rafters. The two men disturb a colony of bats as they walk to the Camper. Musca laughs and points to the fluttering creatures. 'Creepy little fuckers. I wish I had something to shoot them with.'

Serpens pulls back the sliding door on the VW. A small interior light flickers on and reveals the fly-covered corpse. He steels himself for the task ahead. 'What do you want to do with him?'

'Wait. Put these on.' Musca hands him a pair of thin latex gloves. 'Better safe than sorry.'

Serpens stretches them and awkwardly squeezes his hands in.

'Okay, watch and learn,' says Musca. From the tiny kitchen he takes the complimentary food hamper left as a gift by the van hire company and smiles. 'Just what we need.' From cupboards he collects a plate, knife, fork, saucepan and toaster. He opens a can of beans from the hamper, tips them into the pan and places it on the cooking ring. He puts two slices of bread into the toaster and then produces a bottle of vodka from the carrier bag he brought with him. He unscrews it and pours some into a tumbler. 'Almost there, my friend. Almost there.'

Serpens watches in a trance as Musca opens the cupboard beneath the cooker and turns on the gas. He strikes a match, lights a ring on the small hob and then turns it off and smiles contentedly. 'So, that's all our preparation done.' He points to the corpse. 'The scene is set. We have our man left on his own in the Camper after a row with his girlfriend.' He points to the vodka. 'Man gets blind drunk – a reasonable reaction to being ditched partway through a romantic break, right?' He points to the hamper. 'Then, because he's wasted he gets hungry and tries to make himself something to eat.' Musca picks up the vodka bottle and splashes it around. 'Unfortunately, because our heartbroken friend is on his way to being pissed he gets clumsy and spills his drink. On himself. On the floor. On the cooker.' Musca raises his arms violently. '*Voom*! Suddenly he's a fireball. He panics. Falls over and knocks himself out. Within seconds the Camper is on fire, even the barn and he tragically burns to death.' Musca pulls down the corners of his lips to create a sad face. 'Sometimes unrequited love ends badly.'

Serpens is not in any state to fault the plan. 'So the fire destroys the evidence?'

'Right.' He wags a finger. 'But we should take care.' He points to the body. 'First off we pour half this bottle into Mr. Heartbreak. Then we make it look like he fell. We crack his head on something – in the same place where you hit him. That way any autopsy will find the injury is what they term "consistent with the fall" and not with you whacking him.' He grins. 'Finally, we soak him in the last of the voddie, light our bonfire and run.'

Serpens looks disturbed but nods his agreement.

'Okay, let's get it done. Help me sit him upright.'

Timberland's body is heavy and cumbersome. It makes sickening cracking and gassy noises as they pull it into a sitting position. Musca tilts the head back, pulls the lips apart and pours vodka down the dead man's throat. Serpens wants to throw up.

'Best let some of that settle for a minute,' says Musca. 'Or else it'll just come straight back up.' He leaves Serpens holding the corpse while he turns on the gas, heats the beans and makes the toast. 'All done. Let's move him to the drawers there, in the wall opposite the cooker. Open the bottom one. We can make it look like he slipped and cracked his head.'

Serpens flips it open and takes a deep breath. The two men struggle again to lift the body. Timberland was smaller than both of them but he's like a rag doll and weighs a ton. Finally, Musca takes him under the arms, slides him backward and drives the back of the skull down on to the bottom drawer.

He lets the body fall and stands back to admire his work.

A little vodka has spewed out of Timberland's mouth, onto his shirt front and onto the floor. Apart from that it's perfect.

'Finale time. You ready?'

'Guess so.'

Musca takes the open bottle of vodka and pours it over the head and chest. He lays the empty near the hands. He turns off the gas under the beans to extinguish the flames. When he's sure it's out he turns it on again and cranks it up high.

He gives Serpens a look, takes the carrier bag that he brought with him and unscrews the other bottle of spirits. He douses the corpse again and the cooker then points to the door. 'Best stand outside.'

They step out of the Camper into the cold barn and the yellow paraffin light. Serpens watches Musca pour the last of the vodka onto the floor of the van and return the empty to his carrier bag. 'Three, two, one.' He strikes the match. Lets it catch, then throws it o to the floor near the corpse.

'Run!'

They sprint like scared kids through the barn and out into the surrounding field. From the safety of the darkness, they see flames building. The old wood begins to crack in the rising fire. Suddenly, there is a guttural thud. The cylinder explodes.

The barn's rafters splinter and fall in. A scream of nesting bats scuttle skyward away from the spiraling orange flames.

63

SUNDAY 20 JUNE

Caitlyn knows about women who've been held captive for years. Imprisoned in cellars. Even locked in wooden crates. She knows of their horrors because Eric told her all about them. Said it would teach her to be careful – remind her to stay safe. The unlearned lesson chills her. Maybe others have suffered her fate, entombed in a thick stone wall, where you can scream your lungs out and never be heard.

Eric's warnings drift back to her. The horror stories he'd thought would keep her safe. Teenager Danielle Cramer from Connecticut, kept in a secret room under a staircase for a year. Nina von Gallwitz, held for 149 days until her parents paid out more than a million Deutschmarks to get her back. Fusako Sano from Japan, kept captive for ten years. An entire decade.

She can remember them all. All their faces. And they were the lucky ones. Eric showed her the long list of Dutch, American, English and Italian women who had not been so fortunate. Ones who had been taken, held and killed, even though ransoms had been paid.

His words come back and haunt her. 'They take you for sex, for money, for torture, even to get revenge on you or your parents. These are dangerous people, Caitlyn. Some of them are insane enough to take you just to become famous. Whatever you do, don't mess with our security.'

But she had done. She screwed up and she can't make it good. She wants to cry. Wants to sob her heart out. But she doesn't. She won't. She tells herself that she never cried during thirty-nine days of *Survivor* and she sure as hell isn't going to start now.

Caitlyn tries to think of something different. She recalls her time on the reality show. The welcome party, the first tasks, the guys who were hot for her. Thirty-nine days, twenty competitors, fifteen episodes that made her a household name. Once she swam naked during the live telecast. It gave the censors a fit. Damned nearly got the whole series scrapped. But it was a ratings blockbuster.

She'd do it again. Any time. Shock and glamour have become her middle names. It almost makes her smile. Even in this dusty crevice of a prison she can still taste the sweetness of her old life – the money, the fame, the controversy caused by her wild spirit. But for how long? she asks herself. How long before the whackballs holding her send her mad?

64

Gideon is down to the last two tapes.

He's watched close to forty and despite the thunderstorm raging in his head, he's determined to view the last of them before turning in.

He slides one into the player and watches his father appear onscreen. The young professor doesn't look much older than Gideon is now. After a few seconds, Marie Chase can be heard behind the camera: 'I think it's working, Nate. Yes, yes, the red light is flashing. You can start when you want.'

Nathaniel takes a breath to compose himself and brushes a straggle of windblown hair from his face. He's wearing a thick blue fleece, dark pants and walking boots. There's snow on the ground and an all-too-familiar backdrop. Stonehenge. 'I take you back almost five thousand years,' he announces, sweeping his hand across the landscape. 'Back to the days when our ancestors dug this circular ditch, some three hundred feet in diameter, twenty feet wide and up to seven feet deep.' He squats on the ground and places his hands in a furrow where the ditch had been. 'Beneath this spot, archaeologists found the bones of animals that died two hundred years before this ditch was even dug. Why did our forefathers put them there? Why use a pile of old bones to line a new ditch? The answer of course is that these bones came from special sacrifices to the ancient gods.'

Gideon smiles. His father the self-publicist had been well known for spicing up dull university lectures with his own home movies. On the screen, the young professor leaves the ditch and as he walks the circumference of the stones expounds a now familiar theory about the discovery of more than two hundred human skeletons on the site. 'The seventeenth-century historian John Aubrey found these burned human bones in fifty-six different holes. Were they too offerings to the gods? Was Stonehenge both a crematorium and a temple, a ritual slaughterhouse for celestial gratification?'

Having just read the diaries from a decade later, Gideon finds it strange to watch his father pose the questions in such a skeptical tone.

Stranger still to think of what might actually be true. The tape rolls on to the final stage of development: 'Some three thousand years ago, unknown hands moved these bluestones from the Preseli Mountains. We still do not know how they achieved such a feat. They were erected as a circular monument, the entrance aligned toward sunrise at the summer solstice.' Nathaniel walks to the bigger sandstones, his hand stretching to the skies. 'These giant sarsens, some more than three times my height and weighing as much as forty tons. Stood on their ends by incredibly talented ancient builders, they were capped with horizontal sarsens using sophisticated mortise and tenon joints, a technique that seems way before its time.' He walks deeper into the circle. 'Here in the heart of the henge, a horseshoe-shaped arrangement, five pairs of standing sarsens with giant horizontal caps – the trilithons.'

Gideon views the rest of the tape at double and even quadruple speed, making his father comically dash all over the site jerkily pointing out the Heel Stone, the Slaughter Stone and the northeastern entrance.

He takes a short break, makes a mug of tea and returns to watch the last uncatalogued video. He pulls it from its cardboard sleeve and sees a label in the center that hasn't been written in his father's faded hand. It reads: 'To Gideon, my loving son and pride and joy.'

He hasn't seen the handwriting in decades but recognizes it instantly. It's his mother's.

65

Jimmy Dockery pulls on a Tyvek suit and curses the fact that he's the one who's been called out in the dead of night. It always seems to be him that cops for the worst of jobs, the graveyard shifts with their mundane crime scenes. Any bit of mess – get Jimmy to mop it up. First it was chasing missing persons, sweeping up after some old man's suicide, and now it's a burned-out barn. In his head he's a better investigator than that. If his father, the Deputy Chief, knew the kind of crap they sent him on, he'd sack them all.

Dockery flashes his ID and ducks the fluttering yellow tape. An exhausted-looking PC takes his name and he wanders into the blackened ribs of the barn. Soco arc lights illuminate the charred metal remains of the Campervan. A burned-out replica of the one he saw on the footage he recovered from the service station. The one half the police in the country are looking for. Jimmy picks his way over a non-contamination pathway to the vehicle. Inside, a man and a woman are on their knees inspecting the body.

'Is it the girl?' Jimmy asks. 'The one who's missing.'

The question bounces off the back of Home Office pathologist Lisa Hamilton.

She recognizes his voice. 'No, it's a man – and *Sergeant* – just a word of warning, don't crowd me, don't press me, don't annoy me and don't *on any account* mess up my crime scene.'

'Understood.' It's water off a duck's back to Jimmy. Everyone is always giving him a list of don'ts. Besides, he has a soft spot for Lisa. Even at two in the morning, she triggers something primeval inside him.

From over her shoulder, he can see that the corpse looks like badly barbecued meat – a sickening mix of pinks and blacks. Tattered remnants of clothes are stuck to charred bone and tarry puddles of human fat are spread on what's left of the baseboard of the Camper. Jimmy notices part of the vehicle's metal frame is bent upward. 'There been some kind of explosion?'

'Gas canister by the looks of it,' says a young SOCO, a spotty-faced lad with spiky hair. 'From the blast pattern, it seems like it blew under the cooking ring.'

Jimmy moves around them and scans the rest of the burned-out vehicle. 'So no sign of the girl?' he calls over his shoulder. 'You sure bits of her aren't in here?'

Lisa Hamilton cranes her neck upward from her crouch. 'You seriously suggesting I might have missed a whole woman?'

He feels stupid. 'Of course not. It's just that we're all going crazy trying to find her.'

The pathologist continues scowling. 'This isn't about any missing woman. Right now my concern is this man, here. And I'm trying to afford him the dignity and respect he deserves by properly investigating his death.'

Jimmy gets the message and backs off. Other SOCOs are hard at work bagging and tagging whatever can be picked or scraped from the floor and walls. He sees a stack of paper bags containing a broken tumbler, burned saucepan, an empty vodka bottle and blackened cutlery and crockery.

A female SOCO appears at his shoulder with a plastic evidence bag. 'We discovered a driving license and hire documents in the glove compartment. They're smoke damaged but intact.'

Jimmy holds the bag up to a light so he can read through the covering. The writing is just about legible. 'Edward Jacob Timberland.' As he says it, he feels a wave of sadness. Putting a name to the body always alters things. He calls toward the pathologist. 'Prof, I'm going to go back to the station. When will your report be ready?'

She doesn't break from her examination. 'After breakfast. I'll mail through an outline and be available midmorning if you want me to run through it in person.'

'Thanks.' He'd like that. A nice chat over coffee. Who knows what might come up. Jimmy raises a hand as he leaves. 'Goodnight everyone.'

There are muffled replies as he heads out of the barn.

'Good *morning*,' shouts the professor playfully. 'Get your facts right, detective, it's already morning.'

66

Gideon can feel his heart thump as he slides the old VHS tape into the player.

The woman who comes onscreen is barely recognizable as the mother he loved. He expected to see the beauty from the video in Venice. Laughing. Vivacious. Full of life. But it's not to be.

She sits in a sick bed, resting against a plump white mountain of pillows and from the angle of the camera it looks like she's filming herself. The skeleton-thin face, the prematurely white frizzy hair and bloodshot gaze are cameos of pain.

Marie Chase is close to death as she smiles at her son through the TV monitor and through the ages. 'Giddy, my darling. I'm going to miss you so much. I'm hoping that you will have a long and very happy life and know what a joy it is to be a parent. Once you were born, my life felt complete. I never wanted for anything more than you, me and your father to be happy together.' She fights back her emotions. 'Darling, that's not to be. I don't have much time now, but there's something I have to tell you so I leave you this message for when you're older, old enough to see me in this state and not be frightened.'

Gideon has to wipe tears from his face. He realizes for the first time that he'd never been allowed to see his mother in her final days, in the period when she wasted away so painfully. Marie Chase is crying too as she reaches out to her only child. 'Giddy, no one but you *has* ever or *will* ever see this recording. Not your father. Not anyone. Just you. I have something I must tell you personally and your father respects that. He is a good man and he loves you more than you know. I hope you look after each other when I'm gone.' She reaches to the bedside cabinet and raises a glass of water to her parched lips, then forces another brave smile.

Gideon smiles back. He misses her. More than he has ever admitted to himself.

Marie Chase completes her message from beyond the grave, her final words to the son she never saw grow up. Then she tells him what she always told him at night as she switched his bedside light off and kissed his head: 'There's nothing to be afraid of, sweetheart. I love you and will always be there for you.'

The tape turns into a snowstorm of gray fuzz and spins noisily into rewind. Gideon is left gazing at the blank screen, his mind still fizzing from the shock of the secret that she just shared with him.

67

It's three a.m. when Jimmy Dockery turns up at Megan Baker's desk clutching a chipped mug full of steaming coffee. 'You got a minute, boss?'

'Sure.' She waves to a seat. 'What's on your mind?'

He sits, looking exceptionally tired. 'This lad that died in the Camper.'

'Timberland.'

'Yeah.'

'Don't worry. I'm not going to ask you to talk to the parents. The Met can do it. They made contact after we pulled their son's Amex bills.'

'It's not that.'

'What, then?'

He blows out a long breath and takes a steadying sip of coffee. 'The fire scene was a mess. Parts missing from the body, probably blown off, skin melted. And his head was just a big black ball. It was all wrong.'

She understands. He's badly shaken and doesn't want to talk to male colleagues about how it's affected him. 'Do you want me to fix for you to see the psychiatrist?'

He looks aghast.

'Jimmy, when I was training, I saw a guy hit by a train. A suicide. I couldn't sleep for days. Eventually, I found talking to a shrink really helped me.'

'Thanks, but I didn't mean that. I meant *the scene* was wrong. Wrong for what was supposed to have gone on.'

She's intrigued. 'How so?'

He suddenly wonders if he's going to make a fool of himself. 'You'll see the prof's report in a few hours so maybe it's worth waiting until then.'

'No, go on, Jim. If you've got a theory, a gut feeling, I want to hear it.'

'All right.' He rests his elbows on her desk. 'Location, location, location. Right?'

She looks confused.

'That's what estate agents say is the single most important thing.'

She nods, still not sure where he's going.

He tries to explain. 'So you've got a Campervan, a rugged little home from home. You can go anywhere in it. It'll survive whatever the elements throw at it. But you choose to park up *inside* a barn. A building so far off the beaten track, I bet most locals don't even know it's there.'

She gets his drift. 'Strange, I grant you. A barn isn't the right location for a Camper.'

He relaxes a little. 'That's the first thing, okay. So this Timberland guy was a posh nob. A rich guy. Son of a lord, right?'

'Right.'

'So if a guy like that hires a vintage Camper to take his new girlfriend out, what else might he bring along for the trip?'

She thinks about it. 'Soft drinks for the journey. Maybe snacks, probably food. I imagine champagne, maybe a bottle of rosé or a chilled white, some decent glasses.' She gets into her stride. 'Picnic blankets, hamper, sunglasses, maybe a surprise present for her.'

Jimmy smiles. 'Fine. I didn't get as far as you did but look at the list of stuff forensics identified.' He slides a piece of newly printed A4 across her desk and watches as she reads it. 'What you'll see on there,' he adds, 'is a dented can with burned bits of beans inside, fragments of silver tin foil – probably from a chocolate bar – two empty vodka bottles and some staple foodstuffs like bread and butter. Nothing you wouldn't expect. He probably bought some of it, but most of it is likely to have been freebies from the gift hamper that comes with the rental.' He jabs a finger at the bottom of the sheet. 'The little fridge in there protected what was inside from the blast. So here we have some fancy ice cream and a full bottle of Bollinger champagne.'

'What are you getting at?'

'The vodka. Two bottles. To have got through that but not opened the champagne that's hard-core drinking. Surely if you buy the Bolly, that's what you're going to open first?'

Megan jumps to her own conclusion. 'It's hard to start a fire with champagne, but not with vodka. You think the spirits were used as an accelerant?'

He shrugs. 'I'm not even sure you can set fire to champagne, can you?'

'I don't know.' She looks off into the distance, remembers another world, her wedding when she last drank champagne. 'I'm not going to waste any trying to find out though.' She thinks about his hunch. 'You're right, the vodka bottles and the champagne don't make sense. Nor does parking a van inside a barn. And the fact that the girl is still missing makes me even more suspicious.'

Jimmy swings a chair alongside Megan's desk. 'Do you think maybe the two of them had a fight over something and she cracked him one, a bit harder than she meant, then panicked?'

Megan shakes her head. 'Not her. Remember who she is. The daughter of the Vice President wouldn't behave like a halfwit and try to torch the scene, she'd have called Daddy for help.'

He sees her point. 'And I guess it doesn't explain the vodka bottles, either.'

'Quite. What I'm wondering though, is why she wasn't in the Camper with him.'

'They had a row and she stormed off?'

'Doesn't work for me. If she'd have done that, she'd have called home. This isn't a girl who's going to catch a train back to London.'

They sit in silence, both cycling the same thoughts. Jake Timberland is dead because someone killed him. Caitlyn Lock is missing because someone took her. Find Caitlyn and you catch the killer. Hopefully, before he kills again.

68

Serpens and Musca drive separately to Octans' place. They shower while Volans puts their clothes and shoes in two separate sacks, ready to be incinerated later that morning. They put on the fresh clothing and footwear that's been laid out for them.

Plates of cold pizza and cans of chilled beer mark their places at the card table. None of them speak about what has happened. They play poker, gin rummy and crib until streaks of daylight seep through the dusty window of the backroom. Four old mates on a boys' late night out.

Grabb hasn't touched a bite, though he's drinking like a Viking. Disposing of the body has cemented his guilt about the killing. He only cracked the lad with a small rock, no bigger than the palm of his hand. It shouldn't have killed him. The kid must have had some skull defect or something wrong with his brain.

But Serpens can't escape it. He's a killer and it doesn't sit easy. If he gets caught, it will be the end of his parents. They're in their eighties, barely mobile, living in assisted living. They stuck by him when he went to prison. His mother thinks he's stayed out of trouble since then. Gone straight. Grown up. Become someone they are proud of.

'Do you want another card or are you going to stick?'

Serpens looks at Musca and throws his hand in. 'I have to go and get some rest.' He turns to the other two men. 'Thanks for this, for the food and everything.'

Musca gets up, follows him to the door. 'You okay to drive? Do you want me to take you home?'

He shakes his head. 'I'm fine.'

Something has broken between them. Musca feels it. 'Why don't you come back and stay with me for the rest of the day? It might help you.'

'I'm fine, I told you.' There's tension in his voice.

They briefly lock eyes, then Serpens opens the front door and walks out into the cool light of dawn.

Musca follows. 'Hang on.'

Serpens is past hanging on. He zaps open his Warrior.

Musca halts him with a firm hand on his shoulder. 'Wait a minute, we really need to—'

The punch Serpens throws is fast. It's one that's been in his mind for three months. Borne out of frustration, nurtured by resentment, unleashed with anger. It hits Musca smack in the mouth, sends him staggering backward and falling on the pavement.

By the time Musca puts a hand to his lips and sees the blood, the Warrior has already spun rubber and gassed exhaust down the street.

Octans and Volans stand in the doorway looking worried. The noise, the altercation. The scene may well have been witnessed. But they're nowhere near as worried as Musca. He knows Serpens is going to be a problem. A *big* problem.

69

Chief Constable Alan Hunt likes his desk tidy. A tidy desk is a tidy mind. Always end the day with it clear, no business unsettled. John Rowlands, who sits opposite him, would say it's because he came up the modern way. Masters degree in law. Fast-tracked through the ranks. Chairman of the Association of Chief Police Officers. Home Office golden boy with political nous and a financial expertise at stretching budgets.

Sat next to the Chief Super and across from Hunt is the crumpled shape of Deputy Chief Constable Greg Dockery. It's six a.m. and there is only one piece of outstanding business ruining the otherwise clear slab of beech between the three men: a large blow-up of Caitlyn Lock.

Hunt's small and tidy hands touch the photo. 'So where is she, John? Why haven't we heard anything from whoever has her?'

Rowlands scratches gray stubble peppering his chin. 'I expect the kidnappers to make contact later today. They seem to be professional. Happy enough to kill the boyfriend to take her. Now they have her, I'm sure they'll issue a ransom demand.'

'I agree,' says Dockery. 'I would take the silence to mean they've been busy. Probably monitoring the situation. Watching how we react to her disappearance. They may well have moved the girl by another vehicle to a safe location.'

Rowlands taps his watch ominously. 'The first forty-eight applies to kidnapping more than most.'

Dockery sees the Chief frown. The boss's fast-tracked ascendancy evidently excluded force jargon. 'John means the first forty-eight hours, sir. Statistically, our chances of solving a major crime – especially kidnapping or murder – are halved if we don't catch the offender in the first two days.'

Hunt smiles. 'I only believe in good statistics, Gregory, you should know that.' There's polite laughter around the table, then he adds, 'After I got your call about the Timberland boy, I rang Sebastian Ingram at the Home Office to update him. They're putting the SAS on standby and want the Yard to send over a team from its Specialist Crime Directorate.'

Dockery knows better than to doubt the wisdom of such a move. Rowlands is less diplomatic. 'Sir, this is *our* inquiry. We are more than capable of handling it. I've had direct experience of hostage negotiations.'

The Chief tries to placate him. 'It's not about ability, John; it's about political responsibilities and budgets. We are scratching for funds to keep traffic cars on the road. An investigation like this could bleed us dry for the rest of the financial year.'

Dockery tries to sweeten the pill. 'We'll make sure you stay involved. Whoever they dump on us. He's going to have to work every bit as long and hard as you and your team.'

The desk phone rings. They all know a call this early won't be good news. Hunt takes it and briefly talks to his secretary before being put through to someone important enough to make him sit up straight and grow tense.

After less than a minute, he replaces the phone on its cradle and coolly passes on his news. 'Gentlemen, Vice President Lock and his ex-wife have just boarded a private jet in New York and will be with us shortly.'

70

Stripped to the waist and barefoot in black tracksuit bottoms, Draco exercises in the purpose-built gym at his lavish country home. The long, mirrored walls indulge a near-constant checking of the muscles he's painstakingly crafted. He looks ten, maybe twenty years younger than his actual fifty. Serpens is on his mind. A man he never liked. One he is sure is true to his star name – the snake.

A few meters away, his burner rings. The call he's been waiting for. The update. He abandons his sixth mile on the treadmill, guns down the music channel on a sixty-inch plasma and answers it. 'Everything go all right?'

'Not everything.' Musca sounds tense. 'We got the job done as planned but our man has fallen ill.'

Draco understands the code. 'Anything to seriously concern us?' He picks a white hand towel off a bench and mops sweat from his face.

'Possibly, yes.'

Draco drops the towel and reaches for a water bottle. 'Where is he now?'

'At home.'

'Check on him. See if he's feeling any better.'

Musca rubs his jaw, nursing the spot where Serpens punched him. 'I'll wait until lunchtime, let him sleep a little, then I'll go round and have a chat.'

'Don't leave it too long.' Draco thinks on it a second. 'Best not to take any unnecessary chances at the moment. If he's *really* sick, we need to find a cure. A permanent one.'

71

Gideon is almost too exhausted to leave his bed. His mother's video message and her goodbye secret were the final straw. Grief, insomnia and emotional turmoil are now all taking their toll. First there had been his father's revelations – the Sacreds, the Followers, the sacrifices. Then cancer. The CLL that killed his mother. Then her private words to him. Arrows in his heart.

He heads downstairs and triggers a nerve-jangling burst of bells. Still in shock, he turns off the alarm system that he'd forgotten he'd set the night before. Heart still pounding, he makes a mug of dark tea and sits by the kitchen window to watch the last of the sunrise.

Briefly, as golden light comes over the trees and flower beds, he forgets the personal horrors in his life. Then, when the tea is gone and the distraction over, the worries come back. Are his genes ticking time bombs, primed to explode like his mother's did? Or did the strange childhood baptism his father performed with water from the stones cure him? He remembers the words in the journals: 'I will willingly give my own blood, my own life. I only hope it is worthy. Worthy enough to change things. To alter the fate that I know awaits my poor, motherless son. I put my trust in the Sacreds, in the bond I make with them, in the clear blood of mine that I pledge to purify that of my child's.'

Gideon wearily trudges back upstairs to the diaries. They lie strewn where he left them, open at pages that seemed significant. So many refer to the stones. Stonehenge, a site his father published books on, its links to the vernal equinox, the earth's precessional cycle, its mystical connections with the celestial equator, Plato, the Great Sphinx.

Mumbo jumbo. That's what he always felt it was. Yet some of the fragments he's discovered are coming together, forming a path like crazy paving that leads to the heart of his strange and troubled childhood. His father forced him to learn Greek, wrote codes in it and gave him the worst birthday gift a ten-year-old could ever get – a copy of Plato's *Republic*. Not the racing bike he'd lobbied for but instead a wedge of impenetrable philosophy about happiness, justice and the fitness of people to rule.

Looking at the diaries, he sees the old philosopher's shadows in his father's words. Passages emphasise the role of the Sacreds in celestial mechanics and the Platonic year – the time required for a single complete cycle of the precession of the equinoxes. In hard numbers, about 25,800 years. About the same amount of time Gideon thinks it will take him to fully decode and understand everything his father has written.

72

Chief Constable Alan Hunt heads up the eight a.m. press conference. News of Jake Timberland's death and the imminent arrival of the girl's parents have ratcheted up the pressure. He can't let this go wrong. Not when he's in the running for the Met Commissioner's job. He knows that how he handles this inquiry is going to determine whether or not he gets the job.

Reporters settle around a well-planted forest of TV cameras and radio microphones. Flanked by Dockery and Rowlands, he taps the desk microphone and hears thunder crackle across the hall. He learned long ago of the benefits of knowing the sound levels before you speak. 'Ladies and gentlemen, thank you for attending at such short notice.

At two o'clock this morning, my officers discovered the body of a thirty-one-year-old male in a burned-out vehicle. A vehicle we had been seeking to locate in relation to the disappearance of Caitlyn Lock, who most of you know is the daughter of Kylie Lock and Vice President Thom Lock.' The Chief pauses to give the print journalists a chance to get their notes up to speed. 'Given this development, I have asked that our force receive the assistance of expert officers from the Metropolitan Police.' He raises a cautionary hand. 'I need to stress to you that these are preventative and cautionary measures. At this moment we have no indication of Miss Lock's whereabouts and have received no communication from her or anyone else to suggest that her life is in danger. Operational command of the inquiry is currently in the hands of Chief Superintendent Rowlands, reporting directly to Deputy Chief Constable Dockery. They are ready – within reason – to answer your questions, but first they have a request for your assistance.'

DCS Rowlands clears his throat, picks up a press pack and holds it high so everyone can see the photograph of Caitlyn on its front. 'You are all going to receive one of these handouts. Inside is a DVD containing video footage and still photographs of Miss Lock, the man she traveled down from London with, Jacob Timberland, and the VW Campervan they were driving. We are interested in any sightings of this van or these people over the last twenty-four hours. No matter how trivial people think it is, we urge them to come forward and tell us exactly what they saw.'

A reporter jumps in. 'Can you confirm that the dead man is Jake Timberland, the son of Lord and Lady Timberland?'

Rowlands bats him off. 'The family of the deceased has not yet formally identified the body, so that is not something I am prepared to do.'

'Can you confirm that the dead man was murdered?'

Again he reacts cautiously. 'I am yet to receive the full report from the Home Office pathologist who carried out the post-mortem examination. I won't prejudge her findings.'

'Where was the dead man found?'

Rowlands hesitates. 'The exact location is something we are not currently prepared to disclose. I hope you understand there are aspects of this case that we need to hold back for operational reasons.'

An old hack with skin the color of bacon sniffs an opening. 'Is that because you fear Caitlyn Lock has been abducted and only the kidnappers know the location of where they murdered her boyfriend?'

It's an astute question and too close to the truth for comfort. Greg Dockery steps in to field it. 'I have to emphasize what DCS Rowlands has said. The investigation is in its early stages and there is information that we need to hold back for operational reasons. We need you to respect that and help us find Caitlyn. You won't help her, us, or even yourselves with speculative journalism.'

Hunt senses that the reporters are going to keep on poking and prodding unless they get something juicier. 'Ladies and gentlemen, I can't overstate the importance of your role in this inquiry. Responsible reporting is essential. There may be an innocent reason behind Miss Lock's disappearance, there may not. If she is being detained against her will, those people will be reading everything you write and listening to everything you say. That is why we have to be circumspect. At this point that is all we have to say. Thank you for your attendance.' He allows a fractional pause for unrest to grow, then gives them what he knows will be their headline lead: 'Later this morning, I will be meeting in person with Vice President Lock and Kylie Lock, who are flying in from New York as we speak. I hope to have good news for them. I hope we will have knowledge of their daughter's whereabouts and if not, I hope to reassure them that the force and the people of Wiltshire, and the government and people of the United Kingdom, are doing everything within their powers to find her and bring her safely home. Thank you again for your attendance.' He stands, grabs his papers from the desk and walks slowly and confidently off the conference stage.

73

News that the Met has been drafted in doesn't go down well at the post-press conference team briefing.

Jude Tompkins pulls Megan aside at the end. 'The Chief Super has just talked to Barney Gibson from the Specialist Crime Directorate. He'll be here in an hour with a couple of others and they'll take over operational control. John will report to them and I will report to him. I need you to go to see the pathologist, get a briefing on Timberland's death. Once you've reported back, you're off the case.'

Megan is stunned. 'What?'

'Did you mean, *pardon, ma'am*?'

'I thought Rowlands said I was doing a good job.'

'You were. Right up until the point you wanted to dance in the spotlight. Now I need you to go and carry out my orders, not question them. Warren and Jenkins have already been reassigned.'

Megan manages a polite nod before turning away and mouthing a silent stream of obscenities that doesn't stop until she's back in CID.

Jimmy Dockery calls to her from his desk 'Boss—'

She doesn't let him finish. 'Get your coat, Jimmy, you've pulled.' She grabs her jacket off the back of a chair and her car keys off the desk.

74

Serpens is in meltdown.

The guilt is unbearable. Images flash relentlessly in his tortured mind. The young man dismembered and minced at the abattoir. The vodka-soaked body set ablaze in the Campervan in the barn. There is no escape from it all.

Despite this being the busiest time of the year for the security company where he works, he calls in sick. Head pounding, he guns up the old Mitsubishi and drives. He has to get away from it all. Find some peace.

An hour later he's in Bath. A well-scrubbed tourist city where he holidayed as a child. A place with happy memories. Maybe enough for him to come to peace with himself.

He parks at the Southgate Center and buys a six pack of lager and half a liter of Scotch. Wise old locals glare soberly at him as he drinks while he wanders. By the time he's circled Grand Parade and Boat Stall Lane, the beer is finished. He takes a leak in bushes off Orange Grove and meanders east toward the banks of the river.

Resting in the cool shade, his back against a tree by the water, closes his tired eyes. A monstrous mosaic of sounds and sights forms in his head – the empty noise of the rolling bottle that Musca threw into the Camper, the rough scratch of a match, the dull boom that rocked his heart and the fireball that roared through the Camper, splitting the old barn's parched rafters.

Serpens unscrews the top of the Scotch and takes a swig as hot as the flames that haunt him. The more it burns the better. He swallows it down in painful gulps. He killed the guy. Cracked him with a rock and brought his life to an end. One minute the poor sap is on top of the world, making out with his girl, then thwack, he's dead and his corpse is about to be burned to cinders.

Serpens' phone rings. It's not a shock, it's been going all morning. He knows who it is and what they want. He pulls it from his pocket and hurls it into the river. *Plosh*. Makes him smile for the first time in days. He takes another jolt of booze and coughs. It must have gone down the wrong way. Nearly drowned himself. Drowned in Scotch, now that would be a fitting way to end it all, wouldn't it?

Noisy children run past him. A red-faced young boy chases an older girl who's teasing him. Life in the making. He gets groggily to his feet, watches them spin around a tree, giggle and head back to a tartan picnic blanket, where a woman is laying out cling-filmed sandwiches and cans of pop. Happiness. An alien world to him.

Serpens gulps more of the whisky. Pours it down his throat until it kicks back like water in a blocked drain. He drops the bottle to the balding grass, spreads his arms wide and falls like a felled tree into the fast flow of the Avon.

75

Under the brutal glare of the autopsy lights, Jake Timberland's body looks even worse than Jimmy Dockery remembers it. What's left of the fire-blackened and blast-damaged corpse has been opened up and the internal organs extracted and weighed.

Professor Lisa Hamilton reads the minds of the two detectives opposite her. 'It wasn't the fire or the explosion that killed him. The blast blew out some of the blaze in the van interior so there was enough viable tissue, organs and fluid left to establish that he'd been lying dead on his left side for about ten hours before his body was burned.'

Megan double-checks the time. 'Ten hours?'

'About that.' Lisa explains her approximation. 'After death, gravity takes over. Blood stops pumping from the heart and as it settles it marks the tissue.' She gestures to the splayed corpse. 'He was moved a long time after his heart had stopped beating. We know this because of the extent and position that the blood stained the skin. Somebody moved him from the position he'd originally been left in after death and laid him out in the Camper to make it look like he'd had an accident. Unfortunately, they dropped him on the wrong side, his right, with his back slightly raised. Entirely inconsistent with the evidence provided by post-mortem staining.'

She moves around the autopsy table and glides a hand over Jake's gray torso. 'The cause of death is a massive heart attack, brought on by a heavy single blow to the back of his skull with some form of improvised weapon. I found particles of soil and some pretty dense rock embedded in the bone.'

Jimmy paints the scene. 'So, he's hit on the back of the head outside somewhere, then shifted back into his van and laid out on the floor by the cooker. The offender sets the Camper on fire to make it look like our friend here had been on the booze, fallen over and caused the blaze.'

Lisa nods. 'Almost. Remember, I said that there was post-mortem staining on his left side because that's how he'd been lying for ten hours.'

Megan understands her point. 'What you're saying is, whoever killed him spent those ten hours working out what to do. *Eventually*, they came up with the plan to put the Camper in the barn, move him around to look like he'd fallen and then torch everything.'

'Exactly. Another thing: although forensics found two empty vodka bottles near the body, there were no traces of metabolized alcohol in his system. His blood showed only tiny amounts of ethanol but the liver was clean. This is entirely inconsistent with him consuming vast amounts of spirits.' Jimmy is about to ask a question, but Lisa doesn't let him. 'Examination of lung tissue showed no evidence of smoke inhalation. No particles, no tissue damage. Nothing. He'd clearly stopped breathing before the fire had started.'

'The whole scene was faked,' concludes Megan. 'Credit where it's due, Jimmy, it's exactly as you said it was.'

'Really?' says Lisa, expressing genuine shock.

'Really,' repeats Jimmy, proudly.

76

The Master keeps his phone call with Draco as short as possible. 'Have you solved our operational problem?'

'Unfortunately not. Our man wasn't available.'

'Uncontactable?'

'I am afraid so. He isn't on any of his numbers. I've left messages but he hasn't returned them. And he phoned in sick at work.'

'And do you think he is?'

'No. I've been to his house and he's not there. Nor is his vehicle.'

The Master tries to be positive. 'He has been under stress lately. It could be that he felt the need to get away, clear his head. Would that fit his character?'

Draco is not sure. 'It's possible. I have people asking his friends where he might have gone. We're also trying to get one of them to reach out to him. Perhaps he'll return their calls.'

'Good.'

Draco feels the need to reassure his leader. 'We'll find him.'

'I am banking on you doing exactly that. Hold for a moment.' He pauses while an assistant presents him with a file of documents for signature and in a hushed voice reminds him of his lunch appointment with a county judge. He waits until the assistant has left before picking up the conversation with Draco. 'And on the *other* matter, I have a plan to give us some breathing space. Can you meet me?'

'Of course. What time?'

The Master checks the calendar on his desk. 'Three p.m. I'll have about an hour. Don't be late.'

77

Megan and Jimmy park a mile from the burned-out barn. It's in the middle of the largest area of chalky grassland in northwest Europe. A bleak and isolated table of endless land.

Down in a dip dotted with wildflowers they finally see the charred hulk, an ugly black wound on Salisbury Plain's soft green skin. Megan points to tracks through the grass. Vehicle marks and footmarks heading to and from the barn. 'Have we got lifts of any tire prints?'

'I think so.'

She scowls at him. 'You're a DS; you either *know so* or it *isn't so*. Make sure we have them.' They walk on a few steps and she sees he's hurt by her sudden frostiness. She stops. With time and patience she knows he could become a good copper. 'Look around Jimmy and you'll hear the grass tell you stories, tales of who's been coming and going.' She leans close, so that his eyes are guided along her pointing finger. 'Over there – those deep depressions are where the fire trucks came in.' She swings him round and points again. 'Over here – indentations from at least three different kinds of vehicles, much lighter ones than the first. I'd take a guess at some of these coming from our Camper and maybe two other vehicles.'

'Why two others?'

She wishes she had a tape measure to help explain. 'Look at the depth and the width of each track. This gives you the thickness of the tires and indicates the length of the wheelbases. Do you see now that they're different?'

He does. 'So two cars. That would mean at least two people.'

'Good. Get traffic to carry out a thorough inspection. SOCOs will have looked at the marks already but traffic are best at this type of thing.' She squats down and gazes across the grooves in the long grass. 'Question: why would these people be traveling separately rather than together?'

He looks up and down the tracks, then hazards a guess. 'One guy stays in the barn minding the Camper and our deceased. The other one goes away to do something, maybe get the vodka, arrives later?'

'Good.' She gives him an impressed nod as she stands again. 'Let's go further. What does that tell you?'

He's confused. 'What do you mean?'

'What does that tell you about the *relationship* between the two men?'

Jimmy's lost. Behavioral science is foreign to him.

Megan helps out. 'One of them is a doer, the other is a teller. The guy who stays with the body is the doer. It's the worst and riskiest of jobs. He was told to do it by the teller. This is evidence of rank, a pecking order, a structure that those two parties accept.' Her eyes wander to the massive black wound in the earth and scabs of charred barn timbers. 'Of course, it might be *two* doers at the scene and *two* tellers arriving later.'

'Organized crime?'

She shrugs. 'Of sorts. Just how organized, we're still to find out.'

78

By midmorning Gideon needs a break. He makes a short trip to the shops and returns with a newspaper, two-liter carton of milk and stack of ready-meals. He wolfs down a greasy, microwaved lasagna then resumes his decoding of the diaries.

Very quickly it becomes apparent that the more his father learned of the Followers the more he was drawn into their ways: 'I have dispensed with my watch, such a crude instrument. My world is to be governed by an older way, one calibrated to the spiritual: sidereal time, the rule of the great astronomers, the natural instrument that we use to track the stars that guided them and their learning. The real importance of the sidereal zodiac has become known to me, the significant alignments of the great signs with the galactic equator.'

The words are as difficult to digest as the lasagna. His mind drifts back to his childhood. His father had taken him into the garden late at night and pointed out the stars. He'd named various constellations and spoken of the orbits of the sun and the moon. Magical stuff.

Across the room, beneath a dust cover in the far corner, he spots his father's old telescope. How had he not seen it before? It's shrouded in a polythene cover yellowed with age. Gideon bends down and unwraps it like he's been given a surprise present.

The telescope is a Meade. So expensive, so prized, that his father never let him use it unless he was there right by him. It was an indulgence Marie would never have allowed. Thousands of pounds' worth of reflector optics, almost observatory standard, with zero image-shift microfocuser and special mounts for cameras.

As he stands again, he cracks the back of his head on the low roof above. He gives his skull a rub and glares accusingly at the ceiling panel. It looks odd. He presses hard on it and it pops loose at the bottom. As Gideon lets go, the panel swings down on a hinge and reveals a side-sliding window and beyond it a long, flat roof.

Gideon twists a key, slides the window back and climbs out into bright sun. The ledge is bitumen, flat and turns a corner. He walks it gingerly around the hidden room to a wide open space.

Right above the center of the house, on an area between two red-tile apexes, is a small wooden shed about ten feet long by six feet wide and five feet high. It's so peculiar that he immediately recognizes it. One of his father's handmade observatory boxes. A shelter from the wind and rain, equipped with hinged roof.

Inside he finds his father's things. They are spread everywhere. An old camping kettle, cups, tea bags, pens, paper, astronomical charts, reference books and photographs. Lots of photographs. On the walls and on the floor.

It is easy to imagine the old man sitting here stargazing. Lost in his own world. Drawing up charts. Gideon unrolls one of them. It shows the sun aligning with the galactic equator at the time of the summer solstice. He finds another. A depiction of the position of key planets at the point of the winter solstice.

He looks at the photographs pinned to the walls. An exhibition that he's never seen by an artist he barely knew. There are dozens of Polaris, enough to trigger memories of his father explaining the role of the great North Star, how over the ages its position as the leading light for astronomers and sailors passed from one star to another.

He studies pictures of another star cluster: Pleiades. The Seven Sisters. A line from Tennyson comes to him: 'Many a night I saw Pleiads, rising thro' the mellow shade, Glitter like a swarm of fireflies tangled in a silver braid.'

In a nostalgic mood he sits on the floor and slowly sifts the photographs and charts. And then he sees it. A single image that shatters the pleasant moment. Stonehenge.

It's a high-angle, side-on shot that shows the circle, not as it is now, but as it must have been when the ancients first completed it. Gideon looks closer. Faint white lines run from the giant stones to pricks of white above them. Gradually he realizes what he's looking at. Stars and constellations. The stones are aligned with planetary and stellar movements. Thin lines divide the chart into four. Tiny letters mark out north, south, east and west. Two more faded words – one at the top and one at the bottom – are barely visible. Earth. Heaven.

Gideon feels cool air prickle the back of his neck. The Followers evidently didn't just believe Stonehenge was central to all their lives. They believed it was much more.

The center of the sidereal zodiac.

The center of the entire universe.

79

By the time Megan and Jimmy leave the burned-out barn, the roads have started to jam with cars crawling towards Stonehenge. Megan curses the presolstice traffic. They get back to HQ an hour later than she hoped. She immediately calls her ex to check on Sammy.

'How's it going?' Adam sounds surprisingly chatty.

'Good.' She plays with the wire on the phone. 'Or at least I thought it was until a few hours ago. I'm off the inquiry.'

'Why?'

'Her Majesty Jude Tompkins, that's why.'

'Seriously?' He sounds sympathetic. 'What's going on? They scaling the case down?'

'No. Just the opposite. They're bringing in bigwigs from the Met. No room for yours truly. Just as it was getting interesting.'

'You got a lead?'

'Not on the girl, but the boyfriend's death is now officially a murder. Pathologist confirmed it.'

Adam tries to be helpful. 'Look Meg, if you want me to have Sammy tonight, I don't mind. If you think some more time will get you back on the case, then I'm more than happy to have her.'

'You sure?'

'Totally. I love having her stay during the week.'

Adam has Sammy every other weekend. That's the agreement. The routine. She wonders if he's soft-soaping her for some ulterior motive. 'What's the catch? Because if you think I'm going to alter visiting and custody arrangements, I'm not.'

'Don't be cynical,' he snaps. 'I was just offering to help.'

She sees the door of opportunity closing. 'Then okay, thanks. Having her tonight would really be a big help.'

'Great. I'll take her to KFC.'

'Don't you dare.'

They both hang up smiling.

Jimmy puts a mug of black tea down in front of her. 'Don't know how you can drink this stuff without milk.'

'Like everything else, you get used to it.' She leans back in her chair and checks her computer for case updates. She clicks an icon and watches a message pop open.

'Yes! Yes! Yes! Thank you God.'

'What?' Jimmy leans in to read her screen.

'Records found a match for the fingerprints SOCOs lifted from the Camper.' She jabs at the monitor. 'Prints from the handle of the side door and from the interior side of a window belong to one Sean Elliott Grabb. He's got spent convictions for burglary and assault.'

'And a lot of explaining to do,' says Jimmy.

80

Megan feels like she's shaking hands with a giant. The grip crushing her fingers belongs to the new man in charge, Metropolitan Police

Commander Barney Gibson, from the formed Specialist Crime Directorate.

'Take a seat,' he says with a deceptively gentle smile. 'And tell us about the autopsy.'

Megan sits at a table already supporting the elbows of Jude Tompkins, the Head of CID John Rowlands and Gibson's number two, Stewart Willis. She knows this is her last chance to get back on the case. 'Sir, the post-mortem examination was performed by Professor Lisa Hamilton. She puts the time of death at somewhere around ten hours *before* Jake Timberland's body was burned in the Camper. Her findings mean that the blaze was staged to make it look like he'd been killed in a drink-related accident. He hadn't.' She slides a full copy of the postmortem examination across the table. 'This report clearly indicates that Timberland had been murdered.'

Gibson speed-reads the first page. 'Cause of death?'

'It's on the next page, sir. Blunt trauma and heart attack. He was hit on the back of the head with something heavy like a rock.'

'*Not* a rock but something *like* a rock?' He glares at Megan.

'It *may* have been a rock, sir. It certainly wasn't a brick or a hammer but it could have been a boulder or stone.'

'I see.' He reads a little more of the report then looks up. 'The professor mentions soil and grit samples embedded in the skull. Do we have anything back from the lab to suggest where these might have come from?'

'No, sir. But I believe them to be from Stonehenge.'

Gibson seems surprised. 'Why?'

'The solstice, sir. I think it's reasonable to assume that Timberland hired the van to take Lock to see the sunrise there. They would have arrived in the early hours of the morning. Which is the time I think they encountered their attackers and the time Professor Hamilton cited as his TOD. It's possible that Timberland tried to stop Lock being abducted and in the struggle he was killed.'

'Many things are *possible*, Detective Inspector.' Gibson looks towards his DCS. 'Stewart?'

Willis weighs up Megan with his tiny brown eyes. 'Kidnapping someone like Caitlyn Lock takes careful planning, long-term surveillance and expert execution. We're talking about the Vice President's daughter. The type of people involved in that kind of swoop and snatch operation come with full military training and automatic weapons. They don't come empty-handed and hit people with "something like a rock".'

Gibson gives Megan a judgmental stare. 'Anything else, DI Baker?'

She feels humiliated and intimidated. She knows she has one last chance to change their minds about her. 'Yes, there is, sir. SOCOs found fingerprints on the door handle and a window of the Camper. They fit a local criminal.' She glances directly at Willis. 'A *petty* local criminal called Sean Grabb from Winterbourne Stoke. His home is not far from the henge.'

Gibson looks to Rowlands. 'Can you have someone check this man Grabb out? If he *is* as the DI suggests, he may simply have come across the Camper by mistake.' The commander looks back at Megan. 'It's possible your *petty* criminal was lifting tools from barns and sheds and he opened the Camper out of curiosity and got a nasty surprise.'

'Many things are possible,' says Rowlands, pointedly.

Megan sees an opening in the cross fire. 'Sir, I'd be very happy to track down Grabb.'

Gibson slides the pathologist's report across to Tompkins. 'I'm told you and DS Dockery have other pressing duties.'

Megan fights the urge to storm out. 'Sir—'

'You can go, Baker,' the commander nods towards the door. 'We're grateful for your work.'

Megan doesn't breathe until she's outside. She walks into the ladies room, screams and slaps the wall. Those bastards are going to follow up on *her* leads.

81

Caitlyn senses something different about the hooded men moving her from her hellhole. They're on edge. More careful with her than usual. Much slower. Less relaxed. Her heart lifts. It must be because they've decided to let her go. Then her hopes fall again. More likely they're just moving her to another location. It's something kidnappers do. More useless wisdom from Eric.

No sooner has her sight adjusted to the light than a blindfold is slipped over her eyes. She reaches up to her face but hands grab her wrists. They cuff her. Cold metal jaws bite her flesh.

They walk her down a corridor. The loss of sight makes her sway like she's seasick. Unseen hands sail her round several corners and then halt her in a room where the temperature is at least ten degrees warmer.

'Sit her down.'

The voice is male. Educated. English. Authoritative.

She is positioned on a chair. It feels good. Wood and leather, not cold stone.

'Caitlyn.' The voice is calm and measured. 'We are going to ask you some questions. Easy questions. It is very important that you answer us honestly. Do you understand?'

She reminds herself of what Eric said. Build contact – any form of contact – with your captors. It can be the difference between life and death. 'I understand.'

'Good.' The voice sounds pleased.

'Can I have something to drink? I'm very thirsty.'

'Certainly.' He waves to one of the Helpers.

'Not water,' she pleads. 'Anything but water. I've drunk enough to drown. Maybe Coke or juice?'

'We only have water.'

Caitlyn feels a glass being pressed into her hands. She raises it, tips it a little too much and spills some while she drinks. Someone lifts the tumbler from her hands.

'What is your name?'

A different voice. Younger. Thinner. A slight accent. Not so educated.

'Caitlyn Lock.' She says it with pride.

'How old are you?'

'Twenty-two.'

'Where were you born?'

'Purchase, New York.'

'What is your happiest memory about your father?'

The question throws her. 'Say again?'

'Your father, what is your happiest memory of him?'

It hurts even to think about it. There's a long pause as Caitlyn decides what to say to them. 'My dad used to read to me. Every bedtime he'd sit beneath the quilt with me and read until I fell asleep.' She manages a pained laugh. 'He made up stories about a fairy princess called Kay and her adventures, and then . . .' She fights hard not to cry. 'Then I'd fall asleep holding my daddy's hand.'

'And your mother, what is your happiest memory about her?'

She is hurting. The image of her father is clear in her head. She misses him. Aches to slip her hand in his and feel safe again. 'I don't recall much about my mother.'

'Try.'

She takes a minute. She's thought badly of her for so long it takes an effort to remember the better times. 'I guess I remember her tying yellow bows in my hair for my first day at school. 'Cause I hated the blue uniform. I remember making waffles with her at grandma's house. Almost every time we went round. And she used to sit me up on a cushion in her makeup room on the lot and have her own personal artist pretty me up.'

Now she thinks of it, she has lots of good memories of her mom. If only the woman hadn't cheated on them, hadn't left them.

'Okay. That's enough.'

The voice is the older man again.

She hears a click and a dying buzz, like something electric was just turned off. Footsteps cross the floor to her.

'Why are you asking me these things?'

No one answers. Hands start to lift her from her seat.

'Jake, what happened to Jake?' There's desperation in her voice. 'Where is he? Can I talk to him?'

They're turning her around, forcing her to walk.

'Tell me! Tell me what happened to him.' She digs her heels in, leans backward, makes it hard for them to push her. Strong hands sweep her off the floor.

'Motherfuckers!' She wriggles and kicks but at least four of them are holding her, carrying her. 'My father will kill you for this. My father's men will get you and kill every fucking one of you.'

82

The private Citation jet crosses the Atlantic at a cruising speed of almost a thousand kilometers an hour. The flight is less than six hours – almost two quicker than a regular transatlantic charter.

Vice President Lock and his estranged wife Kylie buckle their seat belts as the jet zips into UK airspace. They've barely spoken throughout the journey and the grief-laden silence continues as an armor-plated Mercedes and detail of Secret Service agents whisk them away from Heathrow.

Six police outriders, sirens wailing, accompany them on the last leg of their journey. In Wiltshire, they're held up by a straggling pilgrimage of cars and campers crawling through the country lanes toward Stonehenge. They pass them, corralled by the outriders, and finally arrive at police headquarters in Devizes.

Thom and Kylie Lock are shown into Hunt's office and after a round of handshakes and hellos settle at the large conference table. Opposite them are Commander Barney Gibson and Home Office Minister Celia Ashbourne. The woman, a small but forceful northerner in her late-forties, starts the meeting.'The Home Secretary sends his apologies. Unfortunately it was impossible for him to cut short his visit to Australia. I am here to assist you and to assure you that the British government and all its agencies are doing everything possible to find your daughter.'

'We are making good progress,' says Hunt. 'The vehicle Caitlyn traveled in has been found and although burned out, it is being thoroughly analyzed by forensics.' His face saddens. 'As I think you know, we also recovered the body of the young man she'd been traveling with.'

Kylie Lock reaches in her handbag for a tissue.

Hunt continues: 'Did either of you have any knowledge at all of their relationship?'

She shakes her head.

'It must be new,' says Thom Lock. 'Believe me, the team I had guarding Caitlyn would have reported any meaningful relationship.' He senses his wife's growing distress and takes her hand. The first sign of affection between them. 'Have you had any contact from whoever has taken our daughter?'

'None at all.'

'Do your investigators have any intelligence on who her captors might be?'

'We have the most senior detectives from the Met's Specialist Crime Directorate working on that at the moment.'

'MI6?'

'The Special Intelligence Service has been informed,' Ashbourne cuts in. 'At the moment we don't think it would be advantageous to involve them actively. Should a clear foreign or terrorist dimension develop then we'll reconsider.'

The Vice President exhales. 'Mrs. Ashbourne, my ex-wife and I appreciate your efforts and the hard work of the police service. But – and I hope you don't mind me saying this – we both would feel more comfortable if the operation were integrated with specific people I can send you. The FBI has noted specialisms in this field.'

Ashbourne smiles compassionately. 'I understand how you feel Mr.

Vice President, I have a daughter the same age. Rest assured we are more than willing to cooperate fully in terms of exchanging information with the FBI and appropriately apprising them – and you – of any progress that's being made. However, clear control of this investigation is of such paramount importance that operational integration really isn't advisable.'

The Vice President drops his wife's hand and leans forward. His eyes glint with steel forged in the white heat of campaign trails. 'Minister, Chief Constable, I spoke with the President of the United States before I got on the plane. It was very late but he was concerned and kind enough to call me to express his concern as a personal friend and as the ultimate guardian of all American citizens. We can move forward here in one of two ways. You can accommodate my request and secure the deep gratitude of Kylie, myself and the President. I recommend that you do that. Or in a few hours the President will personally call your Prime Minister and express his grave concerns over how this investigation is being run. He will then hold a press conference on the White House lawn to share those concerns with the American people.'

Hunt nods understandingly. 'Mr. Vice President, we would welcome the assistance of the FBI. I will have my staff officer make arrangements with the Director General's office.'

Kylie Lock speaks for the first time. She wants to ask only one question and the nervous pitch in her voice betrays how frightened she is of what the answer may be. 'Please tell me, Mr. Hunt, honestly, do you think my daughter is still alive?'

The Chief Constable answers without hesitation. 'I am sure she is. I feel confident that we'll soon find her.'

Kylie smiles, relieved.

Thom Lock's eyes tell a different story. He would have said exactly the same if he'd been in the chief's position. He knows the truth. It's unlikely his daughter will get out of this alive.

83

Megan can't face another minute at work. She shuts down her computer, grabs her stuff and slips out into the parking lot. The only consolation is that Sammy doesn't now have to stay at Adam's.

Lost in anger at being dropped from the big case, she almost misses Gideon Chase walking toward reception. His head is down and it's clear he's burdened with even darker thoughts than her own. 'Gideon,' she shouts.

He lifts his eyes, forces a weak smile and turns and heads toward her car. 'Inspector, I was just coming to see you.'

Megan glances at her watch. 'You should have called. I have to pick up my daughter. Is it something that can wait until the morning?'

He looks disappointed. 'Of course, not a problem.'

But she can tell that he doesn't mean it. 'What's wrong? Why did you drive out here to see me?'

He's been rehearsing things in his mind for the past hour but now he's really not sure where to begin. 'You were right. I haven't been telling you the truth about everything.'

'What do you mean?' For a second she can't remember what it was that she had been accusing him of lying about.

'I saw the man who broke into the house, my father's house.' He holds out his mobile. 'I got a picture of him.'

She takes the phone from his hand. The photograph is not good. Shaky. Burned out a little by the cheap flash. Badly framed. Everything you shouldn't do if you're trying to take a good picture. But there's enough to go on. A face to fit her profile.

Megan looks long and hard at the shot of the stocky man with rounded shoulders and short blond hair. He's just as she imagined. White male, midthirties, somewhere around fourteen stone, quite broad, forty-two- to forty-four-inch chest.

'I took it just before I shut the door on him,' Gideon explains. 'If you look closely, you can see the papers burning in his hand.'

She squints at the tiny screen and sees he's right. The photo is better than she first thought. It's evidential. 'Why didn't you want us to know about this?'

He shrugs. 'It's hard to explain. I guess I thought I could track him down before you did.'

'Why would you want to do that?'

'To ask him about my father. Find out what he'd been involved in. What it had all meant to him.'

She senses there's more to it than just a need for personal retribution. 'What do you mean, "*what* it had all meant to him"?'

Gideon freezes. He wants to tell her, have her help him make sense of things but he also doesn't want to seem crazy. 'My father kept diaries all of his life. Every year since he was eighteen.'

Megan doesn't remember any reports mentioning diaries found at the house. 'So?'

'I think they could be important.' He studies her, looking for a reaction. 'Do you know anything about the stones and the Followers of the Sacreds?'

'What stones?'

'Stonehenge.'

She laughs. 'Listen. I'm having a very bad day and I can't work out riddles. What is it? What are you talking about?'

'My father was a member of a secret organization. It was . . .' he corrects himself, '. . . it *is* called "the Followers of the Sacreds".'

The DI gives him a cynical look. 'So what? Your father had a secret club. He wouldn't be the first. The police service is full of Freemasons and the like. I'm sorry, I really have got to go.'

'It wasn't like Freemasonry,' Gideon snaps. 'This group is dangerous. They're involved in all kinds of things, rituals, maybe sacrifices.'

Megan scans him. He's clearly exhausted. Depressed. Possibly even post-traumatically stressed. 'Gideon, have you had any decent sleep recently?'

He shakes his head. 'Not much.'

Now it all makes sense to her. His father's death and the burglary and attack on him must be taking their toll. 'Maybe it could be a good idea to see a doctor? They can give you something to help you rest. Get you through things for a few weeks.'

'I don't need drugs or advice, Inspector. I need you to take me seriously. My father killed himself because of this group, the Followers of the Sacreds. I don't know exactly why. But I think it all has something to do with me.'

She looks from her car to the front door of the station. Only one will take her home to her daughter.

'This has to wait until tomorrow,' she says. She holds up his phone. 'I am keeping this until I can make a copy of the photograph that you showed me. I'll give it back when I see you.'

Gideon nods disappointedly. 'Please come to the house. I'll show you the diaries. Then you'll see things differently.'

Megan hesitates, her own personal safety is always at the back of her mind and Chase is showing signs of becoming unstable. 'My DS and I can come around at ten in the morning. Is that all right?'

'Ten is fine.'

They say goodnight and she walks to her car looking down at the mobile that he gave her and the face of the blond-haired man with a fistful of fire.

PART THREE

84

MONDAY 21 JUNE, SUMMER SOLSTICE
STONEHENGE

High on the hillsides surrounding the stones, Lookers watch the revelers gather like ants around the giant sarsens. The pilgrims hold hands, forming their own human circle against the Megalithic landscape. Throughout the dark hours of the night the men of the Craft have watched them come.

Thousands of strangers. People of multiple nationalities, ages and beliefs. Pagans, druids, Wiccans, heathens, Christians, Catholics and Jews. Some of them to worship. Others just to witness the spectacle. They have come. Just as they always do.

Out in the darkness, in the undulating Wiltshire fields, there are illegal camps and the crackle of small bonfires, lit as in ancient times to mark the passing of the solstice. The site itself has been flooded with a wave of pagan color since access to the stones was opened in the night.

The mystique, the ancient customs and practice of the solstice come up against the machine of modern organization. Crowd control, hygiene, traffic routing. And devotion to one of the oldest gods. Money. Even the samba bands are selling CDs of their own works, with souvenirs as plentiful as drugs and booze.

They have journeyed from across the world for this day and as they near the henge, they become aware that the intense police activity is not only for them. Word travels about the missing American girl and her dead lover and many kneel and pray out of respect and hope.

The drumming that has gone on all night picks up a heavier, more urgent rhythm. The air buzzes with excitement. White-robed druids rehearse their prayers. Bare-chested pagan men dance with retirees in anoraks and hippie women with beads and flowers in their hair.

Primitive horns start to sound, the orchestra of the old infiltrated by new immigrant vuvuzelas. Waves of cheering, clapping and chanting ripple across the pond of people. Innocent eyes, some glazed with drugs, others bright with virgin anticipation, are now all trained on the pink sky, waiting for the magic, straining for the first flash of sunlight to pierce the most famous stone circle in the world.

The sun breaks and penetrates the ringed sarsens. A giant cheer erupts.

Aside from the Lookers, there are no Followers anywhere near the henge. They know better. Instead, they are gathered miles away in the Sanctuary. They kneel on the cold stone of the Great Room. The place where their gods are located.

85

When Gideon wakes he squints at his watch and knows instantly that he'd been right going back to the police. It's nearly ten in the morning of the longest day of the year and he's just had his first real sleep for almost a week. A weight has been lifted from his shoulders.

He showers, shaves and hurries downstairs. The security buzzer sounds just as he's filling the kettle. He presses the electromagnetic release and on the monitor watches Megan's car glide through the grand iron gates and up the graveled driveway.

He opens the front door. 'Good morning,' he says brightly.

'Morning,' replies Megan, less enthusiastically. 'This is Detective Sergeant Dockery.'

The DS smiles from beneath his sunglasses and offers his hand.

'Pleased to meet you,' says Gideon shaking it vigorously. 'Come through to the back.'

The two officers trail him into the kitchen and settle around a rectangular pine table while he makes hot drinks and small talk. 'I guess you're busy with the solstice?'

'Very,' says Megan. 'The roads are crazy. I should do what my ex does, stay away from work at this time of the year. Drives me mad.'

'It alternates,' says Jimmy. 'One year the mob is well behaved and the next they let rip like wild animals.'

Gideon sorts out teas and coffees, milk and sugar and then joins them at the table. Megan sees this as her cue to gear-change the conversation. 'Last night you spoke about your father's diaries and implied that they might shed some light on his death. Can we see them?'

He puts his cup down and stands. 'Yes, yes you can. But you need to know something.'

'What?'

He walks to the foot of the stairs. 'They're not easy to follow. Wait, it's best I show you what I mean.'

He goes to the hidden room and selects one of the volumes that he has decoded. He returns slightly breathless and hands the diary to Megan.

'What is this language?' She holds the book at arm's length, as though it might somehow help.

'Code,' he explains. 'My father wrote all the diaries in code. He devised it when I was a kid, as a way to teach me Greek.'

She squints at the open pages. '*This* is Greek?'

'Not really. It is Greek but Greek backwards. The letters have reverse values to their English equivalents, so Omega represents A and so on.' He reaches for a pen and on the edge of an old newspaper writes out ΜΥΣΩΛ ΨΩΞΥΗ. He hands it to Megan. 'What do you think that says?'

'Megan Baker.'

He looks spooked. 'How do you know that? You barely looked at it.'

She smiles. 'What else would you write? You're trying to interest me, have me take a personal stake in understanding the language. So it follows that you would write something personal, and the only personal thing you know about me is my name.' She turns the pages of the journal. 'Why did your father do this? Why did he feel the need to write in a code that only you and he understood?'

Gideon is not completely sure. 'So no one else could understand it?'

She weighs it up. 'You write a diary because one day you want someone else to read it. People think otherwise but it's true. If what your father has written is important, then he wanted you to read it and perhaps do something with it. Something he thought *only* you could do. Maybe he wanted you to translate and publish it?'

Gideon suspects publication is the last thing Nathaniel wanted. But her words have touched a nerve. 'You think he wants me to approve of all this? Be a part of it?'

'I don't know. What is the "*this*" that you're talking about? Why don't you tell us?'

Over the next couple of hours he tries to. He reads them some of the important extracts he's translated – about the Followers of the Sacreds, the powers of the stones, their roles as all-healing gods. He even discloses some details about his mother's death, her fatal disease and Nathaniel's fear that he may have inherited the condition.

Megan is not sure how to voice what's on her mind without offending him. In the end she just comes out with it. 'It is possible that your father was mentally ill.' She tries to soften the blow. 'He was a brilliant man. He could well have hidden something like that.'

'He wasn't mad,' insists Gideon. 'There's a lot of truth in what he wrote.'

'Provable truth?' queries Jimmy.

Gideon gets up from his seat and goes to the window. He looks out over the lawns that his father walked. He feels uncomfortable having the police in the house, about discussing his father and his private life, but their skepticism gives him no choice. 'When I was a kid, I was ill. *Very* ill. It was probably the start of the same disease that killed my mother.' He looks back from the garden to the officers. 'You know what my father did? He took me home from hospital and gave me a cold bath. A special bath that cured me. The water he sat and bathed me in was collected from Stonehenge. When I could walk again, he took me there and made me touch all of the stones, the giant sarsens and even the smaller bluestones. Since then I've had no trace of that disease. No illness. My health is remarkable. My skin and body recover from cuts and bruises faster than anyone else's that I know.'

Jimmy gives Megan a discreet but telling glance.

Gideon sees it. 'I know you think I'm crazy, but I'm not.' He returns to the table, reaches across it and takes Megan's right hand. 'You cut yourself, right? How long have you had that blue bandage on your finger?'

She looks at the dirty wrap. 'I don't know. Maybe a week. It was quite a deep cut.'

'Look at my face.' Gideon angles his jaw toward her. 'You came to see me in hospital after I was assaulted. You saw the cuts and bruises. Do you see them now?'

She doesn't.

'What happened to the wound to my jaw that they wanted to put stitches in?' He sees a flash of doubt in her eyes and tilts his chin. 'And the split lip? Do you see any sign of it? Any trace at all?'

Megan's heart races. She doesn't. His skin is unmarked. Not even a scratch.

There's a flash of triumph in Gideon's eyes. 'You still have a plaster on a little cut. From a week ago. Now tell me that my father was mad. Tell me that there is no truth in any of his writings.'

86

The top brass had a sleepless night. A call in the early hours turned the investigators' lives upside down. A call from Caitlyn's kidnappers.

By the time the Chief Constable and his team assemble in his office the story is already out. A tip-off, no doubt from inside the force. The world's press is camped outside police HQ.

Commander Barney Gibson kicks off the emergency meeting. 'At two a.m. a call was put through to the incident room. As a matter of routine it was recorded. I will play it for you in a moment. The call has been traced to a public telephone box. No surprise in that. Except this call box was not in England – it was in France.' He waits for the significance to sink in. 'It was made from a public box off Rue La Fayette almost in the center of Paris. French police are at the scene and are looking for camera footage, but I'll be very surprised if they find any. They'll go over it for fingerprints or any other trace evidence that might match against our fingerprint or DNA databases.'

Hunt is anxious to move things on. Thom Lock has been informed and is on his way from his hotel. 'Please play the tape, Barney.'

Gibson presses a digital recorder placed in the middle of the table. They hear a voice. Male. English. The sound quality is poor. 'You've been expecting this call, we know you have. We have Caitlyn Lock and shortly you will hear our demands.' A pause and a click. The girl's voice floats eerily into the room. It's low and sad. 'My dad used to read to me. Every bedtime he'd sit beneath the quilt with me and read until I fell asleep.' She laughs sadly. 'He made up stories about a fairy princess called Kay and her adventures, and then . . .' It's clear she's close to tears. 'Then I'd fall asleep holding my daddy's hand.'

Everyone around the conference table is a parent and the tape visibly distresses them. Caitlyn's voice strums their nerves. 'I don't recall much about my mother. I guess I remember her tying yellow bows in my hair for my first day at school. 'Cause I hated the blue uniform. I remember making waffles with her at my grandma's house. Almost every time we went round. And she used to sit me up on a cushion in her makeup room on the lot and have her own personal artist pretty me up.'

Gibson clicks off the recording. 'Technicians are examining it and checking for authenticity. And Chief Constable, I believe you will be validating it with Vice President Lock this morning.'

'I will. Thank you, Barney.' Hunt turns to his press officer, Kate Mallory. 'How widespread is the leak, Kate?'

'Very, sir.' She's midthirties, balloon-faced with round glasses and straggly black hair. She slides copies of national newspapers across the conference table, her fingers black from print ink. 'All the majors have it.' The *Mirror*'s bold-print front-page headline screams: 'France Now Key In Lock Case.' The *Sun* leads with a giant screen-grab of Caitlyn in a bikini and just one word, *Survivor?*

Kate Mallory reads the first few lines of the *Mirror* article: 'The search for kidnapped American beauty Caitlyn Lock, daughter of US Vice President Thom, sensationally switched to Paris last night as top British cops rushed to investigate a cross-channel call from her captors. Kidnappers made contact via a special line set up by the police for public information. The gang is understood to have played an Al-Qaeda style recording of Caitlyn, in which she revealed intimate details about herself, her father and her mother.'

'Enough,' calls Hunt. 'For what it's worth, I've put a call in to the editor to complain.' He shrugs. 'I guess we have little choice but to hold a news conference and answer their damned questions.'

'You could consider a complete news blackout, sir,' suggests the press officer. 'It's defendable on the basis that the young woman's life is at risk.'

Hunt throws his copy of the paper down on the table. 'What's the point? The news is already out there!' He looks around the faces and then back to Mallory. 'Kate, we can't conduct an inquiry of this scale if the press know about it before our own operational staff. Do your best to find out who leaked. I want a full investigation into this sloppiness.'

The door to the conference room opens and the Chief Constable's PA leans in. 'Vice President Lock is here, sir. He has two men with him who say they are from the FBI.'

87

While Chief Constable Hunt briefs Vice President Lock another tense meeting is underway in an office just down the corridor. FBI agents Todd Burgess and Danny Alvez are face to face with John Rowlands and Barney Gibson.

'I'm really hoping we can help you guys,' says Senior Supervisory Agent Burgess. Tanned and toned, he looks half his forty-five years. 'Both Dan and I know Thom Lock and the President well and we can keep heat off your backs, providing of course you're open and honest with us.'

Gibson understands classic Yankspeak when he hears it. Tell us everything and we'll tell you nothing. 'Who's top of your likely list when it comes to kidnap gangs? Thom Lock especially piss anyone off?'

Both Americans laugh.

'Thom has pissed everyone off,' says Burgess. 'New York organized crime families, Chicago animal liberation groups, west coast environmentalists, even the Russians over in Brooklyn.'

'Then there are the terror groups,' adds Alvez. 'He's a Republican who backs the War on Terror. A hawk in foreign-policy terms. Al-Qaeda, the Colombians, the FPM, PLF, ANO, they all stick pins in effigies of Thom Lock.' He switches the heat back to Gibson. 'What have you guys found so far?'

'Not much,' confesses the commander. 'We're working with intelligence services to grab everything we can. Data, email, voice messages. Anything that's out there about Caitlyn, we're on it.'

Danny Alvez is midthirties, Hispanic with dark eyes and short black hair. He's been waiting for his chance to ask the big question. 'What do you guys make of the tape?'

Rowlands gives him a straight reply: 'We haven't had feedback from the tech staff yet. To me it sounded genuine, though I'm suspicious of why they used audio tape and not video.'

'Agreed,' says Alvez. 'It's certainly Caitlyn though. We talked to

Thom and Kylie and the information about the ribbon and book is accurate and to the best of their knowledge has never been made public.'

'We pinged the tape to Quantico via a secure upload,' adds Burgess. 'Our labs say it contains multiple edits, made on several digital sound layers. They think an initial taping was done with Caitlyn, then it was drop-edited onto another recording device and the completed message played down the line from Paris.'

'Why?' asks Gibson. 'Why would they do all that rather than just put her on the phone?'

'They're real pros,' says Burgess. 'They probably know all recording devices, even digital ones, leave a kind of sound DNA. By over-recording like this, you mix up the sample evidence. Machinery and source become much harder to detect.'

'I just wonder,' says Rowlands, 'if the explanation is simpler than that. If the recording was faked somehow. What if Caitlyn's voice was actually recorded here in England, sent to Paris and then played back down a French phone line?'

Alvez shakes his head. 'Our analysts say the call was definitely made in France. They lifted the background atmos and they're sure it was Paris.' Rowlands' theory grows on him a little. 'Suppose the background noise could have been mixed in from the French side, but it seems a stretch.'

Gibson isn't convinced. 'Come on, they could have gone through the tunnel and been in Paris within four hours of the abduction. Thousands of illegal aliens get across the channel every year, it would be nothing for a professional gang bold enough to target a politician's daughter.'

Burgess agrees. 'Or by private plane, coast to coast in half that time. That's the way I'd do it.'

Alvez nods. 'Me too.'

John Rowlands is outnumbered three to one, but he doesn't care. 'She's here. I'm sure she is. My gut tells me this tape is a wild goose chase. Caitlyn Lock is still within our reach.'

88

Publicly, Kylie Lock hasn't said anything about her daughter's disappearance. She let her husband fix everything with the British police, the Secret Service, the FBI and the President's office. He's good at all that. Despite all their differences, she knows he cares about Caitlyn's welfare every bit as much as she does. If anyone can get those people to find her, it's Thom. No doubt about it.

But sometimes he's wrong. Out of line. Not that he'll ever admit it. Oh no. Even now he won't accept that it was a stupid mistake to have Eric look after Caitlyn instead of a Secret Service detail. Everything always has to be done his way.

Well, today is going to be different. Today it's her turn to step up. And step up is what she is going to do. In a way only a mother can. From the heart. That's why she's called a press conference.

Kylie looks in the mirror a final time, hides her eyes behind her low-profile black Prada sunglasses. She is wearing a midlength gray Givenchy dress, her blond hair is swept and tied back. She's ready for anything the world can throw at her.

After taking a deep breath, she walks into the top-floor conference room at the Dorchester. Settles behind the long trestle table covered in an immaculate white cotton cloth. It's topped with a small angled sign bearing her name and she can see a cluster of microphones and Dictaphones. She looks up and the room seems to convulse. An explosion of shutter clicks and blinding white light. She can see the editorial heads of the BBC, ITN, Sky, AFP, Reuters, PA, CNN, Inter Press, Pressenza, EFE and UPI. And a million others. They have risen from their seats, out of respect for her, not as a famous actress but as a worried-sick mother.

She can feel the heat from the blisteringly hot TV lights strung on their steel poles. People everywhere. At the rear a long line of video cameras are sited on a raised platform. She is flanked by a giant suited bodyguard and a round-faced black woman in her early fifties. Charlene Elba, a rough-and-ready veteran of her Hollywood press campaigns.

Elba taps the main desk mike, gets the ball rolling. 'Ladies and gentlemen, thank you for coming. All of you are aware of the great efforts being made by law enforcement agencies in many countries to find Caitlyn Lock. Both Kylie Lock and Vice President Thom Lock are immensely grateful for the endeavors of those detectives and individuals. However, this morning we will not be addressing any issues relating to the inquiry.' There is a pause. 'Today Kylie would like to directly address whoever has her daughter. Afterward, she will do interviews. The press session will last ninety minutes, after which Kylie has to leave for a personal meeting with the Chief Constable of Wiltshire and representatives from the British Home Office and the FBI. We thank you again for your attendance.'

Kylie takes a second to compose herself before attempting the task of making an impression on the audience. She can feel the cynicism. Hazard of the profession, she guesses. She takes off her sunglasses. Her eyes are bloodshot and it's apparent that she is not wearing more than a brush of powder. The features are familiar to all of them. 'Whoever you are, whatever you want, please don't hurt my baby.' There's a tremor in her voice. 'Think of your own mother, think of your own wife or your own sister. How would you feel if they were in Caitlyn's place? What would you say to whoever had them? You'd say this. Please, please don't hurt the person I love most in the whole world. Please let them go.' She has no notes in front of her, just a plain piece of paper and a pen. She looks down at them for what seems an overlong period of time.

Then she looks up. Her eyes fix on the cameras and the watching press pack and they are brimming with tears. 'My Caitlyn has a heart of gold. She is the most caring, loving, wonderful daughter that a mother could have. Her whole future is ahead of her. Half a century of life in front of her. She has the right to meet the man of her dreams and fall in love, to raise her own family, to sit her own grandchildren on her lap and to know she has made the world a better place with her presence and her legacy. Please don't take that from her. Don't take away all that love that she can give, all her dreams, all her future.' She quickly blots a running tear from her cheek. 'I would gladly give everything that I have to get my daughter back. And that is what I am prepared to do.' She turns over the sheet of plain paper in front of her and holds it up to the cameras. 'This is my bank statement. I am lucky. I have ten million dollars to my name. I promise that I will give you that, whoever you are. Everything I have, everything I can raise. In exchange for the safe return of my daughter.' Her eyes narrow and her face hardens. 'But be aware of this, I am also prepared to give that money to anyone who successfully leads the police or any other investigators to your door and who can recover Caitlyn safely and bring you and anyone involved in taking my daughter to justice.' She takes a long slow breath, seems to relax her shoulders a little. She gestures to the giant beside her. 'This man is Josh Goran.' She puts her trembling hand on his broad forearm. 'He is America's most successful private investigator and bounty hunter.' She takes strength from talking about him. 'He is a former major in America's Air Force Special Operations Command unit. For the foreseeable future, he will be working solely for me and will be completely dedicated to securing my daughter's safe return.'

Goran points a big finger straight down the eye of the nearest camera lens trained on him. 'For those who have Caitlyn, I have a message. Please take the lady's money now and give her up. It's an honest offer that Kylie Lock has made. She means it.' He looks around the room, up at the ceiling. 'Please take up that offer. You'll be sorry if you don't. Real sorry if I have to come and take her from you.'

89

Megan is trying to forget being dropped from the Lock case and concentrate on the silver dog tag Jimmy Dockery has placed in the palm of her hand. It's from around the neck of Tony Naylor, the missing bum case that Tompkins dumped on her desk just as everything else was getting more interesting.

The cheap tag had been handed in by a jogger out on Salisbury Plain and listed on a CID lost and found circular because of the inscription on the back: 'Happy Birthday T. Luv Nat x.' Jimmy had noticed the tag matched the one Tony wore in the train station picture taken with his sister. To round things off, Nathalie Naylor had just confirmed it as the one she'd bought for her brother.

What's interesting Megan is not that it was found but *where* it was found. A lay-by in the middle of nowhere. But not any old nowhere. A nowhere on the closest main road to the burned-out barn where Jake Timberland's body was discovered.

Jimmy is staring at her staring at the small silver block. 'You trying to contact the dead?'

She turns the tag over. 'I wish I could. I'd certainly ask Tony Naylor what he was doing out on that road. Not the kind of place you go for a walk. It's bleak, desolate, unattractive.' She hands the tag back to her DS. 'Naylor was a drifter, no money, no home, certainly no car. How did he get so many miles from a town or village with nothing around but unploughed fields and scrub?'

'Someone must have driven him out there or he hitched a lift.'

'Why?'

'Maybe he heard there was farm work?'

She looks at Tony Naylor's photograph in the file on her desk. The thin-faced twenty-five-year-old has been unemployed most of his life. When he has bothered to earn a living, it's never been far from a town center and a pub. Backbreaking shifts as a crop-picker or farm laborer out in the middle of teetotal-nowhere-land are not his style.

Naylor is dead. She knows he is. She thinks it and she feels it. And she knows that very soon she'll be picking up the phone in front of her and breaking bad news to his twin sister.

'Jim, see if you can get operational support to divert some men from the barn and run radar over the field.'

'You think he's buried out there?'

Megan nods. 'I don't think it. I'm sure of it.'

90

There comes a point when you have to take the game to the opposition.

Change defensive into offensive.

Be proactive rather than reactive.

Gideon runs all the axioms through his mind as he stands nervously outside the office of D. Smithsen Building Contractors. It's an ugly collection of Portakabins on a run-down industrial estate. In the yard are old and dust-ridden flatbed trucks. Potholed tarmac is covered in boils of spilled gravel and cement. Incongruously, there is also a pristine, personally plated black Bentley.

Gideon takes a deep breath and breezes into the latent hostility of a sour-smelling and grubby reception area.

'Good morning. I'm looking for Mr. Smithsen. I have some work I need doing.'

The woman behind the cheap desk looks annoyed at the interruption. She puts her magazine down and gets to her feet. 'Take a seat, I'll see if he's busy.' She jerks open a sliding door, leans in and then turns back to Gideon. 'You can come through.' She drags the door wider and steps to one side.

David Smithsen rises from a torn leather chair to greet his visitor. 'Mr. Chase, how are you?' He gestures to a seat.

'I'm okay, thanks.'

Smithsen sits back behind his desk 'You certainly look better than when I saw you last.'

'That wasn't a good moment.'

'I'm sure it wasn't. Now, how can I help you?'

'Thought it was about time to get that work done. You know, the repairs to the study, the damaged brickwork. And the roofing.'

'Roofing?'

'You mentioned you were going to do some for my father. He'd given you a deposit.'

Smithsen slaps his forehead with his palm and smiles. 'Of course. I'm sorry. I remember now. I thought you meant roofing over the study.'

Gideon smiles. It's time to stop the pretense. He has no intention of hiring the builder. It was simply an excuse to confront the man. 'When you came out to Tollard Royal, you went upstairs and snooped around, went through some of my father's private books.'

Smithsen looks horrified. 'I went to check out the safety of your ceiling, that's all.'

'No, you didn't.' Gideon's voice is calm but he feels increasingly nervous. 'Mr. Smithsen, I knew exactly how and where I'd left those books and you'd moved them, tried to look for something and I think I know what.'

The builder stays silent.

'You were looking for the same thing as the man who broke into the house, the one who left me in the fire.'

Smithsen tries hard to look offended. 'Mr. Chase, really I—'

Gideon cuts him off. 'Listen, I know what you are part of. What you believe in. You think I want to expose you or stop you?' He shakes his head. 'The Craft is thousands of years old. I understand how important it is.' He leans forward across the builder's desk. 'I want to be part of it. Talk to the Henge Master. Talk to those in the Inner Circle who have to be spoken to.' He pushes the chair back and stands. 'Then come back to me, Mr. Smithsen. You have my numbers.' He is halfway out the door when he stops and leans back inside. 'By the way, the books have been moved. And I've arranged for couriers to deliver very detailed extracts and a personal letter to the police in twenty-four hours, unless they hear directly from me.' He gives him a parting smile. 'The clock is ticking. Be sure to contact me *very* soon.'

91

At six o'clock, Megan shuts down her computer and leaves to pick up Sammy. Adam is looking after their daughter and wants to buy them all dinner. Play happy families again. Despite instincts to the contrary, she finds herself giving in.

The Harvest Inn is not far from his house, so they walk over and sit outside. Adam brings a pint of lager, a large glass of white and an apple juice to the weathered wooden table and benches. He takes Sammy to the small swings while Megan orders their food. She sits looking at the evening sun dip behind the play area and for a moment things seem like they used to be.

Sammy runs from the swings to a sandpit. Adam makes sure she's safe, then leaves her there to scrape up a mess and wanders back to the table. 'She's growing so quickly.' He sits down and raises his drink. 'Here's to the great job you're doing with her.'

'And to you.' She tilts her glass his way. 'You're a lousy husband but a good dad.'

'I know. I realize that now.' He looks toward Sammy, bent like a puppy scrabbling sand between her legs. 'She is part of you and part of me. There's nothing I wouldn't do for her and . . .' He seems to run out of courage, then adds, '. . . and nothing I wouldn't do to have you back.'

'Adam—'

'No, please. Let me finish. I messed up. I'm sorry. Really sorry. Can't we wipe the slate clean?'

Megan looks down at the table. 'Things like adultery can't just be wiped clean, Adam. It's not spilt milk.'

The food comes and saves further embarrassment. By the time they've finished, Sammy is asleep on her father's lap. They walk back to his house and Megan puts her to sleep in the spare room. Adam opens a bottle of brandy. The one they bought in France on their last holiday before Sammy was born. They end up talking. About work. About Sammy. About the reasons behind his affair. They talk until all the poison has seeped out and there's no more cleansing and talking to be done.

Megan feels wrung dry. She kisses Sammy's beautiful sleeping face and does what she knows she shouldn't do. She goes to bed with her cheating ex. There's no wild sex. No passionate bridge building. Just a truce, sealed by lying close together. Taking comfort in what they had. What they might be able to have again.

92

TUESDAY 22 JUNE

The morning sun spills through a split in Adam Stone's cheap bedroom curtains and glints off an old mirror on the dresser opposite. Megan has been awake for hours, lying next to the father of her child, watching the warm daylight slip into the room and slowly climb the walls.

She's about as confused as she can be. Her head full of regrets, hopes and warnings. Sammy comes running into the room and chases all her thoughts away. Her cheeks are red from sleep and her eyes are lit up like Christmas. She jumps onto the bed with a squeal and tries to scramble in with them.

Megan slows her down. 'Shush, baby, don't wake Daddy.'

Too late. Adam has been kneed into consciousness. He raises himself, bleary-eyed, into a sitting position, back against the padded headboard. 'Come here, baby girl, give me a big love.' She's in his arms in a second and Megan is left even more churned up than she was ten minutes ago.

The three breakfast together in Adam's small kitchen and he chats easily. Caringly. Just like he used to. 'You got a busy day ahead?'

She pours coffee for them both. 'Do they come any other way? Even off the Timberland murder I'm as busy as hell, and no doubt there's going to be some cleaning up to be done after the solstice.'

He chews on buttered toast as he talks. 'I checked last night with control. By that point, there'd been about ten public order arrests, half a dozen for possession and a couple for dealing drugs.'

Megan is relieved. 'Thank you God for small acts of mercy. Did they say if there was anything new on the Lock case?'

'The press are still feeding on the mother's press conference.' He licks butter from his fingers, hands her the TV remote and gestures to the small set tucked away across the room. 'Try Sky, they usually know what's happening before we do.'

She finds a news report on the film star's presser. It's made up of a soundbite from Josh Goran, a dull interview with a pale-looking Alan Hunt, several shots of men who could be FBI agents, a meaningless comment from someone at the Home Office, random shots of Paris and finally, footage of John Rowlands and Barney Gibson looking wiped out and pissed off as they leave police HQ in separate cars.

'So,' says Adam, finishing the coffee and looking for his jacket. 'What are you doing tonight?'

'Meaning?'

He smiles warmly. 'Meaning, are you coming back here?'

She's not sure. It seems too hard to simply forgive and forget. 'Let me think about it. Right now, I have to go home and change. There's something important that I have to do this morning. Can you drop Sammy at nursery for me?'

'Sure.' He tries his luck again. 'And tonight?'

'*May-be*.' Her face softens. 'Let's just see how the day plays out.'

93

Jimmy Dockery steps into the road and flags down the camouflaged Range Rover. The driver, a sixty-year-old man dressed like a farmer, pulls to a stop in the deserted lay-by, gets out and briskly walks around the back. Jimmy follows him to the rear of the 4×4 with more than a little trepidation.

'Morning, Detective,' says the driver in an upper-class English accent. 'Looks a nice day for it.'

Jimmy isn't so sure. 'Morning. Let's hope so. How are the crazy monsters today?' He peers through the glass of the tailgate at Tarquin de Wale's two Turkey vultures caged in the back.

'They're fine,' says de Wale. 'Did I tell you last night when you came round that I raised them from chicks?'

'You did.'

'They're of Canadian parentage, you know. Best you can get.' He starts to slide the giant cage out of the vehicle. 'Give me a hand.'

Jimmy has a moment of self-doubt. Maybe this is a crazy idea. The extra assistance that Megan told him to enlist from operational support hadn't been forthcoming. Not a sniffer dog for miles around. And the ground radar team is booked up until Christmas. Tarquin's vultures seemed an inspired way to search for dead flesh. Tony Naylor's dead flesh to be precise.

'Can't wait to see if the chaps can pull this off,' says de Wale. Jimmy had read in the *Police* magazine about German detectives using buzzards to detect buried corpses, and exotic animal breeder Tarquin de Wale had been quoted as saying he'd be willing to cooperate freely with any police force in England wanting to give it a try. Well, this is his chance.

According to reports, on every occasion the German birds had been tested they'd found the flesh. Buzzards are said to have an incredible sense of smell. From three hundred feet up, they can detect a tiny morsel of rotting meat. And unlike bloodhounds they don't tire quickly.

The detective slips on his shades and for once they are necessary, the midday sun is high and bright. 'Mr. de Wale, if you make this work then we are both going to finish the day as heroes.'

'Of course it will work,' says de Wale, confidently. 'Have faith.'

Jimmy helps him lift the back of a wire cage big enough to restrain two grown Alsatians. They put it on the ground. Wings extended, the birds' full span is over six feet. They grunt and hiss at the intrusion.

De Wale slips a customized muzzle on the birds' white beaks, then attaches GPS tracking bands to their legs so he can pinpoint the exact spot if they find anything. 'You said you had something belonging to the missing man?'

Jimmy hands over Tony Naylor's silver dog tag and de Wale holds it in front of the striking bald red heads of the two birds. 'If he is out there, even if he's buried, these two will find him. Even without this little trinket.' He hands it back.

The exotic animal breeder walks to the front of the Range Rover to set up the electronic equipment in the passenger seat of the vehicle. After a few moments, he returns with a wide smile and eyes full of childish excitement. 'Ready, old chap?'

Jimmy raises an eyebrow behind his shades. 'About as much as I will ever be.'

94

The hour-long journey feels the longest and loneliest drive of Gideon's life.

He spent most of last night lying awake, worrying about this day. And now it's here. He sits in the car with the engine turned off, staring out of the window, hoping to halt time.

West Wiltshire Crematorium is set in ten acres of tranquil Semington countryside. But none of the beauty of the landscaping distracts from the fact that they are about to burn his father's body. Incinerate it. Blast it in an oven until all that is left is a featureless gray powder. Ashes to ashes, dust to dust. He's heard the phrase a thousand times, but only now does he really understand what it means. From nothing to nothing.

Every emotional connection to his father will be gone. He will be left solely with memories. Mixed ones. Sure, there are Nathaniel's books and tapes, but they're purely factual artifacts. Archaeological reminders of the father he didn't know rather than the one he did.

The morning sun is hot on his face as he gets out of the car and walks along the immaculately clean path. Up ahead, he sees the crematorium, a distinguished and understated building that looks modern with lots of hardwood beams and doors, bright stained-glass windows and a smart red-tiled roof.

Gideon hears footsteps and turns to see Megan hurrying to catch up to him. He hadn't expected her to come and is touched that she has. She's wearing a midlength black dress and black flat shoes, with a black raincoat over her arm. 'Hello,' she manages, slightly out of breath, 'I hope you don't mind me coming?'

'Not at all. It's very kind of you to bother.'

She affectionately touches the sleeve of his new black suit as they walk toward the front doors. 'I guessed you wouldn't know many people down here and thought you might appreciate some moral support.'

He takes a deep breath. 'I do. Thanks.'

Megan misses out the fact that she's also interested to see who else might turn up. What their relationship to Nathaniel Chase might be and how Gideon behaves during what's bound to be a testing ordeal.

An usher shows them through to the chapel, where the coffin is already in place. He had declined the offer of following the hearse from Shaftesbury. Too slow. Too painful. And also rejected the idea of having any kind of eulogy.

Only Gideon and Megan are in the congregation as the casket slips out of public view. He bows his head and she squeezes his hand reassuringly. He tries not to think about his father's corpse slipping into the retort, the special area of the furnace, where it will be exposed to savage temperatures of more than a thousand degrees. His archaeological training means he knows that cremation vaporizes soft tissues and organs. Only hard bones will be left behind. Staff will use some kind of cremulator to pulverize what's left, reduce it to dust, to powder.

Ashes to ashes.

He tries not to think of the man he has lost. The things he wishes he'd said. The words he regrets uttering.

Dust to dust.

He is here to get things done. That's all. To fulfill his father's request that he should be cremated and his ashes scattered at Stonehenge.

The service is over in less than fifteen minutes. No fanfare. No wailing. Nothing but silence and emptiness.

On the way out, a staff member tells him he can collect his father's remains in a couple of hours or in the morning if he prefers. He chooses to come back later. He wants to end the day knowing that it's over. That he never has to return here.

The two of them walk to their cars. Gideon stands at the door of his Audi looking lost.

'Pub,' she says, surprisingly. 'We can't go away from here without having a drink to give your dad a proper send-off.'

95

Caitlyn hears a terrible rumbling.

Cool air wafts into the fetid hole. Hands reach in through the wall and pull at her.

Her body is so stiff and heavy that she feels as though she's been nailed to the hard stone slab. They pull her urgently out of the cavity and stumble her down a narrow dark corridor into a circular room lit by candles. Caitlyn tries to shield her eyes. Rings of small flickering flames burn painfully bright. Behind closed lids, circles are seared into the chemical screens of her retinas. She panics for a second, struggles for breath.

Two men loop ropes around her wrists. They walk her like a seaside donkey. Drag her clockwise. Always clockwise. Twenty circuits of the cold and featureless stone room. Caitlyn is dizzy by the time they stop and let her drink tepid water. Her stomach rumbles. Hunger pains stab and cramp her.

When they are done exercising and watering her, they take off the donkey ropes and retreat to the outer circles of the wall.

Now she can do anything she wants. Only there isn't anything to do. There is nothing but space around her. Space in which she is trapped by the people on the outside of the space. She understands that this is some kind of mindfuck. First they brick her up in a wall so she can't move. Then they give her as much room as she wants. And she still can't move.

Free will. They are messing with her free will.

Caitlyn sits. Crosses her legs. Shuts her eyes and shuts out her world of horror. She tries to find herself. Tries to connect to some iron thread that can't be broken, some invincible strand that she can always hold on to.

Gradually, she forgets the people around her, the smell and light of the candles, the cold of the stone floor, the cramps in her stomach and the burn of the gastric juices in her windpipe. The space. More than anything she shuts out the space. She is nowhere. She is in the safe darkness of her dreams.

Caitlyn feels her legs aching. She is growing weak. She feels herself falling. Tumbling backward. The hooded men snap at her like a pack of dogs. They pick her up and half-drag half-walk her to the cleansing area. They push her into the steaming water. Watch her wash and re-dress. Walk her back to her cell.

Back to the place with no space.

Back to her nightmare.

96

In a black fluttering flash the birds lever themselves into the pale sky above the empty fields. They're gone within seconds. Not even distant specks on the horizon. Tarquin de Wale looks at the sat-nav app on his laptop. He can see their flight lines tracking high into the wild-blue yonder. 'Jolly fast, eh?'

'What if they don't come back?' asks Jimmy. 'You could spend the rest of your life trying to catch them.'

'Vultures aren't built to fly far.' The old eccentric doesn't take his eyes from the computer screen. 'They're lazy scavengers. They ride the thermals mainly. Until they get a whiff of food, then *zoom*.' He smacks his hands together. 'Besides, Wiltshire is the only habitat they know. Their natural home now.'

'Lots of army activity around here,' warns Jimmy. 'I hope they don't get shot down.'

'No problem. Here they come,' says de Wale excitedly.

The vultures swoop down low over the Range Rover and settle in the field about a hundred meters in front of the two men. Instantly, they start to forage. Senses bristling, they flutter and land a few feet away and nudge the earth again. The smaller of the two skips to the side and hammers his beak into rutted tracks two hundred meters from the remains of the barn.

Jimmy watches with mixed emotions. He'd hoped for more. Something spectacular like when sniffer dogs go crazy and start whimpering and digging as though they're trying to find a short cut to Australia. But the vultures don't provide any such show. They lazily forage for almost an hour and don't venture out of the field next to the torched barn. Jimmy is feeling pretty dejected. He checks his watch. 'Let's call it quits. It was worth a shot.'

'I'll get a treat and clap them in,' says de Wale.

'Okay.' Jimmy glances at the laptop screen while the buzzard master goes to get some dead mice out of a sealed sandwich box. The computer has been recording the birds' flight paths using the GPS. Plotting lines on a grid. But these lines go pretty much straight up and down the field, almost as though they'd been mowing a lawn or plowing crops.

It is a thought that he can't shake. Strange creatures. Why would they do that? He goes back to his car. Roots in the boot until he finds some spare evidence bags and then climbs over the stile that leads to the field. Jimmy lines himself up with the pecking buzzards and starts to collect samples. Soil samples.

It is a long shot, but if he is right, the vultures have found what remains of Tony Naylor.

The missing man's body has somehow been pulped and spread like muck across the open field.

97

Megan puts two glasses of wine down on the pub table that separates her and Gideon. It's a schizophrenic kind of place. Half bistro, half old-fashioned boozer. Crab cakes and dominoes. Rocket salad and pork scratchings.

'Thanks.' He pulls the glass toward him but doesn't drink. He's got things on his mind. Things he wants to say. 'Do you remember when you came to my father's house, I told you that I thought he'd killed himself because of this secret society, the Followers of the Sacreds?'

She nods apprehensively, worrying about his mental health. 'Yes, I remember. This was the secret organization you said he mentioned in his diaries.'

Gideon detects the skepticism. 'Do you think I'm crazy? All screwed up with grief and trauma?'

'No.' She tries to be sympathetic. 'You're certainly not crazy. But I do think you're very stressed out.' She leans forward and speaks quietly. 'Gideon, it might well be that your father was involved in some kind of secret organization, but I doubt it had anything to do with his death.' She flinches at the thought of what she's about to say. 'I'm sorry, but in my experience people take their own lives for a lot of highly personal reasons, and it's never about membership of some private club or other.'

He shakes his head and shifts the glass nervously around the table. 'The man who broke into my father's house and set fire to the place belonged to this group.' He leans closer. 'And this isn't a scout group I'm talking about. This is something bad.'

Megan slips into her more official interview mode. 'You might believe that but you can't prove it, can you?'

'I *know* it,' says Gideon. He puts a fist to his heart. 'In here, I know it.'

'In law that's not enough.' Megan can see he's hurting but there's nothing to gain from letting him delude himself. 'Don't you think that if your father was in such a society, such a close brotherhood, then some of them would have turned up today to show their respects? There was no one there. No one but you and me.'

The comment stings. 'Maybe they didn't know about it. It wasn't in any newspapers.' He has another thought. 'Maybe they *chose* to stay away.' He looks at her icily. 'Perhaps they expected the police to be there.'

She sees what he's driving at. 'That's not only why I came.'

'No, of course not.' He realizes it sounded bitter. 'Sorry.' He finally takes a drink of the wine. Sour apples. He has no taste or appreciation of anything at the moment. 'I had a builder round the other day, said he'd heard there'd been a fire and wanted to help fix the damage. He told me he'd done work for my father, so I ended up letting him in to do a valuation. Next thing I know he's upstairs poking around.'

She puts her glass down. 'Did he take anything?'

'Didn't have time but I found him in my father's private room trying to look through the diaries I showed you.'

She's not sure what he means. 'Your father's private room? You mean his bedroom?'

'No. The room next to it. He had built a secret area at the end of the landing. That's where he hid all his journals. If you didn't know it was there, you'd never spot it. But I'd left the door open.'

Megan wonders for a moment whether he'd accidentally let a con man or another burglar into the house, someone sizing the place up for antiques. 'This builder, did you get his name?'

'Smithsen, Dave Smithsen.'

She digs out a pen from her bag and writes the name on a beer mat. 'Do you want me to check that he really is a builder?'

'No need. I went to see him. I asked him outright if he was involved in the Followers with my father. He denied it.'

Megan takes a long look at the tired and grief-stricken man across the table. Hidden rooms. Secret sects. Builders that he mistakes for prowlers. The guy is sick. Paranoid. She wouldn't be surprised to learn he's suffering from some form of post-traumatic stress.

'Gideon, I think you're reading too much into all this. You're all churned up and need some time to get closure on your father's death, the break-in and the attack on you. You'll get respite when we lock someone up, and hopefully that will be soon. We're running face-analysis data on the phone photo you gave us and we've got word out with our informants on the streets.'

He nods.

Megan sees it's not enough. 'We're taking all this seriously. I promise you.'

'No, you're not,' he snaps. 'My father took his life because of something that this group was doing. Something awful. And you're not taking it seriously at all. You're just concerned with the damned break-in and no doubt your crime figures.' He slugs down the rest of his wine and stands. 'Thanks for the drink and coming out here. I'm going to go. Need to get some fresh air. Be on my own.'

98

Megan thinks about everything Gideon said as she drives back to Devizes. She's sure his fears and paranoia are unfounded. He's just mixed up and stressed out. By the time she's back at her desk, she has a simple plan to banish any nagging doubts and prove there's nothing in any of his accusations.

She hits the phone and uses her network of contacts to get the direct line of Professor Lillian Cooper, Head of Hematology at Salisbury District Hospital. The professor is a close friend of someone she knows. Megan dials the medic's number and manages to coax out of her the result of the blood tests Gideon had taken when he was kept overnight following the fire.

'The test results are negative. No disorders of any kind. Your man is the picture of perfect health.' Professor Cooper sounds bored as she flicks through his file. 'In fact, looking at his notes there's been nothing wrong with Gideon Chase since he was a kid.' There's a long pause. The plastic tap-tap-tap of computer keys clacks down the line. 'Well, I'm really not sure about the accuracy of what I'm reading.' There's surprise in her voice. 'It seems he was misdiagnosed when he was young. There's a record here of him having CLL, chronic lymphocytic leukemia.'

'What is that exactly?'

'CLL is an awful disease. Doesn't usually show in people under forty. Must be in the family. It manifests when the production of blood cells malfunctions and the process gets out of control. The lymphocytes multiply too quickly, live too long. You end up with too many of them in the blood, then they fatally overwhelm the normal white cells, red cells and platelets in the bone marrow.'

Megan wants to make sure she fully understands. 'But he doesn't have this – he was misdiagnosed?'

'Yes, that's right. Hang on.' There's another pause while she scans the notes again. 'I'm sure he was misdiagnosed but no one seems to have admitted that they did it. Most peculiar. It says he exhibited an advanced stage of the disease and needed preliminary treatment. Then months later his blood tested clear, just as it did when we screened him.' She sounds exasperated. 'It just doesn't fit. Simply doesn't fit at all. CLL is an incurable condition, it never just vanishes.'

'And professor, you're sure he *is* clear of it now?'

'I have to be cautious. You can never say anything terminal has gone forever, but looking at the file in front of me, I'd have to conclude that he no longer has the disease that he was previously diagnosed as being fatally ill with.'

Megan thanks her and hangs up. It's not what she expected to find.

Not at all. The medical records support Gideon's unbelievable story about being cured because he was washed in water from the stones at the henge.

The next call that the DI makes secures the business trading records of David E. Smithsen. She follows with requests for his work and home telephone records and his credit card bills and bank account details.

From the deluge of documents that electronically floods in, Smithsen appears to be a successful, respectable builder and professional landscape gardener. Megan uses Google Maps to look at aerial and 3D images of his business premises and his house. The home is lavish, detached, probably an old farm that has been converted. At least five, maybe six bedrooms. Several extensions. She zooms in. A swimming pool cum gym by the look of it. Big fences all around. Electric gates and cameras. Somewhere in the region of five to six acres. She values the spread at around three million pounds. Minimum. Megan taps her computer keys. And it doesn't look like he has any mortgage. In fact, no debts of any kind. A DVLC search shows he has a soft-top Porsche, presumably for his wife and a Bentley bearing his personal plate. Another click of the computer keys and she finds he has a cool million in the bank.

Smithsen's business accounts look in order. He and his wife are directors of a limited company with an audited annual turnover of eleven million pounds and a profit of one and a half million. The income seems consistent with his lifestyle. She runs a criminal records check and it comes back squeaky clean. Not so much as a parking fine.

Everything is completely aboveboard, but it doesn't *feel* right. She must have missed something. Megan looks more closely at the mobile phone records. He has the latest 4G iPhone but hardly uses it. She goes line by line down the itemized call list and sees he has rung home on it, booked the same restaurant a few times and downloaded a couple of emails. A guy as successful and busy as he is should be showing high call usage. She goes back to his landline records and scrutinizes them. They show a similar pattern of low activity. Either he is terrific at delegating and has everyone running around making calls and money for him. Or he has another phone. One that isn't billed to his work or home addresses.

Megan is sure he's running an off-the-shelf, prepaid phone. No contract and no trace of owner. A 'burner,' as street kids call it.

Why would a millionaire businessman do that when he's already got a state-of-the-art iPhone? She leans back at her desk and smiles.

He's keeping something secret. That's why.

99

As he walks in the dying evening light toward the stones, Gideon tries to remember exactly when he came here last. Probably twenty years ago just after he'd fallen sick.

He is carrying his father's ashes in a scatter tube chosen for the purpose and he feels sad and nostalgic. He looks out across the field and gathering mist and remembers how his father had held his hand and led him across the misty fields toward the towering stones.

Two decades on he experiences an echo of that fear. A reverberation of the anxiety he had felt when he was eight years old and he'd been left for a few moments in the midst of the giants. It had felt like eternity. The shadowy ghosts, as big as trees, closed in on him. Crowded him. Reached jagged hands out for him.

Gideon recalls it all. His father had spoken strangely that day. Talked about how there were things in life that he wouldn't be able to fully understand but should respect. Like the moon. A goddess watching over him. A powerful force linked to his unconscious powers and the cyclic rhythms of life – human fertility, crop growth, the changing of the seasons. He was too young back then to understand it.

Gideon looks across the great sarsens and bluestones. He sees his father putting a hand on one in the middle of the circle and reaching out to him. Telling him that the soul of the universe was buried deep in this rock, protected and preserved forever.

He hadn't wanted to take his father's hand but he did. It was frightening. Like a charge of electricity surging through two points. A crackling, blistering energy that bound them together. Then his father took him around the circle. Made him touch all the other stones. Pressed him against them and held him there as the current pulsed back and forth between stone and flesh.

'Good evening.'

The voice startles him. Comes out of nowhere. He turns quickly.

It is his father.

For a split second that's what he thinks. His heart is beating crazily. He gasps for breath. The man in front of him is of the same size and shape as his father. Probably a similar age. In the gathering mist the resemblance is unnerving.

The old man smiles. 'I didn't mean to startle you. I'm sorry.'

'It's okay. I was miles away.'

The stranger steps nearer. He is now taller and broader than Gideon first thought and has short gray-white hair. His eyes are piercingly dark. 'You shouldn't be in here, you know. Access is by appointment only. You have to book in advance.'

'I'm sorry.' Gideon looks off toward the parking lot.

'It's all right. I don't mind. What do you have there?' The stranger nods toward the tube.

'My father's ashes. He wanted to be scattered here among the stones.'

The man gestures to the henge. 'I imagine then, that this place meant a great deal to him?'

'It did.' Gideon glances at the nondescript tube. 'He was an archaeologist and studied them in great detail. He thought the stones were magical. Maybe even sacred.'

The stranger smiles. 'Many people do. That's why they come. I'm very sorry to have heard about your loss.' He tilts his head respectfully. 'I'll leave you now to fulfill your father's wishes. Good night.' He turns and walks away.

Gideon stands for a second and looks around. It is now getting really dark and the mist is rolling in like a slow tide. He feels a chill, knows that if he leaves things much longer, he won't be able to fulfill his father's strange request.

The lid to the tube is tight but he carefully levers it free. He doesn't know where to begin and where to end. Should he just shake the tube and walk away, gray powder streaming like a dud flare? Or should he try to distribute the remains as evenly as possible?

He remembers reading in the diaries how human remains were found all around Stonehenge. Hundreds more were buried in nearby fields, ancient camps where the stone workers had lived.

Gideon looks into the end of the tube and walks to the first stone in the opening opposite the Heel Stone. He heads clockwise, shaking the ashes out around the small circle of sarsens and bluestones. The container is empty before he reaches the end but he completes the ritual, shaking it until the circle is closed.

Then he finds himself strangely drawn to the middle and compelled to kneel. He mouths the words he couldn't say when he saw the body at the crematorium. In the darkness he whispers, 'I'm sorry, Dad. Sorry that we didn't know each other better. Sorry that I didn't tell you I loved you. That we didn't find a way to overcome our differences and share our dreams. I miss you. I'll always miss you.'

Black clouds creep across the pale rising moon. Before Gideon can get to his feet a hood is pulled tight over his head.

Four Lookers drag him to the ground.

100

Megan is about to switch off her computer for the night when it pings with a message. Tired, she opens it. It's an alert from the force's facial recognition unit. They've found a street camera match to the fuzzy camera-phone shot Gideon had taken of the burglar.

She reads the text: 'An individual male matching the facial biometrics of your target has been identified by camera XR7 in Tidworth. Click on the icon below to view more stills and to contact coordinating officer.'

She shifts the cursor to a little picture of a camera and clicks it. Her heart jumps. The shots are fantastic. Close to a dozen of them. In several the suspect is standing outside a shop, locking and unlocking the premises. It is a butcher's shop. Damn. She'd thought about a chef or catering worker, not a butcher.

The psychological profile she'd drawn up comes rushing back to her: white male, thirty to forty-five, manual worker, possibly in catering business, local pubs, restaurants. He fits it to a T.

Megan is so elated she doesn't notice her ex and her daughter in the CID office until Sammy shouts.

'Mummy! Mummy!' The four-year-old comes running between the desks.

Megan opens her arms and gathers her up.

'Got a lost child here,' Adam says. 'Told me her mother was a famous detective. So I thought I'd return her in person.'

She kisses Sammy and rearranges her on her knee. 'What are you doing here?'

He gives her a cheeky look. 'I was working a tip-off that you might come out with us.'

Megan thinks about telling him to back off, take things more slowly. But he and Sammy look so happy together.

Adam sits down at her desk, just at the exact moment Jimmy Dockery walks into the room. The two men catch each other's eyes. There's a crackle of curiosity in the air. The kind that makes a cat's tail stand up and fluff out.

Jimmy had come with news for Megan. Good news. Important news. But now he doesn't want to give it to her. Not with her husband sitting there. It'll have to wait until the morning. He waves and wanders out of view.

Adam watches him go and allows himself a smug smile.

101

Gideon is trying to make sense of what's happened. He remembers his head being covered, strong hands holding him, a sharp spike of pain in his leg. They must have drugged him and taken him somewhere to sleep it off.

The hood is off and he's sitting in the dark on a cold stone floor. Candles flicker in all four corners. It's small. Small and has no door.

He's in a cell.

Maybe it isn't a cell. Maybe it's a tomb.

Half-drugged, he struggles to his feet and sways unsteadily. He paws at the walls. There's no way out. His father had written about people being buried inside a Sanctuary. This could be it. He has been walled up in the Sanctuary and left to die.

He feels anxiety climb his chest. There can't be much air in this place. It can't last long. He picks up a candle and extinguishes the others. No point burning precious oxygen. Standing with the single light burning out, he reasons that they're not going to leave him here to die. He told Smithsen that he'd taken precautions, a planned delivery to the police of damning documents, unless he was free to call it off.

The candle burns out.

His heartbeat rises and his hopes fade. Surely they're going to have to come to him, find out what he knows, how much he can hurt them.

There is a guttural rumbling of stone. Narrow slits of light appear in the middle of two opposite walls. Hooded, robed figures flood the small room. Gideon doesn't fight as they overwhelm him, cuff his wrists and drag him through an exit. No hood or blindfold this time. Something has changed.

The corridor they're leading him down is long and winding. Gradually the lighting on the walls becomes more ornate. It even starts to feel warmer. He's flanked by two men. The one on his right pulls an iron ring sunk into a wall. Hidden pulleys go to work. A section of stone slides noisily back. They push him into a chamber.

The stranger he saw in the mist at Stonehenge sits in a hooded brown robe behind a circular table made of honey-colored stone. 'Sit down, Gideon.' He waves a hand to the seating opposite him.

Gideon lowers himself onto a crescent of cold stone. His eyes never leave the robed figure in front of him.

'You don't recognize me, do you?'

'I saw you at the henge.'

The Master smiles. 'I met you several times before, when you were a child. Your father and I were friends.'

Gideon is surprised. 'Then you know what he went through. What happened to my mother and what he had to do to save me.'

'Indeed, I do.' He studies Gideon. 'You have clearly learned much, presumably from your father's journals. But do you actually understand what you have been reading?'

'I think so.'

'So tell me.'

'You are the Henge Master, the spiritual leader of the Followers of the Sacreds. My father was a senior and trusted member of your Inner Circle. You, he and many others give your lives to the protection of the Sacreds and the renewal of their energy.'

The Master cracks a thin smile.'Not quite right. But close.' He's keen to learn how much more Nathaniel's boy knows. 'Do you have any idea how the spiritual energy of the Sacreds is sustained?'

'Human sacrifice. Offerings made before and after both the summer and winter solstice. At specific moon phases. My father described them as necessary for the restoration of celestial and earthly balance.'

The Master looks impressed. 'You are a good scholar. But there is a big difference between theory and practice.' He folds his robed arms. 'You sought us out, Gideon. What is it that you want?'

'Acceptance. My mother and father are dead. You are my family. I am already a child of the Sacreds, you know how my father baptized me as a child.'

The Master nods. 'Indeed. He bathed you in waters from the Sacreds and asked them to protect you from the disease that had killed your mother. He promised them his own life if they afforded you a long and healthy one.'

Gideon's eyes well up. Once more Nathaniel's words come back to him: '*I will willingly give my own blood, my own life. I only hope it is worthy. Worthy enough to change things. To alter the fate that I know awaits my poor, motherless son.*

The Master rises from behind the table and walks the chamber. 'The Sacreds are not monsters. They do not demand arbitrary human sacrifice. It is a fundamental matter of give and take, part of the cycle of life and death. In return for protecting your life, Nathaniel promised them his own. He undertook to become a sacrifice.'

Gideon's mind goes blank. 'The suicide?'

'No. That wasn't an offering. That was a selfish act of desperation. He wanted to stop the Inner Circle following a course that he didn't agree with.'

'What course?'

The Master exhales wearily. 'Your father made great studies and believed that the unalterable doctrine of the Craft was that those who received the gifts of the Sacreds were the chosen ones, the ones who should be sacrificed. He contested that anyone who had drawn from the divine well and prospered should in their later years pay the divine price. The Inner Circle disagreed. They believed that this ancient practice needed to evolve. That the Sacreds should pick their own sacrifices.'

'How so?'

'Easily.' The Master opens his arms in a relaxed gesture. 'People are drawn to them. The Lookers – the men who took you from the henge – they wait and watch. When someone is compelled to touch a specific Sacred, one that is in ascendancy in the sidereal zodiac, then they identify themselves as the correct human sacrifice.'

The Master sits on the stone bench next to Gideon. What he wants to say next will unnerve the boy, possibly shake him to his core. 'The Craft is a democratic body. We follow rules laid down centuries ago. However, the interpretation of those rules is the right and duty of each successive Master and his Inner Circle. When your father took his decision to oppose the Circle's views on sacrifices, he as good as sealed his own fate.'

Gideon looks lost. 'I don't understand. Why was my father's opinion so important compared with everyone else's?'

The Master sees that Nathaniel hadn't told the boy everything. 'Because, Gideon, when the matter was put to the vote, I wasn't the Henge Master. He was.'

102

Caitlyn's screams pierce the foot-thick stone like a high-speed drill. She can't take any more. The blackness, the stillness, it's driving her insane. She hammers her fists, knees and head against the rough walls of the vertical tomb.

The two Lookers guarding her rush to the detention crevice. They can't let her harm herself. She mustn't die before the chosen time. They trigger the release locks and Caitlyn tumbles out and crashes painfully onto her knees. Her body is a patchwork of cuts and her long black hair is matted with sweat and blood. She snarls and kicks out at them. 'Get off me. You fucking bastards, let me *go*.'

The Lookers pin her down on her back. Her face is covered in blood and her manicured hands are cut to ribbons. Her forehead shows several deep gashes where she has crashed her skull against the stones. The men exchange glances. She has gone berserk in there. Thrashed around in some kind of deranged fit and tried to kill herself.

Caitlyn wants to end this nightmare now. Even if it means dying, she wants it to stop. But gradually she calms down. Her mind takes control again and the wild animal inside her is quieted. The men keep pressing her down on the cold stone floor. One is astride her, kneeling on her arms, pinning her wrists. The other is knelt across her ankles. Only now as the bloodrush subsides does it hit her.

They are amateurs.

She has seen Eric and his team carry out restraint techniques. They never do it like this. A twist of a wrist is enough to incapacitate anyone, if you know how. A finger dug into a nerve point can stop a heavyweight boxer, if you know how. These guys don't. They are completely without 'know how.' They're making it up as they go along.

Caitlyn stares into the eyes of the hooded man pressing down on her. 'Okay. I'm okay now.'

He eases himself off her arms. Stands over her. Wary and ready to pin her down again. 'We need to take a look at her head wound,' he says to the younger man.

They help her to her feet and are about to cuff her wrists when Caitlyn pulls her hands away. She drives a knee hard into the groin of the man in front of her. The second Looker grabs her from behind. She leans into him. Uses her body weight to knock him off balance then runs him into the wall behind them. As he hits the stone, she crashes her head up, making sure the back of her skull does maximum damage to his face. It's a sickening blow. He loses hold and slumps down behind her. His nose is broken.

Caitlyn stands unrestrained in the torch-lit corridor of the Sanctuary.

103

Gideon is filled with a dizzying emptiness. The revelation that his father was once the Henge Master leaves him drained. This is not what he expected to discover. He'd sought the truth. Needed a reason for his father's suicide. Someone to blame. He hadn't been prepared for this.

The Henge Master is not concerned with Gideon's feelings. He merely wants to learn how much Gideon knows, how dangerous a threat he represents. 'Do you have any idea what this place is? Where we are?'

'The Sanctuary.' His voice is flat. His thoughts elsewhere.

'And do you know its location?'

It's a tougher question. One that drags Gideon out of his state of shock. 'My father wrote only about the nature of the Sanctuary, not its location. That said, I haven't decoded all of his journals. I am sure there will be passages where he gets more specific.'

The Master tries to read the boy's eyes. It is possible that Nathaniel kept the location secret. It is also believable that his son knows it and understands that to reveal it would be dangerous. 'You are well informed for an outsider. For a noninitiate.' He clasps his hands. 'And that presents us with a problem. What are we to do with you?'

Gideon moves closer to him. 'Let me be part of things. Let me join you. I don't know what else I am to do. Given the loss of my father. His vow. I am to be irrevocably linked with the Sacreds whatever happens.'

'Should we even want to admit you to the Craft, I'm not sure you are ready. Initiation is a searching ceremony. It involves total trust between the Henge Master and the initiate. Trust is all the supplicant has to hold on to as his blood is shed. The pain is excruciating, unimaginable.'

Gideon hangs his head. 'It is what I want.'

The Master puts a hand beneath Gideon's chin, raises his face and looks into his eyes. 'Who is to say you wouldn't continue your father's opposition from within our ranks?'

Gideon becomes animated. 'I don't wish you or the Followers harm. I want to be welcomed into the fold. Just as my father *once* was. I want my life to be lived to the full, under the blessing of the Sacreds. I don't want it to be cursed with sickness. And I certainly don't want to spend the rest of my years fearful that I may be attacked or have my home set ablaze.'

The Master can see there is good reason why Gideon should be motivated to embrace the Craft. And killing him poses the risk of their existence being made public. The Craft would be exposed and the ritual of renewal interrupted. He paces. 'There is a way for you to demonstrate your loyalty, your commitment. If you were to fulfill it, I would personally vouch for your trustworthiness And the initiation would begin tonight.'

'What is it?'

'Your father's books. Deliver them to us and you may become one of us.'

Gideon shakes his head. 'I know what the initiation involves. I am willing to let you put a knife to my flesh and a hammer to my bones. Isn't that enough?'

'No. The books are the knife you hold to *our* flesh and your threats the hammer you raise above *our* bones.'

Gideon thinks of a way to break the stalemate. 'I will give you a quarter of the books before my initiation and I will make the phone call that will ensure nothing is delivered to the police. After my initiation, I will give you another quarter of them. A year from now I will surrender another 25 percent.'

'That is only 75 percent. When will we receive the final installment?'

'Perhaps never.' Gideon smiles. 'Or when I have learned enough of the Craft to please you. When you are ready for *me* to take over as Master.'

104

Caitlyn runs for her life. Sprints as fast as her bare feet can manage. She reaches the end of a short, dark passageway. It goes left and right. She chooses right. Barrels down the corridor, thankful for the looseness of the rough gown she's wearing.

She's fast. Gym sessions every day. Five kilometers on the treadmill. Five on the elliptical trainer. Now she is glad of every workout. They injured her, starved her and scared her, but she's still strong and fit.

The passage curves and disappears into a dark haze. With any luck she's following an outer wall. Outer walls mean exit doors. She glances over her shoulder. No sign of the men. The place is bigger than she imagined. Much bigger. The stones beneath her flying feet are inscribed with something. It looks like someone chiseled writing on to them. Gravestones. Caitlyn realizes she's running on graves. Her heartbeat kicks up another notch. She looks up and realizes something else. The passage is circular.

Dead ahead are the two hooded men she fought off.

Only now there are more of them. Many more. All waiting for her.

PART FOUR

105

WEDNESDAY 23 JUNE

The only investigator not at the Chief Constable's early morning all-agency briefing is Josh Goran. Not that he minds. He's already made sure he's never out of the information loop. His team have a range of journalists, police officers and civil servants on their payroll. The ten thousand bucks he pressed into the palm of field agent Alvez made sure he's bang up to date on everything and anything of note.

Inside the overwarm conference room, Alan Hunt's deputy, Greg Dockery, makes a plea to the seven men sitting with him. 'We need a full and confidential exchange of key intelligence. We have to bury our differences and work together. That's why we're here. Later today Chief Constable Hunt will personally reassure Vice President Lock of the resources that are being deployed to recover his daughter. Commander Gibson, please give us your update.'

Barney Gibson looks across the table and already sees operational fault lines. The two FBI agents have taken up one side, the Wiltshire officers the other and his own Met colleague sits apart from either camp. Cultural schisms, unbridgeable divides during the course of only one operation. 'In the early hours of this morning we received further communication from the group we believe are holding Caitlyn. The call was traced to France, but this time not Paris. It came from a public box in Cannes, in the south of the country.'

John Rowlands throws up his hands in despair. 'I'm sorry, I just don't buy it. They are no more in the south of France than we are.'

The Chief shoots his Head of CID a blistering look. 'John, forget your own pet theories for a moment, we can speculate all we like afterward. Let's listen to the tape first.' He takes a beat then readdresses the whole group. 'From the timing and nature of the recording you'll see that they've responded directly to Kylie Lock's press conference.'

Barney Gibson presses play on the small digital recorder in the center of the conference table. The room's expectant silence is broken by a distorted male voice. 'The price for the safe return of Caitlyn Lock is twenty million dollars. Her mother has promised ten, we expect her father to do the same. The conditions are as follows: the FBI, the British police and that bounty hunter will all state publicly that no surveillance will be mounted on an agreed exchange. And no attempt will be made to arrest any people involved in the exchange. Only when we have this guarantee of safe passage will we give further details of our conditions. Please understand this: we have the resources to hold Caitlyn Lock for as long as we wish. Years if necessary. Sooner or later our demands *will* be met.' Caitlyn's voice suddenly fills the room. She sounds calm but weak. 'Mom, I'm in Cannes near the Carlton Hotel where I stayed with you and François before the film festival at the Palais des Festivals. It's raining today on La Croisette and the Palais is hosting a video gaming conference. Pop, I'm being well looked after. No one has hurt me. *Please* do what they say.' The distorted male voice returns. 'Let me be clear, unless we see the televised guarantees, this will be our last communication with you.'

The tape hisses to a stop. The investigators sit in shocked silence. Barney Gibson knows they're all imagining how Caitlyn's parents are going to react when they hear it. He rises above the emotion and plows on. 'The details given in the tape are correct. The weather in Cannes yesterday was as described and the exhibition mentioned is indeed taking place. Technicians both sides of the Atlantic have confirmed the call was made in Cannes and the background sounds are consistent with those of this particular spot on the Côte d'Azur. Todd, do you want to say something about it?'

'It is a bitch of a recording,' says the FBI man. 'Our techies stripped it down while your guys were sleeping and they confirm that, like the first one, it was assembled on several different levels. The two voices were recorded separately. They spliced them together, then added a third track, a continuous background noise. We analyzed the woman's voice and we are certain it's Caitlyn. The distorted male voice, we think is English, the same that we heard on the first tape.'

'First Paris, now Cannes,' observes the Deputy Chief. 'They keep shifting her. Are probably moving again as we speak.'

'It would explain why they are using phone boxes,' says Gibson. 'They don't mind being traced because by the time we have a fix on it, they're no longer there.'

'Or they never were,' says John Rowlands, still unconvinced that Caitlyn has crossed the Channel. 'It could just be one guy on a motorcycle traveling around Europe sending these clips down the wire. I don't necessarily buy that she is even out of the UK.'

'We have to plan for either eventuality,' says Hunt, ending the speculation. 'Greg, keep me informed of how resources and emphasis is split on this one.'

The deputy nods. 'Sir.'

'What about their demands, their conditions?' asks John Rowlands.

Hunt raises an eyebrow. 'The British Government, police and people do not negotiate with kidnappers. It's policy. We never have and never will.'

Danny Alvez nods in agreement. 'Vice President Lock has said the same kind of thing. It may be different because this is his own daughter, but I doubt it.'

'No way,' says Burgess. 'Thom is hard line. He ain't gonna blink on this one. These sons of bitches can wait as many years as they want, he still ain't going to negotiate with them.'

106

Any moment now the target will appear.

He will be white, thirty to forty-five, and will perfectly fit Megan's psychological profile. She just knows he will.

The DI is parked across the street from a big-windowed shop in Tidworth, her eyes never leaving the area beneath a sign boldly proclaiming: 'Matt Utley. Master Butcher.' Once she's got a good ID on him, she'll get a search warrant and turn his house over. See if there's any clothing to match the snagged samples found at the Chase estate in Tollard Royal. Or maybe tools that serial-match those recovered from the kit bag he left behind.

It's eight-thirty and she's been sitting patiently for an hour. Her mind wanders for a moment, back to her renewed relationship with her ex-husband. Everything seems to be going well. Adam spent last night at her house – *their* old house – and this morning Sammy skipped in with a smile as big as a slice of melon.

At eight-forty a man jogs across the road right in front of her, opens the shop door and turns on all the lights. She watches him pull on a red-and-white-striped apron and busy himself behind worktops and freezer counters. He's in his early twenties, she guesses. Not her target. Just after nine he flips a sign in the door window to declare the place open. She waits a while longer. At nine-thirty, Megan gets out of the car, pulls out her pocketbook and wanders in.

A brass bell dings as she opens and shuts the door. She doesn't wait for a greeting. 'I'm Eileen Baxendale. Council rates review unit.' She puts pen to paper. 'What's your name?'

'Carl, Carl Pringle.' He seems totally flummoxed. 'I don't know nothing about the rates.'

'You don't? Well, who does?' She looks around pointedly.

'You need to speak to Matt. Mr. Utley. The owner. I just work for him.'

'And when can I do that?'

'He isn't coming in today. Said I was in charge.'

'He's sick?'

'Didn't say. Just said I was to run the place and he'd call me later.'

She has enough information to find Utley. He will be on the electoral role, registered with the tax and health authorities. There is little point grilling the kid for any other scraps. 'Okay, I'll come back later in the week.' The bell dings again as she leaves.

On the journey back to HQ, she phones in her requests for background checks on her missing butcher. With any luck they'll be on her computer by the time she gets in.

When she walks into the CID room, Jimmy Dockery greets her with a sheet of paper and a smile. 'I've been to the labs. Look at this.'

He slaps the forensic report down on her desk, points at a crucial part and summarizes: 'The field near the burned-out barn was covered in minute particles of human debris.'

Her eyes widen. 'You got the dogs out there?'

He laughs. 'No, not dogs. Something even better. This is going to sound insane but I read about German detectives using buzzards to search for corpses. So when I couldn't get ground radar or sniffer dogs, I contacted an exotic bird expert and he had two Turkey vultures fly the field we visited.' He proudly taps the report again. 'This is what he came up with.'

Megan is impressed. She reads from the microbiologist's paper: 'Samples of soil were tested and contained human traces. All identified DNA was that of a single individual.'

'You said Tony Naylor was in that field, boss. You were right.'

She forces herself to be cautious. 'Let's make sure it is Naylor before we tell anyone. Try to get a familial DNA match via blood from his sister or parents. Check the national database to see if we ever tested him in connection with an offense.' She thinks of something else. 'Oh, and get the landowner interviewed, I sure as hell want to know how he came to be crop spraying with human remains.'

107

Gideon leaves the Sanctuary in the same way he entered it. Hooded, cuffed and driven in the back of a plain looking builder's van.

After twenty minutes the vehicle lurches off-road and stops. Its back doors creak open and he hears birdsong spill in from outside. It's still early morning. Pre-rush hour. The floor beneath him dips as someone climbs in, swings his feet around and pulls him by the ankles across the van floor. They dangle his feet outside the vehicle, sit him upright and pull the cloth sack from his head.

It's not Dave Smithsen staring into his face. It's the man who almost killed him. The one who left him for dead in his father's burning study. Gideon's eyes drift down to the man's hands. There, on a small finger, is the distinctive signet ring that opened up the wound on his face. Behind the man is what looks like deserted woodland. The perfect place for a grave to be dug and a body to be hidden.

Smithsen walks into view and is smiling. 'This is Musca and from now on you will know me only as Draco. You will treat us both like long lost brothers. Either that or we'll kill you. It's your choice.'

Musca pulls a gun from the seat of his trousers, presses the barrel hard into Gideon's forehead. 'I don't mind which.'

Draco sits casually on the back ledge of the van and puts an arm around Gideon in a gesture of mock chumminess. 'One of our rules is secrecy. Enforced secrecy, if you get my meaning. And the Master relies on Musca and me to enforce it.' He squeezes Gideon. 'If you live, then you live by the rules. On no account do you speak about the Craft, the Followers or the Sacreds to any nonmembers. Ever. You don't telephone us. You don't turn up at our houses or our businesses. You never contact us. We contact you. If we call you on the phone, you don't mention your name or our names. You use the name that you will be given, should you be initiated. You use that name at all times. Don't forget these things. If they slip your mind, my friend's finger might slip too.'

Musca's eyes dance and he pushes the gun harder against Gideon's skull. 'Boom.'

Draco gets to his feet. 'Put him in the front, then you can go.'

Musca guides Gideon around to the passenger's door, helps him into the cab, slams the door and heads to a Mercedes parked nearby. The indicators flash orange as he zaps the central locking.

Draco talks as he starts up the van and drives. 'Here's how it goes. I take you home and stay with you while you collect these books that your father has written. You hand them over to me and I return you to the Master. It is that simple.'

'Then you should be able to manage it, shouldn't you?'

Draco laughs. 'You and I need to get some things straight. The Inner Circle voted a few hours ago on your initiation. The Master's vote carried it. One vote. That's all. So listen rather than talk. All right?' His eyes flash menace. 'For the next twenty-four hours you are *my* responsibility. I will deliver you to the Master's knife and hammer. If you survive the initiation, mine will be the first face that you will see. From that point on, I own your loyalty. You do what I say, when I say, how I say. Do you understand?'

Gideon can see he's riled. 'Clear as day. You're acting tough but really you're just the Master's messenger boy. You don't do anything unless he tells you.'

Draco hits the brakes. The van skids to a halt and the engine stalls. He throws a meaty right-hander into Gideon's face, cannoning his head into the side window. Gideon tries to fend him off with an arm but Draco is already out of his seat, raining blows down on his head and face.

The beating lasts less than ten seconds. Draco holds him by the neck in ironlike fingers and delivers one final blow. The most painful one of all. 'Remember this, Mr. Smartmouth, when we're alone, *I* am your master. I own you. I was ready to kill your father and I'm more than ready to kill you.'

108

The rest of the journey to the Chase estate takes place in a painful silence. Particularly so for Gideon. His lip is busted and a tooth feels loose.

Draco frogmarches him through the front door and straight upstairs to the hidden room.

'Neat job,' he says as Gideon reveals the panel in the landing wall. He taps it with his big perma-grazed builder's knuckles. 'Not bad at all. If I hadn't already been in the room behind here, I would never have guessed one existed.'

Gideon ignores him and steps into the long narrow space.

Draco can't hide his shock when he sees the shelves are empty. Just dust and faded paintwork marking where the diaries had been.

Gideon blots his bleeding lip. 'What did you expect?'

'Watch your mouth.' He smiles at his own joke and walks the room. Knocks on walls. Thumps his heels in a few places. 'Are there any more secret places in here?' He bangs his foot down again on the flooring.

'Aren't you worried about my damaged rafters?' says Gideon sarcastically.

'They're *oak*,' chides Draco. 'It would take the Great Fire of London to burn them down.'

He bangs his way along a line of ceiling panels. Gideon's eyes focus at the far end, the one above his father's telescope.

Draco stops just inches short of it. 'So where are they? Where have your old man's books gone?'

The sound of electric chimes preempts a reply. The gate bell. Draco looks edgy. 'You expecting anyone?'

Gideon shrugs. 'No. There's a security monitor in the kitchen. We can see who it is.'

They go downstairs. The small wall-mounted screen shows a woman waiting in a car idling outside the gates to the house.

'I know her,' says Gideon. 'It's the detective heading the investigation into my father's death. She'll be able to see my car and your van on the drive.'

'Let her in but get rid of her quickly.' He heads toward the fire-damaged study. 'Looks like I've got some work to do after all.'

Gideon buzzes Megan in, opens the front door and walks outside to greet her as she parks. He blots his lip once more on the back of his hand.

'Good morning, Inspector. I didn't expect to see you today.'

She grabs her handbag as she climbs out and shuts the door. 'I wanted to see how you are.' She notices the swollen and bloodied mouth. 'Which doesn't look very good. What happened?'

Gideon touches his mouth again. 'I took a fall while trying to fix up the study. It's not as bad as it looks.'

Her eyes drift past him as Draco comes walking out toward his van. 'You having some work done?'

Gideon glances toward him. 'Yes, Mr. Smithsen did some jobs for my father and he kindly came by when he learned of the fire.'

'That's neighborly.' She remembers their conversation in the pub near the crematorium, what Gideon had told her about the builder's previous visit and how he suspected he was linked to his father's death.

'Can't believe Mr. Chase's bad luck,' says Draco loudly, as he steps closer to them. 'What's the world coming to? You lose your father, then the scum of the earth break in and nearly burn you out of house and home. Terrible affair.' He heads back to the van, rattles a large bag full of tools.

Megan knows they're being watched, given no real chance to talk. 'I came by to ask you a few more questions about your father – is this a bad time?'

'It is,' answers Gideon. 'Do you mind if I call you? I can come into the station, if that makes it easier for you.'

'That would be fine.' Out of the corner of her eye, she sees the builder watching them. 'Before I go, can I use your loo? It's quite a drive back.'

'Of course. Let me show you where it is.'

They peel away from Draco and once through the door she leans close and asks. 'Are you all right?'

'Not really. I have to go with him when you leave. They want my father's books.' He flicks a light on in the corridor and glances back toward the open front door. Draco slams shut the van door and is heading their way. 'I can't talk now.'

Megan has no choice but to slip into the downstairs toilet as Draco strides through the front door and pulls Gideon toward him. 'I saw you both talking. What did she just say to you?'

Gideon tries not to panic. 'Take your hands off me. It was my father's funeral yesterday. She was just being sympathetic.'

He unclenches his fists and lets go of Gideon's shirt. 'Get her out of here. Quickly. Or you'll be going to another funeral.'

109

Gideon walks Megan to her car and holds the door for her. He knows he only has a few seconds.

'I was threatened this morning at gunpoint.' He nods to the house. 'By Smithsen and another man. The burglar who attacked me. They're working together.'

Matt Utley's photo flashes in her mind. She wants to tell him about her trip to the butcher's shop but there's no time. 'Get in the car. We can sort all this out down at the station.'

He glances nervously to the front door. 'I can't do that. I *have* to go with him.'

'Why?'

'My father killed himself rather than condone what they're doing.'

'What *are* they doing?' She looks at him quizzically, remembering again his fragile mental state.

Gideon sees doubt rising in her eyes. 'I told you before. *Sacrifices.* I think they're about to make another one.'

Megan wants to challenge him but spots Smithsen by the side of the house. He's carrying a length of burned timber, trying to look busy. Now is the wrong time. She starts the engine and slips off the handbrake. 'I'll call you later.'

Gideon steps away as she drives off. Smithsen walks toward him, his eyes tracking the car to the electronic metal gates and out on to the country lane.

'What was that all about?'

'Money,' says Gideon. 'My father traded artifacts. Made millions from them. Probably some tomb-robbing in his time. The force's art and fraud people want to interview me about his last set of accounts.'

'She ask about your face?'

'I told her I'd had an accident.'

'Good.' He turns and starts back to the house. 'Come on, we're wasting time. Let's get those books and get out of here.'

'Wait,' says Gideon. 'You think I'm stupid enough to leave them in the house?'

Smithsen's face sets like concrete. Gideon digs his car keys from his pocket and opens the boot of the Audi. The builder peers inside and sees a thick blanket-wrapped bundle. He leans in and tugs off the outer layers. Inside are four A4 diaries, two from each decade of Nathaniel Chase's time in the Craft.

'Is this all?'

'All for now.'

Smithsen opens one up and stares at the coded text. 'How do we even know this is what you say it is?'

Gideon takes the book from him. 'Only my father and I understood this code and that's a good thing. Good for me and good for you. Most people would just throw these things away if they came across them, but they would be wrong to do that. Very wrong.' He closes the journal, rewraps it in the blanket and hands the bundle over. 'That's my side of the bargain. Now complete yours.'

110

By the time you reach the rank of DI, you've usually suffered a few professional wounds. And if you are a woman, you've certainly set some personal rules along the way. From leaving early at end-of-case parties to never marrying another copper, you've laid down the markers. Megan has broken both of those little beauties. But there is one guideline she always follows.

Look at the bigger picture. Don't make knee-jerk decisions. Stand back and weigh everything up. Big. Small. Important. Mundane. Take every factor into consideration.

Which is why she doesn't beat down her boss's door and ask for an arrest warrant and a tactical firearm unit to take in Dave Smithsen. Instead, she talks it through with Jimmy and tries to make sense of it all. 'I saw Gideon Chase this morning. He looked like he had been roughed up. Said he'd been threatened at gunpoint by two men. A builder called Smithsen and the man who broke into his father's house last week.'

Jimmy's surprised. 'I thought you said Chase hadn't seen the burglar?'

'I did. It turns out he had.'

'So why did he lie about it?'

'Long story. Says he felt he had a personal duty to find out what his father was mixed up in.'

'So where did he get threatened and why?'

She shakes her head. 'I don't know all the details. I didn't have the chance to ask him. Smithsen was there with him at the house, fixing the fire damage.'

Jimmy adds it all up. 'So this builder and his burglar mate threaten Chase and then a few hours later he comes round to his house to fix it up? Sounds strange.'

'You're right. It *is* strange. But it got me wondering whether the suicide of Nathaniel Chase isn't somehow connected to the ransom demand for the kidnapped American girl.'

Jimmy's eyes widen. 'Why? How on earth can you connect the two?'

'Cast your mind back to when you saw Jake Timberland's body in the barn. You said you had a gut feeling that the crime scene had been staged. Can you remember what you put that down to?'

'Sure. Location, location, location.'

'That's right. Well, location is the factor that's been bugging me. Both cases share the same focal point. Stonehenge. It's where Lock and Timberland were probably heading for a romantic sunrise before the kidnap and murder. And it's the place Nathaniel Chase wrote books about and where he wanted his ashes scattered. Come to think of it, it's also where his son claims he was cured of hereditary cancer when he was a child and where he believes a prehistoric cult makes human sacrifices so they can benefit from its powers.'

Jimmy screws up his face. 'You don't really go for all that mumbo jumbo, do you?'

'Just playing devil's advocate for a minute. Why not? People have been digging up the bones of thousands of human sacrifices for centuries. The practice has been recorded in the Bible and dozens of other historic documents.'

'I get the history, but even if such a cult still existed, why would it want to sacrifice an American politician's daughter and the son of an English Lord? And how do you explain the ransom demand?'

Jimmy's logic pulls her up short. The cult is a stupid idea but one she's not yet ready to completely write off. 'Cults pick victims for a whole range of reasons. Just like rapists and murderers, they have their own secret criteria. It could be sexual, racial, gender-oriented. Maybe it fits or offends their belief systems. Perhaps Caitlyn fitted one of those categories.'

'And Timberland?'

'It could be that he didn't fit the criteria, that's why he got killed. He was just defending Caitlyn. Being gallant.'

Jimmy shows his ace card again: 'And the ransom?'

She taps her fingers on the desk. Her nails sound like a hungry woodpecker. 'Forget the ransom for a minute. I'm not done with the locational aspect.'

Jimmy thinks that argument is just as flawed. 'Stonehenge. Okay. So how could a cult carry out a ritualistic killing there? The place is slap bang in the middle of two busy roads. Always crawling with tourists. Twenty-four-hour security.'

Megan's eyes light up. 'What if the security team at Stonehenge is involved?'

Jimmy thinks for a second. It would certainly change things. 'Sean Grabb worked security there. I heard he's been missing since the abduction and murder.'

'You sure?'

'Overheard it in the canteen. And remember this guy has previous for burglary and assault.'

Megan looks energized. 'So if Grabb and others working security were part of the cult, they could fix access to the site at any time they wanted.'

'It's possible. I'll check with English Heritage and the security company they use. See what Grabb's attendance record is like. Could be that he pulls sickies all the time and often goes missing. Or maybe this is the only day he's had off for years.'

Megan is only half-listening. 'Good. Good idea. Give it a shot.'

Jimmy has implanted another idea in her head. One more unorthodox than any she's considered in her career. One that could solve the case. Or get her sacked.

111

Cuffed and hooded in the back of Draco's van, Gideon tries to work out the route they are taking back to the Sanctuary. He's sure from the turn out of his gate that they're heading west from Tollard Royal along the B3081 past the King John Inn.

He wriggles into a seated position behind the driver's wall at the front of the van and navigates according to which direction he gets thrown. A jerk to the left tells him Draco has turned right and is driving north. Gideon tries to judge the passing minutes and comes to the conclusion that they've reached Shaftesbury and are now headed in the direction of Gillingham and Warminster.

The last part of the journey is the quietest. Few cars can be heard. From the reduced speed and increasingly bumpy ride, it seems they've gone off road. Gideon is thrown around for several minutes before the vehicle stops and its back doors clunk open.

Three, maybe four men pull him out and manhandle him over hard ground. They walk him into a chilly, enclosed space where footsteps create echoes. Some kind of door is being unlocked in front of him. There's a lot of noise now. Sounds of people grunting. Things shifting. Something heavy sliding.

'Quickly,' someone shouts.

A hand goes around the back of his head, pushes him down, urges him forward. Makes sure he doesn't crack his head on something. He hears rumbling, grunting again behind him. No one says anything for maybe a minute. His mind goes into overdrive. The silence around him feels toxic.

Finally Draco speaks. 'You're going down some steps. Watch you don't fall.' There's sarcasm in his voice.

Gideon hears the slap and echo of footsteps in front and behind as he descends. The steps are solid. Thick stone in a large space, nothing to soak up the sound. Exactly twenty of them.

The descent stops and two sets of hands grab his arms and walk him briskly for almost thirty seconds.

'More steps,' comes the sarcastic voice.

Another twenty.

He recognizes the smell of being deep underground. He knows the odors of the earth – peat, chalk, running damp, sandstone, flint, wet iron, rich molds. They all zing like sharp perfume notes to his trained archaeological senses.

Guiding hands halt him. The hood is plucked from his broiled face. Torchlight. He is deep inside the Sanctuary. A part he has never seen. Those around him are robed and hooded. That's what the delay must have been for, before they started the downward climb.

'Get him stripped and prepared,' says Draco, his voice tough now, as hard as the stone. Gideon tries not to think about what's happening to him. He concentrates instead on forming a mental picture of where he is. A large underground space in open fields at the end of an hour-long drive. He guesses he's thirty miles from Tollard Royal. Thirty miles probably north, perhaps a little west.

Draco interrupts his calculations, leans in close, his warm, sour breath in Gideon's face. 'Listen to me. I am going to teach you how to respond to the Master during the initiation ritual. Don't shame yourself or me by getting any of it wrong. And remember, many agonies will visit your mind and body. If you are truly devoted to the Sacreds, then you will survive.' He smiles. 'If not, you will perish.'

112

Lillian Cooper's pager bleeps on her hip. The hematology consultant unhooks it and curses the message from her secretary: 'DI BAKER HERE TO SEE YOU.'

A long day just got longer. The bath and the glass of chilled white will have to wait. She starts the walk along a zig-zag of hospital corridors back to her office and thinks. Detectives don't turn up announced. Not unless there's trouble. And trouble is what might well be there. She's already behaved unethically, breached internal guidelines and contravened countless clauses of the Data Protection Act by giving the DI confidential information.

'Megan Baker. Apologies for coming over unannounced.' The police woman rises brightly from a chair outside the small office and proffers a hand.

'Not a problem,' says Cooper. 'Please come in. What can I do for you?' She can feel her heart drumming.

Megan takes one side of a desk and opens a cappuccino leather Padovano handbag that Adam bought her in Italy three years back. 'It's about when we last spoke. About Gideon Chase.'

She produces a small sheet of paper and passes it over.

Cooper picks it up and looks at it. 'I don't understand. Who are these people?'

Megan produces her friendliest smile. 'I need your help. Just once more. I want you to access the health records of all the people on that list and tell me what you find. Their hospital and GP surgery records.'

The professor is aghast. She leans away from the paper as though it's white hot. 'Inspector, I shouldn't have helped you the first time. I'm certainly not going to repeat the mistake another half a dozen times.'

'It's not half a dozen.' Megan is steely eyed. 'It's four people. And it would be a bigger mistake not to help.' She sits forward on the edge of her chair. 'The first name on that list, Nathaniel Chase, is the father of the man you looked at for me. We have reason to believe Sean Grabb, David Smithsen and Matt Utley may be connected to Nathaniel's death and to another matter we are investigating. Grabb is currently missing from work and a warrant for his arrest has been issued. All I need to know about him, and about the others, is whether they have, or have had in the past, a major medical problem. That's all.'

'Inspector, I really—'

Megan can see she's softening. 'Just tell me if they have ever been signed off work by their doctors. And if so what for.' She opens her hands in a gesture of simplicity and finality. 'It's not much to ask.'

Cooper looks worried. She shakes her head. 'It would be traceable. Any search I do like that is electronically logged. It comes back to the computer. Even if I use a different workstation, I still have to log in. I could lose my job just for getting you the information.'

Megan scratches her head. She'd been expecting this. It wasn't how she wanted the conversation to go, but it was what she anticipated. 'Doctor, you know from our mutual friend what kind of person I am.

Any assistance you give me is solely for the public good. I assure you of that.'

'That's not the point. It's just not right.'

Megan is going to have to play dirty. 'Lillian, you are married and you are having a long-term affair with a married police officer. How right is that?'

The woman gasps. 'I can't believe that you bring my private life up like this.'

'Believe it.' Her face hardens. A look toughened in the tempering heat of countless interview rooms. 'Please don't preach to me about right and wrong and don't judge me. I'm trying to solve a serious crime and save people's lives. I am prepared to do almost anything I have to in order to do that, and right now I need your cooperation.' She grabs the list of names from the desk and holds it up in front of the medic. 'Now Professor, will you please help me? Or do I have to call my friend at the *Gazette and Herald*?'

113

The main passageway of the Sanctuary is lit only by the smoky, orange flames of an endless line of wall-mounted torches. Long black scorch marks taper up the stone walls like vaporized ghosts.

The passage curves relentlessly downward and inward. It's just like his father described. St. Paul's beneath the earth. A vast cathedral-like area with magnificent chambers and crypts. Gideon is trying to blot out what's happening to him – what is *about* to happen to him. Under different circumstances, he'd be overjoyed to be here, professionally elated at the prospect of opening up the tombs beneath his feet, carbon dating and forensically piecing together the lives of the people buried beneath him.

Four hooded Bearers guide him into an opening so narrow he barely sees it. The top of his head brushes the underside of the thick lintel as he passes through. Another twenty steps and they take a similar squeezed turning into a smaller chamber. A moon face with sagging jowls rises and speaks from beneath a sackcloth hood. 'You must disrobe and shower. Then we will dress you for the initiation.'

They guide him into a separate area where he hands over his clothes and steps into a dark stone trench. There is nothing to wash himself with. No shampoo. No soap. He stands naked and alone. A torrent of water bursts out of the blackness above him. Hits him so hard it whiplashes his neck and drops him to his knees. Gideon shuts his eyes and covers his face with his hands. The flow last minutes and then stops as unexpectedly as it started. He is given a towel and led naked down the corridors to the Great Room.

The sight of the chamber takes his breath away. A life-size replica of Stonehenge fills it. As complete as the first moment it had been finished. His father had declared this to be the true tabernacle of the ancient gods. Their original resting place, while the monument in the fields near Amesbury was built.

A loud guttural rumbling turns Gideon's head. The Great Room is being sealed. A sinister brown tide of hooded devotees swells around him. A surge of bearers edge him to the circumference of a fiery ring of tall, thick candles. Beyond the flames stands the Henge Master, in his hands the ceremonial hammer and chisel. Instruments that may take Gideon's life. Fear wakes inside him. He feels it coursing through his body like a poison.

The initiation has begun.

'Behold the embodiment of the Sacreds.' The Master raises his hands and turns slowly. 'The divinities rested here centuries ago, when our forefathers built this cosmic circle and this Sanctuary. In here, you are in their presence. Out of respect, once initiated, you will ensure your head is always covered and your eyes always lowered. Do you understand?'

Gideon responds as Draco instructed him. 'Yes, Master.'

'You are brought before us because you are deemed fit by members of our Craft to become a lifelong Follower. Is that your will?'

'Yes, Master.'

'Are you ready to pledge your life, your soul and your loyalty to the Sacreds and to those who protect them?'

'Yes, Master.'

'The Sacreds renew us only as long as we renew them. We honor them with our flesh and blood and in return they protect and renew our flesh and blood. Do you pledge *your* flesh and blood to their immortal holiness?'

'Yes, Master.'

Thuribles of incense swing behind him, slowly releasing their sweet and spicy aromas. The Henge Master spreads his arms again. 'Bring him who wishes to Follow to the Slaughter Stone.'

Gideon is led through the ring of candles into the circle. He remembers Draco's warning to keep his eyes averted from the Master. Before him is the terrifying slab they call the Slaughter Stone. He freezes. Unseen hands push him to his knees and then to the floor, securing his wrists and ankles. Fear runs wild inside him.

'Do you believe in the power of the Sacreds and all who follow them?'

Gideon thinks of his father lying in this exact spot. Chained as he is now. About to have *his* blood spilled so his son might escape the agonizing death suffered by his wife.

The Master raises his voice, repeats the question. '*Do you* believe in the power of the Sacreds and all who follow them?'

'Yes, Master.'

'Do you trust unquestionably and unhesitatingly in their power to protect, to sustain and to heal?'

'Yes, Master.'

'Do you dedicate your life to their service?'

'Yes, Master.'

'And do you swear upon your life and the lives of all members of your family and those you hold dear never to speak of the Craft outside of your brotherhood unless given permission to do so?'

'Yes, Master.'

Members of the Inner Circle swing their thuribles over him and then step away. The Henge Master produces the stone blade that was fashioned from the first trilithon. 'I draw the human blood, flesh and bone in the hope that you will accept him as one of your servants and will afford him your protection and blessings. Sacred Gods, I humbly beg you to find a space in your affections for our brother.'

He slashes a deep cut from each of Gideon's wrists up to his shoulders, from each ankle to the top of each leg. Finally, from the neck to the base of the spine. Gideon chokes back a scream. He sees his mother before him, memories of her putting him to bed, kissing him goodnight, smiling at him. Then comes a flash-frame of her in Venice on the film his father made. Then the message she taped for him. The awful secret she revealed to him.

He feels a violent blow to his head. Knows what it is. The brutality of the hammer and the chisel. He hears the Henge Master's voice far away. Blackness steamrollers him. The only words left ringing in his head are those his mother spoke to him from beyond the grave.

114

Megan uses her hands-free device to call Jimmy from her car as she returns to Devizes. 'Are you alone?'

'Give me a sec.' He steps away from his desk and into the corridor outside CID. 'I am now.'

'How did you get on with the check on Sean Grabb?'

'Good. Security firm were very cooperative. They knew about his previous criminal record, he'd told them. They gave him a chance. Say he's turned out to be a model employee. Always punctual and to the best of their recollection, he's never had a day off unless for a holiday.'

'That's because he's never had a day's illness in his life,' says Megan. 'Neither has his father or his grandfather, who lived to be almost a hundred.'

'Good genes by the sound of it.'

'It's more than that.' She glances at her handbag on the passenger seat. In it are the notes she made when Lillian Cooper finally cracked. 'Dave Smithsen, our builder friend, has also never been sick. Not so much as a day off school. And it's the same with Matt Utley, the butcher cum burglar at the Chase estate.'

'They're healthy people. What does that prove?'

'Gideon Chase said the stones had healing powers. Claimed they'd cured him of his childhood cancer and protected people in his father's cult. Remember how quickly his face healed after the fight with the intruder?'

'Boss, you're not from round here but believe me, Wiltshire's a very healthy place to live,' says Jimmy, not sure of what she's driving at. 'Good healthy stock – no big city pollution, not many fast-food restaurants, lots of country walks and healthy living from when you're a kid.'

'Jimmy,' she interjects. '*Everyone* gets sick sometimes. Food poisoning, hay fever, genetic disorders, whatever. Country air and a walk down a farm lane don't stop you getting ill or injured. But these people had none of it.'

'That doesn't prove anything. My father is strong as a bull and has never been injured or ill to my knowledge. Neither has my mum or me for that matter.'

They both fall silent as they realize the implication of what he's just said.

115

Megan lets herself into her house, heads straight to the fridge and a half-finished bottle of Sauvignon Blanc. She kicks off her shoes and flops on the sofa, brimming glass in hand. She and Adam are supposed to be having a romantic night. Her parents have taken Sammy so they can go out for dinner and be alone. If ever she wasn't in the mood for pressured sex, it is now.

She has done a lot of hard thinking on the drive home. About Gideon. About Jimmy. About Jimmy's father – her Deputy Chief Constable. *Jesus.*

She hears a key in the door and shivers.

Adam calls her name from the hallway. 'Meg, you upstairs?'

'In the lounge, getting pissed.'

He appears in the doorway and smiles. 'Are you all right?'

She nods, then says, 'No. Not really.'

He goes to her. She's clearly tense and he thinks he knows why. She's worrying. Stressing unnecessarily. 'Sweetheart, don't get worked up about tonight. I'm fine if you just want to stay in and watch a movie. We can curl up on the couch, like we used to when Sam was a baby.'

Tears brim in her eyes and now she feels embarrassed. Awkward but grateful.

Adam goes back to the fridge and finds another bottle of wine to top up her glass. He grabs himself a beer as well and goes to sit with her. Sit where he used to sit. The way things used to be.

Megan puts her head on his chest, closes her eyes and starts to cry.

116

THURSDAY 24 JUNE

Gideon can't tell if he is regaining consciousness or is still in the middle of a nightmare. Waves of trauma crash in his head. So much pain. So much shock. Torrid images sweep him back and forth like a child in a rolling sea. An underground Stonehenge. Black eyes beneath sack-cloth hoods. A giant ring of burning candles. His mother's face. An ancient stone blade and ceremonial hammer. His father's diaries. The

Henge Master's raised hands. His naked body chained to the Slaughter Stone. The burning stab of the knife in his wrists and legs and back. The taste of his own blood as it runs into his mouth.

Now he sees a boy. An eight-year-old with dark hair and big hopeful eyes. He is holding the hand of his father and they are standing in a swirling mist in an open field. Stonehenge. Only it isn't. They are inside a circle of tall, spectral figures. The vaporous shapes keep shifting, becoming wider then stretching thin like smoke rising from lamps in the ground, then gushing higher like black jets of oil, burning red like the fires of hell, turning gold like the strings of some massive harp.

Now Gideon sees only a waterfall of stars. Galaxies of stars pouring into the center of the henge, swirling in a vast, bottomless cosmic pool. The stars begin to fade. Rocks are falling behind him. Rumbling like an earthquake. The Stone Gods on the edge of the pool are moving, crossing the darkness of his mind. Closing in on him. One grasps his ankle chains. Another lifts the metal restraints around his wrists and then drops his limb like the arm of a rag doll. His heart hammers in his cold, naked body. The giant Gods lean over him. Then they shift. Drift away. Vanish like the mist he remembers around Stonehenge.

The only light in the Great Room, the pale flickering glow from the ring of candles, goes out. Gideon is alone in the stony darkness.

117

Adam gets up long before Megan to make breakfast. Just as he used to. Everything is going to be just like it was.

He hears her come out of the shower. Ushers her back into their sex-wrecked bed. Hurries downstairs and returns with a tray of toast, orange juice, fruit and a flower from the small cottage garden.

She smiles. 'It's been awhile since you treated me like this.'

'It's been a while since you let me.'

They kiss and almost simultaneously glance at the bedside clock. 7:10 a.m. No time for anything except food. She bites hungrily into the hot buttered toast.

'I'll take Sammy to daycare,' he says perching on the edge of the bed. There's something on his mind. 'What you said last night, about crazy cults and Stonehenge. Do you really believe it? Or was it just the messed up day and bottle and a half of wine talking?'

'Bit of both, I suppose.' She hadn't told him everything. Only some of her speculation about Lock and Timberland. Why they'd been drawn to the site, the lure of the solstice and its sacred connotations. She's interested in his professional opinion. 'You think it's daft to consider a cult rather than a kidnap gang?'

He shrugs. 'Aside from the odd one or two, the Charles Mansons of this world, I don't believe cults are anything more than a few nutty fanatics who like a strange dance and the odd prayer or two before a bit of dressing up and frantic sex.'

She laughs.

'Listen, Stonehenge is commercially marketed as being magic, mystical and all that stuff. The security staff over there actually tell you it's a sacred site, they warn you that you mustn't on any account even touch the stones. They are paid to say that, to perpetuate the myths. It's a pagan place of worship. Go there any day of the week and you'll see nut-jobs from all over the world kneeling and praying before those rocks. You're bound to come across stories about cults and all their oddities.'

She's missed being able to talk to him like this. Confide in him. Bounce work off him. 'So you don't buy it? It's all just legend and folk tales. Like turning water into wine and feeding thousands with a loaf of bread and a couple of fishes?'

'You know, Meg, Wiltshire is full of ghosts and myths. St. George is supposed to have slain a dragon over at Uffington. Merlin is supposed to have been at Stonehenge.' He laughs as he stands up. 'Don't get too hung up on it all and I wouldn't go mentioning it to anyone at work who is brighter than Jimmy.'

He bends down and kisses her. 'Got to go.'

'Thanks. Tell Mum I'll call her later.'

She hears his feet thunder down the stairs and the front door slam.

Adam starts up his old BMW, a four-year-old three series he bought cheap at auction. He backs off the drive and calls the station to see if anything urgent is happening. He's struck lucky. Sounds like a nice quiet shift ahead.

Next he swaps phones and makes a private call. The kind he doesn't want Megan knowing about. 'It's Aquila,' he says. 'I'm not entirely sure, but I think we might have a problem.'

118

The Henge Master sits in the flickering candlelight of his chamber and muses on the tricky issue of timing. Three days until the first twilight of the first full moon after the summer solstice. The time the ritual must begin. He must be precise. The sacrificial offering has to start in astronomical twilight on the evening of this coming Sunday and be completed by the start of nautical twilight on Monday morning.

There is much to plan. Bearers to be chosen. Lookers to be detailed. Trusted Followers will soon start arriving from across the world. They will be ensconced as guests in the homes of their British counterparts.

The police activity has lessened but it is still considerable. Too intense to take chances. The newspapers write of little else but the young woman held captive just meters from him. She is less troublesome now. Six days without food has taken the fight out of her. After the pointless escape attempt she has become more placid. He thanks the gods for small blessings.

Then there is Gideon. Spread out in his chamber are the coded diaries Chase brought with him. The Master can't make sense of what they say. The boy has probably made copies of them. He's not stupid. Seems every bit as smart as Nathaniel was. Every bit his equal. Should he survive the effects of the initiation, he may prove an asset rather than a liability.

The door to the chamber opens and the hooded form of Draco enters.

'What is it?' The Master's clipped tone betrays a building tension.

'Thank you for seeing me at short notice. I was contacted this morning by our brother Aquila. His wife, a detective inspector working from headquarters, is starting to make the kind of connections we don't find helpful.'

'In what way?'

'About the American girl and her English boyfriend. She has been speculating that they had been drawn to Stonehenge because of the solstice. That the American had been kidnapped close by.'

The Master is unconcerned. 'I've read as much in the tabloid press. The police won't make it their focus. They know the media make up a new line every hour.'

'But this woman is also investigating the Nathaniel Chase suicide,' says Draco. 'And a missing person. The young man chosen as our last sacrifice.'

The Master nods. 'Now I understand. It is good that you raise this. And good that Aquila reported his concerns with us. I will have the detective taken care of.'

119

Jimmy Dockery is missing.

He hasn't turned in to work. No one has seen him. The computer on his desk is off. There's no response on his radio. He hasn't phoned in sick and from the checks Megan has done he's not at home. No car on the drive. No sign of life.

There could be a perfectly reasonable explanation. But that's not what she's thinking. She's imagining the worst. And with good reason.

Gideon Chase is also missing. He doesn't answer his landline or his mobile. He's not at home either. She just drove back from Tollard Royal and there's no trace of him.

Could Jimmy be with Gideon? It's the obvious connection. But why? Was Jimmy following up on things they'd discussed? She censors more sinister thoughts. Megan would like a face-to-face with Dockery Senior. She'd love to look the Deputy Chief in the eyes and see if he knows anything about his missing son. She can't believe she's thinking like this. She remembers what Adam had said. That it would be professional suicide to start talking to other people at work about what is going on in her head. She shakes off the dark ruminations and determines to busy herself. Wait for either Jimmy or Gideon to turn up.

Master butcher Matt Utley is top of her to-do list. She heads to the property office to take another look at the evidence recovered from the burglary. She now feels sure that the ax she noticed in the recovered bag will turn out to be some kind of butcher's cleaver.

Megan briefly passes the time of day with Louise, the recently widowed property officer, and tells her what she needs. They carry on chatting as the fifty-two-year-old disappears in the back and shouts above the noise of rooting through paper bags and boxes on metal shelves. 'You sure about the dates and case number, Megan?'

'Sure I'm sure.'

Louise reappears. 'Let me check again.' She types in the reference in her computer. 'Sorry, I don't have any entry record.' She looks puzzled. 'There's no trace of anything at all being logged. These numbers you gave me, they don't match anything in the back.'

Megan is thrown. 'Then *where* is it? I saw this evidence personally. I went over it with the PC who recovered it and my own DS said he was—' She runs out of words.

Jimmy told her he'd log the evidence in. She clearly remembers him picking it up off her desk. Her blood runs cold.

Another thought hits her.

She thanks Louise and rushes back to her desk. Opens her computer mailbox. Frantically scrolls down the messages. Panic makes her heart race. She types quickly into the search box.

Nothing.

Types again. This time slower. Scrolls manually through the messages. Still nothing. Flushed with shock, she checks her recent documents tags and deleted files section.

Blank.

They've all been permanently erased. 'Oh God.' She covers her face with her hands. The automated mail that alerted her to the face-recognition match with Matt Utley has vanished.

She has nothing on him.

Every shred of evidence has disappeared.

120

'You don't look so arrogant and full of yourself now,' says Draco, leaning over Gideon and looking into his bloodless face. The Keeper of the Inner Circle knows what he's been through. Hell. He's been there himself.

Draco picks up a wrist manacle, puts a key in it. The chain is dangling to the screwed hook in the stone floor. 'Before I let you out, I need to know if I can trust you.'

Gideon is weak, traumatized. 'You can.' His voice is slow and hoarse.

Draco unlocks the manacles. Two men materialize out of the shadows and lift Gideon to his feet. He is a dead weight and has trouble standing. Blood rushes painfully to his head. He feels incredibly weak, hungry.

He drifts light-footedly across the Great Room, disorientated, as though in the middle of an out-of-body experience. The hooded men around him seem to be shimmering, surrounded by golden auras that expand and shrink as they breathe in and out. When Draco speaks, clouds of white waft from his mouth. Like breath on a cold winter's day.

He knows they are moving him down passageways but he can't feel his feet. Can't feel anything. Yet his sight and hearing are highly sensitized not dulled. He can hear the moisture shriveling up in the hewn sandstones around him. He can see the entire corridor reflected in the dark eye of an ant in the mortar where the wall meets the floor.

They stop in a panic. Their halos mingle and seem to catch fire. Their voices overlap, spill on to each other, their words are green, red, brown. Gideon laughs. They spin him round. He senses uncertainty. There are other men across from him. Men and a woman.

A beautiful woman. Young, dark haired and gorgeous.

His mother.

Gideon knows it is her. She is alive. They pull him away from her. But she sees him. For a split second, he is sure his mother's eyes catch his.

He is wrestled away. He cranes his neck and looks for her over his shoulder. But she is gone.

121

Megan knocks lightly on the door of Jude Tompkins' office and peers in. The DCI is a long way from being a friend, but seems to be the only person she can turn to now.

'Ma'am, I'm very sorry to disturb you. I need to talk in confidence about an important development.'

The office is dark. Tompkins frowns through the puddle of yellow light spilled from a desk lamp. 'What is it, Baker?'

'Ma'am, Jimmy and I have been following up on the Naylor case.'

The DCI looks up, casts her mind back and remembers the file. 'Tony Naylor?'

'Yes, ma'am, that's right.'

She downs her pen and sits back. 'Okay, come in. Tell me quickly.

Gibson and Rowlands have got me chasing my own tail.' She gestures to a seat.

'Thank you, ma'am.' Megan shuts the door and sits. 'To cut a long story short, Naylor is dead.'

Some of the tension on the DCI's face eases. In terms of time, money and resources, a dead missing person is usually better than a live one. 'You've got a body?'

'Sort of, ma'am. Naylor's body was reduced to fertilizer and spread across a field.'

The DCI puts her head into her hands. Wearily. A dead murdered person is a whole other matter. The last thing she wants right now. She scrubs at her mat of lacquered hair, tries to get the blood flowing. 'You have forensic evidence, Baker?'

'We got a sample from his parents, ma'am. The match is perfect.'

Tompkins widens her tired eyes, sits more upright and stares across the desk. 'Have you told them any details?'

'Not yet.'

'You said he was *fertilizer*?'

'Maybe a wrong description, ma'am. Somebody, some *thing*, pulverized his body then spread it across what used to be a crop field near Imber.'

She pulls a sour face. 'So how did you find it?'

'We got a lead from a dog tag found by a jogger. Naylor's sister identified it, from the inscription on the back, as one she'd bought for him.' Megan can see by the exhausted look on her boss's face that now is not the time to mention the rather unorthodox deployment of Turkey vultures. 'DS Dockery organized a search, brought back soil samples. The lab ran quick PCR tests on them and found scraps of human flesh in the earth. These samples were taken from a huge field, from right across it. And all of them contained the same DNA. Labs then matched those to the familial DNA we took.'

Tompkins is impressed. 'Well done. Another time, this would be our major case of the year.' She glances down at the files on her desk, a mass of papers, the photographs of Jake Timberland and Caitlyn

Lock. 'Was that what you wanted to discuss confidentially, or is there something else?'

'There's more.' Megan gestures to a giant map of Wiltshire on the wall of the office. 'It's where we found Naylor's remains that disturbs me, ma'am.' She gets to her feet, walks over to the map. 'Here.' She lands a finger out in the desolate woods and fields of Salisbury Plain. 'It's barely a mile from where Jake Timberland's body was found.'

Tompkins gets up to join her at the map. She peers at the bleak spot. 'So who owns this section of land?'

'That's what's interesting, ma'am. If you look at the Land Registry, it says the Ministry of Defense owns everything out there. But that's not quite true. I dug around a bit and it transpires they own 99.9 percent. The 0.1 percent they don't own is this section. The bit with our field and our barn in it. The place where we've discovered the remains of two bodies within a matter of days.'

'So whose is it?'

'It's owned by Nathaniel Chase. Or at least it was, until he killed himself. Now it belongs to his son. Gideon.'

122

The rule of three. It was one of the first things that producers taught Caitlyn when she went on *Survivor*.

Rule one: humans can't survive more than three hours exposed to extremely high or low temperatures unless they are wearing proper clothing. Rule two: humans can't survive more than three days without water. Rule three: humans can't survive more than three weeks without food.

Caitlyn thinks they should have added a fourth: humans can't survive when they're imprisoned in a block of stone and mind-fucked by whack-jobs in dressing gowns.

The cramped conditions are physically grueling. The lack of fresh air is an agony. She is permanently shivering with cold. But what's really killing her is the boredom. She's being crushed to death by her own fears and imaginings.

Her teeth chatter. She knows her body temperature is falling critically but there isn't enough room to do any form of exercise vigorous enough to generate heat. They are giving her water but she's dehydrating. The persistent migraines are so bad she feels like she's going to black out. Hunger pains are constant and it's so long ago since she ate she can't remember. In the Camper with Jake. That must have been it. A lifetime ago.

Another stomach cramp chews through her abdomen and Caitlyn doubles up in pain. She knows exactly what's happening to her body. Wishes she didn't. It's eating itself. Chewing through her reserves of fat and muscle. Laying to waste all the years of good nutrition and hard work in the gym. Already she can feel her well-toned biceps and quads softening, shrinking.

After her appearance on *Survivor*, Caitlyn was signed up as an ambassador by GCAP, the Global Call to Action against Poverty. So she knows every dirty detail about starvation. On average, it's how one person dies every second. Four thousand an hour. A hundred thousand a day. Thirty-six million a year. She doesn't want to be one of them. Not another awful statistic.

Dizziness washes over her again. She slides to the floor so she doesn't fall and crack her head. A sickening blackness engulfs her. She's uncertain now whether she's awake or hallucinating. Men are lifting her out of her cell and walking her to the showers. Her vision is blurred and she feels faint, struggling to breathe.

Out of the corner of her eye she sees a dark huddle. People moving toward her. Hooded captors, holding someone.

Jake.

He's alive.

She struggles to focus. Sees him surrounded by other men, robed and mean-eyed. Like the monsters who have been guarding her. He looks naked. His chin is sagging on his chest as they lead him by the arms. She wants to say something but her mouth won't work. Wants to run to him but can barely stand. Blood rushes through her like a queasy tingling virus and she collapses in the smothering dark.

123

Megan and her boss are still staring at the map. They've come to the same conclusion.

Two dead bodies found in such a small area, both discovered within days of each other, and on land owned by a rich and powerful man who unexpectedly killed himself. It's a combination of factors that can't be ignored.

'Pull Gideon Chase in and give him the third degree,' says Tompkins. 'Rattle his cage and see if he's a grieving son as white as pure driven snow or whether there's something else to him.'

'Ma'am, I've been trying to get in touch with him all day, without any luck.' She hesitates before adding, 'I've also been unable to contact DS Dockery. He seems to have gone off radar.'

Tompkins fears this is a classic case of the left hand not knowing what the right is doing. 'Is he already with Chase, Baker?' The thought amuses her. 'Is your DS already a step ahead of you?'

Megan doesn't rise to the bait. 'Perhaps, ma'am. But that doesn't explain why I can't contact either of them. Chase's landline is tripping to answerphone and I've tried both their mobiles and left messages.'

'Then perhaps Jimmy's dragged him out to the middle of the Plain. Reception out there can be bad.' The thought jolts her into a more strategic worry. 'Actually, we need to get operational support to cordon off the scene where you found Naylor's remains and find a forensic archaeologist to search the area.'

'I've already had the scene secured, ma'am. I took the liberty as soon as the results came in. You were unavailable at that time, otherwise I'd have updated you earlier.'

The DCI's door opens and her secretary leans in. 'The Chief and the Deputy would like to see DI Baker, ma'am.'

Tompkins looks surprised. 'Why?'

'I'm afraid I don't know. The Chief's PA didn't give a reason, just said I was to find her urgently.'

In Megan's experience, 'urgently' isn't a good word. Never has been. Never will be.

'I'll come with you.' Tompkins pulls her handbag off the corner of the desk chair. 'If it's urgent for you, it's urgent for me as well.'

124

The Henge Master rises and embraces the new initiate. 'My son, it is so good that you are now with us.' He holds Gideon's head to his face. Hugs him like a father embracing a lost child. 'Sit. You must rest.' He turns to Draco. 'Leave us. I will call for you when we are done.'

The Master smiles as he sits alone with Gideon at the circular stone table. 'The ceremony is draining. You will feel weak and tired for some hours, but your body will heal, regenerate quickly.'

On the table in front of him are wooden platters and jugs of water and juice. The boards are piled with chopped raw fruit.

'The food here is perfect for your purified body. Blueberries, cranberries, figs, bananas. Power foods. Please eat. You need to build your strength.'

Gideon picks a little. He has no appetite. He glances around. The dark stone walls seem to suck all of the light from the room.

'Such a famous fruit and such a powerful symbol, don't you think?' The Master holds an apple in the palm of his hand.

'You mean Adam and Eve?'

'No, no, I don't. I was thinking of something Greek.'

Gideon knows he is being tested. His brain slowly moves up a gear. 'Ah, the Twelve Labors. Heracles had to steal golden apples from the garden of the Hesperides.'

The Master smiles then bites the apple. 'You *are* indeed your father's son.' He nods toward the coded diaries spread at the end of the table. 'When we are finished, I want you to read to me. Explain the code.'

Gideon pulls the stalk from a rich red cherry. 'I have some questions.'

'Ask. This is your time. I am here to help you learn to become a valued member of our Craft.'

'I am curious about the Sanctuary. How and when it was built, where exactly it is.'

The Master smiles. 'You will learn the location of the Sanctuary in good time and when you are fit enough I will personally guide you through its magnificent chambers.'

Gideon looks offended. 'I am still not to be trusted?'

The Henge Master sighs. 'The initiation begins your journey of faith, it does not complete it. I think you know that we are approaching an important time in our calendar. One that no one can jeopardize. After that, we will revisit this issue.'

'The ritual of renewal. I presume that is what you mean.'

'I do. In three days it will be completed and then we will allow you to leave.' He smiles. 'On stepping outside you will know the location of the Sanctuary.' He laughs. 'You will know it instantly.'

'And until then I am to stay here? As what? A prisoner?'

'Of course not. As a scholar. We shall talk every day. You will educate me about Nathaniel's writings.' He picks up a diary from beside him. 'And I will educate you about your duties as a Follower of the Sacreds. It will be time well spent.'

125

The two policewomen don't say much as they walk the short distance to the Chief's office suite. They're asked to wait outside for a moment, then his PA ushers them through.

Alan Hunt and Greg Dockery sit at a conference table not far from the door. Neither seems to notice that Tompkins has tagged along.

'You asked to see me, sir,' says Megan, trying to hide her nerves.

'I did, Detective Inspector.' The Chief flashes a politician's smile and nods to a chair. 'Please sit down.' He looks to Tompkins. 'This is nothing to worry about, Jude.'

'Relieved to hear it, sir. With your office saying it was urgent, I thought you'd appreciate me being here.' She helps herself to a seat alongside Megan.

Hunt ignores the comment and turns to his deputy. Greg Dockery fixes his eyes on Megan. 'We have just been informed that the Home Office are about to publish their annual review.' His tone is almost funereal. 'And it will be highly critical of the Wiltshire Constabulary. Particularly, about our attention – or what they see as our lack of attention – to long-term unsolved cases. With that in mind, we need to be proactive and head off any rebukes.' He musters a smile. 'This is good news for you, Baker. As of this minute, you are the acting head of our new taskforce, Operation Cold Case. If you make sufficient progress, if this appointment heads off the criticism, then you can expect accelerated promotion to the rank of DCI. Congratulations.' He stands up and leans across the desk to shake her hand.

Megan is surprised and confused. 'Thank you, sir.' She rises to grip the extended palm.

'Starting when?' asks Tompkins coldly. 'With respect, we're badly stretched, sir. As well as the Lock case, DI Baker has a very full workload, including a new murder. The timing really isn't good.'

'Starting right now,' says Hunt acidly. 'Timing is never good, Jude. There's always a reason to put off change. We'll assign someone else to clear the DI's workload.'

His deputy picks up the impetus: 'This is a major opportunity for you, Megan. It'll be good for you. The posting is in Swindon. You will need to clear your desk today. You start in the morning.'

She swallows. 'Sir, I have a young daughter who goes to daycare in Hartmoor. I need a little more time.'

Hunt cuts her off. 'You don't have time, Detective Inspector.' He glances at his watch. 'Nor do we. You are very lucky. You've landed a hell of a job. Now go and make the most of it.'

'Yes sir.' Megan leaves in a dignified silence, followed by Jude Tompkins. Once outside the door, the DCI takes her by the arm. 'Come back to my office. We need to talk. You're bright, Baker, but not that bright. Jobs like this don't just fall like rain out of the sky. I would have known if a job as strategic as this was in the offing.'

The DCI doesn't say any more until they're back in the privacy of her own room. She shuts the door and shoots Megan an accusatory stare. 'You are being bumped out of here. Shifted doubly quick. What have you been doing? Is it Jimmy? Have you been bedding that ginger toe-rag?'

Megan is horrified. 'I certainly have not.'

'Good. I credited you with more sense than that. So what is it?'

'This has nothing to do with my private life. And, not that it is any of your business, I'm actually back with my husband.'

'So illuminate me. What the hell is all this to do with, then?'

Megan tries to figure it out. Her boss is right. The new job isn't a bump up, it's a bump out. She's not being promoted. She's being shut down.

Tompkins can't sit. She paces and glares with anger. 'Things have never been busier. We've got a suicide, two murders – Naylor and Timberland – and a VIP kidnapping. And the top brass want to ship out my DI in the middle of it all.' She moves closer to Megan. 'Think, Baker. Think hard about anything unusual you have found or that has happened to you. Tell me about it. Is there anything at all in any of the cases that you have been holding back? Doing a bit more work on. I need to know it all. Now.'

126

FRIDAY 25 JUNE

A night spent on a bed of straw in a stone cell has left Gideon aching from head to toe. The Master can call him a scholar all he likes but he knows exactly what he is. He's a prisoner. No less captive than the pale young woman he saw as they led him from the Great Room. The one in his delusional postinitiation state he thought was his mother. It was the girl off the news. He realizes now. Caitlyn Lock. The daughter of the US Vice President. That was the woman he'd seen. From what he can remember she had a lover, an Englishman. He supposes he is also being held somewhere, probably in a cell like his own.

Then he remembers. Remembers his father's book. Immurement. Ancient Britons adopted the practice of the Greco-Romans. They walled-up errant citizens, confined them in tiny spaces until they starved to death. The Followers employed the same practice to purify the body of the sacrifice and rid the mind of any form of visual or audible stimulus.

Gideon pities her. She must be going insane. Pressed up against dark dusty stone with no way to move and nothing to do. A living hell. He stands and walks his small cell. Seven strides long by three wide. Luxurious compared with how they'll be keeping Caitlyn.

He sits on the straw bed and falls deep in thought. The Sanctuary is a circular structure. He can picture the Descending Passage. The corridor of the Outer Circle. The Great Room. The cleansing area. The Master's chamber. Some outer chambers. The cell that he is in right now. From this firsthand knowledge and the descriptions in his father's diaries, he believes he has a good mental map of the entire place. Including where they must be holding Caitlyn.

There is only one gap in his knowledge.

The exit.

127

Megan has spent another night at her parents' house with Sammy. After news of her so-called 'promotion' and the doubts that Tompkins raised, the last thing she could face was an evening with Adam and his bullet-train desires to resume normal family life as though nothing had ever happened.

She steps in the shower and tries to clear her head. All of yesterday's worries are still there. Gideon is missing. Jimmy is missing. She is going to have to uproot Sammy and move to Swindon.

She towels dry and dresses. Tompkins promised she'd put the skids under the whole change of jobs thing. Slow it down. Make it manageable. But Megan doubts even the DCI will be able to get the Chief and the Deputy to change their minds.

Her parents have fed and dressed Sammy and Megan thanks them and drives to nursery, her mind on autopilot. Yesterday's twist in events has brought her and Tompkins closer together. Closer than they'd ever been. She'd even felt confident enough to confide in her. The DCI had typically demanded every last detail and Megan had given it to her. Everything. Gideon Chase's theories about cults. The disappearing evidence that linked butcher Matt Utley with the break-in at the Chase estate. Everything. She was surprised – and somewhat relieved – she hadn't been laughed out of the station.

Having dropped Sammy and kissed her goodbye, she uses her mobile to phone HR and tell them she's going to the doctors' and can't come in today. Maybe not tomorrow either. She looks at the keypad and then tries the numbers she has for Gideon and Jimmy. Another blank. Gideon's absence can only be bad news. She turns the car around and heads out to Tollard Royal.

It's a sunny, clear day and the hour-long trip is almost therapeutic. It's a tiny village on the southernmost boundary with Dorset. Not much there of tourist interest. A thirteenth-century church and a Quaker burial ground. Only Ashcombe House, home to Cecil Beaton, Guy Ritchie and Madonna, is worthy of note.

At the Chase estate the gates are locked. She presses the buzzer repeatedly and calls his phone lines again. Nothing.

Megan gets out of the car and walks the tall brick walls of the perimeter until she's out of sight of any passing traffic. If Utley found a weak spot in the home's defenses, she can.

And she does. After a little tree-climbing and a jump that Sammy would have applauded, she makes it on to the top of the wall. She goes down on her knees, grips the brick edge, hangs low and drops into the garden. She emerges from the soil and shade on to the long back lawn.

'Gideon!' she shouts up toward the house. Doesn't want to spook him, have him mistake her for another intruder.

It takes several minutes to negotiate the lake and the back of the house. There's no one here. His Audi is parked on the gravel out front and judging from the glistening spider webs spun across the wing mirrors, it hasn't been moved for a while.

Megan rings the bell. Bangs with her fist and shouts his name again, even through the letterbox. Nothing. She scribbles a note for him to call her and pushes it through the metal flap. She withdraws her hand and stands frozen in thought.

The last time she saw Gideon was with Smithsen, right here. And he looked scared. At the time she wrote it off as a psychological reaction to his father's death. Now she knows that she was wrong. Maybe he's even lying dead on the floor inside.

She tries to rationalize. Smithsen wouldn't really kill him, would he? Not after seeing her at the house, not after talking to her, a detective, on the driveway. He'd be mad to. The logic is enough to stop her breaking in. At least until she has spoken to Jude Tompkins.

Megan retraces her steps, climbs back over the wall and heads to her car. As she starts up the engine, she sees a flash of something in her rearview mirror. A man in a green jacket moves quickly out of her line of sight.

She is being watched.

They are following her.

128

Once past the King John Inn, Megan pushes hard on the Ford Focus's accelerator as she heads into the open countryside around Ashmore. Sixty, seventy, eighty. Easy for the little car. If they are tailing her, then they are going to have to show themselves.

Just before a tightish left-hander, she catches a glimpse of another car, way back. It's moving fast. Every bit as fast as she is. It could be the lure of the open road that has tempted the driver to put his foot down. She has to find out.

Megan knows that until they get to the aptly named Zig Zag Hill, the B road offers nothing more testing than gentle bends. The Focus is soon doing way over a hundred. She has opened up at least four hundred meters between her and the following car. As she hits the vicious right-hander at the foot of the hill, she pumps the brakes and the Ford deftly keeps its balance going into the left switchback that instantly follows. Her heart kicks like a mule. She works the brakes again, slowing as quickly as she can without smearing telltale rubber.

Megan glides the car off road into the copse of trees on the right. She stops as deep in the clearing as she can manage. Within seconds, the car behind her zips past. It's a Mercedes. Cream-colored. That's all she can make out.

Now comes the real test. If Merc man is just driving for fun, he'll work the hill and put his foot down as soon as he is clear of the bends. She won't see him again. But if he *is* following her, within the next minute or so, then he's going to be wondering where the hell she is. He'll probably swing it around, check he hasn't missed a turning, maybe even double back.

Megan reverses carefully out of the copse and cautiously resumes her journey to HQ at a more sedate pace.

She sees the Merc just past Cann Common. Pulled up. Brake lights on. Two people in the front. A cheap personalized plate ending: 57MU.

Matt Utley.

She remembers Gideon saying he saw Utley with a gun. The brake lights on the Merc go off and it noses out of the lay-by in front of her. She hits the accelerator and burns through the gears, as though she's going to ram the car. She doesn't. At the last moment she pulls right into a small access road to half a dozen houses set back from the road. It runs parallel to the main road and she uses it like a pit lane on a race track. Only Megan isn't stopping.

The back end of the car drifts as it floats over the grass and tarmac. Somehow she keeps control. Swerves out of the close back on to the B road. Heading right past the Merc. For a second her eyes catch those of the driver. It is Utley all right. She has seen his photograph often enough and long enough not to be mistaken. She thinks she recognized his passenger too. She only got a brief glance of the thickset man in a white shirt, but there was something about his outline, the curve of his shoulders and the shape of his head that was familiar.

She accelerates hard along Higher Blandford Road and doesn't let up until she's crossed Christy's Lane and made it on to the much busier A350.

Megan keeps one eye on her mirror all the way back to Devizes. Her brain is reeling from what she's just been through. What she saw.

The man in the front seat of the car with Utley was her husband. It was Adam.

129

They only let him out to go to the toilet.

The rest of the time, Gideon spends locked in the solitary confinement of the stone cell. They bring him meager food and each passing hour makes him feel more like a prisoner.

He realizes there are only two days to go before the Followers complete the ritual of renewal and offer up the life of the woman he saw. They can't take risks. And he could well be a risk. They know his father tried to stop anyone outside the Craft being sacrificed, so there's a chance he might try to do the same.

The bolts on the door are drawn back. It creaks open. Two robed men walk in, say barely anything, except that he is to be taken to the Master.

He walks the corridor his father walked and imagines the secret life of the man he never really knew. How had *he* felt after *his* initiation? What were *his* thoughts after he'd just been initiated into one of the oldest and most secret brotherhoods in the world?

The Lookers leave Gideon inside their leader's chamber. The Master shows him to the stone table, where Nathaniel's diaries are stacked. His voice is businesslike. 'Time for you to read to me. Illuminate me. Then I will enlighten you.'

Gideon opens one of the last of his father's journals. He knows exactly the passage that he's looking for. He clears his throat and begins: 'If this diary is being read, I pray to the Sacreds that it is *you* Gideon who is doing the reading. You were always the most methodical of children, so I presume you will have started from the beginning and this will be one of the last entries you will read. Now you will know of my differences with the Inner Circle, of their desire to force me to accept their will. I cannot bend to their ways. I must not and I shall not. If you take, so shall you give. *You* personally. Not you by proxy or by threat. It is entirely wrong that if you take, you force someone else to give. This is not the way holy people repay their debts. It is the way of the selfish, the untrustworthy, the dishonorable. The way of a man I deemed a friend. A person I allowed into my own house and trusted like a brother. A man who tainted everything in life that I respected.'

Gideon stops reading, turns the diary round. 'Here.' He places a fingertip besides the inscription '**ΟΩΜΥΖ ΙΥΛΦΗΩΣΚΛ**.' 'Do you recognize this name?'

The Master cannot read the code but he knows he is looking at his own name. It is hardly surprising to him to see it written disparagingly in Nathaniel's diary. It proves something to him. The books are truly as dangerous as he feared they would be. 'Your father and I didn't always see eye to eye. Nor was he right about everything. He was a brilliant man, this you know. But it made him difficult. He couldn't be reasoned with.' He stands, moves away from the table and paces slowly. 'Tell me, do you share his views?'

'On what?'

'On me. On the fellowship. He probably wrote in detail about it. Our differences of opinion, especially as far as the rituals are concerned.'

Gideon responds without hesitation. 'He did. I know better than anyone that my father wasn't always right. For years we barely spoke. Now he is gone.' Gideon pauses reflectively, then looks straight into the Master's eyes. 'My wish is only to experience a long and healthy life. To show my loyalty to the Sacreds and if you help me do this, then of course my unquestioning loyalty to you.'

The Master embraces him. It is the best answer he could have hoped for. Gideon returns the gesture, though he would rather drive a knife through the man's heart.

The Master pulls back and holds him proudly by the arms. 'Now it is time for me to illuminate you, to reveal to you secrets that will leave you breathless.'

130

Megan sits in her car in the supermarket parking lot and waits.

She can't go home and she can't go to work. All she can do is dwell on the awful, fleeting image of Adam in the Mercedes with Utley. It was as bad as catching him in bed with another woman. Yet one more rotten, stinking example of his cheating, lying and betrayal.

She thinks of Sammy and wonders how he can have had the gall to come home to them and play the perfect father and husband while keeping all his secrets. Secrets of belonging to other women, other men, anyone except her and their daughter. Now the sadness turns to anger. Her skin flushes and prickles with the rising rage.

It's late afternoon when an old Jag stops alongside her Focus. The window slides down and the driver breaks Megan's festering mood by shouting, 'Get in.'

The waiting is over.

DCI Jude Tompkins listens patiently as Megan tells her about being followed by Utley and her husband Adam. She calls for a vehicle check and confirms the Mercedes is registered to Matthew Stephen Utley of Tidworth. 'I could check on your husband's movements over the last couple of hours but not without people asking me why I want to know.'

'Don't bother,' says Megan. 'I know it was him.' She chews at a blooded nail. 'I feel so stupid. I thought he came back because he wanted to be with me and Sammy.'

'You'll have time to beat yourself up about that later,' says her boss. 'Right now we have to work out what to do about your daughter. Who we can turn to without raising suspicions.'

'Mum has Sammy,' says Megan. 'I called her and said Adam has been aggressive with me. She won't let him in the house or near Sam. My dad is at home too, so everything will be okay.'

'Good. I did some checking this morning. Double-checking, if you like, to make sure we weren't jumping to the wrong conclusions.'

'And?'

Tompkins slides a mugshot out of her handbag. 'Sean Elliott Grabb.'

'Suspect with his prints on the VW Campervan.' Megan takes the picture. 'Worked security at Stonehenge.'

'Right. He's dead. Turned up in Bath. Fished out of the Avon.'

'Murdered?'

'Too early to tell,' says Tompkins. 'Grabb and Stonehenge. That's yet another connection to the Timberland, Lock and Chase cases. There are far too many coincidences for my liking.'

'So what do we do, ma'am? Where do we take this?'

'That's what I'm worried about.' Tompkins gives her a studied look. 'The Chief and Deputy want you out of Devizes, right? They're packing you off to Swindon. So I don't think we can trust either of them.'

'What about Jimmy Dockery? Any sign of him?'

'He's done a Lord Lucan. Completely vanished.' She scratches the back of her head. 'I'm thinking of taking all this out of force, going to Barney Gibson, the Met Commander.'

Megan is surprised. 'He's going to think you're mad.'

Tompkins smiles. 'I know. That's why you are going to tell him, not me.'

131

The Henge Master guides Gideon through the mazy inner sanctums of the Sanctuary. He raises his hands toward the chiseled walls and ceilings. 'The ancients quarried far and near for this stone. It was hand-picked and dressed by initiated builders. The precision was incredible. Each piece sanctified by the Sacreds. Two million individual blocks interlocked. The entire structure erected without mortar.'

Gideon rubs a hand along the smooth walls as they walk. The twisting corridors become narrower and the ceiling height falls as they descend into the heart of the temple. 'Why has this place never been discovered?'

The Master smiles. 'Because there is no reason to look for it. No one knows of its existence and all archaeological digs are focused around Stonehenge. Occasionally there are finds – a wooden henge in line with the Sacreds, a crematorium, the bones of dead soldiers, ancient axes and tools. This is enough to satisfy academic appetitites.'

'But there is more?'

'*Much* more,' says the Master. 'Not only the Sanctuary but other sacred places that are all aligned and linked, blessed and protected. And not just here. Across the world.'

Gideon is dazzled by the extent of the unknown. He has a thousand questions.

'Come,' urges the Master walking again. 'In all, it took more than a hundred thousand people over two centuries to complete the

Sanctuary and Stonehenge.' The Master leads him through a spiraling labyrinth of tunnels. 'They quarried without machines, used rough wooden sleds and their hands to haul titanic weights hundreds of miles, sometimes across deep stretches of water. They built scaffolding from felled trees, ropes and pulleys from grasses, tree bark and vines. They dug a fully functional and entirely original sewerage system. It still works perfectly. Channeled through the plain to the Sanctuary to fall into deep chalk pits fed by underground streams.' He stretches upward and touches an open hole in the sandstone blocks. 'Ancient air ducts ensure a steady flow of oxygen. These vertical tunnels are also star shafts. They point to specific stars, certain constellations. The Sanctuary is a precessional clock that also allows us to keep our charts and calendars, just as our forefathers did.'

The Master leads them through a narrow arch into a passageway running directly below the Great Room. 'While the Sanctuary's initial purpose was to be a temple for the Sacreds, it was also a Neolithic teaching hospital, a form of university cum town hall where science, health and administration were practiced.'

'Their society was that advanced?' asks Gideon.

'Every era has its outstanding leaders, even the Neolithic one.' The Master walks on through the passageway and produces a large iron key hung on brown string around his neck. 'Let me illustrate the point.' He unlocks a narrow oak door and they slide through into the pitch black.

The air is even cooler and their footsteps echo even louder. The Master lights a wall torch and several large, floor-level candles. As their eyes adjust, they see a large and perfectly circular chamber dominated by a dark block in the middle. The vast walls are hewn from bloodred granite, reminiscent of Egyptian tombs. On the walls to the left and the right as far as Gideon can see are dozens and dozens of open coffins all angled so the skulls of the dead have a perfect view of the large Pantheon-like single star shaft in the center of the room.

'A crypt,' observes Gideon. 'Who were these people and why the special treatment?'

'These are the ancients. Our predecessors. The brilliant men who designed and built the Sanctuary, Stonehenge and all the henges, barrows, burial mounds and avenues linked to them.' The Master moves slowly around the room lighting more torches and candles. 'But this is more than a sacred resting place, Gideon.'

The giant stone block in the middle becomes increasingly visible. Fashioned out of polished sandstone, it is at least five meters high and three meters wide. On two sides are shelves filled with maps and scrolls. The other two are divided into what look like dozens of small ovens filled with rubble.

Gideon is amazed. He approaches it like a cat stalking a bird.

The young archaeologist is almost too afraid to touch anything. It is a library. A museum. A time capsule filled with ancient scripts, artifacts, carvings and tools.

'How far back does this go?' he asks.

'Right to the beginning.' The Master points to the top of the cube. 'Up there you will find original carvings. The first plans for the Sanctuary and Stonehenge. Over there in the largest coffins you see the remains of the first sacrifices, those who completed the Sanctuary and the henge.'

'The builders were sacrificed?'

'It was their will. They knew that in offering themselves to the Sacreds, they ensured blessings for their children and the generations to follow.'

Gideon stands in awe. Around him is an archaeologist's dream. An Aladdin's Cave of ancient history and civilization. The discovery of a lifetime. His pulse races. 'I never read anything about any of this. In all the diaries I found, there was no mention of this place or anything in it.'

'Nor should there have been. Speaking of it, or writing about it, is forbidden.' The Master moves closer to him, smiles again. 'Nathaniel knew of this chamber. He did much work in here. Among the parchments and documents in the archive, you will find his own labors, contributions to the star maps and charts that all Masters are obliged to complete.'

So much history in one space. So much knowledge. So many secrets. The Master breaks the spell by motioning to the door. 'We must go. I have more to show you and very little time in which to do it.'

Reluctantly, Gideon leaves the chamber and the Master extinguishes all the lights, relocks the door. They walk to the end of the passage and begin a steep and precarious climb up a seemingly endless flight of open-sided stone steps. They cling like ivy to the outer wall of the Sanctuary. No safety panels or guard rails. A sheer brutal drop beside them.

'Take care,' says the Master. 'You may still be a little weak from the initiation.'

It's good advice. After more than a hundred steps, Gideon finds himself sweating and struggling for breath. The man in front pushes on like a mountain goat, taking each stone slab with a powerful and confident stride.

Gideon keeps one palm on the wall. He notices the intricate carvings in the stone. Ancient art depicting farmers working fields, women carrying babies, herds of cattle gathering by streams. Across the walls he sees other scenes. Workers raising giant blocks of stone, the first outlines of the henge being formed. People at burial mounds, their heads hung low. Scenes showing the orbit of the sun, the constellations of the stars and the phases of the moon. Up above, there is a more frightening depiction.

Men in robes are gathered around a bound figure over the Slaughter Stone, the hammer of the Master is raised. It reminds him that the young American woman, the one from the news, is immured somewhere below them.

He sways on the steps.

A hand grabs a clump of his robing. The Henge Master pulls him tight to the wall. 'Be careful.'

He steadies himself and breathes slowly. 'I'm okay.'

'Good. Then we go on.'

Within a few steps, they reach the top. Gideon sees now that there is another set of stone stairs descending on the other side, running straight down toward the chambers and the Great Room.

The Master again uses the key from around his neck.

The area that Gideon steps into is a world removed from the archive chamber and in its own way even more surprising.

The first thing that strikes him is the light. The bright white fuzz of fluorescent tubes, flickering and buzzing like trapped and angry ghosts. The floor and the walls are gray. But not stone. Concrete. Plaster. It is as though he has walked into a giant modern warehouse or garage.

In front of him is what he guesses is an acre of sealed concrete. Hundreds of meters of plastered walls. The Master walks forwards on to a slatted steel gantry some ten meters above the floor. Gideon follows. There are vehicles parked at the far end. Chunky 4×4s and something distinctly familiar. Draco's white builder's van.

The place is more than a garage. He can feel it in his gut, long before his eye roams over the vast grayness. The space is divided into other distinct areas. There are dozens of metal lockers; clusters of changing benches, tables and chairs. A kitchen section with rows of sinks; endless worktops to cut and prepare food on; lines of tall refrigerators and freezers; microwaves, stoves, ovens and pans.

Enough room and equipment in here to feed an army.

'It's our operational center,' says the Master casually. 'Belowground we respect our traditions in the way our ancestors did. Above the surface, we are an elite force. Tomorrow you will come here and work. You will play your part in the preparations for the great day.'

132

SATURDAY 26 JUNE, ONE DAY
TO THE NEW FULL MOON

Dawn sleepily pulls at the dark curtains of the sky like a red-faced toddler tugging blankets at the foot of its parents' bed. Lookers surround the dew-soaked fields of Stonehenge. They stand in the empty parking lot. No tourists have been allowed to book any early visits to the site.

The Henge Master walks the public footpath trodden by millions, steps across the newly cut grass. Enters the iconic circle. Today will last sixteen hours, thirty-seven minutes and five seconds. The altitude of the sun is 61.9 degrees.

Tomorrow it will make its first major shift for ten days and drop to 61.8. He looks to the ever-changing sky as he enters the horseshoe of trilithons.

Moonset was more than an hour ago. There is no sign of the lady in white. She dances in the unseen darkness almost a quarter of a million miles away. At nine tonight she will return and she will appear in 98 percent of her full virgin glory.

Almost ready.

A gentle wind blows across the open fields. The Master stretches out his arms to feel the energy of the Sacreds. Everything that happens from now on is about precision. Precision, alignment and the final will of the gods.

133

Caitlyn has never prayed. Her father comes from lapsed Jewish stock and her mother from a brand of Protestantism so casual she might as well have been an atheist.

The only things her family have ever believed in are fairness, goodness and kindness. Do unto others as you'd have them do unto you. Not the kind of upbringing that prepares you for being held hostage, immured in stone and starved to death. That's where she has been since she injured herself and they moved her. In a tiny immurement cavity stuffed with memory foam. She can feel it against most of her front and back. Like being sandwiched between mattresses.

Caitlyn closes her eyes and tries to pray. Her mind is such a spiky jumble of fear that she can't even focus a single silent plea to any or all spiritual saviors. For the first time since they locked her up, she starts to cry.

134

It is exactly eight a.m. when Megan follows her DCI into Barney Gibson's makeshift office. She last saw him and his operational sidekick Stewart Willis six days ago, but the two men look ten years older. Endless shifts, sleepless nights and the stress of the inquiry are breaking their health.

Tompkins lays it out for them. 'Almost a week ago, DI Baker sat in this same room and told you that she believed Caitlyn Lock and Jake Timberland had been on their way to Stonehenge when he was killed and she was abducted. We have information that now seems to confirm that. And we think we know who is responsible. Incredible as it seems, there is good reason to believe that an ancient pagan cult may be behind the abduction.'

'Unlikely,' says Willis. 'We have reliable intelligence that an international crime syndicate has Lock. Ransom demands have already been made.'

Tompkins holds her ground. 'I'd ask you to stay openminded, sir. What DI Baker is about to tell you is going to sound fanciful but I assure you that there is strong circumstantial evidence to support it.'

Gibson is starting to think it was a mistake to consent to this confidential meeting. 'Jude, why didn't you take this to John Rowlands or your own Chief?'

She knows she's on thin ice. 'Sir, there is a possibility that my own force may be implicated. Physical and electronic evidence has already been tampered with. The inquiry could be compromised from within.'

'Those are very serious allegations. You put me in a difficult position.'

'I do, sir. And I apologize. But given the circumstances, I believe it is entirely appropriate that we seek your guidance as senior external officers heading this major investigation.'

'Point made.' He turns to Megan. 'So, Detective Inspector, what's the story?'

Megan knows she's only got one shot at maintaining her credibility. 'While investigating the suicide of Professor Nathaniel Chase, a published archaeologist and world-renowned expert on Stonehenge, his son Gideon made me aware of diaries written by the professor about a secret cult dedicated to the stones of the henge.'

'Druids?' interjects Willis.

'No, sir. This society predates any druid movement. If you need a comparison, think of the Freemasons. I believe we are talking about an ancient craft-based order that has matured over centuries and wields considerable power and influence.' No sooner have the words crossed her lips than she regrets them. If either Willis or Gibson is a Freemason, her case is dead in the water. 'Sir, coded diaries discovered by Gideon Chase suggest that the cult derives some form of blessings and protection from Stonehenge providing human sacrifices are periodically made to their gods.'

The two men are looking at each other, thin smiles on their lips. 'I find this very hard to believe. Human sacrifice is unknown in modern day Europe,' says Gibson. 'Even in America, where they have more than their share of extremists, there are only a few documented cases over the past hundreds of years. I'm really struggling to buy into this theory of yours.'

'I was too, sir,' says Megan. 'But certain events have changed my mind.'

Willis glances impatiently at his watch. 'And they are?'

'It all seems to come back to Stonehenge. It is at the center of all our recent major cases. Nathaniel Chase, an expert on the henge, commits suicide. Lock and Timberland are attacked while visiting the stones. Sean Grabb, one of the men we wanted to interview about those attacks, is found dead in Bath. He was working security at Stonehenge. And all of this happens around the summer solstice.'

Gibson seems interested. Or maybe amused. It's hard for Megan to tell. 'Sir, I've checked the medical records of Gideon Chase. He told me he had cancer as a child and the stones cured him. According to the records, his claim seems to be true.'

Willis frowns. For him, it's just not credible. 'Are you telling me that his medical records say he was cured of cancer by a ring of stones?'

'No, sir. They say he had an incurable form of cancer and was cured. They give no explanation, simply because they couldn't find one.'

Gibson lets out a sigh of exasperation. 'DCI Tompkins said evidence had been tampered with. What evidence and what tampering?'

Megan realizes his patience is wearing thin. She summarizes as tightly as possible. 'Someone broke into and set fire to the home of Nathaniel Chase. But not before trying to recover or destroy something of value. We think the intruder was after the secret diaries we now know the professor had written about Stonehenge and the cult connected to it. His son Gideon managed to take a camera-phone snap of the burglar. Our facial recognition software produced a match with a local man. And we also recovered physical evidence from the break-in. Tools in a kit bag that had been left behind. When I last checked, sir, all that evidence was missing from the property store. All trace of it had been wiped from the computer log. As had the electronic bulletin sent to my mailbox about the facial match. Everything had been erased from my files.'

Gibson makes notes then looks up at Tompkins. 'We need to talk separately about this and how we handle it.'

She nods.

The Met Commander sits back and weighs up Megan. As crazy as everything sounds, she seems a first-class officer and not the type to get carried away on flights of fancy. He is also aware that she is supposed to be in Swindon setting up a new cold case unit. What she shouldn't be doing is speaking confidentially to him behind her chief's back.

He leans forward and clasps his hands on the desk. 'You're an experienced officer, Megan, so I'm sure you're aware that our investigation is on a knife edge. We have the FBI, Interpol, private investigators and most British police forces all chasing leads. The strongest of interagency evidence demonstrates that an international crime syndicate has taken Caitlyn and is extorting money from her parents. The asking price is currently twenty million dollars. I respect the manner in which you came to us, but at the moment I cannot risk deploying resources to investigate your claims, I—'

'But sir—'

He stops her. 'Let me finish.' A stern pause. 'I need proof. I need to see the coded diaries you mentioned. I need evidence that there have been human sacrifices in the past. I need something forensic before I even think about switching precious time and people away from where I have directed them. Bring me that and you'll get a different response.'

Tompkins pushes her chair back. 'Thank you, Commander.' She nods to Willis. 'Chief Superintendent. I'd like the assurance that this conversation remains confidential for the moment. For obvious reasons.'

'You have it,' says Gibson. 'But only for the moment.'

135

The day before the ritual is the start of a holy period. A time of reverence. The Master, the Inner Circle and all Followers begin a devout fast. They do it out of respect for the sacrifice. They drink only water. They abstain from any sexual acts of any kind, either practiced or witnessed, until the first evening twilight after the completion of the ceremony.

The Henge Master explains the pursuit of purity to Gideon as they sit in his chamber. 'The ritual of renewal is sacred to us. But that does not mean we are barbarians. No. The most important person among us right now is the one who will be sacrificed.' He rests his left hand on the four diaries. 'I believe that through your father you may well have learned more about the sanctity of life and its meaning in death than most.'

Gideon is unsure where this is leading. 'All I know is, he was willing to give his life to save mine. To give me the chance to raise children of my own.'

'Exactly. A single sacrifice for the greater good of the many.' The Master studies the young man opposite him. 'It is our practice that one of our Followers, usually a member of the Inner Circle, spends the last stressful hours in the company of the sacrifice. To give moral and spiritual support until the very last moment. And to ensure that nothing can happen to them before the ritual begins. This is a role, Gideon, that I would like you to perform for us.'

He can't hide his shock. 'I don't understand. Why me?'

The Master smiles. 'I think you do, Gideon. I think you know why I have shown you mercy and favor. Why I have invested my personal trust and faith in you, despite those close to me doubting the wisdom of letting you live.'

Gideon feels a chill creep through him.

'It is important to me that I go into the ritual with a clear mind and an open spirit. Tell me, Gideon. Is there something your father told you that you haven't shared with me?'

Gideon shakes his head. His denial is true. But he knows what the Master is driving at. He sees his mother again. The frail old woman whom he barely recognizes sits up once more in her deathbed. She speaks the words that turn his life upside down.

Nathaniel is not your father, Gideon.

The Henge Master reads it in his eyes. 'Then your mother told you. *I* am your father, not Nathaniel Chase.'

136

Megan pulls the car into the curb a street away from her house and walks the rest of the way. She's trying to cool down. The meeting with Gibson and Willis had been a waste of time. Made her and Tompkins look foolish. The DCI said as much. The two Met men hadn't believed a word that had been said. They wanted facts. Wouldn't listen to anything else.

Megan feels alone. Vulnerable. Edgy. She's not just walking to cool down, she's also taking precautions. Adam might be at the house. Adam, the husband she thought she was falling in love with again. Adam, the man she saw sitting alongside burglar and police attacker, Matt Utley. She can't see any strange cars near her home. She loiters in the quiet cul-de-sac for almost five minutes before she feels safe enough to go inside.

The house is empty. But he's been here. She knows he has because there's a note propped up on the dining table, bearing his writing. She snatches it away from the vase of flowers.

'Meg. Gone back to mine. Call me when you've got your head together.

A x.

P.S. – we need to talk about me seeing Sammy.'

She screws it up, drops it in a full pedal bin. Her heart is racing. She gathers swimming clothes and thick towels for her and her daughter, takes a quick look around and then steps out on to the drive and locks the door.

There's a man there. A man who has been watching her home and waiting for her.

137

Father and son look at each other across the ancient stone table.

'When did you find out?' asks Gideon.

The Master bows his head. 'Not until Marie was dying.' He looks up, his eyes glassy. 'Nathaniel sent for me when she was in the hospice. She told me just hours before she passed. There was nothing I could do. It was too late to seek intervention.'

Gideon is surprised to feel anger rising. 'And what was she to you?'

The Master scowls. 'What *was* she? She was everything. Everything and nothing. She was the woman I couldn't have but would have married. The person I would have spent my life with had we not argued and drifted apart. If she hadn't met Nathaniel.'

'What do you mean?'

'We were childhood sweethearts. After our relationship broke up, she moved away, to Cambridge. It was there that she met Nathaniel, and married him. I didn't see her until a year after the wedding when she moved back to Wiltshire.'

Gideon does the maths. His sainted mother had apparently broken her marriage vows with the monster sitting opposite him only a year after pledging her eternal love to the man he thought was his father. 'How could you?' He stands, face flushed with anger. 'She'd only just got married and you seduced her.'

'It wasn't anything like that,' says the Master, undisturbed by Gideon's rage. 'It just happened. You'd have to understand how intensely I loved your mother to begin to realize how that one moment of weakness surprised us both.'

'One moment?' Gideon doubts it. 'I was the result of one moment of weakness?'

The Henge Master gets to his feet and comes round the stone table. 'I had no idea until your mother passed. How could I then approach Nathaniel? What could I have said to him about you?'

'Did you know the cancer was genetic?'

He nods.

'And you persuaded my father to join the Craft to protect your own son, to protect me?'

'Yes. It is what a father should do. I needed to protect you.'

The Master embraces him. Holds him tight. As tight as a father would hold his long lost child.

138

Jimmy Dockery steps down the driveway toward Megan. He can see she is scared. 'Don't be frightened, boss.'

But she is. She backs off, retreats toward her own front door.

'I need to talk to you.' He takes another slow step her way.

She drops her handbag, turns the keys in her clenched right fist into a spiked knuckleduster.

He glances at the makeshift weapon, a dismissive look on his face. 'You want to fight me?'

'Come any closer, Jimmy, and I'll kill you.'

He can tell she means it. He doesn't have much time. He lurches forward and makes a pretend grab with his left hand. Megan falls for it. She throws a spiky cross with her right. He steps inside and blocks hard with his left forearm, knocking the keys from her fingers. He could pick her off now with one knockout blow to the jaw. Instead, he snatches her left wrist and whips it up behind her back. Slaps his other hand across her mouth.

Before she knows it, he's bundled her around the side of the house. She tries to kick out but Jimmy is wise to it. He spreads his legs and holds her like an adult would a kicking toddler in a tantrum.

'I'm not going to hurt you.'

Megan carries on kicking.

'Boss, stop it. You were right, okay? I've been following Smithsen and you're right.'

She's not sure that she heard him properly. But she caught enough to stop thrashing and fighting.

Jimmy takes his hands off her.

She turns to face him. 'What did you say?'

'I know where they go. Where Smithsen and the others meet.'

139

The Henge Master opens the diary and points to his own name. ΟΩΜΥΖ ΙΥΛΦΗΩΣΚΛ. 'James Pendragon,' he says aloud. He puts a fist to his heart in a gesture of pride. 'It's a name to be proud of. A family line that stretches back through Celtic times. Back to the most famous king of Briton. Back into the mists of mythology and beyond. We are the stuff of history you and I.'

Gideon is familiar with both fact and the fiction. 'King Arthur is more fairy tale than reality,' he says.

The rebuke does nothing to cool the Master's familial passion. 'Really? Arthur Pendragon, the great Briton King? Or Riothamus the King, or the Cumbrian King, Pennine King, King of Elmet, Scottish King, Powysian King or even the Roman King? You think all these are kings of fantasy? You are a learned man. These legends are rooted in more than mere myth. They have endured.'

'And you?' asks Gideon, a hint of bitterness in his voice. 'What of you is fact and fiction?'

The Master shrugs. 'I am certainly no king, but I do serve and lead our people, the Followers. I am the only child of Steven George and Alice Elizabeth Pendragon.'

'Are they still alive?'

'Very much so. Your grandfather is ninety and your grandmother eighty this year. Both are in excellent health.'

Gideon's emotions are in turmoil. Despite her deathbed confession, he still yearns for his mother, and still feels guilty about what happened between him and Nathaniel. Now he is face-to-face with his birth father and a family tree of mythical dimensions that overwhelms him.

The Henge Master senses the dilemma. 'You will need time to come to terms with things.' He grips his arm. 'Thankfully, we will have it. Once the ritual is over, we can get to know each other. Find ways to bridge the years.'

Gideon still has dozens of unanswered questions but not now. Now is a time of silence. Inner thought.

'So,' says the Master. 'Will you accept the task that I asked of you? Can I rely on you to be the last companion for the girl, the chosen one?'

Gideon nods.

'Good. Very good.' The Master embraces him again.

As they come apart, they lock eyes. 'You are no longer Gideon. You are Phoenix. Your given name is Phoenix.'

He is confused. 'I understood Followers adopted star signs that began with the initial letter of their first name.'

'They do,' says Pendragon, his face suddenly stern again. 'The name I always wanted for my son was Philip. It is what I always called you when I thought of you. From now on, you will be known as Phoenix.'

It feels like a crude trick, a psychological blow to undermine him. This disownment of his name hurts him. Strips him of his identity.

'Our family motto is a simple one,' says Pendragon. '*Temet Nosce.* Thine own self thou must know.'

140

'You nearly broke my damned arm, Jimmy.' Megan nurses her bruised limb.

'Sorry,' he says. 'I tried to stop you without hurting you. I could have been much rougher.'

She straightens out her clothes. 'Bully for you. Where the hell did you learn that physical stuff?'

'Got picked on a lot at school. Ginger hair, makes you a target. My old man took me to taekwondo lessons.'

'Tompkins is going to kick your arse. You've been off radar so long.' She stretches her arm several times.

'You told her?'

'Had to tell someone.'

Jimmy realizes he's at the point where he has to explain things. 'You didn't trust me, I could tell, so I went off to find something that would prove to you that I wasn't part of this crazy cult tied to the dead professor and Stonehenge.'

She looks at him suspiciously. 'And did you?'

'I followed Utley and Smithsen. They certainly know each other. Caught Utley at home and followed his Merc. He met up with Smithsen in a lay-by on the A360. They got into the back of Smithsen's van, maybe he took something out. Then went their separate ways.'

'Which ways?'

'Utley back east toward Tidworth and Smithsen headed west.'

She maps it out in her head. 'There isn't much out there, not until you loop north to Devizes.'

'It's all military. Part of the MOD buy-up.'

'Did you stay on Utley? Or follow Smithsen?'

'Decided to go after Smithsen. As far as I could.'

'And?'

'He went north past Westdown Camp and Tilshead. After a couple of miles, he forked sharp left. Toward Imber.'

'Imber?'

'It's a ghost town. Way into restricted access. No one has lived there for more than sixty years. It's just empty houses. Buildings remain standing but no one is home. The church still holds the odd service every year.'

Megan remembers the map on Tompkins' office wall and her

records search. 'It's where Nathaniel Chase owns a strip of land. One of the few bits that the War Office couldn't buy up.'

'Can't think why anyone would want to own it. From what I know, soldiers just shoot the shit out of the place. Then drive over it in tanks and even bomb the land around it.'

'A lot of work for a builder?' ventures Megan.

'Doubt it. The army would just fix it up themselves. They'd use squaddies to do basic bricklaying and bang up some boards on doors and windows.'

She weighs things up. If Gideon Chase is still missing, it's possible he is being held somewhere in Imber. They could be holding Lock there as well. 'I don't know what to do, Jimmy. I can't go to Tompkins with this and your old man and the Chief want me transferred to Swindon.'

'What?'

'I'm being bumped. Shifted sideways. It's a long story. How do we get to look around Imber without anyone at work finding out?'

'I know exactly how.' He gives her a confident smile. 'In fact, I've already got someone who can help us. He's waiting in my car.'

141

The chamber they've moved Gideon to is much bigger than the last one. About six meters long by four meters wide, he'd say. A penthouse compared with the matchbox they've been keeping him in. But it is still a cell.

The door is open, flanked by two Lookers, one of whom Gideon has seen before with Draco. Inside, high on all four walls are burning torches. On the hard stone ground are two makeshift wooden bunks filled with straw. In the corner of the room, two narrow stone troughs filled with water.

If he's right, the chamber is no more than a twisting fifty meters of corridor from the steep stairwell that leads to the warehouse. It doesn't take him long to work out why that is. They bring the girl here so it's easy to move her into a waiting vehicle.

Gideon hears footsteps outside. A mix of men's voices, shadows across the gated doorway and then four Lookers lumber into the cell. At first he doesn't see the woman between them. Two of the men lift her under her arms while others grab her feet. They swing her on to a bunk.

One of the men is Draco. He hangs back while the first two Lookers leave. 'She is weak, hasn't eaten anything for almost seven days.' He puts his arm around the well-built Looker next to him. 'This is Volans. He's going to be right outside the chamber. He has instructions to fetch a doctor if you think her condition is deteriorating. Do you understand?'

Gideon nods.

'Good, because this woman must not die. Her health is our single priority. For the next day at least.' He gives Gideon a soldierly slap and steps out of the cell with Volans, shutting the iron door behind them.

Gideon wonders if the Master has told Draco about him. About their relationship. It would be the clever thing to do if he was worried about the support of the Inner Circle. It's what he would have done in his position.

He takes his first look at the sacrifice. Easy to imagine that not so long ago she was very pretty. Even without makeup and her thick black hair matted, he can tell she is naturally attractive. Her short hooded robe has ridden up and he can see a flash of a Union Jack tattoo, a sign of another time, a symbol of flirtatious rebellion and youthful defiance. Gideon bends over her and pulls it down to preserve her modesty.

She slaps his hand away. 'Leave me alone.'

He is startled and steps back.

The woman sits up defensively in the bunk. Disorientated. Fear ingrained in her eyes. 'Keep away. Keep away from me!'

'I'm not going to hurt you. Honestly, I'm not.'

She looks around. Her prayers haven't been fully answered but at least she's no longer in that claustrophobic hellhole. She can breathe and stretch. And lie down. She looks at the stranger near her, her eyes almost black.

'Who are you? Why are you in here with me?'

142

A mountain of man gets out of Jimmy's black Golf GTI. 'Josh Goran, ma'am. Pleased to meet you.'

He towers over Megan as they shake hands. He has short dark hair, blue eyes, looks like he has been hewn from granite. Then it comes to her. He's the guy from the TV news appeals. From Kylie Lock's press conference. She guesses Jimmy has already told him about her. 'You'd better come inside. We can talk better there.' They follow into the cottage. And once the door is closed, Jimmy fills in some of the gaps. 'Josh has been retained by Caitlyn's mother to find her.'

'And return her safely,' adds Goran.

'I know,' Megan says. 'You're some kind of bounty hunter cum private eye, right?'

'Rescue and return operative,' he says. 'I have two decades' experience in what is the US equivalent of your SAS. Only better.' He cracks a Hollywood grin. 'Ma'am, I think we're kindred spirits. Seems you and I are both being kept out of the loop. It's why Jimmy here came to me.'

'I don't know anything about that,' she confesses.

'With due respect, ma'am, I think you probably know more than most.'

'Meaning?'

'From the intelligence that I've gathered – and believe me, I've gathered a lot – your local police, the FBI guys, I think they're giving too much credence to this theory that Caitlyn's been kidnapped by an organized gang and is being held in France somewhere.' He nods toward Jimmy. 'I think you and Jim are much more likely to be on the right trail, ma'am.'

She can't help but interrupt. 'Josh, you're going to drive me crazy calling me ma'am. Megan will do.'

'Megan,' he says, through a whiter-than-white smile. 'In my experience if you kidnap someone and take them abroad, you leave traces. Driving's the easiest option. But you do that and you have to dodge a whole lot of surveillance cameras. You got to buy ferry or train tickets, without being seen or recognized. These days that's impossible. You flee the country, you leave signs. But in this case the Feds, your British police and my operatives, they've come up with zip. You know why? Because the perps never left the country. They're still here. Still local.'

Megan agrees. But there are still loose ends. 'What about the recordings of Caitlyn?'

He shrugs. 'Not necessarily what they seem. Be easy enough to have made the recordings of Caitlyn here and then had a guy catch the Eurostar from London and play an edited tape down a French phone line. Point of contact proves nothing.'

'Except that the kidnappers are well organized,' adds Jimmy.

'You can bet on that,' says Goran. 'These guys are very well organized. Part of the reason I think they've set up camp right in the middle of that military no-go zone.'

'Imber is owned and patrolled by UK forces,' says Megan. 'It's impossible for anyone to go in and out of there without clearance.'

Goran grins. 'Not at all. You have working farms nearby and there's a public footpath thirty miles long that runs around the firing ranges. Besides, the military have the dumbest guards alive. Believe me, I've worked with them most of my life.'

Megan smiles. 'So do you think you could work out a way to get in?'

'I'm ahead of you. I'm taking a surveillance team out there tonight. Zero one hundred hours to be precise. You want in?'

PART FIVE

Little Imber on the Downe,
Seven miles from any Towne,
Sheep bleats the unly sound,
Life twer sweet with ne'er a vrown,
Oh let us bide on Imber Downe.'

– *Anon.*

143

SUNDAY 27 JUNE, THE DAY OF RENEWAL,
0100 HOURS

The black Ford Transit that rolls south from Devizes down the deserted A360 bears the green letters 'ATE' and a fluttering red flag. Beneath the official logo of the Army Training Estate are the words 'Specialist Scientific Research Unit'.

The van's six occupants wear high-visibility rainproof jackets emblazoned with the same crest. They carry in their pockets laminated ID cards and official authorization to conduct a nocturnal wildlife survey in and around the IRPP, the Imber Range Perimeter Path, that skirts the live-firing area.

Megan looks around at the team and can't help but be impressed. 'It's amazing what you can pull together when you are chasing a potential pay check of ten million dollars.'

'Indeed it is,' says Josh Goran, sitting in the back on a flip-down seat opposite her. 'Take a bow, Troy my boy.'

Troy Lynton looks up from the submarine glow of his laptop screen and gives a modest smile.

'Troy's our cyber king,' explains Goran. 'The world's best hacker, forger and fixer. Give him a little time and there's nowhere in the virtual world he can't access and nothing he can't steal or alter.'

Megan and Jimmy are crammed in the back with the two Americans. The driver is a man called Jay, who appears to be English. The front passenger is Luc, a former Dutch soldier who has been working with the crew for the past two years.

'Right now there are no major military maneuvers planned at Imber, so troop numbers are minimal,' says Goran. 'Most guys will be lying back at barracks or bedding locals. We should be able to move around without restriction.'

Half an hour later, the van's headlights illuminate a warning sign: LIVE FIRING RANGE CLOSED TO THE PUBLIC: KEEP OUT.

The Transit trundles slowly on, then pulls over in front of a deserted farmhouse. Jay guides the vehicle up behind it, out of sight of the main road.

'Okay,' says Goran. 'Let's move.'

They grab backpacks and quickly spread in different directions. Goran has equipped them all with two-way radios, compasses, night-vision goggles, flashlights and, for the sake of the cover story, cameras and clipboards. Lynton has also briefed them on Imber's stone curlews, roe deer and badgers.

They move silently past shells of buildings, windowless and doorless brick hulks more reminiscent of Kosovo than Wiltshire. Once-beautiful thatched roofs have been replaced with rusted corrugated iron. Wildflower gardens have become mud pits, churned by the caterpillar tracks of tanks. Sprouting in the darkness, they see a red-and-yellow sign declaring, DANGER: UNEXPLODED MILITARY DEBRIS.

Jimmy and Megan stick to the instructions Goran has given them and methodically work their way through the ruins of Imber. English Jay does the same along a northern stretch toward Littleton Down, while Goran scouts the outer parts of West Lavington Down and Lynton works east through Summer Down.

They search for three hours. And find nothing.

As they regroup, Goran lays out a map on the hood of the van and jabs a finger south of Imber. 'This here is the very heart of the firing range. The military call it the danger zone. We've barely been in it. So far, we've just skirted the outer areas.'

Jay glances at the topography. He's still catching his breath. 'It would take all day to drive around that amount of land, let alone walk it and search it.'

No one argues with him.

'So now we have to make a decision,' says Goran. 'It'll be sunrise any minute. If we carry on, there's a high risk of being stopped and no longer any documented excuse for us being here.'

'We need another cover,' says Lynton. 'We simply swap the nocturnal survey for a daytime one. It's Sunday. No one is likely to call ATE and check. But I have to get near a computer and printer to change our papers and pin down some details.'

Goran looks at his watch. 'Zero four hundred hours. I say we pull out of here before we're seen. We grab a few hours' sleep while Troy creates the new documents. Regroup at midday, return and work until nightfall.'

Megan agrees along with the rest but suffers a pang of motherly guilt at the prospect of leaving Sammy with her parents again.

They're in the process of packing the rucksacks in the van when Goran quickly raises an arm. They freeze. From way off in the distance blink the headlights of an approaching vehicle. They take cover behind derelict buildings and the car zips past on the road heading out of the village.

'White builder's van,' says Goran, getting to his feet. 'It had a name like Smith and Son on the side. The back light over the number plate was out, so I don't have a registration.' He looks to Jimmy and Megan. 'Did either of you recognize it? Did it mean anything to you?'

'Yes,' says Megan. 'It meant a lot to us.'

144

The Henge Master sits alone in the darkness of the eastern chamber. He is waiting. Passing time. As he did yesterday morning. And the morning before.

It has always been the chore of Masters to plot the sunrise and sunset over the Sanctuary and Stonehenge. It is the Followers' own geocentric model. Like the Greek philosophers, like Aristotle and Ptolemy, they follow a belief that a fixed point of the earth is the center of the universe.

All things revolve around them. Only the Followers are wiser. It is not the orbit of planetary motions alone that they focus on. It is also their effect that is important. The resultant swirl of spiritual forces. The realignment of souls and energy. The gravitational drift of eternal power and essence.

The knowledge of the Followers predates all others. Theirs is the science that gave birth to astronomy, astrology, geography, meteorology and all others. The wisdom of the ancients.

Through the eastern star shaft, the Master sees the first trace of sunrise. Not dawn. This is different. More precise. The exact time the upper edge of the great orb appears above the horizon. The moment that the balance of power shifts. The split second the rule of night is over.

The first gasping breath of a newborn day.

Eyes fixed on the rising red and orange disc in the morning sky, the Master wonders for a moment about his new recruit. Phoenix. His son. His own flesh and blood. Today will be a telling one for him. For both of them. Blood is said to be thicker than water. Sunset will put that theory to the test. When the ball of fire dips in the west and the last of its trailing edge sinks below the horizon. The answer will be known.

Then history will be written.

145

Caitlyn wakes screaming.

The cell is compost black, wall torches long since burned out. Gideon heaves himself from the straw bunk beside her.

'Eric! *Eric*, help me!'

He follows the nightmare voice, feels his way in the utter blackness. The red glow of torches held by Lookers spills through the iron doors of the cell and he catches a glimpse of her. Knees tucked high against her chest, eyes glazed with terror.

'What's happening in there?' calls a Looker.

'Help! *Someone*, help me!'

Gideon tries to calm her. 'It's okay. You're all right.'

'*Help!*' The screams are louder.

He sits on the edge of the wooden bunk and tries to steady her. 'Caitlyn, you're dreaming. Wake up.'

Two Lookers step quickly into the cell, torches grotesquely illuminating their faces.

'It's okay,' says Gideon, half-turning to them. 'Light the wall torches and she'll calm down. She's just frightened.'

He puts his arms around her and holds her. 'Don't worry. No one is going to hurt you.' The words stick in his throat. Liar.

Light gradually crawls across the walls as the lit torches burn. Caitlyn wakes from the horror of her dreams to face the stone-hard reality of her fate. She holds Gideon for protection. Her voice is rough and raw. 'I need some water.'

The two Lookers wait for Phoenix to give his consent.

'Get her some, please.'

The taller of the two, the man previously introduced as Volans, moves to the back of the cell and fills a pot beaker with water from one of the stone troughs. He hands it to her and she drinks.

Gideon looks again at the two robed men. There is something different about them. The way they are holding themselves, the way they stand. He looks into their faces. Reads their concern, their intensity of focus. Then he notices their robes.

They are armed. Both are carrying guns.

146

Megan wants to chase after him. Wants to get up behind Smithsen's van and put him in a ditch. Find out what the hell he's doing on MOD land at four in the morning.

Goran unclips the radio from his belt. 'Echo Leader, this is Command. We've eyeballed a white van heading east out of Imber. Name on the side is Smithsen – Sierra Mike India Tango Hotel Sierra Echo November. Recon and report until otherwise instructed.'

There is a hiss and then a crackly reply, 'Copy that, Command.'

Megan looks irritated. 'Who was that?'

Goran looks smug. 'I have surveillance units pegged to all corners of the compass,' he says. 'They'll be effective for a while yet, until the roads fill up. After that, it's going to become more difficult. Echo Team is on the van and will report back.'

'I wish you'd told me you had those kind of resources. How can I help if I don't know what you're running with?'

The American grins widely. 'Sorry, lady. I'm afraid you only get to learn about my resources on a need-to-know basis.' He can see she's about to give him a mouthful. 'We don't have time to argue. We've got to get out of here before it's fully light.'

Megan glares at him. 'Wouldn't you like to know exactly where that vehicle came from?' She looks into the twilight, in the direction of the MOD danger zone and the route Smithsen took.

As he is about to reply, Goran's radio spurts to life again. 'Command, this is Echo Leader. We've got a problem. I think the target just made us.'

147

Caitlyn's unsure of the man she's sharing a cell with. He introduced himself yesterday as Gideon but she was too sick to do anything but just stare warily at him. Why is he in here with her? What does he want? He's dressed like all the others but behaves differently. Not as mean. She looks across to him.

He acts friendly. Like he's on her side. But he *is* one of them. She knows he is. The other guards listen to him. He told them to light the torches on the wall and they did it. They did as he said. No hesitation. He has influence over them. So why is he in the cell?

She feels weak and nauseous as she creaks her way out of her bunk and tries to take a step or two. He sees the tension on her face. 'Are you okay?'

'Why do you care?' She glares at him like a frightened animal.

'I'm not here to hurt you.'

Her heart jumps. A sudden rush of hope. 'Have my parents paid the ransom? Am I going home?' She forgets her caution and goes over to his bunk. 'That's it, isn't it? It's why I'm in here instead of that goddamned hole in the wall. It's why you're being nice to me. You're preparing me for my release. Acclimatizing me.'

Gideon stands and steadies her. 'No, Caitlyn. That's not it.' He glances toward the iron bars. 'For all I know, your parents haven't even been asked for a ransom. The people who abducted you are not after any money. I'm sorry.'

She doesn't understand. If they don't want her money, then what do they want? The fear returns to her face. 'So what's going on, then?' She gestures to the room. 'Why this?'

'Sit down. I'll try to explain.'

She sits, nervous as a kitten.

Gideon feels her panic infecting him. What he says next could unhinge her. But he has to let her know, she must understand what is going to happen. She has to realize that these are her last hours alive.

148

Draco's eyes are fixed in his rearview mirror, his hands locked on top of the van's steering wheel. About five miles back he caught a glimpse of something behind them. A dark blur way back. Maybe five hundred meters. Tiny but enough. The road out of Imber is always deserted. Always. But not today. The blur is still there.

'Can you make out what's behind us?' he says to Musca, beside him. 'What kind of vehicle?'

The big butcher swivels in the passenger's seat. He struggles with the shape. Not a van. Not an estate. 'Too far back to see properly. A hatchback maybe. A Focus or a Golf, that kind of thing.'

'Did you see where it came from?'

He turns back round. 'Not a clue. Why?'

'The army doesn't let anyone park down here. So where the hell did it come from and what's it doing out at this time?'

Musca leans forward so he can see it more magnified in the wing mirror. 'Maybe they're lost.'

'Maybe.' Draco takes his foot off the gas and slows the van down to thirty. Another glance in the rearview. A blood-red rising sun and the small black car. It's closing the gap. The builder slows to twenty-five.

'I'm going to brake and pull over without indicating. Get yourself ready.'

Musca eases a subcompact Glock 26 from his waistband and cradles it on his lap.

Draco hits the brakes. The car slides into a gravel run-off.

The hatchback swerves, its horn blaring. But it doesn't stop. A window rolls down and the driver shakes a meaty fist.

Neither Draco nor Musca speak. Their eyes stay fixed on the tail-light of the car as it carries on down the dusty road. They watch until it completely disappears.

'Pissheads,' guesses Musca. 'I'll bet they've been on an all-nighter and are heading off to work.'

Draco restarts the stalled engine. It makes sense. They might be going over to Tilshead or Westdown Camp. 'Let's hope so,' he says. 'Today is not the day we want anyone on our tail.'

149

'You must be fucking *crazy*,' Caitlyn says, backing away from Gideon. 'Cults and and sacrifices? This is not for real.' She paces nervously around the cell.

Gideon glances to the door. The Lookers are out there. Volans and the others. They are waiting. They will hear.

'And this place?' She raises her arms. 'What is it? The room next to the fucking *death* chamber? Are you and your whack-job buddies going to take me somewhere and roast me over a fire?' Her mind can't cope with the madness of what he's been trying to tell her.

He lets her vent. Pace. Blow off steam. Then he completes the picture. 'Just before twilight you will be moved from here. You will be washed and changed into ceremonial robes and taken to the Great Room inside the Sanctuary. There the Master will perform a presacrificial ritual.'

Her eyes widen. He's deranged. Insane. Isn't he?

Gideon tries to reassure her. 'It is not sexual, but it is painful. Your body will be cut with the marks of the Sacreds. One incision for each of the trilithons. This is down your arms, your legs and your spine. Your wounds will be anointed with water of the Sacreds and you will be left for five hours.'

'And then what?'

'The Bearers will take you to the river. You will be immersed in the waters that the ancients crossed to erect the temple that you are in and Stonehenge.'

As she hears the word, she thinks of Jake. The last intimate moments they spent together.

'The henge is where the final part of the ceremony will take place. The offering.'

She stares in utter disbelief. His words are from a lexicon of lunacy. Offering, sacrifice, Bearers, Sacreds. 'How?' The question jumps from her of its own accord. 'How will it be done?'

'It will be quick. Merciful.'

'Merciful? What kind of word is that?' She looks down. Her hands are trembling. It's all so crazy she can't believe any of this is going to happen. 'Where's Jake? Is he . . .' Even saying his name distresses her. 'Is he going to go through all this as well?'

'No.' Gideon tries to be gentle. 'Your boyfriend is dead. The police found his body a few days ago. In a Campervan.'

Caitlyn loses her breath. It's what she feared. Locked in that hole, she's thought as much a hundred times, but the news still breaks her.

Gideon wraps his arms around her and feels her sob against his shoulder. Her whole body shakes as the tears come.

Over her shoulder, he sees a face at the bars of the cell. The face of his father.

150

Sammy is already awake and causing mayhem by the time Megan gets back to her parents' place. She has makeup plastered across her face and over half the bedroom furniture.

'Making myself pretty, Mummy.' She smiles proudly and puckers her newly lipsticked lips.

'Come on, let's get you cleaned up.' Megan sets the shower running and tries to wipe up some of the mess.

Her daughter walks to the low cabinet beneath the sink and collects her own bottle of shampoo. 'I'm a big girl now, I can wash myself, Mummy.'

It makes Megan smile. Her daughter is growing up. Another few months and she'll start big school. It doesn't seem five minutes since Sammy was a babe in arms. Time is going so fast.

The water is fine and she helps Sammy over the edge of the cubicle, careful she doesn't catch her toes, then closes the door. 'You okay in there?' She presses her face to the already steamed-up glass. Sammy slaps the other side, giggles.

Megan holds her head and pretends to be hit, puts her face back to the glass.

Sammy slaps it again and giggles even louder.

This kind of clowning could go on all day.

'Very funny,' says a deep voice behind her.

Megan spins round.

'Adam.' Her head fills with panic. 'How did you get in?'

He smiles thinly. 'Back door. Your mum left it open. I must have told her a dozen times to lock it. She just doesn't listen, does she?'

Her heart is thumping. 'What do you want, Adam? What are you doing in here?'

He shuts the bathroom door behind him. Traps them both in the bathroom. 'Where were you last night, Meg?'

'*What?*' She tries to sound indignant.

'You were out all night. And not in your car. You left it on the drive, and you weren't working. So *where* were you? Who were you with?'

'I think you should leave, Adam.' She tries to step around him but he blocks her. She stares him down. 'Where I go and what I do is my business. Nothing to do with you. Now get out.'

His face colors. A vein in his neck twitches.

Megan tries for the door.

Again he blocks her. Slips his left hand the other side of her so she's trapped between his outstretched arms.

'Let me out.' Megan doesn't shout. She has one eye on Sammy. Her baby girl sits squeezing shampoo down the shower drain.

'When I'm ready, Meg. Now tell me where you were.'

He is so much bigger than she is. She knows she'll lose any fight between them. But it doesn't stop her trying. She drives a knee hard between his legs. He catches it with one hand. His fingers lock like a grip wrench. He squeezes until he sees pain on her face. With his other hand, he grabs her throat and pushes her hard against the bathroom door. 'I hear you've been offered a job in Swindon. Promotion. Good for you. Best you take it.' He glances toward his daughter. 'Best for everyone. That way you keep your nose out of my life and out of everything else around here. Do I make myself clear?'

'Daddy!'

The voice shocks them both. A soaking wet Sammy is out of the shower.

'Princess!' He grabs a towel, wraps it around her and scoops her into his arms. 'Let me take a look at you.' He pulls open the bathroom door. 'Do us a favor, Meg, and make a cup of tea while I get my daughter dry.'

151

The Henge Master sits poring over ancient maps and astronomical charts spread on the stone table. The day's celestial movements are critical. The time is coming.

'Father.'

Both the voice and the word surprise him. Father. How he has longed to hear it. 'Phoenix. Come in. I had forgotten that I'd sent for you.'

Phoenix. The name pricks Gideon like a thorn in his flesh.

'Sit down.' The Master gestures to the stone bench by the table. 'How is the girl? She looked distressed when I saw you.'

'Understandably so.'

'What did you tell her?'

'Her destiny. What will happen to her today. It's right that she be given an opportunity to come to terms with this, make peace with her own god.'

'And perhaps be accepted by ours.'

'Indeed. I would like to stay with her, if that's possible. Right until the very end. I think she needs me to give her strength.'

'The very end. Do you think you are ready for that?'

'I'm sure I am.' Gideon pauses, as if weighing their words. 'Father, we have no more secrets. You think you hold something over me but you don't. I know where we are. I know it from your name, *my* family name, my heritage. I know it from the great forces that you can muster, from the architecture and archaeology of this Sanctuary, from the position of the star shafts and the alignment with the henge. I know it, Father.'

James Pendragon's eyes are glittering in the dark. He walks closer to his son. 'You are right. The time has come when we need to trust each other more. But know this: the ceremony has a certain vividness. It can be shocking. Are you sure you wish to be that close to the woman?'

'I am sure.'

'Very well. You may stay with her until the ritual of renewal has been completed, the Sacreds honored and our debt repaid.'

'And then?'

'Then we reap the benefits. The autumn equinox is but twelve weeks away. This is the time the Sacreds will bless us.'

Gideon's eyes fall on the scrolls of paper on the Master's desk. They look identical to those he found in Nathaniel's observatory.

The Master follows his eyes. 'Do you know anything about archaeoastronomy or ethnoastronomy?'

'Not much,' he confesses. 'The former is the study of how ancient people understood the movement of planets and stars and how they shaped their cultures around those movements. The latter is more the anthropological study of sky watching in contemporary societies.'

The Master looks pleased. 'That's right. Our Craft combines the two. We use historical records, such as those you have seen in our archive, and we keep looking, checking constellations and planetary movements. The alignments with the henge and the Sanctuary are critical to our beliefs.'

'I know.'

'Of course you do. You are one of the few who understands that nothing here is accidental. The position of every building block and star shaft, the physical alignments with sunrise in the east and sunset in the west, the architectural homage to magnetic north, the tilt of the Descending Passages to mirror the inclination of the earth, it all has sacred meaning.' The Master grows thoughtful. 'I must leave shortly. There are things I need to attend to outside of the Sanctuary. We had a problem earlier today. Nothing to worry about but I have to go.'

'Anything I can assist with?'

'No, no. Not at all. It would help if you could keep the girl calm. She will grow more anxious by the hour.' He picks up a long slate knife from among the maps.

The ceremonial blade.

He holds up his right hand and cuts into the palm. Blood trickles in a crimson snake down his wrist. 'Give me your hand.'

Gideon tentatively stretches his hand out and the Master draws the blade across his palm. Pendragon looks into his son's unblinking eyes and takes the blooded hand in his own. 'Blood on blood. Father and son. We are as one.' He holds up their entwined fingers and draws Gideon tight to him. 'When I next see you, it will be after the ritual has begun.' He grips his son's hand tighter. 'Swear to me now, as my blood runs in yours and yours in mine, that our souls and our truths are aligned, that I can lay all my trust in you and in this bond between us.'

'I swear it, Father.'

Gideon watches the crimson drops drip from his elbow and knows it won't be the last blood shed today.

152

Josh Goran flips his mobile shut, amazed at what Jimmy has told him. He and his boss are no-shows. The woman says she's staying with her kid and Jimmy's apparently busy chasing another lead. He can't believe it. The cops here are worse than the FBI. Hundred percent amateurs.

Goran gets his men moving. Things are already running behind schedule and Echo Team has been compromised. Forced to abandon the surveillance on the builder's van. But he isn't worried. If there is anything to find out on the training range, he'll find it.

They get back to Imber by early afternoon. The road into the range is as deserted as it was in the early hours of the morning. But as they cruise past the restricted signs, the empty buildings and devastated gardens, they see ripples of mud on the road.

'Fresh tank tracks,' says Luc from the front passenger seat. 'Not even wet yet.'

'Challenger, most probably,' observes Goran. 'Piece of shit. I saw them in Kosovo. Brits would have been better sticking to the old Chieftains.'

'Or Rotem K2's,' says Luc. 'Korean Black Panthers. They've got fire-and-forget technology and full nuclear, biological and chemical armor protection.'

'K2's are an army equivalent of a Kia,' shouts Lynton from the back. 'Who'd go to war in a Kia?'

They all laugh.

Goran takes the Transit off road down a dirt track, west toward Warminster. It bumps around for about a mile and a half then they park up and drag out rucksacks filled with cameras, clipboards, fake documentation and specimen bags. Their cover this time is as members of the International Entomological and Natural History Society. Insect hunters. Lynton has mocked up IENHS access documentation to the Imber range and even filled their bags with research papers on bees, bugs and all manner of weird creatures.

Luc and Jay drop ramps from the back of the van and unload four Yamaha YZ125 trail bikes.

'Echo, November, Sierra and Whiskey Teams, this is Command,' Goran barks into the radio. 'We are go. Repeat, we are go.'

The four bikes start their outward sweep, while Echo, November, Sierra and Whiskey recon teams begin to walk inward from the circumference of the range.

153

Warminster is eight point two miles west of Imber.

It takes the Henge Master twenty-five minutes to make the journey. On any day other than Sunday he would have done it in only nineteen. But Sunday is a day for churchgoers and tourists, and the old Saxon town has eight major places of worship and the kind of surroundings people don't want to hurry past.

His vehicle rumbles through the main gates of Battlesbury Barracks and halts behind the parade ground. As he makes his way to his office, each soldier he passes stands to attention and salutes their commanding officer, Lieutenant Colonel Sir James Pendragon. Routine and ritual is as important in his public life as it is in his secret one.

Settled behind his desk, he instructs his staff officer to send his guest through. The man he's traveled here to meet. Wiltshire's Deputy Chief Constable, Gregory Dockery, is in plain clothes – a gray wool suit with white cotton shirt and gray tie. In his sacred robes he would be known only as Grus.

'How are you?' Pendragon shakes his hand and gestures to a pair of brown leather Chesterfields.

'I will be glad when tomorrow has come.'

'As will we all.' Pendragon smiles as he sits. 'How are you managing your interested parties, the FBI, Interpol, Home Office? Tell me.'

'Vice President Lock is back in the US. He rings the Chief five times a day. His wife is drunk or drugged all the time that she's not on TV crying or pleading. The Home Office people are bored. They seem resigned to dealing with the fallout when the girl's body turns up. As for Interpol, well, you know how useless Interpol is. Might as well ask the post office to find her.'

'So all is good?'

'Not quite.' Dockery grows fidgety. 'I think we may have a potential problem with the lone American wolf.'

Pendragon nods. 'Major Joshua Goran, former Special Ops Command. I wondered how long it would be before he started causing trouble.'

'Goran has a couple of my men on his payroll. They're only feeding him what we want, but I got word that dogs in his pack are sniffing around Imber.'

'Makes sense. Draco said he saw people out there this morning. They tailed him and Musca for a little while but pulled out when they realized they'd been seen.'

'Any harm done?'

'I don't think so.' Pendragon muses for a moment on the incident. 'Most of our resources are stretched in preparation for tonight and tomorrow morning. But I will increase surveillance at the Sanctuary. I'll make sure Goran is not a problem.'

'Good.' Dockery creaks forward on the leather, places his hands on his knees. 'I also have some difficulties within the force, but I'm hoping they're being dealt with.'

'You mean Aquila's woman?'

'Yes. She's off the case. Hunt was confused of course, but bought the reason for the transfer in the end. She starts a new cold case unit in Swindon tomorrow and we've destroyed any physical or electronic evidence she had put together. I also had Aquila pay her a visit this morning. I'm told it had the desired effect.'

'Let's hope so. And your son, what about him and the woman?'

Dockery flinches. 'He remains a worry. Seems he has a lot of faith in the DI.'

'Son or no son, you can't allow him to become a problem, Gregory.'

'I am aware of that. And your own child?'

'Touché. I don't think I have any worries there though. He passed the initiation of course, and he is more than aware that he already owes his life to our cause.' Pendragon's face hardens. 'So why the visit? What is on your mind?'

Dockery creeps to the edge of his seat. 'I have a suggestion. An unorthodox one. However, one I think you can sanction. If you agree, I'm certain our plans will go ahead tonight without any fear of interruption.'

154

The Apache helicopter swoops across Salisbury Plain at more than a hundred and fifty miles an hour. It banks high into the bright blue sky before looping back over the sun-parched Imber range.

The gunship is fitted with an M230 chain gun, synced to the helmet sights of the pilot and gunner. Even more deadly are its semi-active laser-guided Hellfire II missiles, capable of destroying tanks, buildings and bunkers. It's a flying arsenal.

But this flight is nonaggressive. An impromptu run-out. The pilot Tommy Milner and his gunner and co-pilot sweep the plain to find a group of trespassers reported within the restricted area. A welcome break from the boredom of sitting around.

Milner calls in a result after only a few minutes.

'Targets spotted. Twelve in total. Spread twelve o'clock, three o'clock, six o'clock and nine o'clock. Do you want exact verbal positioning or will you take refs off our data screen?'

'We got the data,' says the base's air controller. 'Processing now. Can you describe movements?'

'Charlie will give you details. I'm just going to hover so we can fix the cameras for you.'

Co-pilot Charlie Golding takes his cue. 'Two distinct groupings. Four on motorcycles moving outward toward Imber circular footpath as just described. Eight more in splits of two, on foot, moving inward.'

Milner hits the zoom on one of the high-powered video surveillance cameras.

A soldierly form, dressed in some type of black uniform, fills the screen. 'I have one of the trespassers full frame,' says the pilot. 'As you can see he is on some form of nonmilitary motorcycle, traveling at slow speed.'

'Thank you, Apache One. We have the imaging. Standby for further instructions.'

The controller turns to Lieutenant Colonel James Pendragon. 'What do you want us to do, sir?'

The Master rises from the seat he'd taken near the monitors. 'Send a ground patrol to clear the range. Lock these fools up until the morning. Then let them go.'

155

Megan has spent most of the day in shock. Adam's surprise visit scared her. She knows exactly what he was doing. He was showing that he could find her, get to her or Sammy, any time he wanted. Well, it had worked. She's still shaking long after he's left.

Adam is still on her mind as Jimmy drives her out to West Lavington to meet a contact of his. A man who sounds almost as frightened as she is.

'He's terrified,' says Jimmy. 'Wouldn't agree to speak to you unless it was way out in the country, somewhere he felt safe.'

Megan glances out of the window at an endless green blur. 'Well, this is certainly way out in the country.'

They pull into the grounds of Dauntsey's, a five-hundred-year-old redbrick boarding school set in a hundred acres of secluded countryside on the northern edge of Salisbury Plain.

'His name is Lee Johns,' explains Jimmy, parking in a line of parents' vehicles near a stretch of sports fields. 'He worked security at Stonehenge with Sean Grabb, the guy who turned up dead in Bath.'

'And what, he just came forward today?'

'No, I only found him this morning. I've been working my way through the security firm's roster and finally caught him at home.'

A few minutes later an old Honda pulls in and parks up.

'This is our boy,' says Jimmy. 'Best you get the rest of the tale from him.' He slides out of his seat and heads across the parking lot.

Megan watches from the passenger seat and weighs Johns up as he approaches. Spotty-faced, midtwenties, tall and thin but doesn't walk proud. He's a stooper. Self-conscious. Doesn't look the kind that makes friends easily. Probably a loner. Lives by himself, doesn't eat well and doesn't have a girlfriend.

Jimmy opens a back door for Johns, returns to the driver's seat and makes the introductions. 'Lee, this is my boss, DI Baker. Tell her what you told me and don't mess about.'

He looks at her like she's about to eat him.

'Go on. I won't bite,' she says.

'You're going to think I'm crazy.'

'Try me.'

'I work – *worked* – a lot with Sean Grabb. He was a good bloke. He sort of took me under his wing when I came up here. Sorted me out like. He got me a job, helped me get my head together and encouraged me to get off the gear I was on. You know about Sean, right?'

Megan nods.

Johns lowers his head. 'He was a good bloke. A mate.'

Jimmy pushes him. 'Tell the DI what you said about the cult and Stonehenge.'

He looks up. 'It's not a cult. It's a religion. A proper religion. Goes back before Christ and everything. Sean was really into it. He believed the henge was some kind of sacred thing that was the home for ancient gods. He would go on and on about it, the power it had. He said the people who worshipped there were good people, doctors, lawyers and stuff, even coppers.' He looks toward Jimmy. 'No offense, like.'

'Go on.'

'Well, I got interested more because Sean was a mate and I wanted to stay tight with him. They took me somewhere weird and held this kind of mass and blessing.'

'Where?' asks Megan.

He shakes his head. 'I don't know. They put a hood over my head. I couldn't see. They drove me somewhere. I remember the inside though. It was like a big old church, a cathedral kind of thing.'

'Warminster?' suggests Jimmy.

'Might have been. I don't know. I've not been in any churches anywhere since I were a kid. Anyways, I didn't get to see it going in or coming out. Sean said it would be some time before I would be told where the meeting place was.'

Megan is anxious not to let him wander too far off track. 'Lee, do you know about Caitlyn Lock, the American who was kidnapped at Stonehenge?'

'Only what I saw on the news.'

'This group and their secret place, do you think they have her there?'

He looks shocked. 'The American? No, I don't see them doing anything like that. No way.'

She can tell he's scared. What interests her is *why*. 'Jimmy says you know about something that's supposed to be happening today?'

He looks uncertain.

'Tell her, Lee.' The DS glares at him.

'All right. Look, it might be nothing. I mean, I'm not that involved with these people, right? I just work security at the henge and went along to the ceremony with Sean.'

'We've heard all that,' Megan snaps. 'What is it, Lee?'

He takes a deep breath. 'There is something big going down at the henge. Extra security has been put on. Dozens and dozens of extra uniforms. I'm on a detail that starts at six and stops anyone getting within a mile of the place.'

'Aren't there prayers, masses and ceremonies happening there all the time?'

'Yeah, there are, but security is usually low level for that sort of stuff. A couple of guards to make sure no one messes with the Sacreds. Tonight is different. The area is completely shut to the public. No bookings from this afternoon until tomorrow.' He turns to Jimmy. 'Look at their records. You'll find it's for maintenance of the stones, but what happens out there tonight is nothing to do with maintenance. At least not the kind most people would expect.'

156

Luc van Daele is the first to run into an army ground patrol. He sees the Saxon armored personnel carrier kicking up dust and spitting out fumes straight ahead. It's not a surprise that they've turned up. In fact, he expected them much earlier than this.

He gears the dusty trail bike down to an unhurried halt and steps off. The engine dies as he turns away from the vehicle and speaks quickly and quietly into his radio. 'I've got visitors. A personnel carrier with four-up. They're just coming over for a chat. I'll keep this channel open as long as possible. Over.'

The big, camouflaged Saxon grinds to a noisy halt and several soldiers spill out. Time to put Lynton's cover story to the test. Van Daele wriggles free of his rucksack and digs out his false papers. 'Hi there,' he shouts with a friendly smile. 'You guys work on a Sunday as well, eh?'

A clean-cut soldier in his late twenties is first to speak. He's kitted out in standard green and brown field gear. The tactical recognition flash on his arm puts him at captain-level with the Yorkshire, one of the British army's largest infantry regiments. 'You're trespassing here, sir. This is a restricted area. I need you to step away from the motorcycle and come with us.'

'I think you're mistaken.' Van Daele holds out a plastic file filled with paperwork. 'I'm with the International Entomological and Natural History Society. My colleagues and I have permission from the ATE to carry out a survey on rare myriapods and isopods.' He can see the soldier doesn't have a clue what he's talking about. 'Centipedes, lice, pill bugs, stuff like that.'

The captain takes the documentation but doesn't look at it. 'I'm sorry, sir. It doesn't really matter what this says or what you're doing, I'm under instructions to remove you from here.'

Luc knows better than to argue. 'Okay. No problem.' He waves a hand resignedly. 'I can easily put up with going home early to my wife and children.' He takes back the papers, shoves them in his rucksack and goes to start the bike.

The young captain steps in his path. 'I'm afraid you can't do that. You have to travel in the carrier with us, back to our barracks. One of my men will take care of your vehicle.'

'Hey, come on now.' Van Daele pushes the officer's arm away. 'I'm happy to ride this off your range, that should be enough for you.'

The captain calls to his men. 'Welsby, Simmonds, Richards.'

Three squaddies quickly crowd van Daele and move him away from the bike. Two of them are no more than kids. He could crack their heads easily enough. Leave them flat on their backs shouting for Mummy. But not without looking anything but like an insect collector.

157

Megan and Jimmy let Johns go and drive toward Stonehenge. She has mixed feelings about what she just heard.

'How much do you believe him, Jimmy?'

He drives with one hand on the wheel. 'Lee is an ex-junkie. Hard for these people to get out of bed without lying. What's on your mind?'

'He used the word "Sacreds." He didn't call them stones. He called them Sacreds. The same word that Gideon Chase used.'

'Sounds like he didn't make it up then, not if Chase used the same word.'

Megan is still chewing things over. 'He's not telling us everything. He's either more involved than he says he is, or less. Either way, he's holding back for some reason.'

Jimmy puts his foot down as they clear Shrewton and join the last stretch of road to Amesbury. A brown sign for Stonehenge comes up on their right. 'You want me to pull into the parking lot?'

'No, not for a minute. Just drive around the place.'

He slows to a crawl as they pass the monument, then turns right off the A344 and heads past it on the other side down the A303. In the grounds around the henge they see more than two dozen black-suited security guards being organized into groups.

'Well, it looks like he was telling the truth about some of it,' says Jimmy.

'Take another right,' says Megan. 'The lane, there. Park up and we'll walk.'

Jimmy indicates and starts to maneuver. As he turns he's confronted by a 'Road Closed' sign weighed down with sandbags in the middle of the lane.

'I'll stop further down and turn around,' he says. 'Otherwise we'll have to go all the way to Winterbourne Stoke and back through Shrewton.'

He pulls out and starts a three-point turn. Megan glances across the open countryside. 'I'm puzzled about something else that Johns said back there.'

'What's that?' he spins the wheel and straightens up.

'He mentioned that he thought people like doctors and police were members of this religion. When he said it, he looked toward you and said, "No offense." Why did he do that?'

Jimmy knows what she's getting at. 'I told him I knew all about the movement. That my father has always been a member but that I never wanted to be. I said my old man was in the force, the Deputy Chief Constable, and he could check on that easily enough if he wanted. That's how I got him to open up and tell us about tonight.'

'Is that true, Jimmy? That your father is a member of the Followers? Is that why I'm being shipped out to Swindon?'

'It's just something I said to Johns to get him to talk.'

Megan looks into his eyes and sees he's masking his emotions. 'You think he is, don't you?'

Jimmy looks away. He's riddled with doubts. His father has been his lifelong hero, the reason he joined the force, the one man in the world who has always been there for him. He can't accept he's mixed up in something as awful as all this. Won't accept it. Not yet. Not until there's overwhelming proof.

158

Caitlyn starts to dry retch. There's nothing she can do about it. She sits on the edge of her bunk, then drops to her knees. The intense heaving comes in painful spasms.

Gideon looks on feeling helpless. He puts an arm around her, gives her a drink, holds the clay cup to her lips. But he can see that he's of no real comfort. Her condition is deteriorating fast.

She sits with her back against the wall and places her hands on her tummy. 'My stomach feels like I've filled it with battery acid.'

'That's pretty much what it is. Gastric acid, secreted by the lining of your gut. Can you remember when you were taken? When you last ate anything?'

'I don't know. I've completely lost sense of time, of day and night.' She thinks. Grasps at the last few days. 'Wait. It was Saturday, the early hours of the morning. The day before the solstice. The nineteenth.'

'Today is the twenty-seventh. Sunday, the twenty-seventh.'

'Oh God.'

'They've done this to purify you. The ritual demands that at least seven days pass without food passing your lips.'

His eyes are on the bars and the two Lookers standing outside. 'Caitlyn, they're going to come for you soon. When they do, they are going to start the ritual and part of it will involve taking you outside. I'm going to be with you. Security will be tight. Even tighter than it is now. But this is the only chance we will have.'

'Chance?' Her spirits lift a little. 'What chance? What are you going to do?'

His eyes hold hers. 'Everything I can.'

159

High in the clouds, the hovering Apache is the first to realize what is happening. The three motorbikes are making a run for it. Dust kicks up from the terrain and the trail bikes are suddenly screaming across the plain in opposite directions.

'Trespassers dispersing. Are you catching this, control?' Milner widens the camera focus to show as much of the ground below as possible.

'Copy. We've got it, Apache. Ground patrols are ready to engage.'

Milner spots the big fat Saxon lumbering across the range, then the trails of two small, faster Land Rover Snatch 2's crossing from the west.

'Don't often see bikers out here,' remarks Golding off-mike. 'Especially ones behaving like those guys.'

'Never mind, good to give the old bird a spin, better than sitting around.'

Golding is as relaxed as the pilot. 'No point having big equipment if you don't use it, I guess.'

They both laugh as they watch the onboard monitor and the run the bikes are giving the army vehicles for their money.

'Could be an op,' says Golding. 'Maybe 76th Foot or the 19th are playing the part of the trespassers?'

'Might even be outsiders,' says Milner. 'You sometimes get the SAS or Marines coming down here for a workout before going out to the Middle East.'

One of the bikes pulls a sharp turn, leaves a Land Rover for dead and then blazes off in an entirely new direction.

'They're going to lose these guys.' Milner points to the monitor. 'Look what they're doing. They've spread themselves so wide, so quickly. The patrols aren't going to catch them.'

'Someone's going to get it tonight.' Golding clicks on his radio. 'We've got one trespasser heading south into the cover of trees near Heytesbury. Do you want us to reposition or stay as we are, covering the others?'

'Keep your position, Apache One.'

Five minutes later it's all over. The bikes have outmaneuvered the ground patrols and disappeared. Only four more of the trespassers, all of whom were on foot, have been captured. Apache One wheels around and heads back to base.

160

STONEHENGE IS CLOSED.

From what Megan and Jimmy can make out, similar CLOSED signs have been posted on all approaches to the historic site. The public parking lot is shut and all nonpublic roads have been closed.

The two police officers walk along the tiny grass verge of the A344 and past the ugly stretch of fenced-off tarmac where coaches and cars normally pull in. They cross the road and peer through another stretch of fencing toward the most complete part of the henge.

'What's going on, Jimmy?' She is staring at the dozens of uniformed security staff. They are all over the site.

'No idea.'

They stand and watch. Groups of guards begin fixing massive sheets of black plastic to the wire mesh fencing. Blocking out any views from the nearby highways. Megan scurries toward the nearest team. 'Hi there. What are you guys up to?'

They ignore her and carry on stretching out a vast swathe of black plastic.

'What are you doing?' shouts Jimmy.

'Minding our own business.' The reply comes from an older, unshaven man wearing a black T-shirt and cargo pants.

Megan slaps her police ID against the wires. 'I'm a police officer. I just made it my business.'

The man gets up off his knees. Stanley knife in hand, he walks her way. 'Carry on,' he calls to the others. He pins a smile against the wires, right next to her ID. 'It's a private party. Booked by a VIP for tonight. Now tell me exactly why any of that can be your business?'

Megan ignores the aggressive tone. He's probably an ex-cop in a dead-end security job who wants to make out to his cronies that he's more important than he is. 'And the sheeting.' She gestures to the river of black now rolling across the field. 'What's that for?'

He looks at her like she's dumb. 'Privacy. Private land. Private party. Get it? If you pay out big money for your own personal pleasure, you don't want nosy parkers at the fences troubling you all night. Understand what I mean? Now if you want to know more, you can ring my office. Maybe they'll tell you who made the booking. Maybe they won't. Now excuse me, I've got a job to do.'

He turns his back and walks away.

Bastard, she thinks.

'I've got the number for the security company,' says Jimmy. 'I'll call them from the car.'

Megan slaps a hand against the wire as she walks away. 'Looks like your informant was right. They're preparing for something big tonight. Something they apparently want to keep very, very private.'

161

The cell door creaks open and the draft causes the torch lighting on the wall to flicker.

'Phoenix.' Musca beckons him away from the sacrifice.

Gideon leaves Caitlyn on her bunk, lying on her side, her eyes glued to the hooded and robed figure filling the door frame.

Musca is wearing white cotton gloves and holding another pair. 'Put these on.'

'Why?'

The big butcher looks at him as though he's stupid. 'Fingerprints.

We don't want any prints on what I'm about to give you.' He leans closer. 'We will come for her in an hour. You need to tell her. So she has this final time for herself. For her to prepare for her death.'

It's more than just a ritual to Musca, Gideon can tell. It's sadism. The thrill of watching someone suffer. The man is enjoying it.

The big butcher steps outside the cell and takes a sheaf of plain A4 paper and a cheap pen from one of the Lookers. 'Give her this. Tell her she's allowed to write a final letter to anyone she likes. You can assure her they'll get it.'

'And will they?'

'Providing she doesn't do anything stupid like try to describe any of us or where she is, then yes, they will.'

'I understand. Anything else?'

'No. Sixty minutes, that's all she has. Not a minute longer. Make sure she's ready.'

The cell door clanks closed.

Caitlyn is sitting up, anxiously watching him as he returns.

He hands the pen and paper to her. 'They have given you this. To leave a message.'

'For my parents?'

He can see that she's got the wrong idea. 'It's not for ransom. I told you, there isn't going to be any ransom demand. These people have no plans to release you.' He sits alongside her and tries to help her through. 'This is it. They are getting ready to start the ritual. You have an hour, that's all. Then it will begin.'

162

Caitlyn writes two letters. One to her mother, one to her father. She wishes it could be just one. But it can't. This is the way that she has to do it. Her parents' divorce is screwing up her death almost as much as it did her life.

Words don't come easy. At first, they don't even come at all. Longhand is an alien lifeform to her. And letters like this, well, nothing prepares you for drafting letters like this. They should be the sole preserve of old people or people with awful diseases.

In the end she just writes down what she's thinking.

> Thank you for bringing me into this world, for giving me your beauty and your love of fun. Momma, I'm sorry we argued so much about Daddy and François. Love whoever you want to love. Love them both if they'll let you! I wish we'd had a chance to kiss and make up.
> Be happy Mom.
> Love Caitlyn xxx

Her note to her father is touchingly different.

> I'm sorry, Daddy. I know I should have done what you said. Please don't blame Eric. I tricked him, that's all. I love you Daddy and will miss you. If there is a heaven, I'll have coffee and pie waiting for you, thick cappuccino like we had in Italy together and a Mississippi mud like the one we made a mess of in the Hard Rock in London. Big kisses from your little girl, I'll always love you, Daddy xxx

Gideon doesn't look at the letters when she's finished. He just takes them off her and folds them in three. 'Are you okay?'

'Not really.'

She looks drained. Like the life has already gone from her.

She pours herself some water.

'Damn it!' She hurls the pot to the floor and starts to sob. 'I don't want to die. Oh, please God, don't let them do this to me!'

163

The security firm's number goes straight to answerphone. A recorded message. No one available until tomorrow.

'Have you got the owner's home number?' asks Megan.

'Yeah, John Doran-Smith. I've got a mobile.' Jimmy thumbs through his notebook again and punches in the digits.

No answer.

Jimmy leaves a message, makes it sound serious, official police business, the man has to call him urgently.

Something's happening. Megan knows now. She switches her thoughts back to Lee Johns. What is he not telling them? There are three main reasons why people like him start becoming helpful to the police. They're afraid of going to prison. They need money for something, probably drugs. Or they're into something they simply don't know how to get out of.

She turns to Jimmy. 'Did Johns ask you for any money?'

'Not a penny.'

'He talked to you solely because his mate Grabb disappeared?'

'Right.'

'We should sack ourselves.' Her face colors. 'How could I be so stupid? He must have been with Grabb when they murdered Timberland and took Lock.'

Jimmy quickly dials Lee Johns' mobile number. They should never have let him go, she knows that now. Half her mind was still on Sammy at the time.

'No answer, boss.' Jimmy holds up the phone as though to prove the point.

'You know where he lives?'

The DS doesn't need any bigger hint. He starts up the car.

'Pray he's there, Jimmy.'

164

The visit of the Master to the henge is unexpected.

Trusted members of the Inner Circle speed up the positioning of the black sheeting. The site is completely cleared. Only when veteran Lookers are in position outside the makeshift privacy curtain does the Master pass through the passageway under the road to the sacred site.

The day is finishing in cloud, the sun sinking mournfully low in the west. Time is of the essence. He walks the edge of the field. As always, he will enter the linked arms of the giant sarsens on a sun-line from the Heel Stone to Altar Stone. He stops at the horseshoe of five great trilithons and kneels.

'Sacred rulers of our universe, I supplicate myself before you, seeking your guidance and wisdom. I do so in all my mortal frailty and loyalty. I dedicated myself to the ritual of renewal and have ensured all preparations to honor you are in place. The one you chose is ready. A small repayment of the vast debts we owe you.'

He glances up, sees a further ominous dimming of the daylight. An unexpected storm may be brewing. A force of nature augmented by the Sacreds.

'Lords, our enemies are gathering. They close on us just as clouds surround the sun and moon. I know this to be a trial, a test of our faith and our resolution as Followers, but I cannot undertake it without your guidance. Without your consent.'

He feels his arms growing heavy. They drop by his side as though exhausted from holding a great burden. There is no need to talk now. The Sacreds know everything.

They are in his mind. In his doubts. They race through every atom of his existence. When they are done they leave him prostrate and gasping for air. But the Master has his answer.

He knows what he must do.

165

Kylie Lock slams the phone down on her husband.

The cheapskate son of a bitch still won't agree to match the money. Okay, she gets that publicly he can't do it. Vice Presidents don't negotiate with terrorists, that she understands. But he could still put his hand in his damned pocket. Do it privately. She could tell the police and the press she raised the extra bucks herself.

But he won't even do that. Can't compromise his precious principles. Oh no, that would bring his *integrity* into question. Would cost him votes is what he means. Thom 'Iron Man' Lock can't be seen to parley with the bad guys. Not even for his family. Certainly not in election year.

She stomps around her suite at the Dorchester. Rage building. Can't even take it out on Charlene. The press aide has gone sick with food poisoning. On this day of all days. Kylie goes to the minibar, looks at the vodka. God she needs it. But she won't. She takes a bar of chocolate instead. Sits chewing on the bed, watching TV and listening to the radio at the same time. She needs some valium. Or amphetamine. She snatches up the TV remote, switches to Sky News. Praying for another fix of news about her baby.

Kylie fires up the iPad and browses the internet, searching for snippets of information about her daughter. She shouldn't. The web gossip is bitter. Twisted. Cruel. There is already a virtual tombstone, spray-painted with messages from fans. Mostly boys.

But she has to read it. All of it. She has to tune in to everything and anything to do with Caitlyn. Because deep down, deep inside her, she feels something she can't explain.

Something instinctual. Maternal. Her nerves are jangling. Something bad is happening to her baby. She just knows it.

166

The sound is the one Caitlyn has been dreading.

Metal on metal.

A worn key turning in an old lock. The cell door is opening. They have come for her. The ritual is about to begin. She is going to die.

Gideon puts his arms around her. 'Be ready,' he whispers. 'Whatever I do, whenever I do it, be ready to fight for your life.'

He can feel her heart hammering against his chest. She is trembling from head to toe.

'It is time,' says an impatient voice by the door.

Caitlyn clings to Gideon.

'Be brave. Be strong.' He peels her off him, holds her hand. 'I'll be with you.'

She takes a deep breath, tells herself to keep her wits about her. Don't fall apart now. It would be the worst thing to do. The fight isn't over until all hope is gone.

From somewhere deep inside, she finds courage, pulls her hand free from Gideon's and walks toward the two robed men waiting by the cell door.

Draco nods to Gideon, gestures to the letters on the girl's bunk. Gideon understands and rushes to collect them.

They walk the corridor of death, flames crackling from burning torches fixed to the walls, and reach the cleansing area.

Caitlyn is pulled from Gideon, undressed and manhandled into the deep stone trench. Clear, cold mineral water powers down on her from the channeled inlets set in the rock ceiling. She shivers, fighting for breath.

Gideon turns away as the Cleansers pull her from the water, dry her and dress her in the long sacrificial robe. One of the Lookers walks over and talks quietly to him. 'Come with me, Phoenix. You must stand for her in the Great Room. The circles of light are lit. They await her there.'

Gideon doesn't want to leave her side. He feels a tug on his elbow and looks back at Caitlyn as they walk. He can't see her face, he wants to see her face, make some human connection with her. But he can't.

Too many people around her.

In the Great Room, he looks helplessly around the chamber, smells the newly warmed wax of the candles. He looks up and sees that the star shafts are open. The sunless sky is gray and edging toward twilight.

Time is running out.

His eyes fall to the Slaughter Stone, the spot where Caitlyn will be strapped down and the marks of the trilithons opened up on her legs, arms and spine. There is a noise outside. Footsteps. They are bringing her in. The ritual is about to begin.

Draco's hooded head appears in the doorway. His dark eyes fix on Gideon. 'Come with me, now! The Great Room must be cleared. There's a change of plan.'

167

'Is there no other way round, Jimmy?'

The DS shakes his head. 'Bulford's a horror. You've got half the bloody army out here: 3rd Mechanized, the Rifles, Royal Logistics, even the RMP.'

Finally, they edge past the slow-moving convoy of squaddies and Jimmy works the car hard down Marlborough Road, takes a right into Hubert Hamilton Road, then a left into Harrington. At last they're in the road where Lee Johns lives.

They slew to a halt, get out and sprint through a communal garden, up white concrete steps to a run-down flat. Megan keeps her finger pressed on the button while Jimmy shuffles along the small balcony to bang on the lounge window.

There's no answer.

She crouches and shouts through the letterbox. 'Lee, it's DI Baker and DS Dockery. We need to talk to you. *Urgently*.'

Still nothing.

'Put the door in.'

Jimmy hesitates.

'Put it in, Jimmy, or I'll do it.'

He steps back, plants a kick below the handle. His foot bounces off the lock but the door doesn't break. He steps back again and delivers a firmer thump with his heel. This time it swings open and they pile in.

Jimmy runs through the lounge into the small kitchen. Megan takes the bedroom. Then the bathroom. Nothing. He isn't here. She goes back into the bedroom. Opens the wardrobe and the chest of drawers. Full of clothes. Into the bathroom again. She finds his toothbrush. No sign of a hurried exit.

They wander outside, thinking about where next to hunt. Forty meters down the street Megan notices a thin man holding a newspaper in one hand and a sandwich in the other.

It's him.

Johns sees them on the stairs. And starts to run.

He's quick too. Much faster than Megan expected an ex-junkie to be. He makes a break for the fields behind Harrington Road. She barrels after him. Jimmy jogs back for the car, hopes to head him off as he comes out on Marlborough Road.

Megan is catching him.

Johns glances over his shoulder and sees her gaining. He also notices Jimmy is not there. It doesn't take a lot of working out to figure he is following in the motor.

Johns peels away from Marlborough Road. He's not going for the open fields. He's not that stupid. Instead he goes north toward a dense copse. With any luck, he'll lose her in there.

But he doesn't make it.

Megan finds an extra burst of energy just as his tank runs empty. She takes him down meters from the edge of the woodland.

They are both breathing heavily but the DI is fitter and stronger. She grabs his wrist and twists his arm hard up his back.

He kicks a little but his lungs are on fire.

'Don't even think about it, Lee.'

168

Six Followers, led by Draco and Musca, briskly escort Caitlyn and Gideon back to their cell.

She is terrified by the men's haste, their infectious nervous energy.

'What's going on?' Gideon asks Draco.

'Wait a minute.'

The Lookers push the sacrifice inside and Draco pulls him away from the bars. 'The Master has changed the plans for the ritual. He has been to the henge and he has himself become a vessel for the Sacreds. The gods are within him. He is in the Great Room right now, allowing them to take their places in the Sanctuary.'

'He is *switching* the location for the ritual?'

'That's right. He believes it safer to take place here, than out in the open.'

'And that accords with tradition?'

'It does. The henge in the Great Room comes from the same tabernacle stone as those on public display. In many ways it is a holier site.'

Gideon realizes the implications of the switch. They're not going to take her outside. He will have no chance to help her escape. He looks through the cell bars. She will be put to death just a short walk from where she is now.

'I have to see my father. I must speak with him.' He tries to push past him.

Draco blocks his way. 'That's not possible.'

'I must.'

'I said it is *not* possible.' His eyes narrow. 'The Master has left instructions that he must not be interrupted. Twilight is upon us. The ritual has begun.'

Gideon is returned to the cell and the door locked. Caitlyn sits on her bunk, her hair still wet, awkwardly holding the ceremonial gown about herself. It is split up the back so the knife of stone may be used on the naked flesh displayed beneath it.

Gideon slips off the rope from around his waist. 'Here, use this. It will help you fasten the gown.'

She takes it and chokes back a sob. 'It's stupid, isn't it? I'm about to be killed and here I am worrying about showing my ass.'

He understands her need to maintain some self-respect, some dignity. 'It's not stupid. It's dignified.'

Caitlyn looks to the door. She's almost too scared to talk. 'What's happening out there?'

'They're going to complete the ritual here, not at the henge.' He wishes he had better news to break.

Her face is heavy with sadness. She looks completely lost. 'Can you just hold me for a moment? I feel like I'm going to fall apart.'

Gideon moves closer. She wraps her hands around his waist and rests her head on his shoulder. It feels good to be comforted. To cling on to someone who doesn't want to hurt her.

'Hey!' One of the Lookers rattles the cell door. 'None of that. Back away from her.'

Gideon gives the man a withering glance. Does the idiot think he's planning to have sex with her? How stupid. He knows as well as anyone that a defiled sacrifice wouldn't be any use to anyone.

No use to anyone.

How could he not have seen it.

He might still be able to save her life.

169

The Henge Master stands clad in a hooded ceremonial sackcloth robe bleached red using an ancient mixture of beets, madder and chokecherries. Beneath his hood there is a moonlike crescent, the outline of his shock of gray-white hair.

The Sacreds have been positioned in their tabernacles. Special sanctuary lights, multicolored glass tubes filled with virgin candles, have been positioned and lit at equidistant spaces around the henge.

Through the star shafts he sees the color of the sky.

Twilight is but a blink away.

The Master is close to exhaustion. The strain of transporting the Sacreds to the Sanctuary has wearied him. But he will not fail.

He raises a ceremonial stone sprinkler filled with water washed from the Sacreds, and creates a divine line from the Altar Stone inside the horseshoe of trilithons, out through the eastern arches of the sarsens, across the Slaughter Stone to the Heel Stone.

From a pocket in his gown, he draws the ceremonial stone knife and gazes upon the slab where the sacrifice will be cut. Five cuts. One for each of the mighty trilithons where the Chief Sacreds reside, the gods of the sun, moon, stars, earth and afterlife.

She will be left for five hours. One hour for each god. Afterward, she will be untethered and washed again in blessed waters. Then she will be offered.

The Master's hand falls to his other deep pocket. He feels that they are there. The sacrificial hammers. He turns his attention to the two Bearers watching and waiting from the other side of the opening to the Great Room. In their grasp is the rough litter made of pine, ready to convey the sacrifice on her fatal journey.

He is ready.

He nods. The Bearers move instantly away.

170

'What were you running for, Lee?' Megan twists his arm even further up his back as she stands over him. 'I don't have time to mess around and neither do you.'

'All right. *All right*, I'll tell you.'

She sees Jimmy crossing the field and lets go of Johns. The kid struggles to his knees. Cradles his twisted and aching arm. 'I got scared. I saw you at my place and just freaked.'

She pulls him to his feet. 'You and Sean Grabb killed Jake

Timberland and you helped him kidnap Caitlyn Lock. In policing terms, you are screwed, my strange young friend.' She jabs a finger in his bony chest. 'We already have the forensics to link Grabb with the killing and the abduction. And I'm sure that once we go hunting for your DNA, we'll find it. Juries love DNA. Three letters that they'll believe more than anything an ex-junkie like you could dream up.'

Johns has been jailed before. He doesn't want to go back. He looks beyond them, down the road to the big open world. Balancing his options. Finally he speaks: 'I want immunity, right? A guarantee I ain't going to get charged with nothing.'

'Dream on,' says Jimmy. 'We're past immunity. It's down to damage limitation now. Hurry up. What have you got before we throw the charge sheet at you?'

He nurses his arm again. 'Not much. It's not like you think.'

She glares at him. 'Don't piss about, Lee. We need everything. No lies. No leaving bits out. Everything.'

He puts his hand to his head. Images are swimming back to him. The man lying dead in the van. The pretty woman screaming and kicking. Him in the Camper suggesting they kill her rather than get caught. 'It was an accident. Nobody meant anyone to die or anything.' He sees their unbelieving looks. 'I mean it. We were after them because the girl touched one of the Sacreds. Things got out of hand. Sean hit the bloke and when we drove him away he died. It freaked us out. We didn't plan it like that.'

'I said don't leave things out.' Megan jabs him again. 'Why were you at the henge? Who wanted them and for what?'

He swallows. 'A stranger has to be picked for the ritual. Sean said it had been decided that it would be whoever touched one of the Sacreds. It didn't have to be that girl or the bloke with her, it could have been anyone, you know? They just got themselves in the wrong place at the wrong time.'

'So where is she?' asks Jimmy.

'She's at the Sanctuary, the place I told you about. But like I said,

I don't know where it is.' He can see their anger. 'Really. I've never seen it from the outside. Out along the A360. Out near Imber, that's all I know. We stopped on a road just before the village, near the range. Sean went on from there with the girl in his Warrior and I waited in the Camper with the stiff.'

Megan wants to crack him. 'You're talking about a young man whose life you stole. Show some respect.'

'Go on,' says Jimmy.

'Sean came back and said he'd phoned someone. A member of the Inner Circle. He looked relieved. He thought it was all going to be all right.'

'So what was all that earlier today?' Megan asks. 'That story about something happening at Stonehenge?'

He colors up.

She reads his face. 'If this girl dies, you're getting charged with murder.'

He understands. 'A man called Matt Utley, we just call him Musca, came to me.' He looks toward Jimmy. 'He knew you were trying to get hold of me, to talk to me about Sean. He says that I'm to contact you, tell you that something's going off tonight at the henge.' Johns glances back to Megan. 'I was confused like, because something was supposed to be going off there tonight. It's the start of the ritual.' He dries up.

'Go on, Lee.' Jimmy's voice is firm.

'Tonight is when the girl should be, you know, sacrificed. And it should be at Stonehenge.'

'Should be?'

'That's the point,' he explains, looking from one to the other. 'They know you're on to them. They know everything. Musca wanted me to say this to you. So you'd go to the stones.'

She lets out a long sigh. 'So where would be the right place?'

'The Sanctuary, I guess.' He puts his wrists together and offers them out to Jimmy. 'You've got to lock me up. Put me in protective custody somewhere. Musca said he'd kill me if I fucked this up. Said I'd go the same way as Sean if I didn't do what he wanted.'

'Get him locked up,' she says. 'DCI Tompkins can deal with him.'

171

The crazy son of a bitch is at it again. Phoenix has his shirt off and his hands up the back of the sacrifice's robe. The bastard is feeling her behind. Volans presses his face to the bars of the cell, he can't believe what he is seeing.

'Hey!' He rattles the cell door. 'Leave her alone, you dog. I told you once.'

The two of them are in the corner trying to hide but he can still see them. Musca appears in the passageway. 'What's going on?'

'That idiot is trying it on with the girl.'

'What? Stop them. Open the damned door.'

Volans fumbles with the keys. Musca catches a glimpse of them kissing. 'Quickly. Come on.'

The two Followers stride into the cell and catch Gideon and Caitlyn locked in a passionate embrace, oblivious to the noise around them.

'Stupid fool!' Musca grabs him by the hair, pulls him away from her.

Caitlyn steps back. Face full of desperation.

Musca spins Gideon around and crashes a fist into his face. But he doesn't go down, he bear hugs him and holds on for dear life. Caitlyn lunges forward. A jagged shard of broken pot plunges into the side of Musca's neck. She feels the warm spurt of blood on her face and knows she's hit a main vein.

Musca shudders. Gideon lets him slip to the cold floor, then pulls a gun from his waistband. Volans is frozen. Stuck between helping his dying brother or securing the sacrifice.

'Get the fuck away from her,' Gideon says. 'I won't hesitate to kill you.'

172

'Caitlyn, take his gun.'

Shaking with adrenaline, she draws the weapon from Volans' waistband and pulls the bunch of keys from his hand.

'Kneel down. Face the wall!'

As Volans moves, Gideon glances at the gun in his hand. He's never held a firearm before, has no idea how to use it. No clue where the safety guard is or whether it's even loaded.

'Let's go!' He pushes Caitlyn out of the cell and closes the iron door behind him. He grabs her by the sleeve and they sprint down the passageway. Behind them come Volans' cries for help.

In Gideon's mind is a mental map. One he knows is incomplete. But it's all they've got. He figures the most direct escape to be past the Great Room, on to the curving passageway of the Outer Circle, then past the Master's chamber. It would lead them to the stone staircase and the warehouse exit.

But that's not where he's heading. He's following a hunch. One that will get them free. Or get them killed.

173

The Master steps hesitantly from the Great Room and looks around. The sacrifice should be here by now.

He hears noises spilling down the corridor, turns and walks back toward the cell. Four Bearers are running toward him. Without the litter.

'She's gone,' shouts one. 'The girl is out of her cell.'

'My son, where is he?'

'Also gone.' The voice is that of Draco, hurrying up to the Master, blood on his hands. 'They've killed Musca and taken Volans' gun.'

'Block the main exit,' says the Master. 'They will head for the stone steps into the anteroom.' He feels ashamed that he trusted his child, personally guided him around the Sanctuary.

Draco dispatches the Bearers. 'And the avenue, what about the passageway from your chamber?'

The Master shakes his head. 'He doesn't know of it, but secure it anyway.'

'I'll go myself.' Draco takes two men, instructs the rest to search the Sanctuary.

The Master looks into the emptiness of the Great Room. He can sense the displeasure of the Sacreds. But he is calm. The place is a fortress. There is plenty of time to recapture the girl and to complete the ceremony before first light.

He walks toward the Great Room, then thinks better of it.

He smiles and shouts for Draco. 'Let the men go. Come with me. I know where they are.'

174

The wall torches are few and far between, the maze of passageways cold and heavy with the smell of damp and death.

Caitlyn clings to Gideon as they run. She prays that he knows what he's doing. Fresh in her mind is her own futile escape attempt.

Something seems wrong to her. They're heading downward. Running deeper into this horrible place rather than up and out into the safety of the outside world. 'We're going the wrong way!'

'Trust me,' shouts Gideon, short of breath.

Caitlyn knows she doesn't have a choice.

As they run down the darkened corridors, he frantically tries to picture the twists and turns of the Sanctuary. In his mind it is like a buried pyramid, only dome-shaped. He sees the upper levels, the modern operational area. The carefully constructed weight-relieving chambers and corridors. Under them the Master's chamber and the Great Room. He sees the Ascending and Descending Passageways east and west of these. Pictures them all built around the central star shaft. The corresponding points of the compass and constellations.

Now he envisages the eastern passageway. The access to the lowest level. The Crypt of the Ancients. The place they are heading toward.

The twisting and tilting corridors remind him again of Egyptian tombs. The kind of places that hold architectural secrets. He sees Khufu's Great Pyramid and remembers its hidden chambers and passages.

He prays the Sanctuary has its own secrets. The star shafts, the varying heights in the corridors, the Ascending and Descending Passageways, and the geographic alignments. They are all clues that he's right.

They slide to a halt in front of a locked oak door.

'Quickly,' he says, pulling a breathless Caitlyn tight to the wall. 'Sit down. Sit here and stay here.'

He backs off several meters, turns to look at her. 'Further forward. Come toward me half a meter.'

She slides along the ground, pulls her shaking knees up to her chest, rearranges the loose sacrificial gown.

'Okay. Stop.' He backs off further, rounds the corner of the passageway behind them, then reappears, looking hard at her.

'Stay here. Don't move. *Whatever* happens, even if you see them coming for you, don't move.'

175

Caitlyn sits shaking on the cold floor, caught half in the light of a flickering wall torch, half in the long shadows of the high passageway leading to the Crypt of the Ancients.

Gideon has vanished. She is alone. Her mind drifts. Back to when she was a child, playing hide and seek with her parents. Only she hides so well neither of them can find her. She waits and waits and waits. Fears they'll never come.

Is he gone for good? Has he left her as a decoy?

There's a noise. Footsteps. Someone is approaching. The waiting is over. Muffled voices. They are coming for her. She remembers what he said: *don't move . . . whatever happens . . . don't move.*

Caitlyn holds her nerve. They're close now. Very close. Footsteps so loud that she knows she is only seconds away from discovery.

She sees them. Two men. One old. One younger. Caitlyn screams. One of them moves to grab her.

The corridor fills with a ball of noise. A sound so loud she flinches in shock. Painful ringing erupts in her ears. The man in front of her clutches his chest. His eyes are wide, his mouth open. He lurches to the side, falls to his knees.

Gideon steps from the shadows. He levels a shaking gun at the older man in the red robe. 'Father—' He spits the word out.

The Henge Master glances at Draco on the floor, his blood leaking onto the stone. 'What have you done?'

Gideon waves the gun. '—I need the key to the Crypt.'

The Master lifts the string from around his neck, his face full of contempt. 'I knew you wouldn't be able to leave without stealing something precious. You're just a grave-robber like Nathaniel.' He throws the key into the pool of blood near Draco.

'Get it,' Gideon says to Caitlyn, the Glock still leveled at his father.

She bends to pick it up.

Draco grabs her by the ankle, pulls her over.

The Master charges Gideon like a bull elephant, crashes him into a wall.

There is another deathly explosion.

176

The two men slump to the ground. Locked together. The Glock clatters over the blood-spattered stone slabs.

Caitlyn's survival instinct kicks in. She stretches her arm through the cloying pool of Draco's blood and grabs the fallen weapon. He's still pulling at her. Strong hands moving from her ankle to her knee. She twists around. She has no choice but to go with the thought in her head. She pulls the trigger. Shoots him in the face. Point blank. The report is deafening.

Blood and brains spatter her. She drops the gun and holds her crimson-soaked hands in horror. She sits frozen until Gideon gets to her.

'Come on, we have to go.'

Caitlyn can't move. Multiple images of what she's done are already branded in her mind. The way he looked at her, then the blood red mist, flaying skin, saliva, flying bone. He's dead. She just killed someone.

'Caitlyn! Get up!'

She feels Gideon grab her hand. It's wet with blood and brain. He is pulling her along, the stones feel soft beneath her feet. Her vision blurs. She stops and retches. Heaves the last specks of moisture from her empty stomach.

'Come on!'

She retches again and looks to the side. Gideon is unlocking a door just a few meters away.

He rushes back and gets her, drags her with him through the new opening.

Blackness. Total blackness.

She stands shaking while he searches. The blood red mist sprays up before her eyes again. Flesh. Saliva. Bone. The final, frozen look in his eyes. Like a broken doll.

Light. A wall torch finally starts to burn close to her. Orange. Orange not red. Gideon has lit it. He leads her by the hand, lighting giant candles around the room. The blackness dissipates, dribbles away like water on hot sand. The room tilts. Her knees buckle and she feels a sickly warmth course through her.

'Caitlyn!'

She hears his voice, tinny and distant, a shout from down a long, dark tunnel, as she falls.

177

The bullet from the Glock has gone straight through the Master's thigh. He's lucky. As a career soldier, he knows two simple truths. First, there's no such thing as a nonfatal shooting. Let any wound bleed long enough and you'll die. Second, unless you shoot your enemy in the skull or the spine, you're not going to incapacitate them with a handgun. They're going to be shocked to hell, but once they're over that, they're going to be up and at you again. And that's what he's going to do.

He wipes away the blood and examines the entry and exit points. Clean. He feels tentatively around the traumatized skin. The bullet was low velocity, so it's a straight hole. Little effect on the surrounding tissue. He presses and watches the cavity fill. If it had been a high-velocity rifle, the injury may have been much worse.

He probes and pokes until he's sure there's no fragmentation in the wound, no shattered bone that has ripped up masses of muscle tissue. He tries to stand, but it's hard to balance. Difficult to straighten his leg and painful to put any weight on it. He leans against the wall and pulls the cord belt from around his waist. He loops it around and pulls a tight tourniquet. It's a temporary fix but good enough for now.

He's risking nerve damage. Better that though, than to bleed to death. He looks down and sees the sticky puddle of blood and brain matter that has seeped from Draco. No point even checking for a pulse. In his peripheral vision he notices the flickering lights from the candles in the crypt. He hears his son shouting. Shouting to the woman to hurry up.

He dips in the deep pocket of his robe. Feels the sacrificial hammers and the ceremonial knife.

Enough to stop them.

Enough to fulfill the ritual.

178

Gideon reluctantly leaves her slumped and twitching in her faint. He carries the torch high and quickly makes his way around the crypt. He has to find the clue. Some proof that he hasn't made a fatal mistake.

From the dozens of inclined coffins, empty eyes in skinless skulls seem to follow him. They trail him like ghosts. He can feel their wispy hands on his neck, cold like a dead-of-night shiver down his spine.

Egyptians ensured the dead who they honored were surrounded by their most prized possessions. From what he can see, it seems to be the same with the Followers of the Sacreds. But the Egyptians equipped their tombs with something else. Secret passages into the afterlife. Long tunnels that allowed the reborn kings to rise again and rejoin their people.

Gideon tries to think of everything he knows about the pyramids. Of the modest structure honoring young Pepi II. The stepped Pyramid of Djoser. Sneferu's Red Pyramid. And Giza – built two thousand five hundred years before Christ, around the same time as some of Stonehenge, and just after the completion of the Sanctuary. The Great Pyramid had chambers similar to those now surrounding him. Mysterious shafts stretched from the King's and Queen's chambers to the outside world. Secret corridors allowed freed spirits to escape to the heavens.

Gideon moves the coffins. Stirs the dead. Hears their bones grumble discontent. Cobwebbed skeletons creak and crack as he searches behind and beneath the caskets for trapdoors or concealed passageways. There are none.

He hears Caitlyn moan and walks over to her, stoops and holds the flame so he can see her face. She is coming round but she's deathly pale. Glassy eyed. Her energy is spent.

He touches her shoulder reassuringly. 'You're all right. You fainted.'

Her eyes flick from him to the horrors of the room. Coffins. Skeletons. Candles. Her nightmare isn't over.

He thinks back to his studies, to the dusty files of his research, his academic past. His mind tries to see beyond the obvious. A fleeting memory of a massive maze. It is that of Amenemhet. Reputedly an architectural work that surpassed the great pyramids, hundreds of rooms, passageways, corridors, false chambers, star shafts and hidden trapdoors.

There had been a hidden exit in the ceiling. Concealed by a stone trapdoor. A small hole opened up into a series of hidden rooms and passageways. An exit route filled with decoy chambers and deadly shafts. But still an exit route.

He remembers Scandinavian archaeologists discovered that the symbol of the maze represented the spring equinox, the time the sun was supposed to escape from the winter's blackness. He looks up. His gaze drifts to the top of the giant cube of artifacts in the room's center. Even if they climbed it, they couldn't reach the stone blocks above their heads. But it looks like the only possible way out.

He hopes Caitlyn is strong enough to make it.

'We have to get moving, come on.' He grabs her wrist and leads her to the giant stone block. Gideon starts to climb and then pulls her up the first set of stone shelves.

'Hang on.' He places her fingers on the edge of the giant sandstone cube. 'Grip tight. I need to climb up another level, then I'll—'

The words shrivel in his mouth.

He can see what she can't. See the shape behind her.

179

Gideon moves too late to stop the stone blade slicing into Caitlyn's calf.

She screams and almost loses her hold on the giant sandstone cube. Gideon grabs her arm and hoists her up a level.

The Master sweeps the knife again. Too low. It misses. He pushes himself closer. Slashes again. He's closer now but not close enough. He ignores the pain in his leg and hoists himself on to the bottom layer of the archive cube.

Gideon is pushing Caitlyn up and around the side of the block. Edging her out of harm's way. He's looking the wrong way. The knife slices into his shoulder. He tumbles from the cube.

The Master lurches after him. This is personal. Pride. Honor. Everything to live – and die for. He attacks again with the blade.

The gun is back on the cube and Gideon has no chance of reaching it. His eyes are locked on the lethal blade in his father's hand.

The Master hobbles and stabs. It's an unbalanced lunge that falls short of its target. Gideon sees the weak spot. Blood is dribbling down the Master's right leg. He launches a wild kick.

The Master howls with pain. The knife drops. Gideon could finish him. He could go back for the gun and shoot him. He doesn't.

He turns and climbs up toward Caitlyn.

'You're a fool!' shouts the Master, lying on the stone floor clutching his leg. 'There's no way out. You can't get away.'

Gideon pulls himself up on to the top of the centerpiece and helps Caitlyn climb the last half meter. As they stand on the apex of the giant sandstone block, he sees that his father is right. There is no way out.

180

The Master hobbles back from the Crypt of the Ancients. He knows there is still time. If he can reach the Bearers, the Lookers, then the sacrifice can be recaptured. The hour is late but it is not yet impossible to complete the ritual.

He's weak, dizzy, losing too much blood. His thigh is twitching and cramping. He stops, quickly refastens the tourniquet. Already nerves are deadening. Every step up the sloping passageway is a form of torture. But as he reaches the middle landing, he sees Grus with three Lookers.

'Here! Over here!' It's the best he can manage as he slumps to the ground.

'Get a medic, quickly,' shouts Grus. He turns to two of the men. 'Help me get him to his chamber.'

'No,' protests the Master. 'My son and the sacrifice are in the Crypt of the Ancients. Get her. Get her now.'

'Watch him,' says Grus to one of the Lookers. 'Don't let him pass out.' He looks down at his friend. 'There'll be a doctor here any minute.'

'Go!' shouts the Master. 'They were climbing the centerpiece. Do whatever you have to, to bring the girl back.'

181

The Master is laid out on a stone table in his chamber.

'You've lost a lot of blood,' says the man tending him.

'I know that,' he snaps. 'Just fix me.'

The medic nods. He waits for the ice and alcohol to come from the fridges in the operational area. He's going to have to cauterize the wound with heated metal. Battlefield improvization. Something he's done before.

The Master's mind is elsewhere. If he can't complete the ritual, there will be repercussions. The power of the Sacreds will wane. Perhaps critically. It will be disastrous for so many people.

But if the sacrifice and his son escape? He shudders.

The Craft will be exposed. He cannot let that happen. He will have no option but to take the ultimate sanction. One that has been prepared. One that only his word can execute.

182

The top of the centerpiece in the crypt is solid. Gideon feels no break in the giant sandstone except for a thin square shaft that runs straight down the middle. He can see no obvious use for it. Was it designed to let something out? Drain away water or gasses? Or let something in?

He looks down the bottomless hole. Did it once house an even taller centerpiece that connected to the roof of the crypt? The shaft is about the width of a waterwell. It's barely wide enough for him to fit into. But it's all there is. There's no sign of anything else that could constitute an exit.

At the edge of the block, Caitlyn sits nursing the gash to her leg. He looks again down the shaft, down into the terrifying darkness. The Lookers will be in the room any second. He sits and dangles his legs into the void.

Caitlyn stares at him incredulously. 'What are you doing?'

'I don't know. Ancient structures seldom make sense. You just have to feel your way around them to discover their purpose.' He lowers himself into the hole, so he is resting on his elbows. His gashed shoulder barks pain.

Gideon scrapes a foot against the wall. He can feel something. A tiny foothold. A gap in the sandstone. He wriggles his bare toe in and stretches his other leg down, searching for a second foothold. After arcing it back and forth, he finds one.

Caitlyn watches him disappearing into the shaft and drags herself over. She's not going to be left here alone. Only his fingers are now visible from the top. He calls to her. 'There are cut-outs in the side of the walls. It's like climbing down a ladder. Feel your way down.'

His hands disappear and in the dim light she can only just see the top of his head. She gets on her knees and lowers herself into the blackness. Back into the dark hole. Her mind rebels, her body freezes. She can't do it again. She can't go into the hole.

But she has to. She has to follow Gideon. Has to trust him.

Her once-beautifully manicured toes rub against the rough sandstone until she finds the gaps and descends into the dark unknown.

Her left foot hits an unusually solid foothold, a knob of stone that protrudes from the wall. It enables her to shift her weight from her gashed leg and move down more confidently.

As soon as she's done it, there's an awful noise. A sound like a train trundling through a tunnel above her head.

'What's that?' Gideon shouts from below.

She has no idea. She looks up.

Something is sliding across the top of the shaft. A stone disc cutting off the remaining light. Caitlyn watches it fill the gap above. There's a clunk. A deathly halt.

They are sealed in. Trapped.

183

As the medic ties off a wrap of elasticized bandage around the Master's wound, Grus repeats his awful news: 'The crypt is empty. We searched it from top to bottom. If they were there, they're not now.'

'They were on the centerpiece.' His voice is thinned by pain. 'They were in there, I saw them climbing it.'

'Do you think I ignored you?' says Grus. 'We searched everywhere. *Including* the centerpiece.'

'I climbed it, Master,' adds one of the Lookers. 'To the very top. The roof above is unreachable. There is no way anyone could have escaped from up there.'

The Master swings his legs down from the stone table and sits up. The rush of blood makes him dizzy. 'Then they're still in the room.'

Grus leans close to his old friend. 'Believe me, they are not. We would have found them.'

'Then they must have slipped out of the crypt behind me.' He stands down and flinches.

'You should really rest,' says the medic. 'The cauterization is fresh and you shouldn't traumatize the wound any more.'

The Master ignores him. 'Sweep the area one more time. Once more and then we are finished.' An expression of defeat washes over his face. 'Grus, you know what must be done, don't you?'

He nods. He understands. Understands perfectly.

184

For a few seconds neither of them move. Frozen in the suffocating dark. They can see nothing. They hear nothing in the hot, still air. Only their own stilted breathing. The scrape of their feet on the stone.

Caitlyn starts to panic. 'We're going to suffocate. Oh Jesus, no!'

'Stay calm.' Gideon climbs up several notches in the stone well. 'Caitlyn, stop it.' He reaches out, finds her foot with his hand. Touches her. Makes contact. The shaft is too narrow for him to get any closer. 'Please calm down. We have to think our way out of this.'

She shuts her eyes. Tries to squeeze out the stinking blackness of the shaft with her inner blackness. She breathes in slowly through her nose. Out slowly through her mouth.

Gideon hears the deep rhythm building above him. He waits, then asks, 'What happened? Did you pull something, stand on anything?'

'I stood on something.' She sounds tearful. 'I'm sorry. It's near my knee now. It was some kind of ridge that stuck out.'

It figures.

He knows ancient tombs were often rigged with devices to stop thieves plundering them. He pulls himself up a little further and feels for the ridge. The stone is smooth. Innocuous in size and shape. It's a strategically placed block counterbalanced by another lodged deeper in the structure. Any sizeable pressure on it, such as a person, shifts the counterweight, which in turn slides the stone disc above across the mouth of the shaft. Simple. Simple and deadly.

'We're trapped, aren't we?' She is trying to sound calm but shaking with dread.

'There's no going back, that's for sure.' Gideon doesn't give her time to dwell on it. 'We need to continue downward. Don't tread on anything else that sticks out. If you feel another of those trigger ledges, tell me. Okay?'

She takes another deep and calming breath. 'Okay.'

She feels and hears him moving away from her. Finds it hard now to hold on. Knows the strength of her limbs is giving out. She's losing the ability to grip securely.

'Stop. *Stop*!' His cry halts her in her tracks.

'I've found another one.'

He runs his toe across it. There's no doubt that it is a trigger ledge. But what exactly does it trigger? An opening? Or another seal? Perhaps one that will trap them in the shaft for eternity.

Or is it just a decoy?

Should they ignore it and press on? But then again, doing nothing could prove fatal.

Gideon's mind spins. The very bottom of the shaft may also be a trigger plate. It's not impossible that standing on it could unleash an avalanche of hidden sand, lime and chalk, or even rocks.

They could be buried alive.

185

'Nothing,' says Grus. 'They are nowhere to be found.'

The Master sits with his wounded leg elevated. 'You are sure?'

Grus nods. 'We have swept it systematically, chamber by chamber, passageway by passageway.'

'Then they are gone,' says the Master. 'That can be the only conclusion. They must have somehow slipped past the Lookers on the surface.'

Neither of them can see how that can possibly be, but there is no other logical conclusion. Grus is reluctant to say what's on his mind, but he has to. 'We are out of time to complete the ritual. We must give instructions to disperse the Cleansers, the Bearers, the Lookers. Our foreign brothers must be alerted. All precautions have to be taken.'

The Master struggles painfully to his feet. 'You are right. We have failed the Sacreds.' He corrects himself. '*I* have failed them. Failed you all.'

Grus knows there is no time for reassurances, forgiveness or sentimentality. 'Do I have your permission to cancel all other activity and revert to the back-up protocol?'

'You do.' He opens his arms to his friend and they embrace. 'Make sure the Sanctuary is cleared within the next ten minutes. I will attend the Sacreds, then use the passageway.'

Grus nods. 'It is the only way.'

186

'What's happening?' shouts Caitlyn. 'What are you going to do?'

Gideon doesn't know.

His heart is beating way too fast.

'Just taking a breather,' he lies as he slides his toes away from the trigger ledge. He finds another foothold and relaxes a little. 'Be careful coming down, there's another one of those traps.'

'Okay.' Her fingers slip. She leans back against the side of the shaft and jams herself against the walls before she falls. All that time immured inside the Sanctuary at last has some use.

'You all right?'

'Lost my grip.' She feels the walls and is relieved to find another finger hold. 'I'm fine now. It's all right. Go on.'

He can't.

Gideon has reached the bottom of the shaft. He pulls his foot back.

Uncertainty hits him again. He tries to calculate how far down they have climbed. At least five times his height, that's five times 1.8 meters. They're a good nine meters down. From what he can remember, the centerpiece was about five meters high, so they are already well below the floor level of the crypt.

The thought gives him comfort. Enough for him to put one foot down and then the other.

Nothing happens.

It's safe.

But there is no way out that he can see.

There is a noise above him. Suddenly, he feels a crushing blow, a great weight thudding into his shoulder, driving him down the thin shaft, making his legs give way. It's Caitlyn. She's fallen on him.

The ground beneath him has opened up. The extra, sudden weight has triggered another trap. The stone floor slab tilts and falls away, and they slide entwined down the slope, sandpapered by the rough surface of the rock. For a few heart-stopping seconds they drop into nothing. Then the slope bottoms out, they slow, then stop.

They're still alive. Alive and excited. There can only be one reason for the final drop. It is a passageway to the outer world. Gideon suddenly understands the centerpiece. It was designed to be filled with the spirits of the ancients. When the shaft was full enough with the weight of the spiritually reborn, it would trigger the opening to a final passageway that would allow them to exit.

Caitlyn groans. Tries to move. Gideon listens to her heavy breathing. He can tell that she's exhausted. He puts an arm across her. 'Rest a minute. We're going to be all right now.'

187

The Apache crew scrambles within five minutes of the call from base.

Tommy Milner had been beginning to think the nighttime operation wasn't going to happen. It seldom does. A routine seek and destroy, something he could do in his sleep. The four rotors lift them high into the black night sky and out across the range. In the distance they see the lights of vehicles clearing the range. They'd been told there'd been some secret recon done out there while they had been stood down.

Milner's radio crackles into life. 'Range now cleared for maneuvers. Confirm when you have target in sight, Apache One.'

'Affirmative base, we're airborne and beginning our approach.'

'System lock,' announces Charlie Golding, the Longbow fire control radar at his fingertips. 'Within range and ready for fire command. Over.'

'You have authority to fire at will, Apache One.'

Golding checks his helmet display. From up above the main rotor, the fire control radar relays data to a matched millimeter wave seeker in the nose of the laser-guided Hellfire II missile. In the middle of his display, Golding sees the first of the enemy tanks that they have been instructed to destroy.

In the dark Wiltshire night there's a blinding flash and an explosive roll of thunder. The ground trembles and groans as it sucks up the brutality of the bomb. Beneath two old Chieftains, the dome of the Great Room cracks like a boiled egg. The Sanctuary's passageways disappear like shriveled veins and the Crypt of the Ancients is buried under thousands of tons of sandstone, earth and rubble. It's like it never existed.

188

Caitlyn and Gideon feel their way through the pitch black passageway. It's getting wider and higher now. They're able to walk side by side. She leans on him to ease the pain in her injured leg.

Gideon is still fearful. The ancients protected the shrines ferociously. There could be more surprises. The whole thing could collapse on them. Or underneath them. He stares into the murk, at the floor, the walls, desperate for any telltale signs. Anything unusual.

He uses his left hand to feel their way along the rock. Holds it high, in case there is a support beam or something worse threatening to smash into their unsuspecting skulls.

From the strain of his knees he can tell they're climbing. Hopefully *up* means *out*. Bearing in mind how deep belowground the Sanctuary was sited, he guesses they still have a long way to go.

Caitlyn says little. The trauma of the last few hours and seven days without food have taken the last of her energy. It's a miracle she's still putting one foot in front of the other.

'Do you want to stop?'

'No. No. Keep going. If I stop, I might not be able to start again.'

They hobble on. A deafening noise erupts somewhere behind them. The ball of sound rolls through the passage. They can't see anything, only hear and feel the shockwaves. The ground beneath them shakes. The walls too. The air fills with dust.

Gideon knows what's happening. A cave-in.

'We have to run.' He grabs her around the waist and gets her moving. 'The tunnel's collapsing.'

It sounds like a giant subterranean beast has woken and is thundering after them, growling and biting at their heels. They charge in a blind panic up the darkened passageway, the jaws of the animal snapping at their heels.

Gideon runs smack into a stone wall. A dead end. The blow knocks him flat. He brings Caitlyn down with him. She tumbles sidewards into the blockage and cracks her hip.

There's so much flying dust and rubble she can hardly breathe. The passageway is filling with soil and debris. They're being buried alive.

'Where are you?' She has lost him in the darkness.

She feels soil and stone flow like a river of dirt over her bare feet. The tide of death is coming in.

'Gideon! *Gideon*, where are you?'

He is facedown in the gathering debris. His chest feels like it is filled with wet cement. There is a pounding in his head and his nose is broken. It takes all of his energy just to get up on his hands and knees.

'Gideon!' She shouts in desperation more than hope.

'Here,' he says. 'I'm over here.'

But she can't find him. 'Over here! Gideon, I'm over here!'

He stumbles toward her voice. His outstretched hands finally find her. Dust is swirling, spiraling above her head.

'Put your hand up! Lift your hand *up*.' There's excitement in her voice.

He does as she tells him.

His fingers find a thin ragged hole. A hole in an exit shaft through the tunnel ceiling. He links his hands together and presses them against her. 'Put your foot in my hands. *Climb*.'

She'd laugh if she had the energy. It's a shaft.

If it's the same as the other one, Gideon calculates they're just nine meters away from escaping.

Nine meters from freedom.

189

They haul themselves upward using the last of their strength.

'*Stop*,' she shouts. 'It's another switch.'

'Work round it,' he says. 'Don't put any weight on it.'

Caitlyn shifts slowly around the trigger plate. But she is high in the shaft. She looks up, hoping to see some light. A glimpse of night sky. A sparkle of stars or fresh breeze. But there's nothing and the air is still rank and fetid.

She climbs, thinking now about her parents, about making up with her mum, holding tight to her dad, saying a long and heartfelt sorry to Eric.

There are no more fingerholds. She has run out of space. Reached the top of the shaft. She bangs it with the palms of her hands.

'It's blocked,' she shouts down, dregs of panic already filtering back into her voice. 'There's no way out. It's all sealed off.'

Gideon wishes he was in front and could explore whatever it is she has found. But the shaft is too narrow to swap positions.

'What do I do?' she shouts. Impatient. Frightened.

'Wait and think.' He tries to imagine the layout of the crypt. They climbed five meters up the centerpiece. They descended a total of nine meters. So the escape tunnel was four meters below the floor level of the crypt but probably rose by the same amount as they made their way along it. He reckons that since entering the second shaft they've only climbed about two meters. So the surface could still be at least three or four meters away.

'Keep your hands off the roof of the shaft,' he calls. 'I'm going to try something.'

Caitlyn crouches low and waits.

He steps across the hole and deliberately puts his weight on the trigger ledge near his right foot. At first nothing happens. Then the stone disc above their heads slowly starts to slide back.

'It's moving. The thing is opening up.'

Her excitement quickly dies down. There is still no glimpse of sky. Just more shaft.

'Keep going up,' he urges. 'After about a meter, you'll find another trigger plate on the right. Don't stand on anything on your left.'

She finds it. Tingles with anticipation. 'What do I do?'

He hesitates. There's everything to gain and everything to lose. He closes his eyes. 'Step on it.'

Caitlyn edges upward and leans across on her right foot. Nothing happens. She slides her other foot across. All her weight is now on the ledge. Soil and stone rain down on her head. She gasps with shock and fear. Turf and sand fall in on her and cascade down on to Gideon.

Fresh air. Caitlyn feels it for the first time in a week. She all but scampers up the last meter. Her fingers touch wet grass. She can hear the sweet sound of outside, feel freedom.

She hauls herself out of the hole and rolls on to her back. She's still laughing as Gideon crawls out of the shaft and collapses beside her.

A cool wind floats across the bomb-blasted fields. They lie there panting and breathing in the early morning air. Neither of them notice the open-top Jeep heading their way or who is in it.

190

'Stop in front of them,' Grus calls to the staff officer at the wheel. He and Aquila ready themselves. Both are still dressed in the Craft's sack-cloth robes. The Jeep's bobbing headlights cut through the gray twilight and fall on Gideon and Caitlyn's wasted bodies.

Everyone had deserted the Sanctuary just minutes before the Master emerged and phoned the military base. In his capacity as lieutenant colonel, he'd given the command for the Apache air strike to take place and had then made his own escape.

Grus never expected to come across Gideon and the sacrifice. He was simply trying to get to his car parked just off the Imber range.

Gideon turns toward the blaze of light. Help at last. He shields his eyes from the glare and is about to shout to the driver when he makes out that the man approaching him on foot is carrying a gun. Even if he had the strength to run, there is nowhere he could hide. No escape.

Grus lets out a shallow laugh. 'One last gift from the Sacreds. The treacherous son and the woman that ruined everything. Looks like she's going to die after all.'

He slips the safety catch off the pistol and walks closer. Night sun lamps from the Apache suddenly unleash a torrent of blinding white light. A megaphone message echoes out of the surrounding field. 'This is the police. Drop your weapon. You are surrounded.'

Grus's face says that's not going to happen. He recognizes the voice. It's Jimmy. His own son. He glances to the side and in the half-light beyond the search beam catches a glimpse of men in black uniforms, no more than fifty meters away. Tactical support. They're running low, dropping into the grass, sighting their weapons. He knows the drill.

The light from the Apache burns brighter and the copter hovers lower.

'Armed police, drop your weapon!'

His son's voice hangs in the air. He's out of time and he knows it. Grus raises the pistol, jams it in his mouth and fires.

The idling Jeep instantly kicks up grass and darts away. Gunfire blazes from across the field. The headlights of the Jeep go out. More shots. This time returned from the speeding vehicle. Sniper fire barks back from the grass, short growls like feral dogs.

The vehicle swerves viciously. It flips on its side. Cartwheels like a clumsy gymnast. Crashes upside down, spilling ragdoll corpses. An eerie silence ensues. No one moves.

Only when birdsong fills the air does one of the firearms team signal that it's safe to move in. Gideon and Caitlyn struggle to their feet and hold each other. The new moon fades in the morning sky.

Dawn finally breaks over the flat Wiltshire plain.

191

MONDAY 28 JUNE

News of Caitlyn's safe recovery is relayed to the suite of Kylie Lock at five a.m. By six, the Hollywood star has sobered up enough to speak to her daughter and to tearfully relay the good news to her father.

Jude Tompkins has a full crime-scene team working on-site at Imber by six-thirty. By seven the bodies of James Pendragon's driver, Nicholas Smith, the Deputy Chief Constable, Gregory Dockery and Inspector Adam Stone have all been examined in situ by a Home Office pathologist and moved to the county mortuary.

By eight a.m. Lee Johns is being formally interviewed in Devizes by Jimmy and by nine he is the first to be charged with kidnapping and manslaughter.

By ten past eight, the media has the story. Newsflashes are filling every radio, television and web bulletin across most of the world.

At ten a.m., Chief Constable Alan Hunt fronts a hastily called press conference in Devizes, congratulating his officers and thanking the Home Office, the FBI and the public for their support.

By eleven, Josh Goran has given the first of what he intends to be many TV interviews, telling how he was responsible for leading the police to Imber and how he is now going to sue the army for the ten million dollars reward that he thinks should rightfully be his. He also shows reporters the foxholes that he and his men dug to escape from army patrols.

By midday someone at the barracks in Warminster remembers they still have several of Goran's team in their cell block and grudgingly releases them.

A little after one p.m., Megan is at her parents' house hugging her daughter Sammy and wondering how to tell her that she'll never see her father again.

Just before three, Gideon wakes in the recovery ward of Salisbury District Hospital, the same one he was in after being attacked in the house of the man he'll always think of as his father. His real father. Professor Nathaniel Chase.

At five p.m. Gideon receives a call of thanks from the Vice President of the United States and a fax from the office of the President.

At six p.m. security teams strip the black plastic sheeting from the fences around Stonehenge and prepare it for a public reopening the following day. By the time the workers have cleared the site, it's twilight again.

Police reports show that no VIP party had taken place after all. There were no crowds and no sacrifice. Nothing out of the ordinary happened. Except for one thing. In the pale light of that busy morning in Wiltshire, there was a solitary visitor to the henge. A tired-looking, gray-faced man entered the circle. He spent a solemn time on his knees, embracing each and every stone.

No one seems to know his name.

And no one has seen him since.

ACKNOWLEDGMENTS

First and foremost my consiglieri and spiritual bodyguard Luigi Bonomi – agents don't come any better. The folks at Little, Brown/Sphere have been amazing – this is as much Dan Mallory's book as it is mine, maybe even more so, and it's been an honor to write this with him. Big thanks to Iain Hunt for all the heavy lifting he did on draft one at short notice. Kudos to Andy Hine, Kate Hibbert and Helena Doree in international rights, you are all goddesses. Thanks to Hannah Hargrave and Kate Webster in publicity for spreading the word. Scary Jack, big thanks to you too. Mrs. M, I couldn't have done this without you x

The Stonehenge Legacy is purely a work of fiction. Scholars will note that while much of it is based on astronomical, archaeological and historical fact, some of those facts have been used in ways to purely enhance the story and don't purport to form a collective truth. That said, despite centuries of research, there is still no indisputable answer to the big question: Why was Stonehenge built?